The Creation Series
Volume One

Where the Shadows Meet the Light

Where dreams become reality,
Where fantasy comes to life,
Where the shadows meet the light...

By Crystal Wolfe

Author's Photo by Julia Nikonchuk
Cover Design by Crystal Wolfe
Interior Design by Crystal Wolfe
Typography by Crystal Wolfe
Edited by Donald Hart, Amber Elizabeth Pearson, and Crystal Wolfe

November 11th, 2018
FIRST EDITION

ISBN-13: 978-0-692-18052-5

Library of Congress Control Number: 2018911060
Darmar Publishing, Maspeth, New York

Publisher's Cataloging-In-Publication Data
(Prepared by The Donohue Group, Inc.)

Names: Wolfe, Crystal, author.
Title: Where the shadows meet the light / by Crystal Wolfe.
Description: First edition. | Maspeth, New York: The Wolfeside Times
Publishing, 2018. | Series: The creation series; volume 1
Identifiers: ISBN 9780692180525
Subjects: LCSH: Multiculturalism--Fiction. | Dictators--Fiction. |
Magicians--Fiction. | Animals, Mythical--Fiction. | Good and evil--Fiction.
| LCGFT: Fantasy fiction.
Classification: LCC PS3623.O5527 W44 2018 | DDC 813/.6--dc23

WHERE THE SHADOWS MEET THE LIGHT

THE CREATION SERIES: VOLUME ONE

"*Where the Shadows Meet the Light* is a brilliant narrative, blending portions of history, magic, and earth sciences, to paint a picture of what life just after Creation might have been like. Featuring Shamanism, Christianity, Jewry, mythical creatures, and light and dark magic, this epic fantasy explores our origins, and lays the groundwork of why things may be the way they are today.

Told from many viewpoints—including animals—one gets a full picture of that colorful life. My favorite is the viewpoint of the wolf, and how he "sees" humans and the things we do. *Where the Shadows Meet the Light* is a spirited read for those liking fantasy mixed with history, and a touch of magic!"

--Darmar Publishing
Queens, New York City

"*Where the Shadows Meet the Light* is a beautifully written and seamless blend of fantasy, adventure, mystery, psychology, and spirituality. The full story itself is unique, with sub-stories based on ancient and magical times. Throughout the novel, Wolfe provides a refreshing outlook on humanity, with interlacing themes on the nature humanity, magical beings, romance, danger, and destiny.

As a psychotherapist, it is a psychological aspect within the novel which most fascinates me. Wolfe's unique style of writing eloquently portrays first-person perspectives of every character in the novel. Thus, the reader is able to perceive deeper thoughts and personality structures of these characters.

Wolfe neatly incorporates and explains viewpoints and belief systems from Hinduism, Christianity, Judaism, ancient Celtic spiritualism, Native American spiritualism, and New Age spiritualism, in clean and insightful ways. Throughout the novel it becomes increasingly clear how intentions, thoughts and actions don't always line up; how misunderstandings and misinterpretations occur; and how visions can be directive or misleading. It becomes clear why the differences between peoples and beings are both vital and valuable. Perspective becomes multi-layered, vibrant, palpable.

Where the Shadows Meet the Light also delves deeply into the theme of trauma, not only from the viewpoint of the victim, but also from that of the perpetrator. This is painful and gut-wrenching—but necessary because it reaches into the core duality of humanity. Wolfe's unique ability to engage the reader to witness such a variety of perspectives is reminiscent of this author's previous publishing's, *Our Invisible Neighbors,* and *The Resurrected Dream,* and is likely to be one of her trademarks as in author."

--Integrated Wellness and Strategies, LLC
Denver, Colorado
www.strategiesintegrated.com

WHERE THE SHADOWS MEET THE LIGHT

Table of Contents

Putting my hands up to the firelight, I rubbed them together to dry and warm them, trying to get the blood rushing back into my hands and body. The light of the fire in the hearth reminded me of my own life, how I'd learned to control my emotions and passions until even I was unaware of my true feelings.

Chapter Seven   Jewel of the Andorra Mountains

A veil passed over Alondria's eyes. Her thoughts were hidden. Usually I could read my twin sister's mind as easily as I could tell the time of day by the changing slant of the light of the shadows and sun.

Chapter Eight   At First Sight

His eyes were so blue, bluer than the ocean, bluer than the sky, deeper even than the luminescent blue of twilight. There was something in his eyes, something I couldn't put into words, something that made me sense feelings from another place and another time, in the future.

Chapter Nine   Scattered Seeds

The seed is split among two men—
Sprung from heaven or sprung from hell?
Is this creature foe or friend?
The truth was hidden well from them.

Chapter Ten   Mirrored Visions in the Crystal Castle

The floors and walls sparkled with all the colors of the rainbow from the light of the sun shining through the ceiling. Only it was made of glass, so that the sun could shine down and make the room dance with a mirage of twirling colors. Walking down a long crystal hall with no windows, we entered a room of luminescent white marble where seven mirrors stood on pedestals composed of sapphires, emeralds, rubies, onyxes, pearls, diamonds and gold.

Chapter Eleven   Dream Weaving

Her fingers were moving upon the wheel faster than his eyes could perceive, her eyes closed in focused concentration. Both Varawynn and I chanted words over the spinning wheel, our contrasting beauty like the green and thorny stem against the bloom of the white rose.

Chapter Twelve   All the King's Men

Winding itself around the men whose eyes never left my sensuously moving form, they barely noticed or cared that I was binding them with my rainbow magic.   Page 177

Chapter Thirteen   The Celtic Shepherd King

I would look back at this moment as the first vision to come to pass from the mirror of desires in the Crystal Castle—when Varawynn and I had embraced in the third mirror. I would remember and recall this embrace with Varawynn many times, for it was to be a desire that was satisfied but once.   Page 186

Chapter Fourteen   King of Broken Hearts

I stood there looking out into the woods for a long time, wondering how Vorseth made me feel as if he was the real King in charge of our fates. Wondering how he always managed to have the last word.

Page 195

Chapter Fifteen   The Mountains of Mourne

Hoods were placed on our heads, so we wouldn't know in what direction we were being taken. We soared through the dark, unseen night in a carriage flying across the terrain, run by steeds of unusual speed and smoothness. Led into a castle by the dim light of an awakening dawn, we were thrown into a dreary, windowless room.

Page 207

Chapter Sixteen   Secrets Come to Light

A shadow fell across the King's face as what happened to his parents played out in his mind. "They were murdered."   Page 222

Chapter Seventeen   Crowns of the Conquered King

My chest pressed against something sharp, as my hand gripped the crown. Losing my grasp, the crown fell to the ground with multiple loud clanks, rolling several feet away. There was a moment of screaming stillness, then it was as if the entire world had sprung to life. The camp of King Mardavian's men came charging towards me all at once.   Page 238

Chapter Eighteen   The Captives

It was always the same servant who brought us our meals I noticed. We'd never seen his face through the mound of his matted hair.

Page 250

Chapter Nineteen   Battles in the Lost Kingdoms

When my five men had all retreated from the fight, wounded and frightened, only then did I step forward. My silver sword flashed by the light of the moon's soft illumination, and the outsider's sword flashed gold.   Page 258

Chapter Twenty   Omens in the Sky

"Yes, it was a very powerful black magic that allowed her to kill him. But as she lay there on the ground beneath me, she looked up at me with these eyes, these eyes that haunted me. Her eyes were so dark and deep I couldn't even make out the pupils, and her movements were like shadows. But there was something else in her eyes, something in the expression…and I just knew she couldn't die."   Page 275

Chapter Twenty-One   How the Mighty Fall

I fell into a dream more real than reality. Every night was like this one, every night the need grew worse, but this night was different, this night she was there in a long lace gown, right there beside me, on the black satin sheets.   Page 286

Chapter Twenty-Two   Healed by Song and Sea

Without pause, Jonlin's fingers knew the notes to play, and the Bird of Eden's wordless song at last moved Varawynn's heart to lift her eyes. The bird was so bright as she flew, it was like a thunderous firelight in the sky. It was as if the sky was caught on fire with her colorful beauty.   Page 312

Chapter Twenty-Three   Fourteen Come Together

As the days passed, the members of the group were slowly finding their place. Only Varawynn stood alone, silent and moody.   Page 325

Chapter Twenty-Four   Ashes to Ashes

I knew that it would be best not to engage the man in conversation, but to catch him unawares. I watched him for a few minutes. Then I came up behind him, with movements of stealth and silence, wielding the knife blade into his back, piercing his heart.   Page 336

Chapter Twenty-Five   Creatures of the Starlight

Flowers of blue and red, violet, white, and indigo were entwined in the silver canopy sprawled out above us. To the left of the sparkling canopy and white tables clad with symbols of the stars, the purple river glistened like the glittering lights on the fairies themselves, as all about us we heard tiny chimes ringing from the bells on the fairy's necklaces and tiaras, dresses and slippers.

Page 356

Epilogue   In the Shadows

"From this child's line a man shall come,

After generations of suffering

He shall be the One—

To lead magickind away from man,

To save the magical creatures from human hands,

To harness the powers of heaven to earth,

To break man's curse—

To break man's curse, and bring peace to earth."

Page 367

Explanation of Symbols:

~ ~ ~ = Change in Time

* * * = Change in Character

~ *** ~ = Change in Character and Time

Note: Sections of the book that are italicized are scenes from the past.

> "And in it a man shall ascend;
> and at its close the house of dominion
> shall be burned with fire, and the whole root
> of the chosen shall be dispersed."
> -- From the Book of Enoch

Prologue
The Prophecy

3rd Millennia BC in the Emerald Isles—

Where the shadows met the light, the battling wizards waged war around them. "Damn you, Arlillyth run faster!" Vorseth yelled through gritted teeth. "Damn you RUN!"

It was the flowers that were slowing her pace, the endless fields of heather, the stones, the roots, and the crooked wayward path of the unsteady surface; that and the poison.

Violently seizing her arm, he dragged her weak body towards the caverns. "Keep it together. You've got to pull yourself together!" The pack was slipping off her slim shoulders. Her body was going numb. "Can't anything go right?"

Pulling the pack onto his own broad shoulders, he cradled her body in his arms like a tired child, running as fast as he could to the secret opening. Her glossy black hair flipped about her face, her limbs moving freely and blindly like the branches of a willow tree in a wind storm.

Behind them, chaos ensued. A land of fire stretched out like hands reaching after them, where the waving wands shooting rays of electric energy had burned the land from the sorcerers who fought in the Eternal War. In the dense forest and high cliffs of Caledonia, the flashing of light coming from the North nearly blinded them.

In the midst of their desperate escape, Arlillyth was hit by a ray from a sorcerer. Now something was working in her system, and there was no time. No time to drain her of its power, or search her body for its source.

"This is the most important moment of your life, Woman! If any moment ever mattered, it's this one! NOW! Wake UP! We've got to RUN!" He could see that she was trying, but then a volcanic explosion burst from inside, and her body began to disintegrate before his eyes.

"Damn them!" he cursed, trekking faster toward the secret sanctuary. Finding the hidden opening, he said the words, and hurriedly made the motions. Entering the cave protected by ancient Eden magic, he made the way, deep into the depths. Her long, dark hair, straight as an arrow, hung limply in front of her face now, her deep green eyes too heavy-lidded with the poison to ever open again.

Impatiently he dropped Arlillyth on the golden throne in the gut of the caverns. Aggressively shaking her, he made a last-ditch effort to revive her, but her body continued to deteriorate. In the final moment of her life, her hands reached out and grasped the jewel-encrusted box Vorseth took from the pack.

"No!" he shouted, terrified the object would disintegrate along with her body. But the jeweled box held its form. In that moment, he resigned himself to leaving the holy remnant hidden inside the locked box with Arlillyth, deep in the bowels of the cavern. But he still held the key, the only way possible, to open it.

Rifling further inside the pack, Vorseth drew from the shadowy folds the vast parchment containing the verse and riddles of the Prophecy. Gently, carefully now, he unfolded the scroll to the hallowed words which governed their existence, and the culmination of his life's work.

Should he leave it here with Arlillyth? No. It would be better to separate two such important sacred objects, and she already held the hallowed relic in her lifeless hands. So, he took the Prophecy in its entirety for himself.

Arlillyth sat on a throne of black marble. Her body and skin had now fully deteriorated into an immortalized form of ash. Her hands held tightly to the sanctified object, frozen in eternal anticipation of who would claim it.

Because of what she was she could have been saved, Vorseth knew that. She was not as other women are. There were ways to breathe life into her ashes, but he was unwilling to make the sacrifices it required to do so for her.

The seeds from the ancestral line of Lillyth would take root in these mystical Emerald Isles, in the obscured caverns of Caledonia, for Arlillyth was a daughter from that line. He would see to it that those seeds were nurtured and guided, to bear the proper fruit at the perfect time.

Her part in the story was now complete, as the Prophecy Vorseth had written himself foretold. Thus, it was up to him for the Prophecy to be fulfilled...

In that silent time of weeping
Whilst the lonely souls lie sleeping
Ere the clock shall chime an hour
When the three shall claim their power.

The tyrannous king who rules with the sulfuric fires
Of the throbbing perversions of his unnatural desires,
Shall recognize in perfect clarity all the tragedies he wrought,
Through the twisted manipulations of the perdition he once sought.

The secret shrouds beneath the simpering veil,
Shall be revealed as a beacon of illumination unto herself—
For that in which she had fought so well to hide,
Were the true illusions of all the good inside.

Soon all shall be revealed for all to see:
The truth of what once was and what shall be—
Infinite life created out of death,
For those who fell shall rise again.

Out of darkness pours the holy light
Of the hope the chosen King of David fights,
Forever he shall be as he was borne—
Wisdom gleaned from the cultures of his birth.

Then every knee shall bow unto the three;
Every tongue confess of the chosen's destiny—
For he shall lead by grace and not through steel
Granting mercy to those whom most would kill.

Through forgiving the pain and tragedies of his life,
He shall conquer death and transcend time.
He shall rise, like blinding sunlight from the consecrated fall,

WHERE THE SHADOWS MEET THE LIGHT

And unite us All as One, for One is All.

Chapter One
Symbol of Immortality

May, approximately 600 AD in the desert town of Haran—

"When the student is ready…the teacher will come..."

In the dream, I heard my name called out by a voice that was unfamiliar. The voice repeated my name over and over. It formed a chanting cadence, like a haunting lullaby with the incomprehensible rhythm of a song long-dismissed from early childhood, but that still hung on the edges of my consciousness.

"Eliju, Eliju, Eliju, Eliju..."

The voice paused, as if it knew that I was listening for his next words, on the edge of my skin in anticipation. "Eliju, I will come for you. I will take you far away from the land of your ancestors, so that together we will fulfill the Prophecy..."

The silence and darkness returned like a heavy shroud, until I heard the voice of someone very different, yet still uncannily familiar. Though I had never heard the voice before, it was a voice imprinted in my soul. When I heard it, it was like I was remembering something that hadn't happened yet, but of which I knew was meant to be.

Her voice was the sound of mists moving provocatively through the shadows, saturated with mysteries I didn't think I'd ever comprehend. Yet I was able to feel and sense the things I could not always articulate into words. The sound of her voice elicited bits and pieces of things I'd seen in visions and dreams.

"Eliju," said the mysterious voice, "you are meant for me, and only I can make you become the man you are meant to become."

We all have a song in our souls. A song only we can play and sing. There are a few people that are tied to our destinies, who can hear the melodies and verses of our song. Her words added harmony to the tenor notes of the song of myself.

I wanted to hear her speak for centuries. I wanted to hear more of that voice that had entered so effortlessly the inner caverns of my mind. It took a hold of me, evoking strange yearnings in my body, with every emphasis of the blue staccato of her words.

The sound of my name in the deep bass chords of the man's voice coupled with the smooth velvety alto tones of the woman's.

Their voices touched and pulled at the strings of my heart, pulling at me with more complex chords than I could have composed singularly. The sounds played a new song between us, like a symphony, which moved like a prism of dancing reflections. The sounds were like endlessly flashing nuances of color and light, creating a mix of notes that together formed the perfect melody.

In this vision of sounds and words, I could sense these voices were linked by a third figure, standing behind them in the shadows. Her essence was other-worldly. Filled by a bottomless void of searching emptiness, she harbored deep and hidden resentments. The first two voices were not even aware of her existence, though her existence, in a way, defined them—and had turned them into all they had become.

When I awoke from the dream, the sound of their voices and their images still echoed in my mind. I knew this was not just a dream—it was a vision, that was bound by Fate to come true...like the proverb claiming, *"When the student is ready, the teacher will come."*

Going about my daily duties as if this were any other day, I determined to follow the routine it had been so hard for me to set. For this was day, and days called for action. Though the *feeling* of the dream was like the remnant of cobwebs that clung to the unswept corners of my mind, I did my chores without rest or pause, in the life I did not choose, or enjoy, or want.

After lunch, I worked on fixing the table inside my hut. My father had built it, and ever since he'd left, it never set right. No matter how many times I fixed it, it continued to break and stood at an angle. As I was working on fixing the table, the sound of a hiss outside my window startled me...

Rushing outside to where the sheep roamed grazing, terror ran through my veins like a lightning bolt striking the rhythmic beating of my heart. A mammoth black cobra bore its teeth at my sheep. *Not Leah! No, not the mother ewe!*

Running towards the pasture where the innocent sheep wandered grazing, my roving eyes zeroed in to where the cobra was nearing its prey. I shouted loud noises, while making wide movements of my arms to shy the sheep away from the predator. The largest cobra I'd ever seen was closing in on Leah, my favorite mother ewe.

* * *

Snake was upon me. I bleated as loud as I could, for Boy to come out and save me. What about my ewe, Rachel? What would become of her, if the snake overcame me, and the poison killed me?

I loved my little lamb so much, and she loved me. I bleated in pain, as Snake overtook me, just as Boy came rushing outside, with a knife in his hand...

* * *

Sheep were such stupid creatures. So easily overtaken. I was on assignment with this one. I even knew the foolish creature's name, *Leah.*

I'd known the first Leah. I'd know Rachel and Jacob too. In Eliju's mind, by naming Rachel as the daughter of Leah, he was trying to redeem and rewrite the hate and jealousy and sibling rivalry that had run rampant throughout his culture's history—from the time of Cain and Abel.

Man had done such things for centuries. It was as easy to rewrite history as the stroke of a quill pen. Kings and scribes had been changing history to suit their own perspectives, since the time Man had first learned to read and write...taught by the Watchers, the Nephilim...the secret things that God had never intended for them to learn.

Enoch was the first to learn to read and write. And he had wrote of the first Serpent, and all that had transpired in the Garden of Eden, from *his* perspective. But nothing is ever quite so simple, or cut and dry.

Evil, he'd called us. Evil. But he'd neglected to write of the love. That some of the fallen angels had loved the humans they had fallen for. It was not just about sex. And some humans had betrayed the angels and done nefarious and underhanded things.

But *God* wanted Man to stay as innocent, as stupid, and as ignorant as sheep. Even though his beloved, mindless sheep were apt to go astray, God would always be on the human's side. God preferred them. He had cursed us serpents to slither on our bellies in the brushes and grasses—our only power in deception.

I slinked around the hut, gathering my bearings. I watched the Shepherd Boy perform his daily duties and rituals. I studied him, stalking him and his sheep for a few days. I knew this was only my first encounter with the Human. Someday he would know me by name...*Onessa.*

He put care into everything he did. I could see that every ritual was done, not just for its function, but for the love of performing each task. Especially with the animals, he was affectionate.

I got to know his habits. Every day after lunch, he worked on fixing his table inside the hut.

This was the time I chose to strike at the sheep—when it was alone and unprotected. It's usually best to attack a creature when they're isolated.

First, I distracted it, leading it away from the rest of the flock. Then I slithered and hissed at her from the brush, striking her neck, my fangs dripping with wet, lustful poison. I was hungry for the kill, hungry for the taste of blood, hungry to hurt Eliju—as was my commission.

* * *

Before I could get close enough to get the sheep away from it, the snake lunged on top of her, baring its fangs deep into the nap of her neck. Plunging blindly forward, I dove on the snake with the knife I kept tied to my ankle clutched in my fists. Thrusting my knife onto the cobra's scaly body, we hit the ground with a painful thud I barely felt, in my pursuit of protecting my sheep, and killing the snake. Leaving an angry gash on her long, dark body, the snake hissed menacingly at me with her displeasure.

With the deft quickness of my tawny muscles, I reached out my hands quicker than the blink of an eye, to grasp her wiggling body, and cut off her head. Struggling in my hands, writhing desperately to be released, I held her tightly in my fists, as she twisted and squirmed. Pulling out my dagger, I aimed the blade for her exotic head. But before I could ensure the kill, she eluded my grasp with the sly movements of her evasive scales, escaping into the underbrush.

I'd been so intent in my attempt with the blade that I hadn't noticed I'd nicked my finger. Yellow gooey blood oozed from my right index finger. I ignored it, and tried to find the cobra. After a few minutes of searching, I grudgingly acknowledged its successful escape, and turned my attentions on the sheep needing nurturing; first bandaging up the small cut on my finger as quickly as possible, so that it wouldn't get infected.

Leah lay on the ground, paralyzed by the cobra's venom. Leah's baby ewe, Rachel, cried woefully over her mother. I cradled the injured mother and her baby lamb carefully in my arms, bringing them both down to the river.

Gently placing them on a smooth, wet stone, I meticulously wielded my knife on Leah's half-unconscious form, carving a precise incision where the cobra had struck. Putting my mouth up to the wound with great care to suck out, but not swallow the venom; it was a thoughtful, but quick process. Eradicating the poison had to be done fast or the sheep would die, but it also had to be done carefully, or I could take in its poison and die myself.

The sheep was unconscious by the time I'd removed the poison from her body. Spitting out the venom from the snake, I cleared my palate with some fresh goat's milk.

Leah lay sadly mewing beside her unconscious mother. I entwined my fingers in their fluffy coarse curls, so light and soft in my hands. In the comfortable familiarity of their texture, the years of my life added to each other, like the rings marking the aging years of a tree. Nineteen-years-old…going on one hundred and two.

I went back to my hut to fetch the healing ointment I'd fastidiously prepared, and fetch a small wooden bowl of water for Rachel and Leah to drink from. For the rest of the day I nursed the mother sheep, along with her baby.

I fed Leah water and food when she could stomach it. I didn't take the time to eat much myself. It was nearly impossible to think of eating while I was in such a state of restless worrying.

Her open wound I treated with the healing ointment I'd prepared in my hut, bandaging up her bite with some old linens and spare twine. I knew very well how dangerous venom could be. If I had an open sore in my mouth, I knew the poison could have gone into my system through the pores.

I'd had run-ins with snakes before, and had prepared the ointment ahead of time. I'd spoken to other shepherds about the correct technique to take out the poison without incurring it myself. I was also very careful not to get the venom onto my nicked finger.

* * *

Boy cared for me so lovingly. He even brought Rachel down to the river with us, as he put himself in danger to take away the poison with his own mouth. He caressed me lovingly as he bandaged up my wounds. There was love in every movement he made toward us.

All the sheep loved Shepherd Boy, but none as much as me and Rachel. For he had saved us from danger more than once. Snake was not the only predator who preyed upon our weaknesses, our softness, our warmth. But I think Boy loved us best for our vulnerability.

~ *** ~

By the end of the day, I was certain the lamb would live, and that my own body had not absorbed the venom. I exhibited no ill symptoms.

After the long day of struggling, to save the one member of my flock, there was no fanfare when I entered my small home, no reward for a job well done. There was no one to speak with about my day, or feed me because I was too tired to prepare dinner for myself.

The loneliness was so strong it was like a separate entity, like a shadow always with me. One step behind every step I took. One step ahead.

That night I went to bed hungry. I didn't have the energy to take care of myself, after taking care of all my regular duties and my poor injured lamb all day. Sleep was long in coming, and after I'd finally succumb to the darkness, I fell into another dream that felt more real than my reality, more familiar then the gentle mewing of the lambs.

This was the second night in a row I dreamed of the familiar strangers…their voices were now etched in my mind. I still couldn't see the woman, but the man appeared before me, hazy, but clear enough to catch the long beard running down onto his chest, the intense dark eyes, and striking brown hair with streaks of red.

"Go with him. You must go with him," she whispered. It almost sounded like the voice of my mother, but it had been so long since I'd heard it, I couldn't be sure.

In the morning, I prepared for tomorrow's Sabbath. I attended to my sheep and cared for Leah. Days of eating little food after nights of little sleep, had me doing my chores and taking care of the lambs in an almost trance-like state of growing exhaustion. In the evening, I dreamt of the two strangers for the third night in a row. This time the man came so close to me, I could see the pores on his face.

"Soon," he murmured. "I will be with you soon. You must be ready."

Ready for what? I didn't know. But given my sense of adventure, and unhappiness as a shepherd, I hoped to find out.

After three nights of dreams with the same people, it was not so easy to put the impressions from my mind by morning's light. I got through the day, but my mind wandered back to my visions more than I would have liked. Towards dusk, as I prepared to eat Sabbath dinner, three steady knocks beat like timed music on my door, and I *knew*, in the same way I'd known that my lamb, Leah, was in danger—that the time had come.

"I know you're there, please open the door, Eliju."

It was the same masculine voice from my dreams, from the stranger who was so familiar. Quickly I went to the door, nervous and excited with anticipation, eager in a way that only those who have lived alone for many years can fully comprehend…

* * *

I knew the boy was at home. After all, the lamp was lit. "Who are you?" the chosen one Eliju called out to me through his heavy wooden door. I was exhausted. I'd been traveling for what felt like a lifetime. Certainly, I had been preparing for this moment for a lifetime.

"I'm known as the Shaman, Wandering Wolfe, lad. I've traveled a long way and a long time to find you. Please let me in, so that I may explain and rest from my journey."

I realized it must be very odd for a stranger to show up on his doorstep in this mysterious manner—I knew that he was unaware that this night was thousands of years in the making, and that every story and moment in the tapestry of my life had led me here, to him…

* * *

Wandering Wolfe…

The stranger's name triggered something in my mind. The memory was almost as unexpected as the man himself. My parents had abandoned me when I was only ten-years-old. Since then I'd tried to forget everything about them. Now my mother's words came back to me, as clear as a cloudless desert sky.

"Surely Wandering Wolfe, the greatest Shaman on earth, will be able to explain to Eliju why we had to leave him all alone and so young." She'd struggled to keep her voice from breaking over the words, and my father had moved closer to embrace and comfort her.

I was only seven when I accidentally witnessed this small exchange. Three years later when my parents abandoned me, I recalled it again. Now, the arrival of this stranger propelled me deep into the subconscious foundation of my life: my pain, my oldest wound, and the most significant of my insecurities. The image of my parents in their brief embrace flooded my perceptions, making me uncomfortable with the depth of emotion it aroused in my psyche.

* * *

"How can I know for certain that you wish me no harm?" the boy called out to me, persisting for his own protection on testing my character. Surely, I was well-reputed to be a patient man, and surely, I understood how he must feel, but I was quite tired, and in no mood for it.

I took a few deep breaths before I answered, searching my mind for the right words. "You don't know me, but I know very well who you are, Eliju. I know them who bore you. Your mother is Isadore, and your father is Kenneth." I knew Eliju's story better than he did. I knew where his parents were, and why they'd left him. I knew all about the young lad. I knew more about the boy than he knew about himself.

* * *

I was flabbergasted. My life felt as if it had been built on shifting sands. Part of me was exhilarated with the anticipation of the unknown. Part of me wanted to resist, wanted to block out forever this man who'd known my parents, and who no doubt wanted something of me, something I might not to be able, or willing, to give.

But shutting out Destiny was like shutting out the light of the sun at dawn. The sun would rise every morning, whether or not you wanted it to. The days would pass, with or without us being a part of them. Life will go on, even after we have lost our lives. So, while I was alive, I wanted to *live*.

Life had certainly gone on without my parents. It had been incredibly challenging, but I had survived. Alone. On my own since I was ten-years-old.

Now this strange man who knew my parents was knocking on my door. There was a rage I'd carried in my heart against my parents since the day they left me. Part of me wanted to take out my rage against this man, but curiosity got the best of me. Beyond my anger, there was a burning need, even stronger than the rage, to understand, *why?*

* * *

Finally relenting, Eliju unhitched the bars and locks for my entry. I was guided into the entrance of the hut. I observed him carefully. I knew all about the lad in theory, but now I was observing him in the flesh, something altogether different. Eliju closed and locked the door in slow, precise movements—demonstrating he took pleasure in the detailed actions of the repetitions of tradition.

His movements were confident. Even though he must be caught off-guard at my presence, he stood straight and tall. Being on his own, from such an early age, had given him character.

His eyes were like quicksilver, flashing between green and blue. His brown hair was unruly, his skin tanned by the hot desert sun, his hands rough from arduous work.

He would do well on our journey; for surely, he was made of sterner stuff than the hard desert soil he had toiled to cultivate. And surely being on his own for so long, and at such an early age, had fortified in him, an indomitable spirit for survival. We would need that fighting spirit to conquer our enemy.

* * *

The man was an intimidating presence. Bearing an air of dignified power and authority capturing my imagination, his demeanor commanded respect. Vivid fire-bird red streaked the full mane of his dark hair. Bulging muscles protruded through his thick robes.

His eyes were intensely penetrating, with an uncanny reddish hue adding warmth to the mahogany brown. His chin bore a long, dark beard streaked with red like his hair and eyes, just like the image of the man I'd seen in my dreams.

Leaning on a staff of withered birch covered in carved symbols whose meanings were unknown to me, the fine lines on his face marked his life and character, yet around his eyes the skin was mostly smooth, as if there had been little laughter during the course of his years, and perhaps little love besides. I sensed the Shaman's mind was like the sky itself, abstract and intangible.

Wandering Wolfe wasted no time on small talk. There was a sense of urgency in his presence, something driving us quickly forward. "There is a Prophecy I studied when I was a young lad, with a prophet of great vision."

"Who is the Prophet?"

"His name was Vorseth, but he is of little consequence. What matters is the Prophecy itself."

Something compelled me to listen, though I was full of questions. "The Prophecy was written thousands of years ago. It tells the stories of the epic battles between good and evil for these past centuries," Wandering Wolfe continued. "The culmination of these battles lies in this moment, in the fates of fourteen Chosen Ones who will either lead us to a time of peace, or of ultimate destruction. You Eliju, and I, are two of these Chosen Ones."

I gulped, feeling overwhelmed and excited at the same time. "I don't understand...how can you know for certain that I'm one of these Chosen Ones?"

"The Prophecy is a book of riddles, in poetry form, that foretells the future," the Shaman ignored my question, and continued his explanation of the Prophecy. "Different peoples and creatures have spent their lives trying to decipher the riddles, so they could discern what would occur. Depending on their alignment with good or evil, some sought to know the future to thwart it, or to further their own agenda."

"Others have gleaned truths to provide useful knowledge in the time that has now come. A battle has been waging in the world around you, which you've no doubt been unaware of. A king named Mardavian is using both brute force and magic to gain dominion over the earth. In his pursuit, he's killed off whole races of creatures and men. The Prophecy specified a group was selected to fight this king, and I repeat, you are one of them."

"But how can you know that for sure?" I asked again.

"Do you have a birthmark on your body?"

I stared at him quizzically, tapping my foot impatiently on the leg of the table, the table that my father had built himself, and that broke on a regular basis. Now just how could he know about my birthmark?

"Yes, I was born with a birthmark that looks just like a horse on my left thigh. Why do you ask that?"

"Because that's my proof, Eliju. Everyone in the group was foretold by the Prophecy to be born with the birthmark of a particular creature or symbol." With that, he pulled back the sleeve of his tunic, to show me an incredibly intricate birthmark of a wolf on his upper right arm.

I shook my head, trying to make some sense of all these new ideas rolling around in my mind. "I don't know how I can believe or process what you're telling me. I'm not sure I even understand what you're telling me—or what you want from me..."

A long, low growl sounded unexpectedly, like a trumpet heralding the beginning of a decisive battle, the sound was both beautiful and menacing, altogether out of place to my ears. Maybe for that reason above all others, it caught my attention.

Over and over, a chant was uttered that seemed to be coming from nowhere and everywhere at the same time. Gaining strength and speed, the wind outside the door cried and moaned like a dying banshee.

* * *

The door that the shepherd boy had so vigilantly locked, came unhitched by invisible fingers, as the full force of the wailing wind flew like a storm of destruction into the room. Despite the tornado of chaos, the wind was perpetuating, everything in the room remained unfettered by the bedlam, except, it would seem, for Eliju himself. The sandy earth of the dry desert soil flew into the room, and almost instantly formed a large wall made of dirt around his tall form.

Fear swept through my body from head to toe. I asked the gods for courage. I watched as the sand surrounded him, the feeling to protect him overwhelming me...

* * *

Growing wider and taller until it had reached the ceiling, the wall of dirt surrounded me on all sides. Suspended there, unmoving, as if to make my tension and fear grow in the anticipation of its destination, the wind at last pushed forward, as the wall of dirt and sand filled my mouth, ears, nose, and even my eyes.

Swirling through my body in every crevice and hole, the pain was both sharp and aching. My body was on fire with the swirling sand that was burning me to death from inside. I cried out in agony, but my cries were lost on the wind.

Sinking fast into a pool of quicksand, my mouth and head were filled with a solid substance never intended for the fluidity of the human body. Choking and coughing helplessly, I was terrified that I wouldn't survive the suffocation. I was defenseless.

With my last choking breath, I fought to keep conscious. I saw the Shaman raise his hands and staff, murmuring hurried words beneath his breath. I knew he was defending me, because right before I succumbed into oblivion, almost faster than my eyes could perceive, the earth came flying out of my body.

Gratefully, I inhaled a long, deep breath. This stranger from my dreams had just saved my life.

* * *

Hastening towards the young man, I laid my hand on Eliju's back, thumping it repeatedly. "Are you all right, lad? Can you breathe?" I was so concerned, I barely realized I'd been holding my own breath while I waited for him to breathe again.

Eliju was still choking, but managed to nod. After being reassured the boy was going to be okay, I lifted my hands into the air, closing my eyes in concentration. Murmuring softly, words I knew Eliju wouldn't understand, I chanted the words of a counter-spell against the intruder to find his whereabouts.

The wind picked up again. The door moved back and forth on its hinges violently. The pounding of feet running, beat in my ear drums, like water beats the beach in the turning of the tides. I heard and saw the mewing sounds of the lambs in my mind's eye. I realized the man must be hiding amongst the sheep.

"He's with the animals!" I shouted to Eliju. Rushing outside, I shouted chants, with Eliju following closely at my heels. Eliju daringly held out his knife, ready to fight with me against the attack on his life. Running purposefully around the hut and into the small dwelling, which housed the sheep and goats, sure enough we found the man hiding with the animals.

Holding out my arms and pointing my right index finger at the assassin, I roared, "Allah longeneva allah longeneva furinor furinora!"

Our opponent countered back, "Hurullah hurullah grimore GRIMORE!"

"Twistio twistio curatio morDA!"

* * *

Wandering Wolfe shouted the words as if he were delivering the death blow in a sword fight. I watched him like I was watching a distant storm, as if I were outside of myself, witnessing some fantastic display of the elements.

The man's body rose into the air, twisting itself like a pretzel. Hanging there in the sky for nearly ten seconds, a burst of light exploded from his chest as he fell, dead and limp to the ground at our feet. A necklace on his chest shone bright gold, as he took his last breath.

He was the first dead person I had ever seen. I stared at the murdered man lying at our feet, out of my head from the shock—because I recognized him.

"I know him," I sputtered out.

"What?"

"I knew him! He is, that is, *was*…Ishmael. I buy my seed from him every spring."

A handful of heartbeats passed. "Eliju, I see now we're not safe here. There's danger everywhere, even in your own homeland."

* * *

The poor boy shook his head. He didn't have the words to express his surprise at this betrayal.

"I don't see this man very often, only a few times a year. Are you saying he meant to harm me all along?"

"It certainly seems that way, doesn't it, Eliju? I'm guessing after this attack that you have more than one secret enemy in these parts. We won't be able to train here as I'd hoped. We'll need to leave right away."

I could tell by the vacant look in Eliju's eyes that he hadn't even heard what I'd said. "But why now? Why after all these years has Ishmael decided this was the time to attack me?"

"Probably because he knew I was here, and he was afraid you'd be leaving soon. If he didn't act now, he'd have missed his chance. Eliju, this is one of King Mardavian's men."

"How do you know?"

I bent down and carefully removed the necklace from Ishmael's chest, without touching the corpse's skin. I knew the arcane symbol well. It was a symbol that defined my own life for reasons I still didn't understand. "This is King Mardavian's crest, Eliju…a snake eating its own tail, the Symbol of Immortality."

* * *

I shook my head. I had nothing left to say. The shock was too much for me. I think he understood my need for silence because we didn't talk as we made our way back to my home. We were seated near the fire for some time, before Wandering Wolfe broke the silence.

"I realize it's a lot for me to ask of you, being that I'm still a stranger, but I'm asking you to trust me, lad. Magic is real and alive even if you've never been aware of it. Though you have no knowledge of the fight that's been waging for centuries, I want you to understand that your salvation is not the only one at stake. I hope that after what happened tonight, you will agree to follow me, and let me guide you in the ways of natural earth magic, which I know as a Shaman. I would like to teach you to fight against this evil. My role in our group, is that of a mentor."

He paused for a moment more. "If you stay here now, you will be in grave danger. It's only a matter of time before you will be attacked again. I want to protect you, but I can't remain here, and allow innocent people in kingdoms elsewhere to suffer. The choice is yours."

I touched my throat, my chest, felt my heart beating in my head, in my stomach, in my neck, in my feet. I inhaled one long, steadying breath. "I respect what you've shown me, Wandering Wolfe. I believe you. At least, I believe that you have good intentions. Most of all, I need to thank you for saving my life."

"It is my honor and duty to defend you, Eliju," he answered sincerely. There was something in the fierceness of Wandering Wolfe's physical display of power, and the sincerity and the straightforwardness of his words, that connected my mind, and what it told me was right and wrong, with my heart, which could feel the wisdom of the man's words, even if my mind could not articulate or understand it quite yet.

In the years since my parent's absence, I'd felt a quiet desperation, a deep longing for adventures in a purpose greater than myself. That lost hope for a different life, was kindled by Wandering Wolfe's mysterious Prophecy. I felt my soul lift when I saw him, felt my spirit rising at his words, rising to meet the man I hoped to become.

I believed that Wandering Wolfe could teach me how to become a man of action, but my actions needed to be led by my visions. My visions had already told me to follow this man. And so, I would.

I would follow him in the same way I was led by my faith. In the same simple way my flock had followed me. In the shadows and in the light, it was my faith that guided me forward.

"I'm willing to go where ever you lead me, Wandering Wolfe. I want to fight this king. I want to make this world a better place, if I am able. Besides, there's no life for me here after tonight. I'd be as safe as a lamb in a den of wolves if I stayed here now, wouldn't I, without the knowledge of how to defend myself?"

Wandering Wolfe chuckled softly, with honest regret for me in his eyes. His eyes were full of warmth, reminding me of the looks I often gave to my sheep. He laid his right hand on my shoulder, squeezing it reassuringly, with unspoken understanding.

We'd only just met, but an intense connection had formed when the Shaman saved my life. I didn't only respect him, I felt indebted to him. And beyond the debt I owed, a bond of trust had formed from the concern over me he'd displayed in his actions. In them, was more love than I had ever been shown. I would enjoy learning from this man. More than anything, I would like to experience more of the caring that had been missing in my life for so long.

When the student is ready...the teacher has come.

Chapter Two
The Wolf Saves the Sheep

I'd never gotten to eat my dinner, and now the food was cold and unappealing. So, the Shaman kindly prepared us a simple meal over a fire outside my hut, after the harrowing experience of Ishmael's attack and death. He said he felt more comfortable sleeping outdoors, and would know how to protect us better in the nature he was accustomed to. As I felt unqualified to defend myself, or to protect him, I agreed to keep him company outdoors.

It was a small thing I know, but I felt grateful watching someone cooking for me. It was nice to be taken care of. My family had left me so many years ago. The food was good, and I was hungry. As I reached over for the last rabbit leg spitting over the fire pit, something heavy toppled over me, bounding into the underbrush. It had only been a flash, but it looked like a wolf.

Instinctively reaching for my knife, I pulled out the small dagger from where it was hidden tied to my ankle. "Who's there? What do you want?"

Wandering Wolfe laughed at me. "Why are you laughing? What's so funny?"

"That was only Flint jumping over you. I think he likes you lad."

"Who's Flint?"

"He's my companion and most loyal friend."

"But he's, he's a *wolf!*" Gripping the knife into the palm of my hand even tighter, I stared at Wandering Wolfe wide-eyed.

"A wolf who is my most trusted ally," Wandering Wolfe replied with a hearty laugh, as he made a yowling cry, beckoning the mythic beast out from where he'd been hiding. In a guttural, animalistic way, he was letting the wolf know in its own language that it was safe and protected here.

"If you want your dinner, you'd better come out. No, Eliju won't hurt you, Flinty, I promise. And I know that you would never hurt this boy, the person we've been waiting for and preparing to meet and join us for so long now."

Fast as a flash of unheralded lightning across the southern

sandy skies, the huge silver-haired wolf, streaked with the color of burnt orange wheat fields, leapt out from the underbrush. With no attempt at pretense, he ravenously ate the last of the roasting hare. Reaching out my hands to try to keep him from the last of the meal, the wolf had already eaten most of it, before I could even get my arms out.

The Shaman chuckled, but I was still hungry. I sighed, looking from Flint to Wandering Wolfe. "Where has he been all this time anyway?"

"Oh, here and there, but you'll mostly see him at night—dinner time to be specific."

* * *

I continued to laugh in amusement at Eliju's fluster and frustration. Eliju had a lot to learn about animals, and their role in the world around us.

"Flint is one of the fourteen, lad."

"An animal is one of our group?" Eliju asked incredulously.

"He bears the birthmark of a fox, the trickster, on his side," I explained to the boy patiently. "And he will not be the only animal—or nonhuman for that matter, in our group."

I knew that the boy loved animals, but he had probably never imagined we'd have creatures traveling with us. To his credit, he knew when to keep his mouth shut, and observe.

Flint was special. I thought back to the first time I met the mythic beast—how he had saved my life, and pet him gently on his back and side with the fox birthmark.

Wolves were often feared and misunderstood creatures. I knew that Eliju's fears were based on such stories as wolves eating babies and killing livestock. Many found Flint to be intimidating at first, but the truth was that wolves were some of the most loyal and family-oriented of all creatures. Flint was my family—more than any person had ever been.

We'd been together all my life, well, at least from the first of my memories of when my life began…so clearly Flint was something more than mere flesh and bone. Like me, he harbored some magic in his blood that kept him living long past the time marked for the inevitable passage into the afterlife.

* * *

Wandering Wolfe seemed close to the wolf, but I didn't trust it.

Wolves *were* a common predator in stories growing up. There was a lot of folklore about the sly manipulations of their ferocious human appetites. Yet I was attracted to its inherent need for freedom and exploration, much like my own.

We slept outside that night, and I knew after what had happened with Ishmael we would be leaving tomorrow. Soon I would leave the only home I had ever known.

As I laid on the blanket, looking up into the sky, I was filled by a sense of wonder and awe at the vastness of the stars that shone like a canopy of sparkling diamonds. I felt a sense of loss about saying goodbye to what my life had been, at the same time electrified wondering what my life would become. It could have been a minute that passed, but it felt like an eternity went by, staring up at the galaxy of stars.

I was pulled from my reverie by voices in the olive grove. Noticing that Wandering Wolfe wasn't in his bed, I decided to check it out. Dragging my tired body from its cocoon, I walked toward the sounds to investigate.

There among the field of trees, as the heady scent of ripening olives filled my senses, I watched as the Shaman conversed quietly with a stranger. I was unable to decipher their words. The stranger's shaggy black hair covered his face. I couldn't make out his features. His torn and tattered clothes revealed little of his form. Observing them for some time from a distance, as I approached them, the leaves rustled in the brush. There was a sudden stirring of motion, then the man was gone.

"Who was that?" I asked the Shaman, as he walked towards me from the grove, the deep smell of ripening olives filling my senses once more.

Wandering Wolfe just shook his head and didn't answer. Suddenly I was overcome with worry…could I really trust this man I barely knew? Then I remembered how he'd saved my life only hours before. I didn't ask him anything more, but I filed the image away in my mind…of the man's shaggy black hair and tattered clothing.

I tried to go back to sleep. But later that night, I was awakened again by a maniacal laugh erupting through the dark stillness. *Could it be part of a dream?* I thought to myself. I'd been having so many lately…

The sounds of fighting and struggling near the hut confirmed that it was really happening. Bolting up off the ground, my first instinct was to check on the flock of sheep. It looked as if the last rung of the gate to the pen where the sheep were kept had been gnarled off. Leah was bleating pathetically, her baby ewe nowhere to be seen. Now it was her daughter, Rachel, who was in danger.

* * *

I was in danger. The golden jackal wanted to kill me. He wanted to rip through my white, coarse curls, and get to my meat. I preferred the taste of green grass and rough shrubs, especially after a rain. It rained so rarely here in the desert. The wetness on the blades of green were so tasty.

I couldn't imagine the desire for blood. I couldn't imagine killing another creature. I lived for the affection of my Shepherd Person, and the caresses of my Mother. I could never be hungry enough to kill and eat another living creature. Then I remembered another time, the time I had lost my way…

~ ~ ~

I caught a glint of the sunshine on the horizon. I thought I spotted a bit of grass the sun was shining on, and I was hungry. It was so beautiful, I decided to chase it! I wandered from the herd, towards the sun, towards the grass. Before I knew it, I'd lost sight of my family and my person. The sun betrayed me as it began to set.

When the dark set in, the fear overcame me. What was I to do? I hadn't meant to stray. But the light had been so beautiful. Distracted by some silly, simple thing, and now I was separated from the safety in numbers.

I wandered for days in the desert. I went hungry and lost weight. I wondered if I would die out here alone. Person would probably never even find my body—for a wild animal would surely find it and eat it before he could…I'd been fortunate a wild animal hadn't found me yet, and I still had hope that my Person would find me—before it was too late.

It was another beautiful day, and I caught a glint of sunshine on the next horizon. This time I stayed in the low desert, and decided not to chase the mirage of wet, green grass upon the gently sloping hill. Surely other sheep would wander, but I wouldn't stray again.

Then I saw him, calling my name across the desert plains, several leagues away. I could hear his familiar footsteps, before I saw him. He had a particular way of walking, a particular stride, with the sound of his boots breaking up the sand on the ground, and I knew it was he.

"Rachel...Rachel...Rachel..."

I bounded and leaped towards him. When he saw me, he rushed to me, and hugged me in his arms, petting my fur and kissing my face. "Sweet little Rachel, your mother and I have been so worried!"

I bleated merrily in response. I was so happy to see him. I never would have found my way home, if he hadn't come to find me...

~ ~ ~

Now there was this strange beast upon me. His sharp, curved teeth were baring down at me. Wolf was there, growling at the ugly jackal. I was shaking with fear, and the cold the fear put in me. I was scared and defenseless. The loud noises made me even more frightened.

My Person came running out. He'd heard the commotion. I could see he feared it was caused by the wolf. But Wolf had been protecting me.

* * *

A low growl erupted from behind the pen, as a dark shadow sprinted to the flock. I rushed towards the sound. What I saw turned me cold.

Flint stood in front of the lamb, his eyes blood red, his fangs bared. *I knew I couldn't trust it!*

Automatically, I unsheathed the knife I kept tied to my ankle, preparing in my mind's eye for a sure aim at the wolf's neck, going in for the kill. Just as I was about to fling the blade purposefully into the wolf, I heard again that maniacal laugh piercing the darkness.

The sound was coming from behind me.

Fear pumped through my wildly beating heart. Sweat poured down my hands unto the knife flashing silver by the shadowy light of the moon. I was terrified to look behind me, and see the source of that freaky laughter. In that split second of hesitation, I was attacked by curved, sharp teeth gleaming white.

* * *

The monster attacked my Person. I let out a loud bleat that sounded through the night. His fangs bared into the Person. I felt the teeth, as if they were in me. I loved Person so much. I'd rather Jackal had attacked me.

* * *

A sharp pain went through me. My side bled profusely, and for a moment, I stumbled with the weakness of the swift loss of blood. In that instant, Flint lunged unto the golden jackal's back.

The jackal's long legs and large feet, which made it good for running long distances, collapsed under the weight of the wolf that had a good twenty pounds on him of solid muscle. The jackal was pinned under the weight of the wolf, foaming at the mouth in frustration and crazed fury.

As Flint held the jackal pinned to the ground, the wolf savagely tore out a huge chunk of the jackal's side. Screaming once more its maniacal laughter, the unruly beast wiggled out of the wolf's grasp, leaping five feet into the air and into a dead run. Flint followed in quick pursuit—into the long, dark emptiness of the desert.

Wandering Wolfe found us just in time to see his companion rushing off after the golden jackal. I looked over at the Shaman, feeling helpless and worried. I didn't know which beast was faster or if Flint would ever return. All I knew for sure was that Flint had not only saved the life of my baby lamb that night, but my own.

Wandering Wolfe sat silently beside me, his presence alone a comfort. I was awestruck at what had transpired, ashamed of my first instinct to assume that Flint had been behind the ruckus and was the cause of danger to my flock. I was still bleeding as Wandering Wolfe bandaged me up, but I was barely aware of the pain, I was so lost in my thoughts and feelings of guilt and fear, shock and gratitude.

* * *

Wolf chased the creature off into the night. The other Person, the Person with a goat beard, came out and sat with Person, dressing his wounds. I could see my Person was in pain—inside and out. I nestled against him, to lend him the comfort of my warmth.

Then I stood aside, watching...to see what would happen. I could see so far in the distance that I was the first to see Wolf coming home...

* * *

Eliju and I waited for the wolf in utter silence, from the dead of night, until the dawn's breaking light streaked across the horizon. I knew Flint had been through fiercer danger than this, and had come out unscathed. I tried to reassure the boy that the wolf would come back to us.

Eliju was clearly a wreck worrying himself over Flinty. That concern endeared me to the shepherd lad. I could see that the boy was beginning to recognize the majesty of the wolf's essence, and the inherent defense and protection Flint would provide for him and all he loved, as Flint had protected me and all whom I had loved, all my life.

~ *** ~

It was by the light of an awakening dawn that Flint returned to us, dragging the body of the dead jackal in the grip of its ferocious jaws, to lie at my waiting feet. After Flint released the golden jackal from his mouth, he sat there expectantly, looking up into my eyes, with his own black soulful ones so faithfully—that I realized now held warmth, wisdom and spirit.

There were thoughts and memories behind those eyes, and an intention of fierce defense. Wandering Wolfe looked upon his companion with great relief, as he again placed a fatherly hand on my shoulder.

I couldn't help it. I was overwhelmed with my feelings. My eyes filled with tears. Putting one hand on Flint's muscled shoulders, with Wandering Wolfe's hand on my shoulder, so that we three were connected by touch, one to the other, the only words I could get out without breaking down were, "Thank you."

There was a moment of stillness. Then the wolf gave me a lopsided grin, and licked my face. With my unshed tears still in my eyes, I laughed. The Shaman smiled. And that was how the wolf saved the shepherd boy and his sheep.

~ ~ ~

Chapter Three
Time Waits for No Man

June-July, moving north through the regions of Western Europe from the Middle East—

The next morning, I woke to discover that the Shaman had packed his belongings, and some of my own as well. Something broke in my heart, when I thought about leaving my flock. I was overcome with sadness and fear.

"We have to leave, Eliju. You know we must go, for your own safety, as soon as possible. We've been attacked twice already since my arrival."

My heartbeat quickened with nervous expectation. I wasn't certain I was ready to go yet, but I didn't voice my misgivings. He was right. We were in danger here, and even though I had mixed feelings about beginning our journey, it was time.

The Shaman and I ate a light breakfast, while I packed a few more things. I took the morning to get my affairs in order. I sold my sheep to the most humane shepherd I knew a couple farms over.

My heart ached when I saw the last of Rachel and Leah, and the looks of hurt and betrayal they gave me as I walked away, but the memories of our time together, I'd carry with me forever. After all, it was the sheep that had kept me alive after my parents abandoned me. I had lived for them, and their love had been the only I'd known for nearly a decade.

I hid the deed to the hut and the farm in a safe place, in case I'd ever need to return, after the last of our adventures were over, or we needed safe housing. Most of the crops would go to seed, and depending upon how long I was away, it would take a lot of work to get everything back in working order. But chances were I'd never return at all.

The thought was both exciting and disheartening. By the time the loose ends were tied up, it was mid-afternoon before we began our journey. Even so, by nightfall I'd already traveled further from my home than in the whole of my lifetime.

The days and weeks passed, marked by the lessons I had with

Wandering Wolfe, and the change in terrain. We never slept long, and never ate much along the journey, yet I was full of energy. I was even losing weight, growing tall and lanky.

"Your height befits a king," Wandering Wolfe told me one day, a couple weeks into our travels, as we took an afternoon break for tea. We were sipping on some steaming hot mint tea he had brewed for us. The mint was fresh and crisp. We'd found it in the bushes, and plucked it up for our tea time. It tasted heavenly. Sometimes I felt I could lose myself in simple pleasures like this one. My thoughts and worries were not so simple.

Sometimes I thought about how the Shaman had said he knew my parents. I wasn't ready to bring that up to him—and yet I stewed over it often. We were getting closer as the days passed, our relationship slowly building, as I learned to trust him more each day, and that his intentions were good. Even though I felt safe and protected by the Shaman and the wolf, the nightmares and my visions persisted, and I was haunted in the day, by the shadows of the night...

~ ~ ~

Hands covered with wet, sticky blood groped in the darkness. They were my hands, but whose blood? The smell of death overwhelmed my senses. Should I be able to have my senses in a dream? It was so real.

My skin was yellowing and graying. My body was passing from life into death; my body was weakening and deteriorating. My energy waned. My life force ebbed, as I became light, like air. I felt as light as a feather, as if a sudden gust of wind could lift me up and away.

My skin became loose and cracked. More than sixty years passed in an instant, then in the thin veil between life and death, a voice of song and beauty cried out, in a sound both grotesque and lovely, as if half its soul had ceased to exist in that moment. This soul's cry scared me out of my own body.

Her pain was my own. It pierced through the wall that separated me from everything, and everyone. In an instant I was torn, half in my body and half out. Half physical, and half spirit.

Ashes blew on the wind all around me, as an erupting laugh pierced through the sounds of the air, so twisted in its gleeful joy at the sound of the girl's sorrow that an anger and hatred welled up inside me. As I turned towards the sarcastic laugh, I glimpsed a flash of long, dark hair against the grey green sky of an impending storm. When I turned to face her, I sensed her anger was my anger too. It was just another version of the same pain we all felt.

A small view of the woman's back and deep purple dress imprinted itself in my mind. A blend of fear and desire came over me when I saw her, so strong it diluted the anger almost entirely.

~ ~ ~

When I woke up, I knew without the shadow of a doubt that the woman was real, and I believed that she was someone from my future. Last month I'd had my first encounter with death, and already that death was causing me nightmares. Last month I had heard her voice in my dreams, now I was beginning to feel and know her, from the inside. I wondered how much longer it would be before she stood before me, as real and tangible as my own skin?

~ *** ~

I was concerned about Eliju. His nightmares showed themselves around the dark circles beneath his eyes. Yet I also realized that Eliju was a visionary. Even though he didn't share with me what or who he saw in his dreams, I knew this was a spiritual gift he had that needed development.

His maturity at this stage in his life was not as apparent as it was bound to be in later years. He'd had little experience with social interactions, and only a few years with his parents in the earliest stage of his life. As far as his relationships, his social experience was so slight, he was still very much a child, needing to learn the basics of love and respect that were so essential to creating lasting associations. Yet his desire to be good was evident to me.

I had so much to teach to Eliju. He had so much to learn about simple things that many others take for granted. He had been so isolated for most of his life, but I could sense when I looked at him that this was a man of unusual destiny.

In other ways, his parent's abandonment had forced him to grow up before his time. Eliju was a hard worker. In his life as a shepherd and farmer, he'd risen with the sun to begin his labors. In the seasons when the sun burned brighter, longer, and hotter, he rose even earlier. But I rose hours *before* the sunrise, no matter the season, for my occupation was the study of life and the earth itself. The more frequently I was a part of the birth and life, and death and rebirth of physical nature, the more I learned as a scholar of human nature.

Almost a month into our life on the road, I woke Eliju while it was ever in the still and hollow darkness. The boy was deep in the throes of another nightmare, but he got up without complaint.

"The lessons begin after breakfast, boy, so dress quickly. We have a long day ahead of us, and I want our lessons to begin as the sun comes up." Eliju nodded groggily.

I sensed Eliju's longings and fears. I had compassion for his life of isolation. It wasn't a natural life for anyone, let alone an extrovert like him. I was more patient with the boy in our lessons than I had been with many of my past students.

Yet I also sensed I needed to be firm with the boy or he'd never learn. Teaching him would be something like walking a high wire—always careful of tottering to the left or right, between toughness and kindness. For one misstep could mean a fall, from which he'd never be able to stand on his own two feet again.

As we ate breakfast, I asked, "Have you ever witnessed a sunrise, Eliju? Tell me, have you heard it too?"

"Of course, I've seen a sunrise," the boy responded quickly, then stopped and stared at me confusedly, when my full words set in. "Heard it? How could I *hear* a sunrise?"

I stood proudly to my full height of six feet four inches, puffing out my chest in stately dignity. "I am a Shaman, at one with the earth. I intend to show you how to not only see a sunrise, but hear it, *feel* it, until the pulse of the earth beats in time with your own heart's beat. It is important to go with the flow of life, with the flow of nature that is life itself."

* * *

I stared at him in wonder. A fire ignited in my spirit, when I thought about being able to do the things this extraordinary man wished of me. After finishing breakfast, I hurriedly pulled the small cracked mirror from my pack, smoothing down my wild hair.

I saw myself in the reflection, light olive complexion darkened by the daily pummeling of the hot desert sun, and intense, large eyes, sometimes a deep sapphire blue, sometimes a dark emerald green. A fair amount of matted brown hair fell about my face. It was crooked and moderately long, for I was the only one to cut it, and I never cut it well. I knew I was bold and rebellious by nature. A fiery spirit burned in my essence that hid the silent loneliness of my days, before the Shaman had come.

I was glad he had come. Words could not express how glad I

was that he had come to take me away.

The fulfillment of my life had been in caring for my flock, but there was so much missing in a life spent only with animals, as much as I loved them. I had farmed the food I ate, and sewed the clothes I wore, not well, but well enough that they should keep me covered. My hard life showed on my tough skin, the worn hands; my tired eyes. I missed my sheep, especially Rachel and Leah, but I felt in my soul that I'd been created to leave my life as a shepherd, and that I was born for something more than toil on the hot desert sands.

Somewhere deep within, I'd been longing for the company of *human* companionship, friendship from another human heart. More even then the promise of adventures in faraway lands, I was grateful to be with the Shaman, so that I wouldn't be isolated anymore—alone with my questions and desires. I was a natural seeker and adventurer. Traveling had already begun to soothe my restless spirit. Yet I longed and hoped, for more...

"Hurry boy," Wandering Wolfe said, as I finished dressing. "We need to hurry, for our lessons to begin with the sun."

I placed the comb and cracked mirror back into my pack, and hastily walked with my teacher into a quiet grove. The sky was a brilliant blue, and the stars had completely faded. The day was an open canvas, to be filled with the pastel colors of the sunrise.

* * *

Eliju started to say something, but I interrupted. "Be quiet, Eliju. There's still time for a dawn's grounding exercise. Now close your eyes. Listen carefully to the sounds you hear. Lay down and let your body relax into Mother Earth. Feel each part of you becoming one with the soil beneath you...from your legs, all the way down to your feet, from your arms, all the way down to your hands, from your back, to and stomach, and even your head...all now one with Mother Earth. What do you hear, Eliju?"

He wisely took a moment to reflect, before answering me. "I hear birds singing around us. I hear the footsteps of other animals in the forest." An owl sat on a nearby perch behind him, hooting softly. "I hear an owl, though it's an odd time for an owl to be out."

"Can you hear anything else, lad?"

"No, not yet."

"Listen closely. Listen to the air. Listen to the wind. Listen to the heat hissing like a snake. Listen to my heart beat. Hear your own heart beat pounding in your chest. Hear it. Feel it. Go into the beat. What can you sense now, Eliju?" I watched as Eliju's worried, anxious face, dissolved into peaceful serenity before my eyes.

* * *

The world stood still in this moment. Time itself stood still. How could being so conscience of the present, cause me to see and feel so much I'd missed before? Time and life were endlessly ebbing and flowing like the ocean. Yet I felt as if I were a still, motionless stone on the moving waters. My mouth felt gummy, and I couldn't find the words to articulate what I was feeling.

Somehow the Shaman must have sensed it, because he didn't press conversation further. He let me lose myself in my senses, at least for this beautiful moment in time, where and when I was truly *present.*

It felt like a lifetime passed, but after what must have been only a few minutes, the Shaman spoke again. "Do you feel so light you could fly, and yet heavy, as if you couldn't move even if you tried?"

"Yes," I whispered, full of awe at the expansive feeling of my spirit.

"Come back to your body. Plant your feet. Ground yourself on the earth beneath you. Now open your eyes."

I felt my body molding itself into the ground, as if there were no distinction. Opening my enlivened eyes to a sun which was just beginning to rise on the horizon, the backdrop of dark blue was swiftly turning to an azure so beautiful it took my breath away. The sky was painted like a canvas with oranges and streaks of pink and gold.

The new day was like a new world swiftly changing. Beneath me, the grass was greener than I'd ever seen it, and when Wandering Wolfe told me to touch the dirt, it felt lightly wet with dew and yet dry. It felt so crisp and fresh, I almost wanted to taste it.

I'd never felt this way before, so wild and free, and yet more grounded than I'd ever been. It was only the beginning of our time together, yet Wandering Wolfe had already changed my life, simply by opening my eyes to the world around me.

~ ~ ~

One night when we were both sleeping outside, near the fire pit, I woke up to the Shaman shouting. "Ahhh, ahhhhhh, ahhhhhh! Get it off me, get it off me; get it off me!"

I pulled the dagger from my ankle. My eyes never left him. But I couldn't see anyone there. Was he having a nightmare like I often did?

Wandering Wolfe brushed his hands frantically over his robes. A Black Widow Spider flung off his face and onto his shoulder. The fire's light illuminated its furry body. *So that's what was attacking him!*

It was hard to see it in the dim lighting, but I dove toward the poisonous spider, my small dagger missing it by several inches. Wandering Wolfe yelled out again, as if I had stabbed him. I lunged at the Black Widow again, this time slashing off one of its dangling legs. I cut off part of its head, then another of its legs, until it lay in pieces beneath the Shaman's bed. Surely stabbing the ugly little thing was overkill, but it seemed as if the Shaman's fear required it.

"Thank you, oh Father Sky above and Mother Earth below, I thank you for aiding Eliju," the Shaman breathed deeply, falling back onto his pillow with a heavy sigh.

"Are you really that afraid of spiders?" It was hard to believe so skilled a warrior as the Shaman, could be afraid of something that small, even ones that were poisonous like the Black Widow Spider.

"Deathly afraid," Wandering Wolfe admitted. "And that is a story best left untold, my dear boy. Suffice it to say that once upon a time, someone used them to torture me, and I never quite got over the experience."

I did a double take. He had no problem killing a man or any formidable opponent sent by King Mardavian, but a Black Widow Spider sent him into hysterics? Whatever had happened to him must have been bad. I felt sorry for him. Yet his reaction to the Black Widow made him even more intriguing to me. He was a man of endless mysteries and contradictions.

After the Shaman went back to sleep, I took the poisonous Black Widow Spider, and smooshed her mangled body into a small, empty vial from my pack, to be utilized later when I had some spare time, to concoct an anti-venom—in case one of us was attacked by a spider or snake.

I'd gotten into the habit of making these, after my first lamb was killed by a snake when I was 12-years-old. I'd carefully researched how to make the anti-venom, and how to administer it, to not take in the poison myself. I understood well how the very poison of a certain beast used to kill, could be used to save.

With the midnight interruption, the next morning came early. We were both tired, and not very productive, until after our midday meal. Every day after lunch, for two hours, Wandering Wolfe taught me weapon training with bow and arrows.

I was surprised Wandering Wolfe was teaching me this at all. It was even more surprising to discover how good the Shaman was at teaching combat. I enjoyed these lessons more than I thought I would. I was better than I thought I would be at them too.

* * *

Eliju took to his weapon training, like a bird takes to flight. He was a natural. I suspected his fencing lessons would be even better suited to him. The young man's mind was quick and bright, grasping onto things swiftly.

He loved learning how to fight. But I also noticed how he was with Flint, and how he had been with the animals on his farm. He was gentle with those who were weaker than he was. Indeed, he even seemed drawn to weakness. Knowing this about him, I didn't think there was too much cause for concern that he would use his weapon training to defend the innocent where and when needed, not attack and strike out with his own willful impulses.

"It's important to learn how to defend yourself and others, Eliju. If you don't, your life could become disjointed, like a broken arm that never righted itself, and you will never have peace. Killing must be the last resort, but for every death there is a life. To kill to protect, or to die as a sacrifice to preserve the life of another, is the most honorable passing into the light of all."

"Like how you killed Ishmael to save my life?" Eliju's forehead was creased with worry and guilt.

I put my hand reassuringly on Eliju's shoulder. "Kind of like how you killed that Black Widow last night. Eliju, that man wouldn't have stopped until you were dead. I didn't enjoy killing him. But yes, to protect you, I will do what I must. I know so much about fighting, not because I'm not a peaceful man—but because many others are not."

I could tell Eliju was perplexed by these ideas, but he didn't comment. Taking his last arrow out of the bull's-eye, he held the bow and arrow in his hand, focused and steady, moving several yards back, ready to begin again.

~ ~ ~

Heavy footsteps coming toward us, sounded like an elephant running through the forest. Tree limbs were falling, crushed beneath the weight of the creature's movements.

"What could be making all that noise?" I asked, slopping my rosemary mint tea down the front of my shirt, in haste to get into an upright and defensive position.

Then the "monster" was upon us, over seven and a half feet tall, wearing worn and dirty clothes, and with a broad sword at his side. It wasn't just the height that set this monster apart—it was his third eye brazenly open in the middle of his forehead! I stared up at the monster, my eyes widening like saucers.

How amazing! I'd learned from the wolf, Flint, that appearances can be deceiving, but my excitement when faced with such an unusual creature, surprised me. I could tell by the Shaman's expression that my response surprised him too.

"What, who *is* that?"

Wandering Wolfe laughed. "That's a Cyclops, Eliju and his name is Cleo. I know him, so don't worry. He doesn't wish us any harm."

* * *

As I defended the creature to Eliju, his third eye closed. "I'm sorry if I frightened you, Eliju, but I wished to see into your mind and heart. First impressions are important."

"I wasn't scared! You just took me by surprise! It's not every day you meet a giant with three eyes! But really—I think how you look is marvelous!" The Cyclops laughed and smiled.

"You're on your way to Anak are you not, old friend?" he asked me.

"Yes, we're going there to collect the sword for Eliju I commissioned for him during my last visit. Anak is the land of the Cyclops, Eliju."

"Are your kind...friendly creatures?" Eliju looked at the giant Cyclops and gulped. It was hard not to be amused with his reactions. His face so often expressed exactly what he was feeling and thinking.

The giant laughed again, hitting Eliju so hard over the shoulder, his bottom was pushed into the ground—though Cleo didn't seem to notice, even with his extra eye. I turned my face away, and chuckled into my beard, as quietly as I could manage.

"My kind are friendly to the friendly," Cleo said with a smile, but there was something *behind* his smile that hinted they weren't so friendly to the unfriendly. Cyclops could be fierce warriors when the occasion arose.

"I was sent here to be your guide. There are creatures in these parts that will rip you to shreds if you don't have protection."

"We're very thankful for your help, Cleo." I told him, with a respectful bow.

For the next few days, Cleo joined our travels, and I delayed further training with Eliju. I couldn't very well teach Eliju anything with the Cyclops with us. Eliju listened to our conversations courteously, smart enough to keep quiet himself.

Cleo was an avid hunter, so we ate more heartily in those few days than we had in a long time. I was usually more intent on studying and teaching Eliju than on our meals. The vegetation and herbal teas were good enough for me. I tried to hunt a little on the way, for Eliju's sake, and I certainly enjoyed good venison, but rarely took the time required to get it.

I was good at hunting, but I didn't enjoy doing it regularly. When I did take the time, the meat usually lasted for a while, depending on how big the creature was I'd caught. Cyclops, however, could eat half a doe by themselves each night, and they loved to hunt. They practically lived to hunt and eat. Tonight, we ate a bear Cleo had killed, and cooked it over an open fire most of the afternoon and into the evening, making the farm boy quite happy.

I was far more tickled with my daily ritual of concocting special teas to drink with whatever fresh ingredients were in our surroundings. My tea breaks during the day had a way of lifting my spirits. Its consistency was a ritual that comforted and soothed me, keeping me centered. To each their own I supposed.

Over dinner we conversed. "Where's your companion, Wandering Wolfe?" asked Cleo. "I've never known him to leave your side."

"Nor has he," I answered, taking a hearty bite of bear meat, and hankering for some potatoes with it.

"Then where is he, old friend?"

I quickly chewed and swallowed my food, doing some quick thinking at the same time. "It's no dishonor to you Cleo, but Flint is my protection too." Gratefully the Cyclops took the hint and stopped prying. Cleo's eyes (all three of them) registered understanding, and he asked me nothing more.

Then, as if on cue, the silver wolf streaked with strands of burnt orange, appeared out of nowhere, into the midst of our campsite. He was nothing but a mere shadow when it was this late at night, and Eliju gave a start when he saw him. The wolf licked Eliju on his cheek—his way of apologizing for jumping up on us.

"He's been watching us all this time?" Cleo asked.

"Yes, of course. Flint is always close to me, but he doesn't like being in cities, so he stays on the outskirts of the towns. But I think he'll be wanting some dinner now." I'd saved some large scraps of meat for him, which he obligingly devoured.

"He's the biggest wolf I've ever seen," noted Cleo.

"He'd never hurt one of my friends, unless they gave him a reason to, of course. He's been my companion for many years, and has saved my life more times than I can count. I owe him a great deal."

He'd guided me to safety at a time in my life when I was lost and still couldn't explain, covered in blood as a small child...but this was not something I wanted to speak to Cleo about, nor was I ready to speak to Eliju about something in my life which was still a mystery, even to myself.

I recalled when Flint had viciously attacked King Mardavian, who I'd once considered a friend. It was the only time I'd yelled at Flint and struck him. It wasn't long after that, Mardavian had shown his true colors. Then I knew that I'd been wrong, and Flint had been protecting me. Similarly, Eliju had misjudged him at first. It seemed that the instinctual wolf could judge the content of a human's character faster and better than we humans ever could.

"Somehow in my brief encounters with Flint, I don't doubt it," Cleo laughed. The words of the Cyclops pulled me back to the present, with Cleo and the shepherd boy, who was so critical to our future. For a moment, I'd been transported back into the past, with the people who held such importance to our present.

"I owe him too—for saving me and one of my lambs. Though growing up, I always dreamt of having a horse." The note of longing in Eliju's voice was not lost on me.

"Why, for it to make your work lighter? So that you could ride it, and he could carry your load?" Cleo goaded him.

Eliju was clearly insulted, too forthright to pretend Cleo's words hadn't offended him. "Of course, not! I don't feel that way about animals! I respect animals more than most people. I *have* heard that horses can be quite stupid, and would run off a cliff if spooked, but I also know there are special horses, just as there are special people. It's their spirit of freedom I so admire." I liked and respected the boy's honesty, while being concerned over his lack of diplomacy, and how others would take it.

Wanting to protect him from the Cyclop's wrath, I interjected,

"It only makes sense you feel that way, Eliju, as your birthmark is the stallion. We'll have to get you a horse at some point, but I'm afraid I don't have the means to purchase you one now."

"I don't want a bought horse, Wandering Wolfe! I want a wild thing; it's no use to have a horse if its spirit is broken."

Cleo grinned. It was clear that he at least found Eliju's frankness a worthy trait. "There's more to you than meets the third eye, boy. I think I like you."

The Cyclops patted his back, no doubt leaving a bruise on him, with his exceptional brute strength. "Perhaps you are a good pheasant's egg after all." There was a moment of silence, until we all burst out into laughter.

That night Eliju had a tough time getting to sleep again, as Flinty was howling up at the moon in a haunting cadence, both eerie and beautiful. It was often hard for fellow travelers to get used to the wolf's strange cries, but the sound was comforting to me, like a lullaby. His howl was the sound I'd heard since I was a young child, and I'd often fallen asleep to the sound of his cries.

~ *** ~

The next day we arrived at my beautiful city. Our warm, wooden homes stood out, as if greeting us as friends. Our most prominent buildings were made of polished stones. I puffed out my chest, and held my head high with dignity. As the Shaman and bright lad entered our city gates, I could see they were impressed.

I had enjoyed my time with the humans. To my surprise and pleasure, I had especially enjoyed the young lad, whose honesty and humor had amused me. I was bolstered by my time with them, knowing our bards would interview me after they'd left, and add my tales to their songs. I would be famous among my people, for my small part in helping to protect them on their journey to our land of Anak, and the brilliant swordsmith who had worked so laboriously to make for Eliju, a sword worthy of a King.

After I'd gone to retrieve the pair, I knew my fellows were busy bustling about preparing a grand feast for the special duo which would make our people proud. I was looking forward to the succulent meats being prepared by our finest chefs. I knew the Shaman and Eliju would remember and celebrate our city far after their adventures were over…

* * *

The homes were crudely constructed wooden settlements. The

most prestigious buildings were made of cold, gray stone. I couldn't help but doubt what kind of sword could come out of a dingy place like this one, but I was smart enough not to voice that question to the Shaman or Cleo. It was clear our guide was proud of his city, but I wasn't too impressed.

The town wasn't big enough to be a real city, so it wouldn't have taken us long to get through it, had it not been for the countless Cyclops coming up to Wandering Wolfe to talk with him and brag, which was halting our progress. I didn't want to make waves, sensing these creatures had a quick temper. I didn't want to find out what they might do to us if their temper was incised.

Flint had disappeared again, but sometimes in the distance I thought I caught a glimpse of a dark dot on a distant hill. *I'm with you, Flint. I'd rather be with a small group, or enjoying my own company, than to feel alone among so many strangers.* Yet I *was* curious about the Cyclops and how they lived. After all, they were my first experience of a culture and race outside of my own—other than the Shaman.

* * *

As we slowly made our way through the town, our progress often delayed by the admirers of our mission, I couldn't help but remember the last time I was here. I remembered that day very well, as it was the only day of my life I'd been bested in magic.

But that wasn't my focus as we made our way through the crowded streets. I was considering how my presence and commission of Eliju's sword had transformed this whole town.

Only a few years ago, it had been so poor and defeated. Centuries of oppression, of moving and starting over—due to the hatred and prejudice of Man, had taken its toll.

When I came to Orkin, asking him to make a sword worthy of a King who would unite all creatures and humans, the Cyclops and their city here had been totally altered by the respect I had shown them. I could see the pride they were taking now in their homes, and in their person. There were countless new buildings and businesses that were clearly flourishing. There was no denying my coming here had been the catalyst for this change.

I was so humbled and gratified by the improvements in Anak that I felt tears rise into my eyes. What power we each had in improving the lives of our neighbors! Or even better yet, what power we had in respecting those who were the most different from us.

Sometimes that makes all the difference in their world.

By the end of the afternoon, we'd entered a tall stone building where the sword maker, Orkin, held Eliju's sword. "I've come for the sword I commissioned for this boy here, Orkin. I hope you've fared well these past years, and have completed the project. The city of Anak certainly looks to be much improved!" Eliju stared at me wide-eyed. There were some things it took a long time for a young man to understand.

* * *

"I've fared as well as can be expected, Wandering Wolfe, while Cyclops elsewhere, some my own kin, are annihilated at King Mardavian's hands."

I glared at Eliju. He was too young. He could not yet appreciate the time and effort it had taken to yield such a masterpiece. He could not yet appreciate the lives that had, and would be lost, to see his rise as King.

I shook my head. "Such an important sword for so young a boy, though at least he is of an impressive height."

"Yes, he's growing very tall, isn't he?" Wandering Wolfe agreed with a smile.

I could read the look and mannerisms of the old Shaman all too easily. It was plain as the days of the week, and the order of the seasons from spring to summer to fall to winter. He already loved the boy.

He looked at him as the hope for all mankind. He looked at him with the indulgent air of a father, when what the boy really needed most was a good, hard look at the reality of what King Mardavian had already cost the world—and the duty and responsibility he had to correct it.

I had a mind to pierce Eliju through the heart with his own sword I'd been commissioned to forge for him Make him feel the pain of the centuries we'd all had to endure, of lost people and races, lost cities and Kings. Wound him with the pain of their loss, so that when he held the sword, he understood its worth was in the lives of all those who had gone before him—making it possible for him to rise as King of all, at all.

But instead I only asked the foolish old Shaman, "Do you have the silver?" I was abrupt, making it clear I was too busy for social niceties.

"Yes, of course." Wandering Wolfe shuffled through his pockets to throw down a large pile of silver coins, wrapped up in a delicate blue silk. "The sword is ready I presume?"

"You commissioned the sword seven years ago, sir. I've been forging it ever since. It was completed two months hence. I am prepared. I have been waiting for you."

I'd put my heart, soul, sweat, and full-time hours every day for years on this sword. Much as I resented the young, foolhardy lad, I couldn't deny the majesty of my masterpiece, nor the significance of the person I had forged it for. I knew the boy did not yet deserve such a sword, but perhaps someday he would understand its real weight and worth was not in its craftsmanship, but in the heart of the one who carried it. For all of us.

* * *

Seven years to make one sword? I'd expected the sword to be ill-shaped and poorly formed, if I went by Orkin's crumply and haphazard appearance, but if it'd taken the Cyclops nearly seven years to forge, perhaps I could expect more from the swordsmith.

When I saw the weapon, my breath caught. The handle was made of pure, refined gold; rubies lined the length of the handle, and in the center, one large, well-rounded diamond with six black onyx, stones surrounded it in perfect symmetry. The blade itself was long and sleek, with a dark sheen over the fine silver.

Orkin held out the sword to me. There was something in his eyes…making me see it as a priceless object, a true masterpiece. Relishing the feel of the sword's light weight, when I gripped the handle between my fists, it fit like a glove, like silk against satin, like sapphires set in silver. I didn't know how it could even be possible. It fit my hands like an extension of my own body.

How could he have done that? How could Orkin have made the handle fit me so well?

"It's spectacular," I told him in awe. "And I know I don't deserve it, but thank you."

"A sword befitting a Chosen One," Wandering Wolfe consented with a smile. Suddenly the pile of coins on the table seemed awfully small.

Orkin noticed my expression and took in my words. I saw his eyes narrow, knew he was analyzing me. "I would have been honored to bequeath you this sword without charge, but your master insisted on paying me a penance for my laboring."

"It really is an incredible sword…" I murmured.

"You didn't think it would be possible for one such as myself to make a sword so fine, aye?" The swordsmith asked with a grunt. I was caught off-guard by his insight.

"All that is lacking is a little magic," Orkin lamented to himself.

"We can ask the Elven folk to give it that," assured Wandering Wolfe. Unexpectedly, Orkin hmphed and turned away, in a not-so-polite dismissal of our presence. Why was he so angry?

"Come along, Eliju, it's time to go."

"Not so fast," said Cleo, as we walked out of the swordsmith's shop, appearing out of nowhere. "We've been preparing a feast for you of meats—beer, elk, fish and more. You do realize wherever you bring him, you'll find a feast? It would be rude not to partake in it."

"I will grow stout," Wandering Wolfe fretted.

"And it will become you," said Cleo with a laugh. "Besides you won't be eating so well on the journey itself. You should store up fat in the cities, like camels store up food before a long journey into the desert."

"I suppose you do have a point there," Wandering Wolfe relented, while I was salivating at the thought of all that juicy meat.

We moved to the center of the town quickly, to a large, long table in the center of the square. The tallest and best dressed Cyclops brought out tray after tray of whole bear, venison, goat, lamb and fish. The feast lasted into the wee hours of the morning. Wandering Wolfe got so drowsy, twice I had to catch him from falling head first into his plate of food.

Cleo finally noticed our exhaustion and guided us into a guest house with two plush beds and our own rooms. Tonight, I slept dreamlessly and peacefully beneath the soft folds of a delectable feather bed, and didn't even wake up once until mid-afternoon. Jumping out of bed, I quickly dressed and packed my things just as Wandering Wolfe came in.

"You slept late Eliju, but we have a lot of traveling to do. I thought it kind to allow you one good night of undisturbed sleep. But now it's best we get a move on, and I'm glad to find that you're ready for me!"

"HAH! I bet you slept in yourself! You almost passed out last night you were so drunk!" Wandering Wolfe smiled slyly and winked. As we left the city of Anak, Flint rejoined us, moving swiftly and deftly in the underbrush along the path we took.

~ *** ~

A week after we left the town of the Cyclops, Eliju and Wandering Wolfe sat outside roasting their catch of fish over the fire, with me at their feet. I liked to be near their feet so that I would always know where they were, and to be sure to follow in where they were going. I liked to follow in the underbrush, so that if someone sneaked up and captured them, I would be able to figure out a way to save them later.

Licking the blood off my paws from my latest kill, I gnawed in-between my toes, grooming meticulously. I enjoyed the grooming process almost as much as the eating. Wandering Wolfe stared down at me with eyes full of a lifetime of love. I could feel his love like the rays of the moon shining down on me, like the call of the moon to my soul.

The shine of the moon made my spirit soar as the lure of flight calls to the eagle. The moon moved my spirit as the tides were compelled to turn by its pull.

My person turned to Eliju and asked, "Tell me, do you know much about the moon cycles, Eliju?"

"I know a lot about the moon and its phases. I know there are rare times when no moon is in the sky at all. I've heard of blue moons, but I haven't seen any. I know about the lunar and solar eclipses as well."

The Chosen knew more than my person had anticipated. I thought about the time of the red moon, when I had found my person wandering around caked with blood on his skin.

"Do you also know about the twelve signs in the zodiac system, Eliju? Do you know that in some years there are thirteen moons and thirteen signs? Some calendars go by a solar cycle to divide the year, but it should go by the natural cycle of the moon. Shamans follow the lunar cycle, and in my Medicine Wheel, you will find thirteen moons."

I could see that Eliju wasn't really paying attention. He was staring absentmindedly at the winking stars in the sky, and the pregnant moon which illuminated the blonde soil and deadened fields. giving them an almost translucent glow of bluish white. He was contemplating that look of love Wandering Wolfe had given to me, and wondering if anyone would ever look at him that way.

I felt his heart. I felt his pain. I sensed his wound of abandonment from his parents that still hung off his skin like icicles off the trees in the winter snows.

"As I was making up your own individual chart Eliju, I found that you're currently under the influence of the thirteenth moon. Hence, this will be a time of great transition for you. You'll begin to question your old beliefs and traditions, and are likely to experience profound changes in your life."

"That makes sense," Eliju admitted, turning to him now, finally giving him his full attention. "But how can you always be so certain about everything?"

"Do I really have to explain that, Eliju? It's called faith." Spontaneously the Shaman reached out and hugged Eliju. I think the Shaman sensed his pain too. He was sensitive, at least by human standards.

But the boy wasn't used to any sort of affection. The Shaman's tenderness brought tears to his eyes. He was nearly broken down with the suddenness of the realization of how much he'd always needed the affection he'd never had...in those moments when he had most needed it.

Eliju's heart was heavy. He was remembering the years he'd spent in isolation and solitude. I saw it in his mind. He had suffered. For all those years, he had grieved alone. He worked hard all day—then at night he retreated to his bedroom, where the darkness overcame him, the denser emotions of rage, and anger, and grief.

Wandering Wolfe waited until Eliju blinked away the dampness in his eyes, and said softly, "All this is in your Medicine Wheel, my dear lad. This will be a time when you'll become more reflective and are meant to listen to your innermost thoughts and hearing the voice of—"

"Hearing what voice, Wandering Wolfe?"

"The voice of Mother Earth."

"*Oh.*"

He'd thought just maybe Wandering Wolfe was referring to the same woman he'd been seeing in his dreams. I knew the woman who haunted Eliju's sleep. I sensed his curiosity.

"This will be a period of restlessness and transition. You may have trouble coming to decisions. It's important not to deny or fight the change and the desire for inner analysis. If you deny or repress your more challenging emotions, like anger, they'll become more powerful and you may become harmful to yourself or others. There is nothing wrong with being challenged, Eliju. Challenges force us to grow. You must accept the metamorphosis you're going through, and if you do, the change will occur much more seamlessly. Now I would like to go through a full moon meditation ceremony with you. Hopefully it will cleanse you of any doubts."

Going back inside to gather the objects they needed for the exercise, they began the rituals of grounding and cleansing in a small clearing. Wandering Wolfe cleansed Eliju and then himself by splashing water around Eliju's form, and asked him to perform the same exercise for him. Meditating together in silence, Wandering Wolfe told Eliju to let his mind begin like a cup, full of images and thoughts inspired by this moon phase.

The moon was special to me. I was akin to the moon. It called and pulled at me in strange ways, as if stretching me outside of myself. When the moon shone in luminosity, it connected me to the earth, and all the suffering upon it, as if all the tears and blood shed upon the ground, urged my soul to express itself in the cry of the moon.

Like the nightingale's song, or the raven's flight, or the dolphin's dive, we each have our own ways of expressing what is in our hearts. Our howl is the cry of a spiritual being, grounded on an earth laden with cares, lifted up into the skies. What the world doesn't understand is that the immortal, defining cry of the wolf—is our way of praying for peace.

~ *** ~

Chapter Four
The Minstrel's Lullaby

August-September, traveling into the City of Hebron, and North, out of the desert—

When we reached the next town, Flint again disappeared into the obscurity of the forest. As we made our way through the dusty sand-strewn town of Hebron, a haunting melody, carried on the skirts of the dancing wind, bewitched us like a belly dancer sensuously moving in the rhythm of an Arabian night. We were compelled ever closer to the sound. I could tell that the song was a lullaby, but the song itself was unfamiliar.

At last we were upon the music. It was coming from a young man with sandy-brown hair and eyes closed in concentration. His fingers swept over the fiddle with great feeling. His hands were not smooth, but neither were they as rough and worn as mine were. He sang,

"Echoes of darkness descending
Beating the shore like the tides.
Silver beams of shadows ascending
Into the open expansion of skies.

A song sung is unseen, just like faith is—
What was meant to be, said to be, long before,
Is the hope—like a white bird that's rising,
Somewhere on the sky of another shore.

Soundless and wordless the melody,
Living hidden as a child of the light.
Born from the tribe of Israel and the race of Joseph,
I'm longing for the kindred spirits of a future time.

Gleaming gold is on the horizon,
Distant love is calling my name,
Colors and light are sweeping through the skies and
With my song, I take flight to another shore and a new life."

I was only a simple farm boy, but I felt as if I could sit down and easily while away the rest of the day watching the bard play his music, but curiosity got the better of me. "What's that song you're playing, lad?"

The bard's eyes were a gentle brown, with flecks of gold so bright they appeared as liquid gold in their luminescent warmth. "It's a song I wrote myself. I call it, 'Another Shore, A New Life.' Then he smiled a wide, sweet smile, meant to set me at ease. I was quick to return his smile, as I'd always admired people with musical abilities. Maybe he could teach me how to play the song of myself.

* * *

I recognized the young man and his beautiful music. Stepping forward, I pushed back the hood of my coarse cloak, so that the young bard could see my face. Looking up into my eyes and visage, his smile faded into an expression of recognition.

"You're familiar to me, sir. I think I remember hearing your likeness in a legend."

"And what legend might that be?"

"I don't know. I can't place it."

"Well, I know who you are, young man. Jonlin, the famous Bard of Hebron, whose music could coax the venom out of a snake, the sticklers from a porcupine!"

Jonlin chuckled at my description. "I don't know about all that—but I am the Bard of Hebron. And how do you know these things, sir, if I may ask?"

"Because I've heard about your likeness too, but I'll explain how in that tavern just yonder—the only one you have in this small town of yours. My name is Wandering Wolfe, and this is Eliju."

"Alright, sir, please just allow me to tell my parents where I'm off to."

* * *

The elder man agreed to wait, so I went home to tell my folks where I was going. Moments later we were heading down the small hill, to the tavern on the outskirts of town. The old Shaman with those intense, knowing eyes was so familiar. There was something good in the young man's big, round eyes, full of life. I liked him.

As we walked to my town's quaint tavern run by Judith and her son, Taruth, Eliju asked, "So where did you learn to play the fiddle like that Jonlin?"

"I was taught by a visiting gypsy."

"A gypsy?!"

"Oh yes. She saw I had a natural gift for music, and took an interest in teaching me the basics—though I've mostly learned by ear, how to piece the melodies and harmonies of a song together."

"That's a skill most can only dream of," Wandering Wolfe noted. Eliju was wide-eyed. He clearly appreciated the ability to make song out of wood and grain.

Perhaps I would try teaching the lad how to play some notes on my fiddle. I had often fantasized about having my own school where I taught students how to sing and play instruments. Perhaps Eliju could be my first pupil...

It was a nice thought. Oh, how silly I was! I had only just met these two men, and already I was day-dreaming about my friendships with them! My dear father would tell me I was at it again, fantasizing my life away. He always said it was a good thing that there was a place for bards in our world, as music and performing was the only thing I was good for. In a world where I couldn't make my living from music, I would be lost.

* * *

The motley crew finally reached the unkempt tavern where I sat waiting for them, in a quiet corner of the dimly lit interior. I'd been a tenant of this dirty place for the past few weeks, renting a room upstairs, as I awaited their arrival. Wandering Wolfe knowingly walked to the table in the back where I was sitting, sipping from a cup of steaming hot black tea.

I looked over the young men intently. Wandering Wolfe, I knew. He'd visited my tribe several times over the years, and was well-acquainted with my Medicine Man—as the legend of the tortoise on my belly and my name-sake, Shadow Rain, was well-known among my people.

I let them sit down before I asked, "So you must be Eliju and Jonlin?"

"Yes, we are. And who are you, miss?" Jonlin asked her gently. He seemed very sweet. The sound of his voice was like a melody.

"I'm Shadow Rain, though I usually go by just Rain, and I'm in training to be a Shaman, like Wandering Wolfe." I was surprised by the flash of instant curiosity on Eliju's face. I felt strangely flattered, and blushed profusely. I had not expected the Chosen One to be so handsome. His good looks caught me off-guard.

Jonlin turned to the Shaman. "So that's who you are! Wandering Wolfe, only the most famous Shaman on earth! Am I right?"

Eliju nodded proudly, "Yes, and he's *my* Master!"

"No, he's *our* Master," I corrected. "He's going to be teaching ALL of us." I watched Eliju carefully. His face lit up when I let the cat out of the bag that we'd be joining the group. My heart skipped a beat for a second. I was excited to leave this little desert town. I was excited to begin the journey…with him.

* * *

I was elated. TWO new people in the group! I was elated to have Jonlin, a *bard* of all things, joining us…and I'd always wanted a little sister!

Yet I was a little scared to be around girls. I wasn't used to them. What if I said or did the wrong thing—which I was all too likely to do with my clumsy ways—and made her cry? With her long dark hair, wide, slanted dark eyes, donning strange garbs the likes of which I'd never seen, I wondered where she'd come from—I'd never met anyone like her before.

"Just as you are all *my* masters," said Wandering Wolfe, deflecting their attentions. I was still off-put when he said things like that, wanting him to accept the praise he deserved, but Rain only nodded. It felt like they knew each other.

Abruptly, Wandering Wolfe turned his burnt autumn eyes to Jonlin, and told him he'd come to be his teacher as well. This time the boy looked taken aback. "But I'm just a bard. There's nothing special about *me*!"

"I'm afraid there is, Jonlin. You've been foretold as one of the fourteen Chosen Ones to fight King Mardavian—as is evident by your birthmark."

"My birthmark?"

"Yes, Jonlin. You do have a birthmark somewhere on your body, don't you?"

Jonlin nodded, "Yes, I suppose I do, though only God knows how you know about it! I have a birthmark of a lamb on my chest over my heart."

A *lamb?* My mind was flooded with images of my flock,

especially Leah and Rachel. *I hope they're doing okay without me...*

After a pause, Wandering Wolfe added, "And it's *your* name that is written in the scrolls of the Prophecy. Have you ever heard of the Prophecy, Jonlin?"

"Yes, though I never imagined I'd be a part of it!"

"Each of the fourteen members has a special marking on our bodies we were born with. By this, there can be no doubt that you are one of us."

"But I can't leave my family and friends! They need me here. I mean, I would like to help all of you, nothing would make me happier than to see King Mardavian overthrown, but how can I leave my whole life behind? Besides, I have a tough time believing you could really need me. How could *I* possibly be of any use? I'm not being falsely modest, sir. I'm only good at playing music. What help could I be in times of war?"

"Jonlin," Wandering Wolfe answered solemnly. "Your parents already know about this. They knew this day would come. I've known your parents since you were a little boy. They've kept me updated about your progress as a bard."

"Really?"

"I understand your feelings. I've been where you are, Jonlin," Rain interjected, in a sympathetic voice holding a note of resigned sadness, and a wisdom beyond her years. "I understand why you feel you shouldn't leave your village, your home and friends, and I'm sure they do need you here. I left my own tribe as I was in training to be its Medicine Woman. My tribe still needs me, but the world needs me more."

She paused for a moment before continuing. "It wasn't easy for me to leave them, but it was the right thing to do—for them, for all of us. We are called to a greater purpose. Somehow, you're a part of this, just like me, just like Wandering Wolfe, and without you, without all of the fourteen Chosen Ones coming together, we have no real hope of victory."

Shadow Rain's speech convinced Jonlin. He nodded his consent, but said nothing. There was a way about her. She seemed approachable, and at the same time she made me uncomfortably aware that she was sizing me up. Her name was so unique, *Shadow Rain.* Time would tell its meaning, and the historic legend, that was behind it.

~ ~ ~

That night we slept in the dirty tavern in Jonlin's poor village of Hebron. For dinner, we "feasted" on an overcooked helping of mutton and moldy bread, drinking a dark, warm ale that made me sick to my stomach. We were up early in the morning to start our journey as a group of four—five, including Flint.

Jonlin briefly brought us into his home, and introduced us to his parents. I tried to be respectful to them in their hut, but I really didn't pay much attention, figuring I'd never see them again. Wandering Wolfe expressed appreciation and gratitude to Jonlin's parents for allowing their son to join our journey.

Surprisingly, with two new people in the group, we managed to get around faster, but now when Wandering Wolfe and I took a break to do exercises and lessons, Shadow Rain usually participated with us. I was impressed with how much more advanced she was than I. I didn't mind a girl being better than me at something. I was rather impressed by it.

Jonlin had declined learning the Shamanic rituals, saying he didn't wish to fight. Nor did he condone practicing magic, being a deeply religious man. I felt a pang of guilt after Jonlin said this, for I was religious too, and knew the people who I'd worshipped with would have shunned me had they heard I was now practicing magic.

Yet magic spoke to a part of my soul I'd never been aware of. It felt like a part of me was expanding with every lesson. It felt like I was coming alive. It felt like I was coming home, to a place I'd never known.

There had been nothing negative about anything I'd done or learned. I remembered what Wandering Wolfe had said about accepting these recent changes and concepts into my life. I was coming to accept this as part of my destiny, refusing to be afraid or ashamed of it—magic was simply a greater expression of the spiritual realm, and what is God if not spirit?

Life was more than mere dust and dirt, and man was more than mere flesh and bones. Magic was only a means of tapping into the spiritual part of our being, the spirit beyond the flesh. Magic was something to be attained—like knowledge, wisdom and faith.

What were miracles if not magic? And what were miracles, but God's fingerprint on the earth, and the intervention of angels on a human's behalf? Using magic didn't make me love God any less, only understand one more aspect of God's anatomy, as if I was learning to understand the facets of a star in a galaxy of planets, moons and stars, in a timeless vacuum of limitless space, bound by eternity.

Though I was learning much in these meditations, and evolving in my values, my background had been one of such extreme isolation compared to others, especially those my age, that I was excited to have the new people in the troupe. I'd always wanted to be a part of a big family, with lots of sisters and brothers. I'd always dreamed of having a large circle of friends.

I admired Jonlin's musical ability, and Shadow Rain's magical skills. I longed for people to be close to. I longed to be known, seen, and loved, just as I was. I was hoping that we would become close friends, even a family.

Wandering Wolfe understood all this, watching me with the new people like a proud papa. It was never really said, but deep down, I think Wandering Wolfe knew that I felt he was like the father I never had. And I think he felt it too—that I was like his son. There was something special between us, a bond of kindred spirits that defied explanation.

Jonlin smiled at my looks of admiration and awe when he played his instruments and sang, taking it in stride with a grace and humility that made his talent even more outstanding. Shadow Rain took my awe and awkwardness to her advantage a little, teasing me when we did our magic lessons with the Shaman, and making me make silly mistakes, which wasn't too difficult, as I was so unused to being around girls, I was already a little jumpy! She scared me a little. But the truth was, I loved each one of them already, and had from the beginning.

~ *** ~

The air was warm and dry, as the desert sand blew all about us in the night wind. Inhaling deeply the scent of olives in the air, thick and rich, my bare feet felt the ground full of the gnarled roots of old olive trees, tangled up beneath me.

In my mind's eye, images of fall colors flooded my perceptions. In our midst, the full moon shone, like the lighthouse's beacon in the middle of the ocean, beckoning me home, calling me to focus my attention on the light, and the source of the light itself.

Wandering Wolfe passed me a translucent crystal, staring deeply into its depths. Then he shared his impressions. "I'm imagining all the leaves falling off the trees, and the trees and ground blanketed in soft, fine snow. I'm imagining a land of crystals. I'm imagining at last finding the true purpose of my journey in this life."

"I'm imagining open fields after its crops have been gleaned. I see its ground is sparse and barren, after the last of the harvest. I see a woman with long black hair, but I can't make out her face. I imagine a deep blue sky, and the ground beneath it covered with crisp white snow. This is the 'Full Green Corn Moon.' Soon the Harvest Moon will come, and the seeds planted in faith, shall come to fruition."

Flint came stealthily into the clearing where we stood, so quietly I barely took notice. I couldn't help but feel the wolf came just to watch and study how well I carried through the foreign Shamanic proceedings.

Wandering Wolfe was intent on the ritual, oblivious to my musings. Lovingly, he laid the crystal in the center of the circle he'd made, and because the moon was transited in a water sign, he placed a small chalice full of water from the river near the altar. Wandering Wolfe chanted softly,

"Oh, lovely Mother Moon,
Your soft white glow of light
Illuminates our night,
Giving purpose to our lives.

Oh, lovely Mother Moon,
We ask of you this night
To guide us to the light,
Revealing the purpose of our lives."

As Wandering Wolfe chanted the words, my imagination wandered. A scent of blue silk floated on the underlying currents of the wind, like the first fall of snow sometimes surprised the ground with its cold purity. Feeling as though there was someone there watching us, her form was not of physical substance. It was as if she was there in the scent of blue silk, as if she were the wind itself.

I was instructed to send out positive images to Grandmother Moon, so I lifted a silent prayer into the sky. Instead of directing my thoughts to the moon, I spoke to the woman of my dreams.

"I don't know who you are, or why I keep seeing you in my dreams. I feel your presence with me. Your scent is haunting me, the flash of your hair, and the sound of your voice. Who are you, and what do you want with me?"

Wandering Wolfe thanked the moon for the energy and love she'd given us, as he quietly took up the crystal, and lightly shook it in the chalice of water. The crystal made fluid ripples on the surface. The ritual closed, as my mentor rattled and chanted the poem once more. Then he cleansed and renewed the crystal and the bowl.

"What did you think of our little ceremony, Eliju?"

I took a deep breath before answering. "I feel calm and peaceful...and tired," I admitted, as if somehow seeing the woman from my dreams, prompted me to go to sleep.

"Go ahead and sleep, Eliju. Flinty and I will sleep outdoors as usual. I'll see you in the morning."

"Thank you, Wandering Wolfe."

"What are you thanking me for?"

"For bringing me this peace. I guess I really *have* been feeling restless lately, and these ceremonies have a way of energizing and grounding me."

"It's when you learn to accept these changes, you'll feel peaceful *most* of the time, Eliju. You will think on that," Wandering Wolfe said the words as more of a command than a request. I nodded, and went into my tent. In this meditative state, it only took me a few moments to fall asleep.

When I did, I saw once more that long, black hair moving gracefully in the night sky. "Are you Mother Moon?" I asked. I heard her laugh, and knew the answer was no. "Then who are you? What do you want with me?"

"You'll find that out soon enough," the phantom taunted before disappearing. I sat up straight in bed, realizing that it was already daybreak.

~ *** ~

"Now let the real magic begin."

The terrain had changed drastically in our weeks of travel from the desert landscape Eliju and I had met in. I was used to traveling, but I knew the rest of the children weren't. It was hard for them to travel for hours at a time. We weren't yet as far north as the mountains, but the woods were a pleasant change for the boy, who found he loved the trees of the forest.

I loved Eliju, in a way I'd never loved anyone before. It was as if loving him was using a part of a muscle in my heart that I had spent a lifetime without using, and was now getting exercised. He really was becoming the son I'd never had.

I loved Jonlin and Shadow Rain too, but Eliju...well, he was like a clumsy colt ungracefully stumbling on his feet. And for some reason, that endeared him to me in a way I couldn't quite explain.

Another month passed before I gave Eliju and Shadow Rain their next lesson together. They were also given a separate lesson each week. It was a full moon, the perfect time for experimentation.

"What are we going to learn tonight?" Shadow Rain asked.

I gathered the objects needed for the ritual before answering her. "We're going to learn some moon magic."

"First we'll perform a ritual, and then we'll begin the magic." I cast a clockwise circle. In the center, I lit a white candle to represent the Harvest Moon.

"Visualize this circle surrounded by white light, which will protect us from negative energies entering the circle, and keep the positive energies within the circle. Now, we begin:"

> "We ask of you this night
> By the power of your sacred light
> To protect us with this rite
> To show us, to change us, to remake us.
>
> We ask to go to the shadow lands
> Where those we seek are found again
> Upon the ever-shifting sands
> Of time and distance, we shall cross.
>
> We ask for our senses to be heightened
> For our discernment to be sharpened
> We only ask to be enlightened
> To be transformed by all we see.
>
> Oh, Mother of the Harvest Moon
> Your name is One and All
> Guide us in our transportation
> Teach us how to heed your call..."

Shadow Rain went first. After I held out my wand to the moon, and spoke the words over her, her body spiraled faster and faster in a circle and then disappeared altogether.

Eliju blinked in surprise. "Where did she go?"

"She probably went to her old village to see her family and tribe."

Many minutes passed, until Shadow Rain spiraled back to us, landing ungracefully with her face in some moss beneath a tree. As she stood up, spitting out the grass that'd gotten in her mouth, she turned towards Eliju, who burst out laughing when he saw her looking so disheveled...with tears in her eyes.

She ignored him and said to me, "That was a powerful spell. Can you use it anytime, anywhere?"

"No. This is a special spell of transportation that can only occur once a year during the Harvest Moon, which occurs in the full moon in the month of October or late September. It's said to be the moon of the greatest magical power."

"But there *are* other spells of transportation aren't there?"

"Yes, of course, but they have different requirements, and are difficult to attain. Please trust me when I tell you that you aren't ready for them. Now, Eliju–it's your turn."

Eliju looked as white as a ghost, but I chanted the words and made the symbols with my hand motions. "Rumina, rumina, rumina transporta rumina."

It happened so fast, he was knocked off his feet, as he spiraled faster and faster through time and space. I felt a little concerned about him. After all, this was his first major spell...

* * *

I didn't know where I was, but I knew who I was with—the woman of my nightmares. Wearing a ruby red cloak, all but her long black hair was completely covered by a shroud of mystery and darkness, but I knew it was her. Her visage was like the thick fog on a moonless night, but she was real. She was alive, somewhere in the world.

Chanting softly under her breath, she was standing over a black cauldron. The air was heavy with a sweet, yet bitter scent I couldn't identify.

"I've been expecting you," the sorceress said, without skipping a beat.

"Why won't you show me your face?"

"You shall see it sooner than you would like, Eliju." I'd expected she wouldn't answer my question directly, as she was almost always evasive. *I wonder if I'm even here.* Without even being aware of what I was doing, I reached out my hand to touch her body. All I touched were mere shadows, but it sent a shock of fire down the length of me, like a volcano erupting from the inside out.

"You shouldn't have done that, Eliju."

"I'm sorry," I said immediately, not usually so quick to apologize.

"You've thought of me much I see. What do you think I want with you?"

"I have no idea."

"You have no idea just how important you are, do you, Eliju? You've been proclaimed to be King of all. At least that's what the Prophecy would have us believe."

Who is this woman? What does she want with me? I didn't know about the Prophecy. I didn't know if I would be King, but I knew that I wanted to meet this woman for real.

As usual she read my mind. "As I said, we shall meet soon enough, Eliju. Until then, I shall continue to visit you in your slumber, imparting messages that shall become important in time. Now leave me to work out this spell, and go back to where you belong. I have much to do tonight."

I watched her for a moment more. Her movements were deft and quick, with a poise and grace I had never encountered in another female.

Spiraling downwards, faster and faster, I landed on the ground at Wandering Wolfe's feet, with a loud, kur-plunk! It was hard to transition from the other-world back into reality so suddenly. I hadn't been ready to leave her.

"What did you see? Or rather, who did you see? You have a strange expression on your face."

"Where's Shadow Rain?" I asked, ignoring Wandering Wolfe's question. I didn't want to talk to the Shaman about this woman in my dreams.

"I sent her to bed. Now please answer me."

"I, I can't."

"You're keeping something from me, but I can't force you to tell me what you saw. Go to sleep Eliju, we'll talk again in the morning." I heard Wandering Wolfe sigh to himself after I walked away, but I didn't go back.

~ *** ~

Chapter Five
Legend of Shadow Rain

Late September-October, continuing through the regions of Northwestern Europe—

Our next day's travels were dark and ominous. Even the sun was obscured by the clouds. No light shone on the path, as we walked in silence. "A storm is coming—I can feel it," Shadow Rain whispered. "A storm is brewing in the air, among the clouds; I can smell it on the wind."

"That's not all that's coming," said Wandering Wolfe. None of us responded to him, no one wanted to know what he sensed out there in the darkness.

Continuing to walk in silence, our ears were perked for the slightest noise. Our eyes were searching for any movement in the shadows. Just as we were finally beginning to relax, a twig snapped not far off.

"What was that?" Eliju asked nervously.

"Should we hide?" I asked, clutching my small case which held my fiddle against my chest, for safekeeping. It was my most prized possession. They could take my clothes and pack of food, but I would be inconsolable without my instrument, which was like an extension of my own body.

"It's too late for that!" We felt our minds explode in our skulls, in a bursting of light and noise. In a flash, it was still once more, and all thoughts dissipated in an endless, dreamless sleep...

~ *** ~

Eliju was the first one to come to. There was blood all over his clothes. Wait, but was it blood? He felt no pain. No, it was paint, not blood.

Shadow Rain had blue paint all over her, Jonlin had yellow and Wandering Wolfe had gray. The second thing he noticed was that his hands were tied behind him, and his legs were bound together. They were in a crude hut, and he could smell the grass and heather, though there were no windows and no doors. By the weight of the silence, he knew the walls were thick. They were in a circle: Wandering Wolfe beside Eliju, Eliju beside Rain, Rain beside Jonlin and Jonlin beside Wandering Wolfe.

We had taken all their weapons, but humans often hid their weapons in unseen places on their person. We had not considered it important; however, to run too thorough a search on them, as our powers were so much greater than daggers and swords.

If only I could get to my dagger, Eliju thought. I could read his thoughts. Rain moaned. She was waking up now too. Her bright eyes fastened on the young man immediately and darkened.

"Are you *bleeding*?"

"No, it's just paint."

Relief washed over her face. "Did you dream anything?" she asked.

"No."

"Neither did I, and I always dream. What do you think they want with us?"

"I think they want to stop us from doing something that's in the Prophecy."

That was astute of her. "What makes you say that?"

"I don't know. Just a feeling I have."

"I've never known you to have such feelings."

"I have a lot of dreams. Always have had. And they often come true…"

I made a mental note that he might have the gift of precognitive dreams. These two were of interest to me. I was glad to have this opportunity to view their interactions in secret, without the interference of the others in the group.

Rain's eyes changed—the dark blue turned to grey. "And so, it's begun, but how will it end?"

"What? What did you say?"

"I said that's really interesting. It sounds like that's one of your gifts."

"Really?"

Eliju grinned from ear-to-ear. She hadn't laughed at him, or discounted his words. That made him like her much more. It brought them closer. Humans invariably sought the approval of those in their circle, bonding to the ones who understood them the most.

"Do you think we should wake up the others?"

"Let them wake up naturally. Eliju—what kind of dreams do you have at night?"

He was visibly caught off-guard by her question. She clearly just wanted time to talk alone with him.

"I don't mean to be rude, but I'm kind of nervous to say."

"Just tell me."

"I'm afraid some of the dreams I've had lately could come true—and I don't want them to. I don't want to give them too much power by putting them into words."

Eliju was wise to recognize the power of words to manifest our thoughts in the physical.

"I think I know there's a woman that comes in your dreams."

"Why do you think that?"

"Because sometimes I dream of her too."

"So…you have the gift of dreaming about the future too?" he asked her.

She nodded. "That's how I can recognize it in others."

There were strange feelings growing stronger, and taking shape in the pauses of their silences.

"Do you think Wandering Wolfe knows who she is?"

"I don't know. I haven't asked him."

"I thought you told Wandering Wolfe everything?"

"Not this. This, I've only shared with you."

His words made Shadow Rain feel special. Their feelings were bonding them, as humans often connected by sharing secrets and from having things in common; whereas, spiritual beings like myself preferred the company of differences—differences in race and skills, in looks and purpose, to learn from each other. This secret might come in handy later, to be used as a weapon of division against the Shaman, their leader.

The silence grew stronger; the shape of their pauses became like a separate entity. Rain sensed something, something within him, some great fear; some uncertainty.

"Tell *me* then. Tell me what you're so afraid of. You're bound to feel better telling your secrets to *somebody!*"

"I'm not afraid…that is, I'm just concerned we're being watched," he whispered, looking around covertly. Perhaps the boy's perceptions were keen enough to feel my eyes on them.

"I don't think anyone is with us. Please tell me about your nightmares, Eliju."

She was so close to him, she could smell his breath, like berries glistening after a rainstorm. She didn't really care if there was someone watching, she was as curious as a cat about to lose one of its nine lives. From her senses, I could sense the same impressions, smell the same scents, feel the same feelings. Just as the young man looked as if he was seriously considering telling her about his dreams, the Shaman and bard came to.

I hadn't learned everything watching them, but I'd gleaned enough of their secrets to cause some problems among their ranks. I was satisfied. This was a good start.

Wandering Wolfe yawned tiredly, but Jonlin's eyes took in their expressions, and sensed something meaningful had been exchanged while they'd still been unconscious. For all the Shaman knew about life, sometimes the dynamics of the relationships directly in front of him eluded his notice. He'd barely looked over at the children yet.

Perhaps our magic had affected the Shaman more than the others. Wandering Wolfe seemed disoriented. Jonlin was the most alert, like a fox ready to begin a chase. At least the Shaman first appeared to be out of it—but it took him only a moment more to sense my presence, stronger than any of the rest of them had.

"We're not alone," Wandering Wolfe whispered. "Children—let *me* do the talking."

"What?" they asked in unison. It was then that I decided to make myself seen.

* * *

A tornado erupted in the middle of our circle, growing louder and stronger until it came to a standstill before our stunned eyes. After the wind and dust had settled, a creature appeared before us unlike any we'd ever seen before. It stood to a commanding height of fourteen feet, and was so dark and beautiful, it took our breath away. Clearly, it was not human. It spoke in a language we'd never heard, and yet understood.

"I've been observing you," the sinister being said softly.

"You're a Nephilim...I've read about your kind in legends, but I didn't know any of you remained after the Great Flood," said Wandering Wolfe with reverence, looking awestruck, but speaking in even tones.

I knew Wandering Wolfe enough to know that those well-measured words of his were hiding his own secret agenda. The Shaman said and did nothing without purpose.

"We are immortal beings. No natural disaster can eradicate our race. My name is Ramuel. I am a leader among the Nephilim. And I've heard of you as well," the giant being spoke sharply; it's long tongue hissing like a snake.

"Oh? And what have you heard?"

"It is I who will be asking the questions! Give me the name of the boy marked in yellow."

"That's Jonlin."

"He is quiet, unlike you and the two others! I like that."

No one said anything. We were waiting.

"Why have you trespassed through these forests?"

"We were on our way to Avalon. The only way to get there is through your woods and mountains."

"You're going from whence my people sprung. We have a colony in those mountains. They belong to us. We were the first to set foot on that land many centuries ago. Its original name is Pishon. Tell me, what is your business there?"

"Our business is our own," I interjected firmly, determined to show no fear, determined to show the creature I was made of sterner stuff than he imagined me to be, and that I was not so easily intimidated. The Nephilim hissed again softly, his gray eyes blinking.

"Now you will tell us what you want with us...why you've kidnapped us," I demanded.

The being made a horrible sound—it must have been a laugh or a cry, but it sounded like a howling scream. "You're quite the impertinent young man! You speak rashly, without any thought to the consequences, do you not? But I must know you wish us no harm before I am to release you."

Wandering Wolfe interjected, "Let us show you something. But you will have to untie me first."

"How do I know I can trust you?"

"You don't know. But there's only one way to prove to you who we are, and that's if you untie me."

"I warn you not to try anything sneaky, whatever magic you possess shall not compare with *mine*," the being glowered at us threateningly. As its deft fingers pulled at the air, the ropes untied themselves, falling effortlessly from the body of the Shaman.

Pulling up his sleeve, Wandering Wolfe showed him the mark on his shoulder in the uncannily intricate design of a wolf. "We all have a marking that was foretold by the Prophecy," he explained, as he covered his skin. "The girl Shadow Rain has the birthmark of a turtle on her stomach, Jonlin has the birthmark of a lamb over his heart, and Eliju has the birthmark of a stallion on his upper left thigh."

The Nephilim recoiled backwards, his slanted eyes widening in surprise. "You are...*they*," he murmured, in the strange language they all understood.

"Yes," said Wandering Wolfe.

"Is *he* the One," he asked, pointing at Jonlin. Wandering Wolfe shook his head. "No, it is the other—Eliju."

"Ah, yes. The name is vaguely familiar, yet the other radiates light and peace, and there is much hidden rage in the Chosen. I do not trust him."

"I do."

As he drew closer to me, the peculiar creature's cold breath gave me shivers. Studying me closely, his gray eyes were colder than his breath. "There is something in his eyes I do not like. I am surprised you do not see it, old Wise One."

"I do see it."

I wondered what they saw. Wondered what they knew.

"Then how can you trust him?"

"You don't know him as I do. You see into his eyes, but I have seen into his heart."

"Ah, but the eyes are the window to the soul. It is his heart that leads him astray with burning emotions..."

"His intentions are pure."

"I wish I could be so certain," the strange creature whispered. "I will give you safe passage in exchange for a favor."

"What sort of favor?"

"That, you shall know in time, but before I leave you, I'd like to speak to the Golden Boy alone."

"The Golden Boy..." I murmured, wishing deep down that Jonlin was meant to be our King—for surely, he would do a better job of it than I could.

"Yes, that is what my people shall call him!"

"What will you call me then?" I asked tensely. Ramuel looked me over me again, the expression changing from pondering to knowing. "The Chameleon," he answered. I felt disappointed with the title. It must have shown on my face, as nearly all my emotions did. I knew he was right about that.

"Yes, 'The Chameleon!' For your eyes change from blue to green so fast, and your emotions change just as quickly. If you were the earth, you would be the shifting sands, ever-moving from cold to hot, from wet to dry...yet as inflexible as the boulders on the Silverine Waters, as unstable as the Volcanos of Kilgo, the volcano—whose chief purpose is to erupt. Come, I shall show you a safer way through these woods. If I let you go of your own accord, it won't be long until you're taken captive again."

* * *

"Thank you, Ramuel." Something in my spirit had stirred with his presence. My hands and voice were shaking. I was not afraid exactly—but I felt as if I had encountered my Destiny, several years too soon. The Nephilim moved towards me, now looking me up and down. "You're familiar to me as well. Who are your people?"

"I am a descendant of the Shiwanna tribe, from the people of the clouds in the silver region of the moon."

"We knew them long ago. I see the ancient ones in your eyes. There's a blue flame behind them that burns when it rains, for that is your namesake is it not?"

"Yes, Shadow Rain," I whispered.

His expression was impenetrable. Holding a mysterious note in his voice, he recited:

> *"There shall be a rain that floods the sea,*
> *And dries the land with naught for green—*
> *A shadow rain that burns the wet*
> *Among the souls that cannot rest.*
> *When the moon is full on the eleventh day,*
> *This shadow rain shall be our grave."*

"Where did you hear that?" There was something familiar about the poem, something that brought back the memory of my own legend.

He looked at me sharply, curiously, his black eyes narrowed. "It is in the legends of the Fallen Angels. Tell me, why did your parents name you this...*Shadow Rain?*"

"I was born on a moonless night, when a storm was brewing. The air was wet, but it did not rain. We have a legend about my name in my culture too."

"What is it?" he asked me. "Let me hear this legend." In a tense, strained cadence, I recited:

"The Legend of Shadow Rain"

"When the night is silent in unquiet rest,
As the Watchers gather on the mountain's crest,
When the symbol on her skin burns bright blue,
Then the namesake of her birth shall come true.
As the chanting power brings forth the rain,
The race of the Nephilim shall be erased.

Destroying them with the powers of the Shadow Rain,
With a fury like the ocean's tempestuous waves—
The meaning shall be lost on her until the day,
When her daughter's birth shows the way.
She must use their destruction for her own gain,
Or their ancient souls shall have lived, and fallen, in vain."

Ramuel stared at me so intensely that my stomach felt queasy. Then he continued speaking, as if I hadn't spoken at all. "I shall speak to the Golden Boy alone tonight. There shall be two fires, and we shall sit apart from yours."

Agreeing with him with a silent nod, the ropes that had bound us, and the hut, magically disappeared with a nod from Ramuel. We were instantly surrounded by the heather Eliju had smelled. Their green leaves danced in the soft wind, their red berries dripped in the dew of the afternoon rainstorm. Picking some berries to eat with dinner, we moved on, this time apart from the path.

"Remember that sometimes following the path others have set before you can be dangerous. Sometimes it is better to forge your own way," said Ramuel.

* * *

"Thank you. We will remember this," said Jonlin respectfully. I already knew that lesson. Humans were often the last to learn. Traveling in silence, the humans were deep in their own thoughts. Usually Eliju and Wandering Wolfe talked, with Jonlin and Shadow Rain speaking and following behind. Tonight a stranger was among them, and none of them wanted him to overhear their thoughts, though they were aware that he probably sensed them anyway.

I looked up at the Nephilim. I dug my paws nervously into the earth. I hoped he could not sense my thoughts, read my secrets.

But the Nephilim were magical creatures with more powers than even Wandering Wolfe knew about, for they were deeply secretive, as well as fiercely self-protective. No one knew they even existed anymore, for many men and beasts had come to their land seeking to be taught their magic.

When the Nephilim couldn't be persuaded to reveal them, either by bargaining, or blackmail, or promises of wealth, or threat of annihilation—they were massacred almost to the point of extinction. Still, some lived on, and that was a comfort, for magic was always welcome and needed on an earth ruled by Man.

As the night slowly crept upon us, the sky was silent. There was no storm tonight. The air was cool and softly fragrant with the white blossoms that languidly twirled around us, on long, slender vines wrapping around the giant oak trees. They were unusual vines, in that they made the trees they clung to stronger. It didn't choke and kill, as most ivy is wont to do.

"Lilies are what we call them where I come from. There's a legend in my tribe of an Indian Princess who was named after them. Snow Lily was her name. She was murdered along with the rest of her tribe centuries ago. The sad thing is, she was said to have been killed the night before her wedding day."

"That is sad," said Shadow Rain.

There was a haunted, faraway look in Wandering Wolfe's eyes. "Strange I should remember that story. It happened so long ago." Wandering Wolfe looked away, lost in his reverie. The Nephilim stared at Wandering Wolfe intensely, and they resumed their stubborn, self-protective silence.

Just as Ramuel had requested, two fires were built that night. The Nephilim and Jonlin sat apart from the rest of the group. Only I knew what Ramuel and Jonlin spoke about, watching them from the shadows in the underbrush.

The next day, Ramuel and the group of Chosen Ones parted ways. We all knew deep down that this was not the last we'd seen of the Fallen Angels.

~ *** ~

Chapter Six
Memories in the Firelight

October, traveling North along the coast of Western Europe—

As the days passed, the air outside grew colder. The season of silences had almost begun. Sometimes when I couldn't sleep, the Shaman would give me lessons in the dead of night, or we would talk the night away. Wandering Wolfe liked to keep watch. I enjoyed keeping him company.

I was doing so well with the Shamanic exercises and weapon training during the day that Wandering Wolfe thought it was time to teach me a little fire magic. So that night, standing in the middle of a small clearing, while Jonlin and Shadow Rain lay fast asleep, Wandering Wolfe said he'd teach me the magic of creating a fire using only my mind. My religion would've warned me against participating in such an exercise, but my spirit soared at the prospect.

"Someday, Eliju, I may get you a wand to aid you in your casting, but you don't need it. Shamans use staffs not wands. Wands, staffs, incense, are only tools. The mind can create magic as easily as these objects, if it uses its knowledge to focus its power. The mind is the most powerful weapon we have, Eliju. A wand is only as good or bad the person holding it. Even wands with special abilities must be controlled and developed by their owners, like swords."

"But getting back to the exercise at hand, I want you to close your eyes, and briefly go through the centering exercise I taught you," the Shaman continued. I followed Wandering Wolfe's instructions obediently.

"The source of inner sight is known as the third eye, lad. Like the eyes of the Cyclops, but invisible and spiritual. It has the power to see the images and memories in another person's mind—even to make the images in your own mind come to pass. There are endless possibilities for the power of the third eye hidden within us, to be discovered through our own seeking and introspection. Like the Cyclops' third eye, it is located between your left and right eye. It functions as a secret balancing act between logical reasoning, and creative intuition—or the right and left parts of the brain. This inner eye is the key to your spiritual power, and the key to the uniting of cynicism and idealism, lending itself to practical ideals and insights that are grounded firmly in reality."

"Center all of your energy, emotions, desires, and power into this third eye. Squeeze your inner eye. Feel the rush of fire that burns within your mind. There are no words necessary for this spell. Its power lies in the depths of the mind's consciousness. There are words I could give you to aid you in forming a fire from your will. There are words to incise fire from a wand you do not yet possess, but it is imperative for your inner strength and will, to be the basis of your magic. No object, or even the ancient universal truths of the origin of words themselves, are more powerful than what's inside of you."

"Focus your inner eye to the ground a few feet away from your feet. Feel the steady ray of light that comes forth from this third eye, and bring the full force of it onto the ground directly in front of you! WILL and ORDAIN the fire you feel burning from within, and IMAGE it to the ground. NOW!"

Without warning, a tree a few yards away from us caught fire. The fire burst up the tree trunk, and the leaves at its top fell at our feet, smoking and blackened. Wandering Wolfe's hands moved up and down the length of the trunk, like they did in the smudging process, in quick, rapid motions. When his arms were completely raised, his hands remained spread out. He called out, "ALUM!" and the fire went out with a dramatic poof.

"That was an excellent first try, lad. You just need to learn to *focus* the line of fire from your third eye. I'm quite impressed. I think you're beginning to feel the first stages of the spiritual power that is your right as our King."

I felt my skin crawl. "Wandering Wolfe, I wish you wouldn't say such things."

He shook his head, "Eliju you're going to be King of every person, and of every type of race, religion, or creature in our world. You're going to be *the* ruler that's been foretold for centuries to bring all people and magical creatures and cultures together."

I wasn't pleased with Wandering Wolfe's words. I found them unsettling. "I don't deserve such a future. You should be King, not me! You or Jonlin."

"I was destined to teach you what you'll need to learn to become the kind of leader that unites the good, and protects the innocent. I'll be your guide on every step along this journey. Of course, you're not yet ready for that future. With my guidance, hopefully someday you will be. Don't dwell upon a future position you can't even imagine yourself capable of. Have a little faith—Fate took you this far didn't it?" Wandering Wolfe winked and smiled.

The heavy mood was slightly lightened by the confidence Wandering Wolfe had in me. Yet since the arrival of the Shaman into my world, I'd never had more doubts about myself...or questions about my future.

Wandering Wolfe demonstrated for me the correct way to start a fire, and we finished eating the rest of the fish that were left over and dried from supper earlier that night. Just as I'd eaten one fish, and was reaching for the last one, Flint snatched it up, gobbling it up in a few seconds. "Hey! I wanted that!"

"No matter," Wandering Wolfe said with a laugh. "I have some mushrooms I gathered earlier today that I can roast up, and it won't take too long."

Then I laughed with him. It was so nice to be up in the middle of the night, cooking with a friend. It felt so good to sit in the open air, feeling the breath of fresh air on my face. It felt good to share in the company of another human soul.

I loved traveling, being in constant motion every day. I loved the changes of landscape, and experiencing for the first time, the changing of seasons. At this moment, I wished in my heart I would always be in the company of my teacher, my mentor, and my best friend.

~ ~ ~

A week later, we were sitting outside again and enjoying the fire, keeping watch together while the others lay sleeping. Just as we settled in for the night, a lightning bolt struck a rock a few feet from our campsite.

Without warning, thunder boomed in the distance, as rain pelted us from the sky. Forced into our tent after many moons sleeping outside, by the fire, in the fresh air, it took a while to shake the excitement off us enough to even consider sleeping. The rain had revived us.

The storm hadn't stopped either. The wind picked up and the hail started, piercing through our tents like a chisel through ice. Jonlin and Shadow Rain came running from their tents, in a bundled mess at our feet.

"There's a town near here, let's see if we can find an old abandoned building," Wandering Wolfe suggested. "We can make some new tents with stretched deer hides tomorrow, or after the weather calms down."

* * *

Flint barked. As usual my wolf was going to guide us to safety. Flint guided us to the town, and a small, abandoned home that would make a good shelter, at least for the duration of the stormy night. Shadow Rain sneezed. There was a definite chill in the air, and the old house was full of dust and cobwebs.

Eliju went to work right away, making it comfortable for all of us. He was becoming such a considerate young man. His lack of upbringing was quickly becoming a distant memory, as he blossomed in the constant company of the people he viewed as his family. It was so clear how much he enjoyed our company.

I knelt on the hearth to get a fire going with match and flint, while the rest of the group checked out the bedrooms, and looked for some blankets. They hauled them back into the living room, where the fire I'd built was blazing merrily.

I had an especial liking for roasted potatoes as a midnight snack, and I felt like it would be fun for all of us to have a bite to eat, so Eliju helped me prep the potatoes to be roasted over the home fire. After the potatoes were carefully placed in an old heavy iron skillet we found in a lonely kitchen cupboard, Eliju brought up a term from the first night we met. The term popped out of his mouth as unexpectedly as the sudden downpour.

* * *

As soon as the group was all settled around the hearth, inhaling deeply the mouth-watering smell of the roasting potatoes, Eliju asked, "What are the Akashic Records you mentioned the first night we were together, Wandering Wolfe? I know I've never read about them in the Torah."

The Akashic Records. The term didn't ring a bell. Shadow Rain and I were as expectant as Eliju as we waited for him to answer, but the Shaman remained silent.

* * *

Turning to stare into the red-hot flames, for a moment I lost myself in the swaying movements, and the familiar crackling of the carefully contained heat. Putting my hands up to the firelight, I rubbed them together to dry and warm them.

The blood rushed back into my hands and body. The light of the fire in the hearth reminded me of my own life, how I'd learned to control my emotions and passions, until even I was unaware of my true feelings. It had all been done before, by many men and women in history. Being alone for so long, they tell themselves they're meant to be alone—despite the intrinsic message from the first story in the creation of time…

Now it was only foolish forgotten lore from an unexplored wisdom that after Man was created, "it" was not good, "it" was not done, *life*, until Woman was made for him. ***"It is not good for man to be alone,"*** God had said, and so Woman had become the zenith of creation.

Women were the crowning glory of all of life itself, as the last creature made by God. Women were the most complex and beautiful of creatures, and the human representation of God being able to produce and carry-on human life…

The memories came flooding back to me of a long-ago time, before the losses that had changed the course of my life, and broken my heart beyond repair. The memories returned, of the only woman I had ever really loved…

Something in my subconscious recounted for a moment, the moment of love long ago, so long past I wished it could be completely forgotten, and the moment my unnatural fear of spiders was born. Yet I also wished, somewhere deep inside, that I was still a *man,* and not merely a Sha-man, and the memory could be fully retrieved. If only that moment of love could have lasted longer than a season, but truth to tell, a mere moment of love can last for a lifetime, and I was grateful, to have loved at all.

Half a dozen more flashes of lightning lit the sky, before Eliju broke the silence. "Wandering Wolfe, can you tell us more about the Akashic Records?" he asked again.

Eliju's voice pulled me back from my reverie, and the longings in my heart the memories had incited. I realized that no matter what age they are, men and women always long for love.

I sighed. "Yes, now that I've rested a bit, I'd be happy to tell you about the Akashic Records, and much, much more." I took one more deep breath, fully dismissing the cobwebs of memories from my mind, and the painful emotions from my heart.

"The Akashic Records are the history of the earth and everyone in it. They're the voice and actions of people past, present, and future recorded on the ethers. These records can be tapped into by anyone at any time, if they're tuned in enough to the etheric."

"What's the etheric?" Jonlin asked.

"The etheric is energy. It is a halo of white light surrounding humans, animals, plants, objects, everything and anything. In spirit, whatever is created lives on. For example, the table that Eliju built and fixed in his hut every other day, became a part of his spirit. His spirit brought life to a simple table. Jonlin brings life to the instruments he plays. Anything that is built, holds the breath of life of its creator. Just as a child, carries something of their parents in their spirit. I think the fact that your old table never stayed fixed, means there's something in you, Eliju, that's broken."

I could tell that Eliju felt a little exposed in front of all of us after I said that, but Shadow Rain kindly came to his rescue. "We all have broken, fragmented pieces in us. That's what soul retrievals are for."

"What are soul retrievals?" Eliju asked her, grateful the heat of the attention was taken off him.

"They are what Shamans do for their people, to heal them."

Before Eliju could ask her to expound on that, I continued as if Shadow Rain had never interrupted. I was still in such a dream-state, I was barely aware of her interjection.

"In this darker time of year, physical senses are in a heightened spiritual state, and if you learn to harness this heightened state, you can learn to focus it, and tap into the Akashic Records. Voices, light, speeches, conversations, the scenes and memories of human experiences are a few examples of what are in these Records."

"Like a bird, unpredictably flying in the flow of where the wind takes it, life itself is like a wheel. A circle, or a serpent eating its own tail, is the sacred symbol of immortality because there is no end and no beginning, as all of life is a continuum. At the beginning of life, babies often resemble old men, and at the end of life, little old men often go back to acting like babies. History and patterns repeat until someone with enough strength and courage, forges their own way, making a new path...but I am digressing now."

"You've said the Akashic Records are somehow the manifestation of the history of the world, right?" Eliju asked.

"Correct."

"So, these Akashic Records are a history of the past?"

"Yes and no. It is the history of the past, and the present, the future, and every possibility therein. Again, imagine a circle."

"So, are you saying that we could change the future included in these 'Akashic Records,' and we could even change the past, and what has already occurred?" Jonlin asked incredulously.

"We can change the past literally and figuratively, merely by altering our own perceptions of it, and our evolving comprehension of universal truths inherent in all religions and higher octave meditations."

"I'm not sure if I agree with that. Not every religion is right," said Jonlin gravely.

"No, but there is truth in all religions, just as there are truths every person has to impart. Every person you meet has lessons to teach you, and has lessons to learn from you. The key is to discern the objective truth that hangs in the balance between biases, personal opinions, and perceptions that may be tainted by individual experiences. Wisdom and the intellect may know the inevitability of certain courses of action within our lives and those near to us, but if our hearts believe this inevitability *could,* and indeed *can,* and *will,* be changed through faith and love; then they *shall be.*"

"I'm afraid some of your teachings damage my religious beliefs, and my beliefs are the foundation of my world. I've never heard of these Akashic Records. It scares me that you're leading us astray, Wandering Wolfe," said Jonlin.

"It concerns me too," Eliju reluctantly agreed.

"I would never want to lead you children astray. Not in any way. If my teaching makes you uncomfortable, you don't have to accept it. I would only ask that you at least let me make you aware of these concepts. The Akashic Records may not be included in your holy books, but consider this: the river that is flowing just beyond us, would it not be there even if you didn't believe it was, and wouldn't you still get wet if you walked out into it, even if you thought it was not there? If you still refused to see it right before your eyes, wouldn't you drown if you refused to swim in it?"

"I'm sorry," Jonlin said politely, "but I don't think what you're saying proves anything."

"Perhaps it doesn't. Or perhaps it does at least prove that it would be wise to have an open mind to the possibility that your texts don't hold *all* the answers to the questions of the universe. Fear is never the answer. Fear never leads to truth. Knowledge is power."

"To study religions besides your own, leads to the questioning of one's faith, which ultimately strengthens it. If being open to other people's ideas, makes you lose your beliefs, then my question is how strong the foundation of your belief system was to begin with?"

"And after studying so many different religions, you identify most with Shamanism?"

"As I've told you before, Eliju, I don't consider Shamanism a religion, but a way of life, a way of being at peace, and in sync with the earth around us. I believe for a human soul, our connection to the earth, and to the ground, is essential to our connections with those around us and ourselves. I have beliefs I share with different people in other religions. In seeking to find the universal truths that bind us together in love, I learn to appreciate our differences, and not fear them."

"The Akashic Records I've been telling you about are not specifically a Shamanic belief. It is a universal concept that merely adds to the understanding in religion therein. It's not a religion, meant to be worshipped."

"What harm is there in an idea? The Akashic Records are merely an idea that may help to further our understanding of the world. It does nothing to interfere with your traditions or its precepts. It is when we fear each other's ideas that wars start. When we understand an idea, even if we don't agree with it, fear dissolves."

"But what proof is there of these Akashic Records? Maybe it would help them to understand it better," suggested Shadow Rain.

"They are in the Apocrypha. The Book of Enoch talks of them especially." I knew this could be a comfort to Eliju and Jonlin. "It is mentioned in Eliju's original Torah and Jonlin's original Bible. You can look up this information yourself."

Shadow Rain smiled at the boys triumphantly. To be honest, they did look relieved.

"I have been able to comprehend the Akashic Records, though of course, only in part. Humans have a limited capacity to understand such deep mysteries, but I can see the etheric with my naked eye at times, when I am in a meditative or evolved state of being. This gives me an advantage of belief. Since I've experienced going into these Records, I know there's nothing to be lost or gained from them, except wisdom and understanding, and I am not alone. Others have been able to tap into sections of the Akashic Records, and can see the etheric with the naked eye."

"What's the etheric again?" Eliju asked.

"It's the source of energy inside the aura, our life-force. An aura is the color, or colors in which a person resonates to, in personality and spirit. Some people believe that energy and light are what lives on of us after the decay of the physical body, the soul. It is our souls that are eternal."

"Can you see the 'aura' as well, Wandering Wolfe?" Shadow Rain asked, intrigued.

"Sometimes, when I'm in a very spiritual state…but not always."

"What colors are the auras of people?"

"They can be any color, Eliju, and they all have many different meanings. It's a matter of being able to interpret the meaning behind the colors."

"What color are our auras then?" asked Shadow Rain earnestly.

I looked at them all closely. No, I decided, this was not the right time to share that knowledge. "I'll tell you another day, once I've fully come to understand their meanings." Even Jonlin looked disappointed, but I didn't want to go into those concepts yet—we'd had enough to deal with discussing the Akashic Records.

"But about these Akashic Records, are you really saying that the history of time: past, present and *future* is recorded in them?" Eliju asked again.

"Yes, that's exactly what I'm saying."

"It's so hard to understand." Jonlin and Eliju looked at each other in agreement. They felt very similarly about these ideas.

"Why is it any more difficult to remember the past, than it is to remember the future?" I asked them. Eliju couldn't help it—he laughed.

This annoyed me a little, and I spoke more firmly now, and with more authority. "People find proof through science, which is apt to change as we learn and evolve, but the truth is that their opinions are simply glorified theories, which will ever divide these scientists from the world and even from each other. Those who are obsessed with a world of facts are fools. These self-imposed facts only exist in their own biased perceptions…"

"No matter how carefully an experiment is conducted, there will always be exceptions and uncontrolled variables. People also find proof through philosophy, which is apt to change to suit the needs and desires of changing societies. So in the end, is not the only proof of anything at all—in the faith we hold for it inside? Don't fear my teachings. Test them, try them, and I don't believe they will interfere with your religions at all."

"Let's say I integrate this theory, the Akashic Records into my own religious doctrine. Let's even say your practices of our exercises with nature, I adopt into my own way of life and culture. Eventually, won't my own traditions, which I was raised with, become weakened or diluted at best, discarded as out-of-date at worst...the way the Christians feel about us?" Eliju looked at Jonlin warily.

Jonlin twitched uncomfortably with Eliju's look. Jonlin spoke softly when he added, "You must understand that we believe in one God, Wandering Wolfe. And though I don't want to take liberties and speak for Eliju, I think we do both worry that magic could detract from our beliefs because God is the source of power and life. And our faith in this God is what has seen us through the hard circumstances we've faced. We don't want to jeopardize it."

Eliju nodded at Jonlin. He was right. This did obviously worry him. I knew it was Eliju's faith that had seen him through when his parents abandoned him. I would never want to take faith away from him, or Jonlin, or anyone.

I softened; feeling, rather than seeing Eliju's deeper feelings. "I understand your concerns, boys. I can only say that if God is the one true thing for your faith, that will remain strong regardless of the kind of people you meet, or the ideas you hear along the way. In this world full of colors, things are not so clearly black and white. White is, after all, the symbolic representation and containment of ALL colors, Jonlin."

"I believe truths gleaned from these ideas would add color and dimension to the core of your foundation of one God. The Akashic Records are simply the record of time. That idea does not interfere with the idea of one God, only that God has a record of history in a dimension which people of heightened spirituality are able to occasionally tap into."

"I understand your worries, and I'm glad you've voiced your concerns, dear lads. You may well be the cornerstone of all our hopes, and perhaps my own redemption. I would do well to not only share my beliefs and way of living, but also learn from you about your own beliefs."

"All we can truly offer you is a listening ear, Wandering Wolfe, and an open mind, and I think we'll keep in mind that your intentions are good," Jonlin said, as he looked at Eliju, who nodded that he agreed.

"Do you remember the story of Enoch—the man who walked in the Garden with God, and never died, who is in both the Bible and Torah? When God brought him up into heaven, it is written in the Apocrypha, that he became the angel, Metratron, and that it is he who guards these Akashic Records. Please look into this, boys; it may reassure you." Jonlin and Eliju nodded. I knew that they would.

"Do you think you could tell us more about King Mardavian now, Wandering Wolfe? Mardavian sent a man I'd known all my life to try to kill me the first night the Shaman came," Eliju explained to the others.

"Wow," said Shadow Rain. "That must have been pretty scary."

"It was," Eliju admitted. "I'd only met the Shaman moments before this man attacked me."

"I'm sure it was a plan on King Mardavian's part—to make you distrust him," said Jonlin.

"But it didn't work," smiled Eliju. "Wandering Wolfe killed the man with magic and saved my life—which only made me trust him much sooner than I would have otherwise."

I hadn't missed Eliju's changing of subjects. "King Mardavian is cruel and twisted, Eliju, in ways you may have never imagined. Jonlin and Rain can tell you about him as well. He—*enjoys* hurting others, in any and every way he can. I always look for the redeeming qualities in people, but I've never managed to find any in him. It's as if he has no heart or conscious. And without a conscious, he's dangerously powerful because he can so easily hurt anyone that gets in the way of his agenda, without remorse."

"I was there when he changed the direction of the winds on Mount Cristo. I was there when he stopped the sacred burning of the Valley of Kilgo, turning the Valley of Eternal Fire into a Valley of Ash. I was there when Mardavian, along with his father, killed his own sister, Eliju."

With those words, and that memory, I had to stop for a moment to catch my breath. My eyes flooded with tears. I didn't allow them to fall, but the children saw them. I took another deep breath before going on.

"He uses his power in the vilest ways a man ever could, killing off whole races, to gain dominion over their lands and assets. It's going to take a lot of studying, practice, hard work, and more than a pinch of good fortune, for us to defeat him."

It was clear to me that Eliju felt woefully inadequate. He gave a helpless look to the others. Jonlin put a steadying hand on his shoulder. Shadow Rain smiled weakly. She felt frightened to face King Mardavian herself.

I studied them, seeking to measure the depth of their hearts, weigh the potential of their minds. Emotionally I cared about them, but intellectually I detached and analyzed them apart from my feelings.

"You're all young and inexperienced in many ways, yet I see in each of your souls, the potential for greatness. Eliju has a natural courage that will be crucial in our fight against King Mardavian. Shadow Rain has magical skills to help aid us. I think both of you share visions of the future that will give us important knowledge in advance."

"What about Jonlin?" Shadow Rain asked quietly. "What is his role in our troupe?"

I felt my chest ache as I looked at him. "Jonlin will become our heart..."

I paused to stir the potatoes, in the skillet over the hearth. By the delicious scent of them wafting throughout the room, they were nearly ready.

"We are destined to experience war and all the consequences of it, children," I continued. "The repercussions of taking another person's life, and of watching the life of those you love stolen before their time will–"

"Will what?" Eliju prompted.

"Will change you. It will either change you for the better, or it will destroy you. There will be temptations and just cause to become bitter and angry, consumed in revenge—or its other false twin of justice—taken without due respect for the law, and obedience to authority. If you take revenge on for yourselves, you could easily become a warped mirror image of King Mardavian himself."

"We all face evil and suffering in life. It is our reaction to it— choosing to overcome it, or choosing to become a part of it, that defines us. Life either makes us better, or it makes us bitter, children. Regardless of the circumstances that are beyond our control, it will be your choices that decide your Fates. Each of us will have to decide for ourselves."

Eliju gulped, groping for a way to lighten the mood, he said, "How about bittersweet? It's my favorite combination of flavors. How about rosemary and oregano for the potatoes?!"

Shadow Rain laughed, and said she thought that sounded good. Jonlin, who was grateful for the interruption, added, "Sure why not?" The mood of the conversation shifted. Nothing more was said about soul retrivals, the Akashic Records, or King Mardavian that night.

I listened as they talked and laughed about simple things from their simple lives, before they'd started out on this journey: of Shadow Rain's training to become the Medicine Woman of her tribe, of Jonlin singing for his bread, as the beloved Bard of Hebron, of Eliju's farming and shepherding of his beloved flock in Haran.

Not long after the conversation shifted, I pulled out the roasted potatoes from the pan over the hearth, and we ate and laughed far into the night. I let us sleep into the early afternoon hours. We remained in the abandoned house for a few days, while we stretched hide to make new tents.

The night before we moved on, as we ate, I became more and more detached watching the children chatting and chattering away, becoming entranced once more in the fire and flames.

The traumas we endure in this life change us. They lacked the experiences I did, so they could not understand my thoughts, and I could barely relate to theirs sometimes. In the turning over in my mind, of the memories from so long ago, the feelings I'd buried, in a moment of burning, returned.

~ *** ~

Chapter Seven
Jewel of the Andorra Mountains

October-November, traveling West through the Kingdom of the Franks, to the Southernmost border of countries in the mountain peaks and valleys of Andorra—

Bang! I was suffocating beneath the water. Someone was holding me under. The icy water flooded my lungs.

Gasping for breath, my whole body was on fire with the cold prickly movements of the swirling undertow. Right before I succumbed to the freezing pulsating of the frigid water, I was raised up, high into the air.

I floated there for an instant, high above the reach of human hands. Off in the distance, I made out a tall, gray tower with imposing black spikes and gargoyles, in front of stain-glass windows depicting torture and war.

My body fell to the ground, and was immediately dragged before the ornate black front door of the castle trimmed in gold, and stained with fresh, splattered blood with a strange tint of yellow. My blood. Pulled inside, lying face down on the floor, I looked up to see the woman I'd seen in my recurring dreams, wearing a long, black dress.

I could make out every minute detail of her body, but not her face. I had never seen her face, but I knew her well now. Her matching necklace and ring glowed ruby red, and held moving swirls of black and fiery burnt-orange within.

Sharp pain echoing all over my body, made me cry out. My body was shoved onto the cold stone floor. Over, and over, and over again, I was beaten and bruised, until my bloodied body held little strength to live.

As the group of men who'd beaten me, lifted me up, and then pounded my chest down onto the cold floor, I felt my heart exploding in my chest. Right before I fell into complete oblivion, I woke up sweating...

Sitting up from the ground where I'd made my bed of fallen autumn leaves, I wiped the sweat off my brow with a corner of the blanket. *I need some fresh air...*

Walking away from the campsite as quietly as I could, I sat next to the "Virgin Lilies," as Rain called them, inhaling their sweet fragrance. I felt my anxiety slowly begin to dissipate into a peaceful meditative state, as I took in multiple slow, deep breaths, just as Wandering Wolfe had taught me to do when my restless spirit overwhelmed me.

"Your nightmares are getting worse, aren't they?" I heard Rain say from behind me. I twitched. "I didn't mean to startle you."

"You didn't mean to—it's okay…" But really it wasn't. I needed some space right now to let go of my nightmare. I felt nervous and awkward about being alone with a female at night. What would my old Rabbi say?

"Will you please tell me about your dream?"

"No, I'd better not, Rain. I'm sorry."

"Then do you want me to tell you about mine?" I didn't answer right away, but I was curious. She smiled—she was probably smart enough to know this.

"It was about that woman you see in your dreams."

"You dreamed of her too tonight? Could you make out her face?" I didn't want to be inappropriate talking here with Rain, but I *did* want to compare notes. I was compelled to find out who this lady was. The desire to meet her was getting stronger.

"No, but I heard her voice. She spoke to me."

"Would you mind if I asked you what she said?" I knew Rain was a sensitive girl, so I was really trying to be delicate with her.

"She told me you would choose evil in the end."

I felt my heart expand with hurt. "No, I *won't* Rain. No matter what anyone says, I won't. I can't. That woman we see in our dreams wasn't telling you the truth."

"Eliju–"

"Rain, I don't want anything to do with evil. I want to do good for people, give them the things they need that I never had. I especially want to protect the animals and magical creatures. In my life, I've been far closer with animals than people. I'm sorry I raised my voice to you just now, but it wasn't directed at you—I just want you to believe me."

For this one moment I let down my mask, to show her how hurt I still was from my parent's abandonment of me. The traumas of our lives don't always go away. They stay with us as imprints, becoming scars that make us who we are.

I looked at her as my friend and little sister. Her good opinion meant a lot to me. I felt naturally protective over her because I saw through her exterior, realizing how caring and vulnerable she was. I hoped she would understand me...

* * *

I saw into his core, the source of his pain. "Eliju—"

"Please Rain, say that you trust me, that you believe in me," he pleaded with me. I began to see that he longed for the approval of others nearly as much I did.

He pretended the negative comments people made about him didn't bother him, but they did. As he came closer, my heart skipped a beat. I was glad it was this dark, so he couldn't see me blush.

I couldn't believe how my heart ached for him, how I was so easily overcome with compassion. I'd always been an empath—having the ability to feel other people's emotions as my own was one of the reasons I'd been chosen so early on to become my tribe's future Medicine Woman. The more intensely felt the emotion, the more I shared in it.

Both Eliju and I were emotional, but our feelings expressed themselves in different ways. As his painful emotions filled my heart, I felt again my own desire surface to become his friend.

"I believe you," I whispered. It was all I could manage to say. My mouth felt tight and gummy for some reason.

His eyes were so beautiful. Why hadn't I realized that before? His eyes were so blue, bluer than the ocean, bluer than the sky, deeper even than the luminescent blue of twilight. There was something in his eyes, something I couldn't put into words, something that made me sense feelings from another place and time, in the future...

"Thank you," he said softly, softer than the brush of the cool breeze against my skin in the night. He smelled like the burning embers from the fire at our campsite. He was masculine and bright. I was water falling into a stream, the force of my energy was in a storm or an undertow. My emotions could carry me away, but when they did, I usually just wept the day away.

He was looking at me in a way I didn't quite understand. He was so very different than I was, and yet we shared similar gifts, and similar fears. What happens to a fire when a storm comes?

In those few brief moments when his eyes met mine, my heart felt more than in the culmination of my whole life. I was dizzy with the intensity, almost sick with it. Was I being affected by the heat of his energy of fire?

I understood now what Ramuel had meant when he said Eliju was full of hidden emotions, so many emotions to a degree even I as an empath had never encountered. They were fiery, and yet roving and restless like the tides. I felt like I could get swept up and away in them, or just as easily drown in them.

There are levels of emotions, just as there are levels of knowledge and love. Eliju's emotions were high, extreme. He lived on the edges of things, had lived on the outskirts of the world, isolated for so long. But that didn't reflect his true nature, and his emotions had burned deep inside him all his life, and being held down for too long, they now threatened to erupt.

"Was there any more to your dream?" he asked.

"Yes."

"Please tell me."

"She told me one of us was going to die."

"She's lying. She was trying to scare you."

"I'm afraid she was telling me the truth, Eliju. I'm so afraid that—" I stopped and stared into his eyes. *If only he could hold me— that would be such a comfort.* But I knew somehow deep inside that his arms would never hold as much comfort for me as Jonlin's steady faith. What I felt for Eliju, was far from calming.

The heights of Eliju's passions frightened me. Like my birthmark of the tortoise, I preferred staying closer to the ground, solid and stable. Whereas, he was like the stallion on his left thigh, desperately craving to run free.

"No one is going to die—except King Mardavian," he insisted.

"I hope you're right."

"I know I am."

"Where do you get your confidence?" I feared and worried over everything. Even what I knew for sure, I tended to doubt. In this too he was different from me, he was far more self-assured.

He smiled at me with a bitterness beyond his years. "I guess from years of disappointment."

"I don't understand that."

"Neither do I, but it's the truth."

"What was it like?" I asked him, tentatively, not wanting to pry, but sincerely curious.

"What was what like?"

"Growing up without a mother, without a father?" Looking down, he turned away. "I'm sorry, I didn't mean to–"

"I don't want to talk about it." That hurt ran too deep. The years that went by without them had still not become a scar. His wound was still raw. Time heals nothing, not without understanding and forgiveness. In not being able to understand, he had not managed to find a way to truly forgive.

"I'm sorry, Eliju. I guess I don't understand why they left you."

"I don't understand it either, and I never will."

Moving closer to him, I said, "Don't pull away from me. Please let me try to comfort you. Rain is healing, cleansing, and I know it's a part of my purpose in the group."

"You can't heal me. No one can," he insisted, as he withdrew further away from me.

"I can try."

"I'm sorry, I don't mean to be impolite, but no, Rain. You can't."

"Maybe Wandering Wolfe could–"

"No."

"Can't you just talk to me?"

"No. Don't you see I can't?" His face was contorted in an agony so painful to see, I had to look away to keep from crying myself. He finally broke down, and the words rushed from his mouth, like water that had been dammed for too long. Now the water of his words overflowed too hard and fast over the wall he'd kept them safely controlled behind.

"I was just ten-years-old when they left me. I don't even remember them, just vague images—in colors really. I know she had dark, brown hair, and he had red hair. I see her hands, olive skin, and, and somewhere in me I know she was beautiful, but hard. My father was softer. I don't know how I know that."

"I remember the feel of my mother's lips on my cheek," he continued. "It was the last kiss she gave me. They left in the night. I was sleeping, but I still remember her kiss. I remember that more than anything else. It was so light, so gentle, and so cold. My father stroked my hair...I remember."

He turned to me, his face looked distorted in this light, distorted by the pain. "How could they leave me when I was just ten-years-old? How could anyone abandon an innocent little boy? How could they–how could they–how, could, they, how–"

He had to stop before he lost control completely, and wept with all the tears, he'd kept inside for almost ten long years. I couldn't help myself, as he spoke, I'd started crying. I was crying now for him, hurting with him, feeling his emotions and pain as if they were coming from my own heart.

"Oh Eliju, they must have loved you! You were their only child!"

"How can you say that? How could they love a child they left behind? They CHOSE to abandon me!"

"I don't know, Eliju. I just don't know. I can't understand it." Tears were always near to the surface of my essence, and I let them fall now freely. "All I know is that you're wonderful, and I don't understand how anyone, how *everyone* couldn't love you."

I could see in that moment, his soul in perfect clarity—radiant with strength and courage, borne of a pain that most would never experience and could never have overcome. I couldn't imagine the fortitude it would take for a ten-year-old boy to survive on his own.

"Don't lie to me Rain. I know who I am, and I know I'm not ever going to have love. I will never be loved."

Eliju's face was down, he couldn't look at me—he felt so unworthy. It still hurt how his parents had left him, as if it were just yesterday.

"Don't say that! Eliju, you *are* worthy of love! *Everyone* is! I think I might know now why you were chosen to be the King among us."

"Why?"

"Because of your strength, you're incredible, superhuman strength. I don't know any other person who could've lived through what you went through—especially at ten-years-old! I think you're the strongest person I've ever known in my life! Maybe they left you so you'd become stronger than everyone else."

"The only reason I'm so strong is because I had to be. What other choice did I have, to lie down like a dog and die? I almost did. But if I'd done that, what would've become of my flock and land? I never could have let the sheep, or the farm, suffer by my own laziness or despair."

"The reason they left isn't important to me—there's no excuse that would ever make sense to me," he persisted passionately. "I've already tried to make some sense of it, and I just can't. It's monstrous. My parents are monsters."

"You're right, of course you're right, and I can't understand it either. I don't think I'd ever be able to forgive my parents for abandoning me like that."

"That's what I'm most afraid of. Don't you see? *They're in me.*"

"No, Eliju, you mustn't think of it that way. They're your parents, but you're separate from them. You don't ever have to be like them. As you said, what they did was a choice. You don't have to make the same choices they did."

"I would never abandon my children the way they did. No, when I have kids, I will be with them every day, teaching them, talking to them, doing things with them, loving them."

I felt myself smiling at his words. Eliju would make a good father someday, but Eliju was shaking his head, seething with anger.

"No, they *were* my parents. Now they're only ghosts that haunt me. I'll never be completely at ease, until they're gone from this world."

"What are you saying, Eliju?"

"Nothing. Let's go back to sleep."

"But Eliju, wait, what do you mean? What are you saying?"

Changing the conversation subtly, he asked, "What was it like, Rain? What was it like to have two parents loving you your whole life long?" Ironic that I couldn't understand not having two parents, and he couldn't imagine having them.

My compassion for him swept back over me, and I forgot my questions and concerns over his words, until I was safely in my bed and too far away from him to bring it up again. My mind was so easily impressionable. It didn't take much to steer me off course, as Eliju did.

"I really don't know how to answer that, Eliju," I told him sadly, longing to give him a hug, but afraid to reach out.

"I know. It's not really a question you would know how to answer anyway. The only way you can explain what it's like having two parents, is after you've already lost them."

"I'm sorry, Eliju. I just—" He held up his hand to stop my words of pity.

"Let's go back to sleep, Rain. Wandering Wolfe will probably have us up at the crack of dawn."

Before I could reply, or ask him to stay, he turned his back on me, and in his quick, confident stride, walked back to camp, and into the sanctuary of his tent, away from the questions he wasn't prepared to answer, even inside himself. Nearly six months had passed since he'd begun this journey, he would be twenty next month, at the end of

November, and I knew he didn't feel any closer to finding the woman of his dreams...or any nearer to understanding his purpose in the Prophecy.

~ *** ~

Our group had been heading northwest for a couple months, on turgid hills and mountains much harder to traverse than the flat deserts. The trees were growing thicker and closer in proximity, though their leaves were mostly bare this time of year, so we could see further into the landscape than in other seasons. This was helpful to me, as I'd never seen a real mountain, let alone climbed one before.

Holding on to the roots of the trees as I climbed, twice I caught myself from falling. Hardened by the frost; the grass was mushy from a recent snowfall, but there were still traces of green and colors left from the fall season, like the leaves of yellow, orange, red, and gold.

The way was rocky, full of stones, and to my surprise it was more difficult going down the mountain than up; my sure footing was threatened more so in the descent. By the end of each day, my body was sore from head-to-toe, with the effort of crossing the tough terrain. These mountains were beautiful, but treacherous.

"How much longer do we have to go?" Shadow Rain asked tentatively.

"We're almost there," Wandering Wolfe assured us. "We should get to the next town by nightfall."

We traveled for the remainder of the day in considerably better spirits. By the time we came to what appeared to be a grand city, it was so dark that we couldn't make out much of the buildings or landscape, which was a pity, for it appeared to be the prettiest and largest town we'd come across yet.

We made our way to an opulent fifty-foot-high castle. We merely walked up to the castle's gates, and the door opened. We didn't even have to knock, before we were ushered in.

Eliju and I were particularly awed by the grandiosity of the estate. Shadow Rain was too tired and hungry to be very observant of her surroundings, but as we were ushered inside, I think all of us sensed a sweet harmony in the air. A harmony not just in the aesthetic and lavish beauty of the interior, but in the atmosphere of the castle itself. The castle's energy was warm, bright, and light—like a roaring fire at midday.

The floors were made of white marble, and inlaid with pearls, silver, and onyx stones, making lovely patterns and symbols on the floor. The walls were painted a pale cream. Filling the walls were murals and tapestries of landscapes with bright blue skies, white clouds of various shapes and sizes, rose-tinted waters, and light-green grass.

There were murals of castles in the sky, lakes where fairies danced, and elegant ladies in ball gowns of pastel pinks and purples and blues, walked along the shores of the waters. Swans glided on glittery silver seas, while angels flew in the sky above them, with faces of calm serenity. I drank in the beauty of the castle, like a man deprived of water in the desert.

As we came upon the lavish dining room, an enormous crystal chandelier, resplendent with twirling colors, hung above a table of deep mahogany. The table could seat up to one hundred people comfortably, and was inlaid with elaborate designs and symbols, with threads of gold strewn within the floor of white marble.

As soon as we'd entered the dining hall, two people who were clearly related, gracefully glided into the room, with such poise and elegance, it was as if their feet didn't touch the ground. I wondered if they could be more than human because their grace was so perfect, and their features were so flawless.

The first to enter the room was a young man with rich brown hair and golden highlights. His round brown eyes were so warm they seemed composed of fire.

Wearing a meticulously intricate golden crown with diamonds ingrained around the entirety of it, and with the largest of the diamonds in the center, it was an ideally symmetrical and aesthetically pleasing design. He was magnificent in robes of gold, with a white rope tied around him that cinched in his masculine V waistline. Even wearing his heavy robes, it was clear this rather tall boy was solid muscle beneath his clothing.

Just after he'd entered the hall, a lovely, slender girl floated into the room, like one of the ladies from the tapestries on the wall. She, too, had rich brown hair, but instead of just blonde highlights she also had highlights of brilliant red.

Her eyes were as warm and inviting as the finest of chocolates, and her countenance held the sweetest expression upon the most feminine and delicate features any of us had ever seen. There was the purity and innocence of a child about her; she seemed to be totally unconscious of her effect on others. Her beauty and elegance were as natural to her personality as the sun's nature was to shine.

Instead of a large crown like his, she wore atop her lustrous head of loose, flowing curls, a gold circlet with rubies surrounding a stone that was akin only to this land. The stone looked like fire, with streaks of red, orange, gold and black trickling through it.

Eliju pulled me aside for a moment, to tell me that the stone in her circlet was in one of his visions. She was not the elusive woman from his dreams Shadow Rain and I often wondered about, nor was this the same castle where he was imprisoned in his nightmares, but she did wear the same strange stone. I felt honored Eliju shared this with me. We were all becoming closer.

This gorgeous girl wore robes of pure snowy white, with a golden silk sash that cinched her incredibly tiny waist, revealing an hourglass figure, and dramatic curves that were wonderfully womanly. The gold sash lit up her pale olive features, and the white robes gave her the look of an earthly angel.

"My name is Alondria, and this is my twin brother, Aldoran," the angel said. Even their names were like a melody, from a much more attractive world. I'd assumed rightly that they were related, but I had always had a fascination with twins, and this made them even more appealing to me.

Alondria was so effortlessly beautiful; she took the breath away of even Shadow Rain. Her skin was radiant. She positively glowed from the love radiating from within her, from the inside out. There was a moment of silence as everyone studied each other, then, with an impossibly graceful movement of her arm, the girl asked us to be seated.

"You are welcome to take your seat at the table. We'll be eating shortly. We're only waiting for our parents to arrive." Her voice was like the soft tinkling of toasting crystal glasses, full of sparkling pink champagne, and it *moved* my spirit in a way I'd never be able to put into words, though bard as I was, I was determined to try.

As if on cue, a woman entered who, if possible, exceeded her children's otherworldly charms. I felt like if I didn't play my fiddle and sing, I would burst.

Before anyone knew what I was about, I had my fiddle out, and was singing a song to serve as a prayer and toast. Afterwards, I was red-faced and shocked by the inspiration to sing, which had so overcome me.

"I praise the God that led us here—
To the Kingdom of the Franks,
I praise the beauty offered here,
By the royalty of high rank.

I praise the feelings evoked here—
An inspiration to make me sing,
I cannot contain the joy found here,
Bubbling over from inside of me.

I thank the God who brought us here,
And the peace that we have found.
And with this song I raise a toast:
I praise the food we are about to eat,

I praise the wine we are about to drink,
I thank the prince and princess,
And I thank the king and queen,
For we are honored by this feast."

The twins' mother, Selena, smiled as I played, nodding to her daughter, and looking up, as her husband entered the room. He was her opposite. Short and stocky with a bird-like nose and a balding head, we could see the twins obviously got their looks from their mother. I wondered what this beautiful lady had seen in this man to make her want to spend her life with him.

As soon as we were seated, a dozen or so of their servants brought in plates of the finest food and drink I'd ever seen or tasted... There were wines sweet and dry and fruity and deep. Hot spiced wines, chilled fine white wines, sweet rose wines, and deep, rich red wines were displayed in opulent goblets of gold.

Everyone in our group found ourselves drinking more goblets then we'd care to count. It was all so delectable and decadent, even I couldn't stop myself from trying one wine after the next. I was usually the sober one, but no sooner had our goblets emptied, then a servant poured us a hearty portion of another exotic wine to try. I didn't want the night to ever end.

The food we were served was divine. There was a feast of many meats prepared in countless ways, with breads of every shape and type. There was chilled fish, baked fish, broiled fish, and fried fish whose crust was as light and flaky as an angel's kiss.

There were side dishes of baked potatoes, mashed potatoes, sweet potatoes, potatoes broiled in a pan of marinated wine, and Eliju's favorite dish of roasted lamb with red potatoes, seasoned with fresh herbs of rosemary and oregano, with three different gravies to choose from.

Salads were dished out with several types of cheeses from this region of the Kingdom of the Franks, olives and tomatoes from Basques, fruits and candied walnuts, pecans and almonds. Plates full of cheeses from regions across the continent, were displayed on dishes of ornately designed cut glass of ruby, sapphire, and emerald hues, making the table a sea of jeweled colors, especially as the plates emptied.

For desert, there were fruit pies, cream pies, a light mousse pie, grandiose strawberries dipped in dark and milk chocolate, a pound cake liquidized with heavy wine and cream, chocolate cake with a side of fresh, finely chopped coconut, a vanilla cake topped with vanilla frosting as light as air, and fresh strawberries; tall angel food cakes with chocolate and berries, short pound cakes with fresh cream and jam, and bite-sized, multi-layered chocolate raspberry tortes. We were each given a dainty dish of crème brûlée, so light and creamy it dissolved just as soon it touched the tongue, and on and on came the trays of delicacies, in an endless display of blatant hedonistic culinary delights.

Without question, our group ate more in that one meal, than in all the time we'd been traveling together. Without question, it was the best and most diverse meal any of us had ever eaten in our lives. No one understood how these people could have fresh fruits and berries and salad in the late fall, but we were all too drunk and happy to care.

Yet, as everyone ate and relished the feast—talking loudly and often at the same time, I was quiet. That is, after I'd burst out into song I was quiet!

As I stared at Alondria, I found I could barely look or think of anything else. She was the most beautiful girl I had ever seen. She inspired me. She moved me. She enthralled me like a story out of a fairy book that I simply could not stop reading until I'd finished it.

* * *

Throughout dinner, I studied the bard Jonlin, studying my daughter. On Jonlin's pensive face, expressions of awe, fascination, and most of all, an almost hero-worship respect, passed over his even features. I also noticed that when Alondria looked at Jonlin, there was an expression in *her* eyes I'd never seen there before. The warm eyes usually so open and transparent for me, were impossible to read.

Alondria was the only person who ate little at dinner, and kept trying not to look over at the bard. Theodore and I, of course noticed Alondria and Jonlin's strange quietness too. I knew my children well, and my eyes missed nothing. I noticed at one point, the bard and my daughter's eyes meet. I felt the heat.

After dinner, I pulled Jonlin aside to thank him for his lovely song. He blushed helplessly—and quite appealingly modestly.

"You are very talented, and my husband and I respect talent above all else. He is very talented himself. He painted the murals on the walls throughout the castle."

"Wow," Jonlin said, obviously impressed. Who would not be? Theodore's talent set him apart, as one of the great artists of our time. There were few opportunities I missed to brag about my husband.

"And he writes…poetry mostly, and lyrics to songs. It would be wonderful if perhaps someday you both could write a song together."

"I would be honored to do so," said Jonlin, looking as if I'd just dubbed him with knighthood.

"I'll mention it to him. Goodnight," and before I left him to retreat to my chambers, I gave the boy a motherly kiss on his forehead, and smiled to myself about what I hoped was to come.

I liked the bard a great deal. He would be good for my lovely daughter. He would suit my husband and I well. I could see Aldoran and him becoming like brothers. A mother can always guess her daughter's feelings.

I realized of course, that they had only just met. But these things often occurred instantly. After all, hadn't I fallen in love with my husband before I'd ever even met him?

By one of his paintings, I'd fallen in love. His looks hadn't mattered. I'd fallen in love with his talent, before I'd fallen in love with him…and Jonlin was very talented.

Alondria would be perfectly suited to inspire a bard. I didn't care that he was poor and of humble birth. We had more than enough riches, without adding to them. What would we do with more gold? I cared that he could serenade my daughter in the moonlight, and that with him, she would always live in love.

* * *

My beautiful wife, Selena, the descendent of a muse, had inspired my best works of art. We had lived our days in a romantic state of shared bliss. As I drew, painted, and sculpted pieces of art for our gardens, my wife's love and adoration blossomed like a winter rose, with a love that did not die, but grew stronger over time.

We shared a love at first sight. In my experience, the only way a relationship can last forever, is when the connection is instant from the start. Of course, no marriage is all roses, but the thorns make the good times that much more meaningful. All epic loves have their battles—from the people who are jealous of the love they believe they will never possess themselves.

Selena and I had gotten through these hurdles together. Difficult circumstances had only brought us closer. Our unique city, apart from the wars and battles being waged around us, from all sides, had been won through the battles we had fought as a couple.

I had always hoped for my sweet daughter, Alondria, to share the same kind of life, and marriage, as Selena and I had, as the inspiration of an artist. Her romantic nature would be well-suited to such a love.

Of course, art could be many things—music was certainly an art, and the Bard of Hebron, Jonlin, had much potential. I liked the young man. Not only was he talented, he was humble and kind. I could tell already that he would be suitable both in skill and personality, for my beloved daughter.

I knew Alondria better than anyone. I knew she felt something for the boy. I knew she would want her parents' approval, so Selena and I would be encouraging to the pair.

I'd been concerned for my daughter in her adventures, but meeting the Shaman, Wandering Wolfe, and the Bard of Hebron, set my concerns at ease. I was leaving my daughter in good hands.

There would be love found along her adventures. This I could already foretell. It didn't take a muse to see the love at first sight that Jonlin and Alondria shared. My fatherly concerns were appeased by the end of our first dinner with the Chosen Ones.

* * *

After everyone had gone to bed, I helped my sister wash and dry the dishes. Although we had many servants to keep up with the castle's pristine conditions, we'd been raised not to be above working hard alongside the servants to help clean. We'd been raised to get our hands dirty and pitch in on occasion. After a feast such as we'd had tonight, the servants welcomed our help.

Besides, privately and away from the newcomers, I knew my sister would be more apt to answer my questions. During dinner I'd been unable to read her.

"So, what do you think of the Chosen, my sister?"

"He's not like I imagined he would be."

"How did you expect he'd be?"

"More like Jonlin perhaps…" she answered carefully, looking away, as a stray piece of her auburn hair fell across her face, and she brushed it aside. Watching my sister at dinner, and just now as she spoke about Jonlin, for some reason I couldn't explain, I hesitated in asking her directly what she thought of the soft-spoken bard.

Pausing for a moment, I asked, "And what do you think about Wandering Wolfe?"

She smiled brightly. "He's everything I'd hoped for and more! I'm looking forward to learning from him."

"I'm sure you are. I know I would be."

Alondria turned towards me, looking up into my brown eyes pointedly. "You want to ask me about something, but you're holding back."

"You're right, I am."

"You've never been afraid to ask me anything before."

"It's not that I'm afraid exactly. It's just that I felt you were acting strangely with Jonlin, and I was trying to figure out the best way to ask you about it."

A veil passed over Alondria's eyes. Her thoughts were hidden. Usually I could read my twin sister's mind as easily as I could tell the time of day by the changing slant of the light of the shadows and sun.

"Your group ate and drank and laughed and talked much tonight—only the bard Jonlin was quiet. And you."

Alondria looked away, clearly not wanting me to read the expression there. Twirling a glossy rich curl in her hands was her self-conscious feminine trademark. I knew she played with her hair when she was nervous. She was usually a charming hostess. But tonight, she was as quiet as the grave. Why?

"What is it sister, what thoughts are you keeping from me?"

Her words were so quiet I almost missed them. "He is…familiar to me, my brother."

"How is that possible? I know you've never met him before."

"No."

"Then what're you saying?"

"I can't tell you yet."

Her words stung. "You've always told me everything."

"Yes, but I can't talk to you about this, not yet anyway."

"But you *will* tell me eventually," I said it more as a statement than a question.

"Yes, when the time is right, and I feel more comfortable." It hurt me that she didn't feel comfortable talking to me about this.

Putting my broad hand on her slight shoulder, I sighed resignedly. "Then I'll have to accept that, and wait until you're ready."

"Thank you for not pushing me."

"As if that would work on you anyway! I'll see you in the morning."

I started to go, then turned back to add, "I'm sure you feel as if your whole life has been preparing you for this, for this one moment—a future that will affect the lives of our people, of *all* people. Your life is just beginning tomorrow, dear sister. Oh, how I wish I were going with you! You are so blessed to be Chosen as part of the most important troupe in history!"

"Yes, I am so blessed," she whispered, but there was something in the tone that was about more than what I'd just said—more than the lessons with Wandering Wolfe, or the journey to conquer King Mardavian, and all the adventures they'd have along the way, but what more I knew not, nor would for some time.

~ *** ~

The next morning, a gentle snow storm filled the sky, blanketing the peaks of Andorra in its splendor. After the snow stopped falling, the sun shone upon the white world making it glitter in the light.

Jonlin's eyes sparkled at the wonder of it all, for he'd never experienced the magical miracle of millions of unique falling snowflakes, laying the world beneath it in a holy land of divine purity, symbolically covering a multitude of sins. I watched as his eyes sparkled as much as the snow.

Theodore, my beloved father, pumped Wandering Wolfe's hand before we left. "I know you will take good care of my little girl." Then he placed his hand for a moment on Jonlin's shoulder. "Be well, my son," he told him. "Go in peace." Jonlin shyly nodded.

My beautiful mother, Selena, smiled at all of us warmly, as we departed, particularly the Bard of Hebron. My parents embraced Aldoran and I for a long time, before they let us go. Their love for us was as warm and transparent as the sun shining down at us from the sky. I saw the Chosen King, Eliju, watch our embrace with tears sparkling in his eyes.

As we left my home, Eliju was wide-eyed and child-like, as he held out his hands and tongue, letting the soft flakes wet his mouth and hands. I couldn't help but smile at his enthusiasm. Lifting his arms to the sky, he danced a jig, and laughed like he was a little boy.

I'd grown up in a place with four seasons, so I was amused by Jonlin and Eliju's reactions to what was, for me, natural and commonplace. Yet the boys' reactions to their first snowfall made me experience afresh the miracle of snow.

After eating a light lunch, Jonlin broke out his fiddle, singing to us a song inspired by the snow, inspired by the feelings in his heart:

> "Many towns have I passed through
> With open skies of brilliant blue,
> But never have I seen such grace,
> As the smile on Alondria's face.
>
> The majesty of the snow that falls,
> And blankets the earth like a million stars,
> Echoes the happiness of my own heart,
> With a beauty that could never be bought.
>
> Peace washes over me, as I look at this land,
> Renewing my faith and strength
> For the battles awaiting us ahead,
> Knowing we'll fight them together, as friends."

My eyes welled up at the poignant sweetness of Jonlin's voice. I'd never heard a man's voice sound so tender. It was so tender, I could feel it caressing the softness of my skin. Touched by his love for my land, as much as his tribute to me, as he sang, I rested my head on Aldoran's shoulder, sighing at the rush of emotions I was feeling inside.

Shadow Rain looked over at me, and I threw her a warm smile. Her dark eyes widened, then narrowed. Her mouth pursed, then opened into a surprised grin. She was good girl, and I liked her. I had a way of communicating my sincerity through my smile, to let others know I wished them only kindness and goodwill.

It was freezing as we walked through the city and climbed the Pyrenees Mountain Range, but we were warmed by the hot drinks Aldoran had prepared for us ahead of time. He would take us as far as the borders of our land; then give a regretful adieu. I knew he wanted to accompany us, but it was I that had the mark of the cross on my left palm.

Even the poorer homes in our town were well-kept. For much respect was given here to all people, in all stations of life. More amazing than the town's beauty, was the energy of love and peace in the air. I was glad that Eliju and Jonlin could sense our kingdom's positive energy. I hope that it comforted them to know there were still a few spots left in the world where kindness was the norm, and leaders were willing to be the servants of all.

Soon the city and valleys of Andorra were behind us, as once again we climbed the mountains scattered through these lands in silence. Each of us were deep in our own thoughts, and having to conserve energy and pay close attention to our footing, as we climbed the mountains; the inclement weather making travel more dangerous. By the time we stopped to rest, atop the last mountain in our region, we were panting from hunger and exhaustion, and it was nearly nightfall.

Andorra served as a border between the countries of the Kingdom of the Franks, and the Visigothic Kingdom. The Kingdom of the Franks was the side we lived on. Its people, the Andorrans, had been named after Aldoran and I. Ours was an Independent City.

The way my family ruled over it, created a haven of paradise, surrounded as we were, by countries that were fraught with discord. This was just one small part of the Pyrenees Mountain range, and we would be traveling up into the lands of Caledonia. As such, we still had a long way to go.

~ *** ~

Chapter Eight
At First Sight

Eighteen years ago, on the Isle of Apples in Avalon—

"Girl!" High Priestess Boann said insistently.

"Boy!" her husband the High Priest Dagda insisted.

"Girl!"

"Boy!"

"Girl!"

"Boy!"

They both laughed, as he put his rather large hand on her belly, and felt the baby kick. "It won't be too much longer, now will it?" he asked her, in his deep bass voice.

"No, she'll be here any day now my darling."

"I can barely wait!" he laughed again. "You know I don't really care what the gender is. I just want it to be healthy. I love him already."

*"I know darling, and **she** will be." But her laughter didn't affect his somber expression.*

"I have a feeling that—"

"A feeling that what?" she asked him, knowing her husband's "feelings" were really messages from the gods. Doubling over in a severe contraction, she was forced to lie down.

"Shall I get the midwife?" he asked her, and at her nod, he quickly ran from the room to fetch her.

"What sort of feeling?" she called after him, but he didn't hear her—and if he had, he wouldn't have taken the time to answer.

Seventeen hours later, the midwife was pulling the baby from her mother, as she let out a scream. "What is it?" Dagda yelled, for he'd insisted on staying in the room with his wife during the labor.

"There's something, something on the leg, and her leg is turned, twisted. It's, it's unnatural…"

"Twisted back? Let me see," he said, as he took the baby from the midwife.

"You're right, our baby will be lame—her right leg is misshapen. This mark though, what is this mark?" His face went through a range of emotions—fear, disbelief, joy, then overwhelming

pride.

"What is it darling, tell me!" his Lady demanded fearfully.

"A mark is on her right thigh—a birthmark of a raven in flight."

"A raven?" she cried, as her face went through the same range of emotions. "She's 'the One' then isn't she?"

"Yes, my darling!" he cheered, grasping her tightly, into a fierce embrace. "We shall name her Varawynn, and she shall have the best training, and the best suitors, and–"

"Darling, you're getting ahead of yourself, as usual," she noted, laughing at her husband's excitement that matched her own.

"I can't believe it!" he yelled, as he ran from the birth chambers, to announce the news to his beloved town, after handing his precious baby girl back to his wife.

"I can," she said, with a mother's intuitive wisdom, her tears of sadness now turned to tears of joy. "Such a gorgeous baby girl," she said, caressing lovingly Varawynn's unruly black curls, full of a mother's fierce love already.

"And what does it matter that she's lame, when she has such an important destiny?" Laughing merrily, well-pleased, she could never have imagined how wrong that assumption would be…

~ ✳✳✳ ~

November, traveling north through the regions of northwestern Europe, and into England—

Within the golden rays of the sun, I kneeled and prayed to my Christian God. Serenity was reflected on my upturned face, alight with the rays of the sun, hands clasped tightly in holy reverence. My faith was different than the Shaman's–tamer perhaps, less wild and free, but more peaceful too, for in my steady heart was a quiet, inner knowing that could never be shaken, for it was too strong.

My faith was like a white flame, like the hot sand. It was what gave me the spirit to be strong, and fight King Mardavian's forces without fear or aggression. I fought in my own way, through tranquil reflection and prayer. In times of trials, it was my faith that gave me hope.

"Death is not the end of life," I said to myself, in a moment of deep reflection. "It is but the beginning of something greater–a life more real and beautiful than anything on earth could ever be."

I often stole away in the early morning light, to solitary places, praying and thinking alone, but never lonely. I tried to slip away before anyone else was up, by doing chores like gathering kindling for the fire. These times of silence and reflection, restored my soul and renewed my mind. I needed these times apart to keep me energized for our travels.

Standing and wiping the dust off my knees, and the sweat off my brow, I walked back to the camp in a state of deep peace. When I arrived back, all the tents were packed up, and the food was put away in our packs.

"Excellent timing," said Wandering Wolfe. "I want to get an early start, so we can be there by supper time."

"Where's there?" I asked with mild interest.

"You'll see," he answered evasively, ever the mysterious one. The sun dipped behind a grey cloud, darkening the clear blue sky. The wind picked up, swirling some of the powdery snow through the obscured horizon.

"Looks like we're heading into some harsh weather," I noted.

"What kind of land will we be heading through today?" asked Eliju. "Will it be difficult terrain?"

"To some degree. We'll be going over a few hills, but mostly some heavily wooded areas. Everyone needs to watch their steps! I'm hoping by the end of the day, we'll get to the lake we need to cross over into Avalon. Have you ever heard of Camelot?" the Shaman asked.

Eliju just blinked, and I responded quickly, "Yes, of course, in my history books."

"Well, this land we're traveling through today is that ancient land. We're going to Avalon, the Isle of Apples."

"What are we going to find there?" I asked.

"What or who?" Wandering Wolfe asked, answering a question with a question, as he was often apt to do.

"I'm guessing what *and* who," said Eliju.

"Well done, my boy!"

"So, I'm going to assume we'll be adding another member to the group?" Alondria said, more as a statement then a question.

"And what's the significance of fourteen anyway?" Shadow Rain piped in.

"All of us have specific skills, and unique backgrounds meant to protect and support each other—you in particular, Eliju. But thirteen is the significant number here. Twelve disciples and one master, who is sacrificed. In our Prophecy, it's the fourteenth that will be sacrificed, and the thirteenth will remain the master."

"How will the fourteenth be sacrificed, Wandering Wolfe? You're not telling us that one of us has to *die,* are you?" Shadow Rain shot Eliju a significant, worried look. Wandering Wolfe didn't answer her. That was answer enough.

We walked the rest of the day without further conversation, as it was hard enough to hike the land. At least the mountains of the Kingdom of the Franks lay behind us, but there were still fallen branches, and large and small twigs beneath us, so we had to be careful not to fall or stumble, which took a great deal of concentration in and of itself.

* * *

I was so tired, after another night of fitful sleep, that I tried to focus all my energy on the physical traveling, not talking or thinking. Shutting off my thoughts and feelings, I turned my mind from the woman of my nightmares, emptying my mind so that I could find some peace.

We traveled through the forests, until we came upon the object of the last leg of our journey, a shining purple isle sparkling like liquid diamonds in the light of the fading sun. Glowing with an otherworldly intensity, holding a life of its own, I had never seen a lake so beautiful.

The water was multiple shades of purples: violet, lavender, and indigo hues, shimmered with an iridescent light, on the waves of the water. This lake made me feel as if a part of myself I'd never been aware of was now, here, home.

The stretch of grass beyond the water, was a deep green, like the sparkle of vibrant emeralds. Something about the green forest behind us, and the purple lake in front of us, and whatever lay ahead of us, gave me a peace and a comfort I'd never had in Haran, or anywhere else along our journey thus far. Somehow this lake filled me a calmness I'd never been able to find within myself.

Its familiarity defied logic, but nevertheless, was just as real to me as my own flesh. I was just as comfortable here, as I was in my own skin. Grappling for peace all day, seeking a calming for my passionate, restless spirit all my life, as I stared into the indigo waters, I felt a stillness and serenity I'd never known before.

There were two boats lying at the shore, and Jonlin, Alondria, and Shadow Rain went in one, while the Shaman and I took the other. Still in silence, we rowed to a small stone castle several stories high.

"Follow close behind me, and don't look anyone in the eyes," Wandering Wolfe warned.

"Why?"

"Because these people possess magic, and can read your thoughts."

Wandering Wolfe knocked on the door of the castle just beyond the shore, and a lovely blonde-haired maiden opened it. "Hello, this is the home of High Priestess Boann and High Priest Dagda. Whom may I say is calling?" she asked pleasantly.

"This is a private matter, miss. We're here on a business of sorts."

"May I please have your name good sir?"

He hesitated, then answered curtly, "I am the Shaman Wandering Wolfe." Nodding, as if she'd been expecting him to say this very name, she said simply, "Come in."

Opening the heavy oak door, she gestured us inside with a graceful wave of her arm, like the gentle bending of a willow branch in the wind. Single file we walked through the door, as the young girl guided us to a large dining area, with a table that could easily seat fifty people. Tonight however, there were only four people seated at the table, who immediately stood as we entered. The room was spacious enough, with a tall, domed ceiling made of stain glass, almost like a cathedral.

* * *

The stain-glass was dark, a depiction of the Celtic forests just beyond our castle gates. The tree leaves in the glass hung over the table, as if the leaves sheltered us, giving the room the illusion of being outdoors, with the privacy of a canopy of tree leaves. Red roses and ivy entwined themselves up the bark of the trees, providing the most vibrant color.

In Caledonia, the grass was renowned to be the greenest in the world. The reason for that was due to the frequent rain. So, the often grey, overcast skies, made the stained-glass dome dark, even during the days. When it rained, the rain beat against the glass, like a melody. On sunny days, the sun shined in disjointed shadows through the heavily wooded glass scene.

Even now, after all these years, I felt intimidated by the

grandeur of this castle, and even more so, I was intimidated by my handsome husband—though he said the reason he'd married me was because I was the only person who'd ever been brave enough to stand up to him. It was not a usual occurrence, however. I tried to pick my battles wisely.

In some ways, this castle still didn't feel like my home, as I had grown-up with the nomadic clans in tribal tents, living off the land. Though my husband was of the same clan, he was among its leaders, and had been brought up in this castle. That made a big difference in our backgrounds and upbringing.

Those differences had lent problems in our marriage over the years, but our mutual love and respect had kept us together. In the end, it is with the people we love, we make our home. With my husband and two precious children, I would always belong. I loved my family. They were my life. They were my home.

I would miss my special daughter terribly, on her journey to make our world a better place. At least the gods had allowed me my sweet son at home, to keep me company, in the times I still felt out-of-place. Gus was a good boy, and he was so much stronger than he realized.

* * *

The woman at the head of table said graciously, "We've only just sat down to dinner, would you care to join us?"

"Yes, that is precisely what we had in mind," replied Wandering Wolfe, with a thankful grin, and a merry twinkle in his warm brown eyes.

I turned my head briefly, to stare at the people in the room. The man was tall and thick, with graying, dark hair and a short, carefully trimmed grey beard. His eyes were the same color as his hair. The woman had wavy, black hair with a touch of copper and vivid green eyes.

The boy was tall like his father, thinner though, lanky and springy like a grasshopper. He looked much shyer than his sister, for he kept his face down in his dinner; whereas, the girl looked up and studied everyone.

Their daughter had the same green eyes and flowing black curls as her mother, though hers had none of the red in it. She was enchanting. Once my eyes rested on her, they couldn't be convinced to move elsewhere.

Yet there was a coolness in the fair skin, dark hair and green-colored eyes of these people. A watery quality that was as elusive as the wind. You couldn't peg them as stubborn as rock, before they shifted like a chameleon into humble sheepishness or brash joking.

There was a proud dignity in the girl and her father's expression, a high-backed royal bearing—a lifting of the chin, which expressed a certain conceit. Her brother and mother had a gentler quality to their mannerisms, wearing a subservient air next to the more strong-willed personalities of father and daughter.

* * *

I studied the group covertly, under heavily-lidded eyes. I hoped that in these people, my dear sister would find friends, and make a family with them apart from our family in their travels. I was in awe of my sister, of her Great Soul, her Epic Destiny, her formidable strength. She took after our father. She was so capable. She was everything that I wasn't: persistent, confident, and a great leader.

Truth to tell, I never felt I fit in. I feared the great unknown. I loved Lake Avalon and the Isle of Apples. I had a way with flowers and growing things. I spent most of my time on the garden grounds of the castle, and in the woods, among the trees, plants and flowers. But people scared me. I didn't know how to deal with their emotions. I had a hard time connecting.

My mother was so beautiful inside and out, my father was so strong and good at every job he undertook, while I was gangly and awkward. I could not walk down the road, without tripping over my own two large feet.

I had not the brains, nor the heart, nor the strength, nor the magic in the pores of the skin that my kin had. There was no one so great, in the whole of our tribe, then my sister, Varawynn.

I loved my big sister for being better than I was in every way. I loved her for being everything I wished I could be. I loved her for being everything I knew, I never would be.

I'd miss her terribly while she was gone, saving the world, and protecting our lands. I could never rule our tribe better than she could.

She should have been born the son. I would never allow my gender to place me above her. I had too much respect for her character. I would insist that she rule over this land, whenever she returned.

I would not reach for a crust of bread that she wanted. She

deserved every gift that life could give. I'd gladly give my life in exchange for hers, in a heartbeat—for she was so much worthier than I could ever hope to be.

* * *

"We've been expecting you for some time. My name is High Priest Dagda, and this is my wife, Priestess Boann. These are our two children, Aengus and Varawynn. You may call him Gus. I am a descendant of Morgan le Fay."

The High Priest paused for dramatic effect, before resuming his carefully rehearsed speech. "Our scrolls foretell that the girl with a raven birthmark, who is a descendant of Morgana le Fey, shall be our High Priestess, beginning a new reign from an ancient line."

"We also know enough of the Prophecy, to know that our daughter is destined to join your group, and do wonderful things in the world, before returning to start her reign here," added Priestess Boann. "Varawynn has the mark that reveals she is meant to be our High Priestess and the sorceress in your group. Show them my dear."

Obediently lifting her skirt, their daughter revealed her birthmark of a black raven in flight on her right thigh, the detail of which was extraordinary.

"I'm quite impressed, my Lady," said Wandering Wolfe. "And that does prove she belongs with us."

Varawynn smiled at her brother Gus triumphantly. He met her look with awe and wide-eyed respect. Varawynn reached out and ruffled her little brother's hair.

"Yes, I believe it does," the High Priest Dagda agreed proudly. Making small talk as they ate, when they had finished, Lady Boann asked, "I'm sure you must all be very weary from your travels. Would you like to be shown to your chambers now? They're all on the second floor, and I hope you'll find them accommodating."

"Yes, thank you, that would be most appreciated," Wandering Wolfe said gratefully. His eyes had gone bloodshot from exhaustion.

"I'll show them the way, father," Varawynn volunteered, as she stood up, with a twisted cane of birch clutched in her hand. Our eyes opened wide at her stance. The girl was lame! Even the Shaman looked surprised by it.

* * *

I watched carefully, the way the group watched my daughter, as she stood up, and revealed her lame leg. My daughter was so vulnerable to the perceptions of others. I worried about her so much.

She was everything that I ever could have wanted in a daughter—beautiful, brilliant, courageous, and sensitive. She had her dear mother's heart. She was drawn to suffering, and to the alleviating it.

So few realized how much my daughter suffered herself. It hurt me to see how people viewed her, as she used her cane to walk. It hurt me to think that anyone could look down at her, as anything less than she was.

Her magical ability would be the stuff of legends. She was a member of the fourteen Chosen Ones—fourteen destined saviors, from lands and countries all over the earth, would protect our Freedom. She would come back, after her adventures, and rule over our beautiful lands, as renowned as her ancestor, Morgan le Fay.

I was so proud of her. I had no doubt in her abilities and the success she would have in life. I wanted everyone to see her as I saw her.

I knew that her glorious Fate was inevitable, but I still worried about her, as her father. As her father, I knew how quickly she became attached to certain people and things she admired, then clung to them for dear life, even though letting go of them would have been healthier and more beneficial to her.

I knew she would never stop believing that the Isle of Apples was the most beautiful place in the world. No matter where her journey in life took her, she would always return home, to her first love.

Varawynn had a stubborn streak, that was certain. She was the most stubborn in regards to the people she loved—and the people she hated. If she didn't like you, you could do nothing right. If she did like you, you could do nothing wrong. She would refuse to see any warning signs in whomever she fell in love with, until it was too late, and her heart was broken.

She was not the kind to get over things quickly. She held onto hurts and grudges, nursed her wounds like her closest friend. There would be no dissuading Varawynn, once her mind was made up, and her heart was in it.

She was so pure in her perceptions, so good at looking into a person's soul at first glance. She had that ability to see through to the heart of any given person or situation, to the foundation of a person's character. She could lay bare a strategic war game, with the mere yanking of a single thread. She had the mind of a general, and the heart of a jewel.

Her good heart was from her mother, my better half. Her brilliant mind, she inherited from myself. She was the best of both of us. My son, Aengus, Gus, we called him for short, had neither his sister's brains, nor her noble heart, and was as much a disappointment to me, as Varawynn was the apple of my eye. Gus was ill-equipped to rule our tribe as well as Varawynn could.

I hoped she'd find a good man who recognized her greatness, seeing through her tough exterior, into her vulnerable heart. I hoped my daughter would find a man who would cherish the part of her that could never give up on those she loved.

* * *

"She can still get around just fine," my father said defensively, though no one had put him on the defensive. I could see shame written all over his proud demeanor.

"Let's go," I said, pretending not to see their looks, though my words felt strained. *Can't he conceal his embarrassment at my disability any better?* It was all I could do to keep my temper and features even.

"But didn't you say our bed chambers were on the second floor? Would you like me to help you with the stairs, Varawynn?"

* * *

The group, and I who knew him best, as his teacher and mentor, gaped at him in surprise. Eliju had been friendly with Jonlin, Shadow Rain, and Alondria, but I could tell there was something about this new girl that brought out Eliju's protectiveness. The protectiveness he'd only shown towards his sheep.

* * *

"No, thank you, I can get up the stairs just fine," I snapped back at him, with a defiant toss of my thick, dark curls.

"She's very independent," High Priestess Boann said, attempting to explain away my rudeness with superficial pleasantries, like she *always* did. My roughness didn't seem to bother Eliju.

"Let's *go*," I commanded. "Follow me." Finally, after much ado about nothing, the group followed me to the stairs.

In amazement, they watched as I used my cane to get my one good leg above me, using my good leg and both my hands to pull my bad leg onto the step. This all took place in maybe half a second.

Again, I tried to ignore the look of shock on their faces,

though this time Wandering Wolfe did a better job of hiding it. Eliju's room was the last one down the hall.

"Do you want to go do something? I'm not really tired," he asked, now that we were alone.

"Well, what do you want to do?" I was surprised enough into asking.

"Why don't you show me around Avalon?"

"Okay," I instantly agreed, beginning to warm towards him—as I adored my land, and all the people in it, more than life itself.

"Show me where you go when you don't want anyone to know where you are."

My eyebrows rose at this strange request, but I liked it. This land was my treasure, and no other request would've been harder for me to resist.

"Follow me," I told him bossily. This time Eliju didn't offer to help me with the stairs. He learned quickly. I liked that.

Slipping unseen out of the castle's servant's quarters, a million memories rained down on me. I pulled Eliju through the corridors of the castle, which had been in my family for hundreds of years. So many generations of my blood had dwelt within the same rooms. Some of their blood had been stained upon its floors. Every family's history carries the burdens of secrets and betrayals.

I knew every hidden passageway, every carefully chiseled stone that made up the castle's walls. Although my Celtic royal line was comparatively poor next to the castles of other kingdoms, we were rich in magic that was without rival.

I could tell Eliju how the change in seasons altered the color of the stone, by the strength or weakness of the light. When it rained, the grey stone looked almost black. It rained here often.

I loved the rain. The way it made the grass smell so fresh. The way it beat the moving waters, stirring them into frantic motion. I loved the dark skies. I loved the gray clouds. I loved the feel of the moisture in the air. I loved how our castle was at the foot of Lake Avalon. Lake Avalon, with its mysteriously purple waters glittering in the light of the sun, shimmering by the glow of the moon.

I loved it here in the spring, summer, autumn and winter. Whether the sweetly-scented rosebuds were drifting upon the waves, or the summer heat sizzled over the water, or the brilliantly colored fall leaves were falling into the lake like pouring rain, or the isles were iced and blanketed by several feet of snow, the water gave me peace. When

I was near Lake Avalon, I was both calmed and energized by it.

There was magic in the air in the Isle of Apples. All the magical creatures were welcomed and worshipped here. We embraced the Lady of the Lake, Vivien, and her daughter Ileona, half-human, half-magical sea creature, who had made her home in the Crystal Castle on the other side of the lake.

The Castle of Camelot used to be just over the forest and hills. It had been abandoned for many years, and had fallen into disrepair by the time I was born. I used to visit that castle when I was a little girl, until it was burned to the ground in the last Clan War.

I used to sit at the Round Table, imagining the queens and kings, and the knights and wizards, and lords and ladies, who had once graced its halls. I would walk down the spiral banisters, tracing the rail of the spiraling staircase on my fingertips, and imagine myself to be a great lady from those days, coming down the steps to meet my destiny, square in the eyes—as I met all my challenges.

It was hard to believe that the Castle of Camelot, the Castle of the Clouds, in the gently-sloping highlands beyond our forest, was gone now, forever. Yet who I really was, a Celtic princess, was of even greater importance than the ladies of the court, and I was proud of who I was.

I was proud of the raven birthmark on my thigh. I was proud to be one of the fourteen Chosen Ones of the ancient Prophecy. I was proud to have been a descendant of the King of that once grand castle—a descendant of both the highlands, and the lakes and forests at the mountain's feet.

King Arthur and Morgan le Fay were half-brother and sister, so my blood entwined within itself like our Celtic Spirals, like a snake. The magic in my blood was in the blood of these lands. It was buried beneath the grounds of the sanctuaries. It was buried out at sea, wrapped in cloth of gossamer white linen, and sent out ablaze, in the funeral ritual of our gods.

I believed my destiny would be something special. Something like the flaming phoenix, burning itself alive with the depth of its passions, then rising among the ashes, stronger still from the death and destruction it rose victorious over...

The grass really smelled green in the forests. The flowers were deep-scented. The sorcerers came here in droves after the tragedy of Morgan le Fay's death, and after the religious Catholic Order took its endless judgments and fire and brimstone homilies, elsewhere.

Now the magical creatures roamed freely over the wild landscape, and were given free reign to express their powers. They came here to learn from my family, of the magics that were then taken across the earth. Our symbols and gods lent them power, but our magic could only be fully possessed by our own elite tribe.

I took Eliju back to the shores of the Isle of Apples. We climbed into a boat, and I rowed us to the shore of Camelot's dense forest. I wanted to show him the Sword in the Stone. The Sword was missing, but the stone where the sword had stood for hundreds of years, remained.

Eliju's dawdling pulled me from my reverie. My impatience kicked in. "Come on," I said, for I was walking faster than he was.

He laughed, and said, "I can't keep up with you!"

"Well, you'd better, because I'm not waiting up on you!"

We both laughed this time, and true to my word, I didn't slow my pace for him to keep up with me. Pausing at a small clearing, where a large, ornate stone was prominently displayed in the center of the ring, we stood and stared at the light from the moon shimmering down on it. The stone was emanating an eerie, translucent white, and shadows of light splashed themselves on the dark ground beneath us.

"What is this place?" he asked.

"They say this is the stone where Arthur took out his sword."

"What sword? Who's Arthur?"

I looked at him incredulously. "Haven't you ever heard about Camelot?"

"No, I haven't, would you please tell me about it?"

I grinned, relishing the pleasure of knowing more than the Chosen One, I dove into relaying the story with gusto. "Arthur was a King who brought the feudal kingdoms together. He started out as a peasant boy. His line of Kingship began when he pulled a sword from this stone. The name of the sword was Excalibur."

"Excalibur?"

"Yes."

"The Lady of the Lake, Vivien, helped the boy, the future King Arthur, pull the sword from the stone."

"Who's the 'Lady of the Lake?' "

"She's a relative of the sirens, an enchantress of the waters. She was the mistress and master of these waters…ultimately, it is she who conquered Merlin, the greatest wizard of the day. He was the mentor to King Arthur, and they say it may even have been his magic that lent

Arthur his power. This is that very lake, the Isle of Apples in Avalon."

"Wow. That's incredible. No wonder the water here seems so magical! But what happened to King Arthur?"

"My ancestor, Morgan le Fey killed him. Well, the son she'd bore from him, the result of her clever trickery, killed him. That, and the heart break he experienced over the betrayal of his wife, Queen Guinevere, having an affair with one of the Knights of the Round Table, Sir Lancelot."

"What a story!" Eliju was clearly impressed. He continued to stare admiringly at the forest and lake. "It's so beautiful," he whispered, but he was looking at me when he said it, not the water.

Turning to him, as the glint from the stone shown like a beacon, the small clearing was bright with the pale moonlight. His eyes were green like mine, but they became as luminescent as pearls in the starlight. I was amazed by his eyes.

I had intended to tell him the rest of the story, but I was dumbfounded by the sudden light illuminating the small clearing where we stood. The way the emerald green of his eyes shone so brightly...

I completely lost my words in the familiarity of his eyes, so like my own. Eliju looked as if he was falling into me, when my words jarred him back to reality.

"Do I know you?" I asked him, caught off-guard by the familiarity, as much as the rays of light from the stone. The cool air sent shivers up my spine. "Did you see that?"

"See what?"

"That light?"

"What light?"

"Do I know you or not?" I demanded, off-kilter with all the strange impressions.

"I don't know, but I think I have the same feeling as you do."

"We have the same eyes."

"Yes, I know."

"How can we have the same eyes?"

"I don't know."

"What can it mean?"

"I'm not sure."

"You're so familiar to me. I *must* have known you before."

"What are you talking about?"

"In another life, I mean."

Eliju laughed. "Well, how else do you explain it?" I asked him.

"I *can't* explain it."

"I feel as if I've known you all my life."

"I wish I *had* known you all my life."

I frowned at his compliment. "Don't use lines on me, Master Eliju."

"Master Eliju, I like that, and it wasn't a line at all, it was the truth. I'm not even sure what you mean by 'lines,' " he laughed good-naturedly.

There was something honest and open in his face. I didn't think he was the type to play games. It was so hard to trust someone with something as priceless as your heart. Yet in that moment, I could not control the fluttering in my chest, or the stirring of my spirit, by the look in his eyes.

I was silent for a moment to collect myself, then said more quietly, "I'd like to see the stars over the water."

"Okay," Eliju agreed.

I could sense he wanted to hold my hand on the short walk to the water, but he was smart enough to restrain himself. I sensed his want, but neither of us said anything as we walked to the shoreline and sat down on the grass.

I was still unsure of him, but as we stared up into the open sky of moon and stars, watching the gently rhythmic movements of the water, I was overcome with the serenity of the knowledge that came to me.

Both of our eyes were glowing in the night. I felt as if I would be content to just sit next to him, looking into his eyes, forever. "You're so beautiful," he said, so softly I thought I'd imagined it.

"I think I know who you are," I told him, matter-of-factly, ignoring his compliment.

"Who am I?"

"You're my twin soul."

"Does that mean I'm your soul mate?"

"Yes, the second highest in fact."

"*I'm the second* highest?"

"Yes, and that means we're very much alike."

"That makes sense."

"Indeed." He would later find this was my favorite word of accord. Without needing to suggest it in words, we both lay down on the grass next to the water, our hands close, but still not linked, as we fell asleep beneath the stars. He was the star, the Chosen King, and I was the water, a reflection of his light.

~ *** ~

Chapter Nine
Scattered Seeds

From a cottage in Caledonia, on the Isle of Skye—

I remembered this poem from the Prophecy, "The Legend of the Split Seed." It was a story about a girl with two blood fathers. Things like this were possible. Rare, but possible.

Sometimes two men's seeds germinated and split in the mother's womb. It defied the laws of nature and science, but then again, so did miracles. I found the passage pressed inside an old book of spells. It brought back a lot of memories. I hadn't read it since before the couple who had raised me, Elijah and Ruth, had been murdered...

"The Legend of the Split Seed"

The seed is split among two men–
Sprung from heaven or sprung from hell?
Is this creature foe or friend?
The truth was hidden well from them.

Split three ways, most by two,
Living in obscurity.
Her power hidden beneath the truth
Of the life she did not choose.

Dead and buried beneath the ground,
Who is that within the earth?
I can hear the trumpets sound!
I can see her black hair crowned!

And the dead babe, will she speak—
And confess the sins of man?
Will she reveal the secrets they keep?
Buried well and hidden deep?

All their weaknesses unveiled
By the light of death and shame—
Heard by a mother's solemn wail
In the Prophet's long, lost tale.

There shall come an appointed time,
When all planets in the sign of Scorpio align--
For the Ashes of Avalon shall rise
In a moment of day ebbing into night.

Then as the sun becomes obscured,
The truth at last shall come to light—
Of the life that existed
For the sake of another life.

She shall then reveal her true name,
The name known to very few,
Given to her in God's glory and shame—
For destined for her is unending fame.

The power is there for her to use,
Written in blood beneath the ground...
What only she has the magic to choose—
To save a life, she must lose the life she found.

Sadness washed over me, as I read the poem. I tried to ignore it and keep busy. Vorseth was coming tonight. I needed to be doing something purposeful as I waited for him.

The light from the dripping candle shone on the passage, but I ignored the wax falling on my desk, and pushed my focus away from the Prophecy, concentrating on finding the *Spell of Illumination*. I was going to partner the spell with my crystal ball, to give me greater vision, not into the future, but into the past.

For I sensed that the whole of my long life, was based on lies. I felt hidden away, but I knew there must be a reason for it. I was always searching for the truths I could never seem to find...

* * *

She was flipping through a book when I arrived. "You're late again," she said, not looking up.

"I had other business tonight." Business with her kin. She continued looking though the book of spells. "What are you looking for, my dear?"

"Don't you know?"

"A spell?"

"What kind of spell?" she asked, knowing I could read her mind if I wanted to.

"A spell of magnetization?"

"I will not say."

"Every day I come I am afraid to find you gone."

"Gone? Gone where? Wherever would I go? Like it or not, this island is my home."

"Sometimes I think you might run away, to look for your blood relations. I know you've been lonely, my dear." She was silent. "It's not time for you to know your family yet."

"I know that."

"I will tell you when it's time." Turning her back to me once more, she continued searching through the book. "You already know so much, my dear. So many different spells for so many different things."

"But this spell was perfect. I remember seeing it a few months ago, when I was looking for something else."

"When the time comes for you to know who and where they are, you won't need a spell to find them. Rest assured, my dear, they shall come to you. Now tell me what you've learned today in my absence."

"First tell me more about my blood relations. You've told me next to nothing for so long, and I won't wait any longer!"

I sighed. "I should have waited to tell you that Elijah and Ruth weren't your kin—"

"I already knew they weren't my real parents."

"How?"

"I sensed it of course. Their ways were not my ways. We were always so different, though they were very kind to me."

"But you never knew any other ways."

"No, but I've sensed other ways, and you taught me other ways after they were gone. You took care of me."

"That's true."

"But I miss them. They were good people. At least tell me about my mother. Does she have power like mine?"

"I cannot say."

"No, you *will* not say!" Her narrowed eyes contained an icy malice more dangerous than fire's flames.

"She is beautiful, I can tell you that."

"How beautiful?"

I paused. "Her beauty is like the blue of the flame, the deepest and hottest part of the fire."

"What do I care about her beauty? Did she love my father?"

"Yes and no."

"What do I care if she loved my father? Was he a good man?"

"Yes and no."

"What kind of answers are these, Vorseth? I want to know about my family, and where I come from!"

"You shall learn all the answers in time. Perhaps if you did your lessons you would understand the Prophecy, and wouldn't need me to explain such things to you, nor would you believe a spell would help you in fulfilling your part in it."

"You want me to study, and then you criticize me for studying my spell books. I already know most of the Prophecy by heart, Vorseth."

"Yes, but not all of it. You don't realize how privileged you are to have the entire book of scrolls in full. People would kill for it, my dear. People would kill you if they knew you had it."

"I only care about my kin."

"Perhaps that is right."

"I don't care what you think is right!"

"You dare to be disrespectful of me, when you owe me so much?"

"I owe you nothing. All you taught me I would have learned one way or another...if not by you, then by someone else, or on my own. All you taught me was already within me. You're the one who first told me that all answers lie within—if we have the courage to ask the right questions."

"Yes, that is right, but still, I—"

"No, I'm tired of your games—I want answers!"

"When the time is right."

"How much longer do you expect me to wait?"

I knew her coolness was only a pretense concealing her anger, ever hovering beneath the surface of her poise. I also knew that when she was angry, she pretended that she wasn't grateful for my taking care of her after Ruth and Eliju had died, but most of the time, she was appreciative of me.

"If you try and kill King Mardavian too soon, he'll wind up killing you. Then you'll never get your revenge on the King."

"Elijah and Ruth did not deserve to be killed. Especially the way that King Mardavian tortured them." I closed my eyes for a moment, as an image of their mangled bodies passed through my mind. "But there's another reason you don't want me to leave yet," she said astutely.

"Yes."

"But you won't tell me."

"Correct."

She sighed, and switched tactics, knowing she wasn't getting anywhere. "I wonder, how one such as I could be born on a place like earth."

"What do you mean?"

"I'm so unlike the other humans here. My heritage is so different from others...with a blend of four races of magics: Egyptian, Celtic, Shaman, and Hebrew. I wonder if any other person on earth is like me." Her words were met with the not-so-distant howling of a wolf.

* * *

I'd been watching this woman from a distance for centuries.

Periodically, I'd cross over the waters onto the remote island, the beautiful Isle of Skye, with its sunsets painted in lavender, sapphire, rose, and sea green. She had always lived on this island, with the grass the color of emerald gems, and where an air of beauty and enchantment tinged the edge off the loneliness of the isolation, in gold.

Every few months or so, I came back to the island, just to keep a paw in. I had my ways to travel quicker than the average creature. I had my special ways of moving across the terrain. I liked to keep an eye on my people, and the people who were important to my people, and my person.

I'd known this woman from birth. I knew where she came from. I knew her real kin. I bided my time, for the right day to come, when the yellow sun went dark, and the white moon, and distant earths corresponded with the black Scorpion in the sky. Until that time, I watched—from a distance.

* * *

I felt the wolf watching me, from time-to-time. I felt his dark eyes on me, and when I gardened outside, I often found his paw prints on the earth, and in the forest. I knew he didn't wish me harm. After all, if he did, he would have harmed me long ago.

For as long as I'd lived, the wolf had watched over me. We'd never come face-to-face, but I knew it was the same wolf. He had a uniqueness to his howl. After all this time, his cry was comforting. The Isle of Skye was so isolated. In a way, the wolf's presence eased my loneliness.

Staring out the window, into the forest lying beyond my small cottage, thinking of the wolf, and all the years of loneliness I'd endured, I said, "I've waited for so long to prove my powers, and take the life of the man who killed the only people who ever loved me. I've waited so long to discover who I really am. But I shall wait until the moment when the Sun and Moon, and all the planets, are aligned with the Sign of Scorpio, as they are in my chart. I do not have so long to wait now."

Yet there was something in the warlock's expression that worried me when I said this. There was a strange sadness in him as he looked at me, with regret and resignation in his withered grey eyes.

* * *

She was right about the timing, but I knew there was nothing I could say, to prepare her for what was to come when the planets were aligned in the sign of Scorpio—the sign of the Phoenix, Eagle, Grey Lizard, Snake, and Scorpion.

She could never know what she was meant to do, or the truth as to her heritage. Not until the very last moment of her tragic life as the Shadow of God in the Legend of the Split Seed...

No, there was nothing I could do, or would do, to alter the fulfillment of the Prophecy. And so, I let it be.

~ *** ~

Chapter Ten
Mirrored Visions in the Crystal Castle

November, in the region of Camelot and the Isle of Apples in Avalon—

When we woke in the morning, our hands had somehow found a way into each other's hands. Eliju pulled his hand away quickly and stood up. My heart hurt when he did that, but I pretended not to notice.

"Oh no! They're probably all looking for us by now. It's already ten o'clock!"

"How do you know that?"

I shrugged. "It's one of my gifts. I always know what time it is."

"That's a very handy kind of gift."

"Indeed. But we'd better head back now, Master Eliju...I really don't know how we're going to explain this." I felt the worry starting to show on my face, and tried to even out my features.

"I don't care what they think," Eliju said.

"Well, *I* do!"

"That's because you belong to them." With the way I felt already, maybe he would one day too.

Shaking the thoughts from my mind, we crossed the lake to the other shore. We weren't even out of the boat, before my brother had accosted us.

"Where have you been all this time, Varawynn? Mother's been worried sick!"

"I don't owe you an explanation, Aengus!"

"Maybe you don't owe *me* one—but you'd better be ready to explain where you've been to mother and father! They've been waiting for you for hours, you know."

"Okay, okay! Just take us home, Gus!" Gus shook his head, his pale face red and puffy with lack of sleep and worry, he accompanied us back to the castle without another word, where High Priestess Boann met us at the door.

I knew for the good ole mild-mannered Aengus to be this

furious, there must be some real raucous going on at the castle. It was embarrassing to consider what the rest of the people in the group must be thinking.

"Where have you been young lady?"

"Oh mother–"

"Don't you 'oh mother' me! We've all been worried sick! We have the right to know where you've been. Your father is beside himself."

"We were in Camelot's forest just beyond Lake Avalon. We fell asleep on the shoreline, watching the sun going down. We really didn't mean to worry anyone."

"Are you telling me that all this time, you've been *sleeping*?"

"Yes, and it was the best sleep I've gotten in a long time," laughed Eliju. I stared at him in horror—he was amused by this!

"Shut up! You're not helping matters, Master Eliju." Easy for him to poke fun—it wasn't his family that was mad at him.

High Priestess Boann glared at us both. "We don't have time for this now, the Oracle needs to see you two."

"The Oracle wants to see *me*?" My eyes shimmered with excitement. Ileona was the most magical, the most unique creature in our lands. As the descendent of the Lady of the Lake, she was intricately linked to my ancestors, and I admired her beyond compare. I felt so special she had requested to meet with us.

"She wants to see everyone who's going on the journey, so you'd better hurry and change."

"Do we have time for breakfast?" Eliju asked, as his stomach grumbled in protest.

"No! You should have thought of breakfast, and been home sooner—better yet, you never should have traipsed off last night, and caused such a raucous this morning. Now hurry up! The Shaman is waiting for you both at the Gathering Corner."

"Who's the Oracle?" Eliju asked, as we walked as quickly as we could, to meet up with Wandering Wolfe and the rest of the group.

"Ileona is the most revered person in our town, for she's the daughter of the Lady of the Lake, Vivien. I told you about her and Merlin last night." Eliju nodded, recalling our conversation.

"Ileona lives in a remote area far from the center of town, on the other side of the lake, preferring to be separated from the rest of us. People come from all over the country to ask her to do readings for them. My family is the most magical of the land because we're descended from Morgan le Fay, but she's even more magical and respected than we are because she's not fully human."

"Yes, children we're going to go into a room with seven visionary mirrors in the Crystal Castle," Wandering Wolfe was saying as we arrived where the rest of the group had been waiting for us.

"So, beware of her," he continued, paying us no mind. "She can read people's minds which gives her an unfair advantage against her opponents. She's not beneath using your greatest weaknesses to win a fight. Don't ever look her in the eyes. For it's through the eyes she can read your thoughts, see your past, and glean your weaknesses."

I wondered how he presumed to know all that nonsense about Ileona. His perspective of her certainly seemed skewed. I felt anger rise up in my heart against the Shaman, and glared at him.

* * *

I glowered at Varawynn. I felt protective over Eliju, okay maybe a little possessive too—and I didn't like the looks of the girl. It took me a while to trust people. Eliju, on the other hand, eager for friendship and over the moon about having so many people to be with and talk to, tended to attach himself quickly. Too quickly sometimes.

He'd done so with the Shaman, and Jonlin, and me as well. I realized that Eliju was by nature, a people person. After being isolated for so long, he was like a cat with cream every time someone new came into the group. His fascination with Varawynn seemed different than his attachment with us, somehow. I was worried Varawynn would hurt him.

I couldn't deny she was gorgeous. With her long dark curls, big green eyes, like two emeralds, pale skin like a porcelain doll, and cherry red lips, I was sure she was used to getting her way. Pretty girls like her usually *did* get their own way.

Eliju, being so inexperienced, would almost surely fall for her smooth words and pouty lips. She looked to be clever and manipulative on top of beautiful, so most men would.

It was Wandering Wolfe who had discovered Eliju wasn't in his bed, and Lady Boann who found Varawynn wasn't in hers, and that neither bed had even been slept in. It had caused quite a stir around the breakfast table.

High Priest Dagda had fired away questions at Wandering Wolfe like a general, as to the boy's intentions. He was the girl's father afterall, so he was bound to be protective, but really it was Eliju who needed protection from *her.*

The High Priest didn't know Eliju. Eliju was wild and brash to be sure, as many young men are, then considerate and pensive by turns, but mostly he was like one of the little lambs from his farm, innocent as a babe. Lord Dagda didn't know that Eliju had been isolated and alone throughout his life, and was deeply religious, so there was NO WAY he would do something intimate with Varawynn on the first night they met—but he sure gave Wandering Wolfe a talking to in concern for his daughter.

Poor Gus got the brunt of it when Dagda barked and ordered him about all morning, taking out his frustrations on his son, and letting him know that if he didn't go out and come back with his sister there'd be hell to pay. As if it was *his* fault for Varawynn's total lack of consideration for anyone's feelings but her own.

"We don't have time now for explanations of where you two have been, so let's go to the Castle and we'll discuss your whereabouts later," said Wandering Wolfe. He was unperturbed by their absence. He seemed to have total faith in Eliju's *and* Varawynn's "intentions."

"Yes, but there's nothing to explain, we only took a walk last night, and fell asleep accidently," Eliju told him.

Wandering Wolfe nodded, as if to say he'd figured as much. I still didn't think it excused their inconsideration of our concerns. As usual the Shaman was letting Eliju off the hook too easily. He clearly had a soft spot for him. I didn't entirely blame him for that, knowing how hard his childhood had been, but I still would have said a little more to Eliju than he did.

"Now come along," said Wandering Wolfe.

Eliju and Varawynn walked together, continuing to talk away, like two long-lost friends. They're already as thick as thieves. I looked over at Jonlin, silently asking for his help with my eyes, but he just shrugged.

We were all a part of the same group, so shouldn't we all be friends, or at least find a way to get along? His eyes seemed to say.

The Crystal Castle stood seven stories high, and was composed entirely of crystals. It was a sunny day after yesterday's gloom, and the Castle was resplendent with every color of the rainbow.

Flowers of every color and varied types surrounded the Castle, bringing even more glorious colors to the castle's majestic appearance. The miraculous thing was, it was the dead of winter, so there shouldn't have been so many blooming flowers. Varawynn explained it was the

Oracle's magic which made them bloom all year long, lending color and fragrance even when it snowed.

At the Castle gates, we were greeted by a watchman. "We've been expecting you," he said. Wandering Wolfe nodded, and the gate opened.

"Walk slowly, and kneel before her. Don't forget–do *not* look her directly in the eyes whatever you do," warned Wandering Wolfe urgently. "She's a very powerful sorceress. She speaks in riddles and is as brilliant in her knowledge, as the sun that rises every morning. Her eyes will weaken your resolve, and her words can confuse you. Don't pay her too close attention, or look at her too long or intently. She's powerful enough to make you lose yourself."

"It sounds like you know her," said Alondria.

"It sounds like you don't like her," Varawynn accused.

"That doesn't matter, just be wary of her, understood?" He wouldn't let us inside until we'd all agreed.

Entering the beautiful Crystal Castle, we walked through a grandiose entrance with mirrors on the walls, and even the ceiling. Coming upon a throne room where the Oracle was seated, awaiting our arrival, we immediately bowed low in reverence of her. After a few moments, we raised our heads, to study this enchanted woman.

Her hair was such a flaxen blond it was almost white. Her eyes held a nobility of strength and character, glowing white-gold like the sun itself. Her eyes flickered from Eliju to Varawynn, then back to Eliju.

"I've been waiting a long time for this moment," she said, in a voice lyrical like the tap dancing of rain on cobblestone. Eliju went to his knees, bowing his body low beneath her.

"Rise up, and come to me," she commanded him. Throwing a glance back towards Wandering Wolfe, who adamantly shook his head at him, Eliju got to his feet, and walked to the Oracle, Ileona.

"Look me in the eyes, Eliju."

"But–"

"I said look me in the eyes."

I feared for Eliju. If Wandering Wolfe was right about the Oracle, what would become of him if he obeyed her request?

* * *

Wandering had specifically told us not to—but what could I do now with such a direct order, but obey?

"Yes, m'lady."

Brazenly, I met her eyes. Her eyes were the color of pale gold. I felt myself being drawn inside them, as I'd been pulled into Varawynn's eyes. It was a strange power this race had in their eyes, drawing you in until they'd taken what they wanted of your memories, or essence.

I knew now that I was not an ordinary person. Realizing this, maybe for the first time in my life, I stared back confidently into her eyes without blinking. Many moments passed, until the Oracle herself finally looked away. I knew this had been a test, and I knew that I had passed it.

"No one has stared into my eyes without losing their senses. Your thinking, however, seemed to become clearer by them. You are indeed the Chosen One."

I grinned, and Varawynn looked proud of me, so supportive of me already. Alondria smiled back at me encouragingly. To my surprise, Wandering Wolfe looked disgruntled, Jonlin was day-dreaming, and Shadow Rain just seemed generally grouchy today. She had a look on her face like a fish that had just been hooked.

"Come with me, Eliju. I'd like to speak to you privately," the Oracle requested, less demanding now.

I followed her without question. "How long have you known you were Chosen?" she asked me, as we entered a more private room.

"Not very long, m'lady, I've only known these past six months or so."

She raised her eyebrows, though I doubted this woman was often taken off-guard. "You mean no one told you before you met Wandering Wolfe? Have you even read any of the Prophecy?"

"I've only heard a few things from Wandering Wolfe, and Shadow Rain once recited a piece of the Prophecy we think has to do with her. I haven't heard very much of it though, no."

"You should've been told," said Ileona, her smooth, honeyed voice rising slightly in anger. "Your parents should have prepared you, Eliju."

At the mention of my parents, my body stiffened. "My parents abandoned me when I was ten-years-old."

Ileona took another good, hard look at me. After a few moments, she nodded to herself. "I understand things a little better now, Eliju. Please, you must give your parents a chance to explain when the time comes. It's important."

Something about the Oracle made me comfortable to speak my heart with her, sharing things I'd never shared with anyone before. "*If I ever see my parents—they won't last the meeting.*"

Ileona's watery golden eyes widened. She comprehended what I was eluding to immediately. "Have you ever killed before, Eliju?"

"Just sick animals on the farm, but those were acts of mercy—putting them out of their misery. Wandering Wolfe has been training me with weapons, and I'm not afraid to use that knowledge to kill them."

"To kill one's parents, even if they are evil, is a great iniquity, Eliju."

"They left me alone as a young boy. If any parent deserves to die, it's ones who abandon their children when they're so young, they're barely able to fend for themselves."

"Oh, but they knew you wouldn't die. They knew you'd grow uncommonly strong with their absence."

"How do you know that?"

Smiling at him, with a slightly condescending air, she replied, "I just *know*, Eliju."

"Why did you test me like that in front of everyone, Lady Ileona? What is it about the eyes of your people that are so powerful?"

"The soul of a person is revealed in the depth of their eyes, Eliju, for the eyes are the window of the soul. That's why our people's eyes are so powerful, for through careful study and analysis, we've grown in our ability to perceive others with an intuitiveness that cannot be matched. Varawynn and I share knowledge of spiritual truths that most dare not dream of."

"What did you see when you looked into my eyes, Lady Ileona?"

She paused, giving more weight and consideration to her words. "When I looked into *your* eyes I saw conflict—the two opposing forces of love and hate, light and darkness. You are very passionate. Your emotions run deep, and you're ruled by an intuitive force. You are naturally gifted spiritually, and you have visions of the future through your dreams; you have within yourself the power for true greatness, and ultimate destruction—both."

"It will come down to your choices, as life always comes down to our choices. You may feel confused about what's right and wrong. The wrong decisions will sometimes seem right. The wrong choice is a choice of the mind and justice, and the right choice is of love, selfless mercy in its purest form. Blind faith does not mean a faith that is blind to reason; blind faith is the belief in the unseen things, which are far more powerful and real, in the higher realms. Love cannot be seen by the naked eye, but it can be shown and felt, and most of all, it can be chosen."

"Now," she said brusquely. "Let me take you to the mirrors. Most who enter the mirror room may only choose one mirror, but because you're the highest of the Chosen Ones, you'll be looking into them all. Speak to no one about what you see in this room, and don't touch any of the mirrors, or you'll be cursed to remain trapped within them forever. Please trust me. Don't test me on this. *Do not touch the mirrors.*"

"There are seven mirrors. Seven is the number of spirituality, creation and completion. The first mirror will show you your past. The second mirror reveals your deepest fears; the third mirror, your deepest desires. The fourth mirror shows how others perceive you. The fifth mirror shows your potential best act during your life, the sixth shows your potentially worst act, and the seventh mirror will show you your future."

"Realize, the mirrors can show you your *future* desires, as well as those you have now, as well as different, alternating futures that depend upon your choices taken at the crossroads of your journey in life. Before leaving you, I will share with you my Crystal Castle's poem in the Prophecy:"

"The Seven Mirrors"

"Within the golden mirror
Imparted through its light
Your past is revealed
Like a beacon in the night.

All that you have seen,
All that you once were,
Is reflected from the golden wall,
Of the shimmering glass that's first.

After this, you'll find the second mirror
Whose fears are deep and cold—
Some fear the dark unknown,
Or the slow decay of growing old.

WHERE THE SHADOWS MEET THE LIGHT

Some fear the loss of love,
Some fear the depth of their own hate,
But whatever you do fear,
Shall surely control your fate.

The third mirror reveals your desires,
Which may someday come to pass.
All who look into this mirror
Will see a million wishes pass by fast.

Do you covet all the riches
Of this greedy, turning earth?
Do you wish for a true love, or
Do you wish to return a hurt?

The fourth mirror reveals how others see you,
All your pain and love and rage.
Do they look at you with tenderness?
Or an envious, jealous hate?

This mirror can be a blessing;
This mirror can be a curse.
This mirror can be rewarding,
But it is the culmination of your worth.

The fifth mirror shows the best act
You could perform within your life.
It is the key to the real you—
The you that lives by love and light.

May this act be remembered
To remind you who you are.
Careful not to stray from virtue,
Or rising again, better after a fall.

The sixth mirror reveals your worst act
From the hidden secrets that burn inside.
It's the you of darkening shadows,
From the power of the night.

This act is but a choice,
A hand dealt you don't have to play—
It is the path of least resistance—
The corrupt and easy way.

This last mirror shows your future,

Two differing paths that could occur—
Like the choice between your best and worst act—
You choose the path of king or fool.

Choose the path of love lit by the light,
Let it lead you to a destiny of glory divine.
For if you choose the path of least resistance,
Then destruction shall surely conquer you in time."

After the Oracle recited her castle's part of the legend, she brought me through more rooms composed of crystals. The floors and walls sparkled with all the colors of the rainbow, from the light of the sun shining through the ceiling. Only it was made of glass, so that the sun could shine down and make the room dance with a mirage of twirling colors.

Walking down a long crystal hall with no windows, we entered a room with floors of luminescent white marble, where seven mirrors stood on pedestals composed of gems of sapphires, emeralds, rubies, onyx, pearls, diamonds and gold.

"The marble protects the mirrors. Take all the time you need, but again, do *not* to touch the mirrors, or you'll be pulled within them, lost to us forever."

I nodded, not turning back towards the mirrors until the door was completely shut behind her. The first mirror was made of pure gold. Looking inside it carefully, at first I saw nothing—then slowly an image began to emerge in the glass...

A woman with long, dark hair was rocking a tiny baby, singing it a haunting lullaby in Hebrew, with a sad smile. A red-haired man came in, and stared lovingly at the baby, with the same sad smile. The song was familiar.

A shock of electricity passed through me, as I realized these were my parents, and I was seeing myself as a baby. Then I saw something that turned my blood cold. I was made witness to my parent's abandonment of me...

I was asleep when they packed their few possessions of clothes and small, sentimental items, like the drawing my mother had made of me. It was winter when they left me, and there was an enormous pile of wood outside to use for heat. My mother had stored enough food in jars to last me a year.

She had tears in her eyes, as she went into my room, to kiss me for the last time. A single tear fell down her cheek. I stirred in my bed, but didn't fully waken to her touch.

"We have to go now, my beauty," my father said from the doorway.

"Must we?" Hesitating in the half-lit space of the doorway, her expression held equal parts horror and longing.

"You know as well as I do that we have no choice. It's in the Prophecy. We must leave him. We're merely pawns in the story of his life."

"We're not just pawns, we're his parents," she insisted forcefully. Her face melted into a look of exquisite agony, and in that fleeting moment, the true depth of her feelings was revealed. Her gentle face contorted itself until she appeared ugly, with the intensity of her guilt and suffering.

"I don't want to leave him either," my father's tears fell resolutely down his face, "but we *have to go.*"

After those words, the mirror lost its clarity, and my mother's response was lost. *So, they didn't want to leave me,* I thought to myself. "As if that really matters,*"* I mumbled. But my voice quivered.

Then the image changed, as I saw a woman with bright red hair speaking to my father, though they were speaking so softly I couldn't hear them. *Who is that woman?* The moment the thought entered my mind, the image had faded.

I saw myself, as a small boy sobbing underneath the sheets. Shaking with cold, I'd been unable to get the fire rekindled, and was too distraught to try again. I had to look away for a moment. It hurt to remember that time.

The first three days after my parents left, I'd shook and sobbed in bed, willing death to come and claim me. I hadn't eaten, praying to God over and over again to take my life.

On the morning of the fourth day, I woke up to a flooding of light on my face from the window. Famished, I got up and ate. At that moment, something deep down inside willed me to live; to fight to survive. A supernatural strength propelled me forward.

Faith made me get up. Faith made me keep going. And the sheep. They needed me. They couldn't get on without me. I hadn't fed them in three days either.

Opening a can of food my mother left me, my hand was gouged and cut open by the lid. Terror struck me at the blood rushing out of my palm. I was overcome by fear it would get infected, and what that meant for me, so alone.

Enraged, I watched my ten-year-old self, break every last jar of food my mother left me. At least a year's worth of food was smashed against the walls with my fury, until my whole body held shallow cuts of glass, and the walls were caked with food of all different colors and textures.

Standing there shaking, a mere boy, now with no food left to him at all in the winter months, my face was crazed, but purposeful, as I remembered thinking *if I'm going to make it through this, I'm going to have to learn to make it on my own.* I went outside and fed my starving sheep, vowing to never neglect them again, and to give to them, all the love I had to give.

I had kept my vow. Rain or shine, while sick or well, in raging heat or bitter cold, I had taken care of my sheep, and loved them as the only family I had left.

The next mirror was made of sparkling sapphires which contrasted beautifully against the clean, silver mirror. Looking into the second mirror, I saw for the first time the infamous King Mardavian. Mardavian was torturing the Shaman to death with imaginative methods of brutality and cruelty.

One scene that flashed across the surface of the mirror, was spiders climbing all over the Shaman. *So, this was the root of his unnatural fear of spiders. It started with Mardavian.*

After this scene, the mirror showed a crown being taken from my head by two people in masks and long cloaks. The deaths of the people I loved, and people whom I'd never met and yet obviously cared for, were being tortured. I was imprisoned: a fate to me worse than death, for I valued nothing above my Freedom.

I moved on from this mirror, glad to reach the third. The third mirror, which revealed your deepest desires, was made of sparkling emeralds.

When I peered into this mirror, I saw a quick flash of my parent's embracing me which made my jaw tighten angrily. I saw another quick flash of Varawynn and myself in an embrace. In a third flash, I saw the face of a woman with full red lips, and a deep olive complexion. It could have been Varawynn, but I wasn't certain. Varawynn's skin was fair.

In the brightness of the flash, I couldn't catch the message in the liquid pools of her eyes, the gateway to the hidden yearnings of her soul. She was stunning, but images passed so swiftly by in the mirror that I almost missed them.

There was a fourth flash of being crowned King with a woman by my side I couldn't make out…only a halo of dark hair. This mirror intrigued and perplexed me, as I secretly wondered if the woman could be Varawynn.

The fourth mirror revealed how others perceive you. This mirror was comprised of blood red rubies, and the mirror itself was a glossy dark sheen, appearing almost black as I looked into it. The mirror flashed red as I saw myself yelling at Rain years into the future.

For a brief moment, I looked in the mirror, and the pain I caused Rain flooded my heart until I couldn't breathe. I couldn't believe I could ever yell at Rain this way. I liked her, I cared about her. What would make me so angry as to disregard her feelings so completely?

The image changed. Now Wandering Wolfe was staring at me while I was sleeping, with a look of deep pride and respect, like that of a father to his son. Then for a moment I felt Jonlin's feelings—he had a general compassion for all people and things that amazed him.

In a time near in the future, Varawynn looked at me with such devotion in her eyes, it made my heart feel fluttery. From a grey stone castle in the distance, a powerful hatred and resistance dwelled for me inside its walls. Its source was uncertain, but powerful.

On an island in a small cottage, I felt an otherworldly presence that felt sinister. A puppet master watched all our moves from a distance, making the hateful people dance with his overseeing fingers and well-contrived manipulations.

Then a love stronger than any emotion I'd yet experienced overpowered every other perception, like the sun shining full bore down on me in the heat of the day. It was the love of a father for his children.

The next mirror revealed your best act, or at least the potential, for your greatest act in life. This fifth mirror was comprised of hundreds, perhaps thousands of snowy white pearls, pure and clean, and perfectly formed. The glass in the mirror was so bright it was almost glowing.

To my surprise, as I looked inside this mirror, I saw myself much older, kneeling before a woman who had a wand in her hand she pointed directly into my face. I saw myself falling to the ground, as if I *let* her kill me. How in the world could this be my best act? I didn't understand the message at all.

The sixth mirror, which was said to reveal your *worst* act, or the potential of your worst act, was composed of dark, onyx stones, with tiger's eye placed randomly amongst the smooth jet-black stones like flashes of golden hope in the darkness. The glass was the shade of gloomy grey storm clouds.

When I peered into this mirror, nothing happened for a moment. Then I saw a sword going through the heart of a boy with dark hair. There was a flash of green, then oblivion.

The last mirror was the one I was most interested in seeing into. It was supposed to foretell your future. The mirror was covered with diamonds sparkling against the white marbled walls surrounding it. There were two different scenes playing out in its undulating depths, concurrently.

First, I saw what appeared to be a grand celebration. I saw a young woman with long brown hair and almond blue eyes, and a young man with ebony hair and deep green eyes, dancing and feasting together. I saw a lady in a white dress coming towards me, but the image was shadowy, and all I could make out was that her hair was dark. I saw the death of King Mardavian and the Shaman alive and well, and older still.

Simultaneously, as if the scene was juxtaposed, another scene was playing out. I saw myself standing over endless stacks of dead bodies lying in ruin on the ground—not just men's bodies, but women's and children's bodies too.

Magic erupted from the tips of my fingers, magic I'd used to kill them. Savagely, I saw myself slay my parents as they lay sleeping, before turning my rage on the pretty young girl with blue eyes I'd seen before. In a dual with the boy with the flash of green, his tall form lay crumpled on the ground beneath me, his black hair and freakily pale skin covered with blood.

In the background of this dual, a great stone castle lay beneath a moon that shone blood-red. As the boy lay there, weakly spitting out blood, he called out a name. A word that shocked and defined me, making me feel a myriad of emotions deeper than I knew I could feel, higher, lower, calmer, wilder, than I'd ever wanted to go—

"Father!"

Warmth enveloped me like a mouth opening before a kiss. My knees gave way. As I started the slow descent into the glass, I witnessed my own death in the mirror.

The mirror was pulling me into itself like crystal quicksand. Just before I'd touched its undulating surface, lost forever into its mysterious veil of inviting oblivion, I felt myself being pulled up and away, just as I lost consciousness.

When I came too, Jonlin was sitting over me, slapping my cheeks. "Where am I?"

"In the Oracle Ileona's castle. In the mirror room."

"How long was I out?"

"Only a few minutes. When I came in, you were about to fall into the mirror. I saved you."

"Saved me? From what?"

"You know…they've all said that if anyone falls into these mirrors, it will claim their life."

"Oh, hog wash. I don't believe that would've happened for a second!"

"I don't believe it either, but that's what they said."

"Well, I'm okay now, thanks to you, Jonlin. Whether or not the myth is true, I'm grateful for your help." I gave a pump to Jonlin's shoulder. "Have fun looking into the mirror of your choice."

I wobbled away shakily. Turning back for a moment, out of curiosity, I asked, "Which mirror are you looking into by the way?"

"The seventh mirror—my future," answered Jonlin.

"That's the one *I* would have chosen too. That is, if I wasn't lucky enough to look into *all* of them." I threw him a clownish grin and winked, before leaving the mirror rooms.

* * *

After Eliju had left me alone in the room, I stood there for a moment staring down the length of the long room resplendent with color and light. For reasons I couldn't explain, tears filled my eyes. Tears often came to me, and I was easily moved in my heart by kindness. But now, a sorrow filled me as I walked down the hall to look into the last mirror.

This was the mirror that had nearly pulled Eliju in. It was composed of countless clear diamonds making it radiate like a rainbow. The colors blinded me, the love overwhelmed me, and I let my tears fall freely.

I couldn't see anything at first, and thought it was because of the bright bursting of color, or perhaps the tears flooding my eyes. But as I stood there, in front of the mirror, and my eyes adjusted to the wash of colors and light, the mirror still stood silent, revealing nothing.

I stood there for a while more, willing the mirror to come to motion. I walked to the left. I walked to the right. I wondered if perhaps my lack of belief was the root of the lack of revelation. I considered looking into another mirror, as this one seemed not to be working for me.

I stood there, considering which mirror would be most important for my life. Ultimately, I felt it would be cheating to try my hand looking into another mirror.

I left the room feeling confused and perplexed. I said nothing to anyone for a long time. It must be that the mirror's magic was a mere myth, folklore that wasn't real. Rain was next, and she chose the sixth mirror, which was said to reveal the potential for your worst act in life. I hoped that she wouldn't be as disappointed as I had been.

* * *

I stood before the mirror where Eliju flashed before my eyes— not just Eliju, but a feeling arose as I looked at him. A feeling I didn't think I was capable of. A feeling of *lust*.

I felt ashamed. Even as I saw myself in the mirror mixing together a potion of herbs and liquids, I was ashamed.

I watched myself traveling to the lands of the desert, Jonlin and Eliju's homelands. I'd never seen much of the deserts, but I saw a lot of the desert in this mirror.

Then I was with Eliju, dumping my concoction in his tea…and what happened next was so shocking and shameful, I couldn't repeat it, even to myself. I left Eliju asleep that night and stole away back to my home with my tribe. But my body began to change, and the repercussions of my worst act would last for a lifetime…

I came from the room pale and wane, worried and anxious. I felt by the results of that night, I would have to follow through with my worst act. But it was so hard for me to believe I could do such a thing.

Alondria came after me, and she chose to look in the second mirror, revealing your greatest fears. I wondered why, of all the mirrors, she had chosen that one?

* * *

I was in awe of the Crystal Castle…it was like something out of my dreams, or a fairy tale. I wished Aldoran was here. I knew that if he was, he would have chosen the mirror showing your potentially best act. He was always looking up, looking for the next hurdle, the next challenge that would make him grow. He was always trying to improve himself, to be the best man he could be—when he was already the best man I knew.

We hadn't been apart long, but I missed him terribly. We'd grown-up doing everything together, and he was more than my brother, he was my best friend. We'd never been apart this long before. I was homesick.

Up until now, my twin brother had been the most important person in my life. But I was not my brother.

I walked down the long hall, with the mirrors and the Crystal Castle. I thought the Crystal Castle was the most beautiful castle I had ever seen or heard of. The sapphires on the second mirror sparkled against the gleaming silver surface.

I stared for a moment at the bright blue gems, to steady myself. I hoped that whatever fears I saw in the mirror, I would be able to conquer or defeat.

I saw Jonlin's face flashing before my eyes. He was smiling. Then the scene darkened. I saw flashes of a battle—swords and shields, blood and bodies that lay dying on the ground, soldiers on steeds bearing King Mardavian's crest—the snake eating its own tale.

Eliju was in my arms, blood all over his chest. I was crying uncontrollably as a shadow moved above us. The shadow of an impending storm, like a cloud obscuring the light of the sun as it moves to cover it.

From Eliju's death, destruction covered the earth. The earth became a red river with human blood. I saw King Mardavian's power expanding over all continents of the earth. The magical creatures were no more.

In my homeland Andorra, there was no peace. My greatest fear was the annihilation of the magical races, the destruction of humanity, the loss of our freedom that would occur if Eliju died, and our group's cause met with defeat.

My right hand, bearing the cross in its palm, pressed into Jonlin's bare chest, with the birthmark of a lamb over his heart. Moving towards him, we kissed. The taste of his tongue was metallic. Then the mirror went dark and still.

I closed my eyes, and stood there for a moment in silence, committing the images and impressions into my soul. I willed myself the courage of my twin brother, but deep down, I knew I could never be as strong. My greatest strength lay in my ability to love. But therein also lay my greatest weakness.

Wandering Wolfe met me at the door. He nodded to me wordlessly as we passed each other by. I turned back for a moment, to see that Wandering Wolfe stood in front of the first mirror, the mirror of the past.

~ *** ~

She was sitting quietly reading by the water the first time I saw her. As quiet and still as the soil beneath her. The gray stone castle and grey green sky were the background for her halo of dark hair and the elegantly chiseled features of her divinely feminine face. She looked up in languid displeasure when she heard the heavy booted footsteps of her massively formed father and saw me.

"This is Wandering Wolfe," King Yaldaboath said with a sweep of his arms towards my shy half-smile and awkward stance. "He's come to be taught magic with you and Mardavian."

She smiled curiously, her phoenix-shaped eyes narrowing with suspicion. "Why?"

"It's in the Prophecy," he told her simply. After that, there were no more questions about my intrusion in their lives. My presence was taken in stride, for the whole of their lives and education was governed by the interpretations of the Prophecy.

She was tall and slim with slight, hugging curves; she walked in the refined movements of royalty bred with class, in a natural, effortless style. Her intimidating beauty was merely a softened façade for the even more intimidating quicksilver brilliance of her mind, the heart that burned and beat with an ambitious desire for power, and passions and desires deeply insatiable. She and her brother Mardavian were like the sunset over the waters. He was merely the reflection of the colors in the sky; she was the source of his every idea and lesson learned.

"In the beginning was—"

"The Word," she answered the wizard Vorseth immediately, our master in all things.

"And the Word was—"

"Without form or substance."

"So, the world was—"

"Borne from thought the words breathed form to life."

"Very, very good," Vorseth nodded, as Mardavian and I looked at her in awe and wonder. There was no outwitting her.

"And hence, Mardavian, what is the most powerful force in the universe?"

"Words?" he'd answered hesitantly.

Vorseth shook his head. "Any ideas, Wandering Wolfe?" He

smiled at me as if he knew me, though I still really could not explain why he had chosen me for his pupil. His familiar way with me was unnerving.

"Words created life, but why and what was the intention of creation?"

"Very good, answering a question with a question, and digging deeper than the surface." Vorseth smiled at me again, as Mardavian scowled.

"Words created life, and thoughts gave birth to words. Words then are more powerful than the action, as thoughts are the source of action. Without first the thought, and the words revealing our intentions, our actions are stagnated. Creation is borne from words which are borne from thoughts, hence in theory, our thoughts create our world," she said.

"So, what is the source or intention of our thoughts?" Vorseth asked, to no one in particular.

"Aren't our intentions individual?" I asked.

"Individual intentions may be, but we have lost the original question in the answering of it."

"Is the greatest source of power creation?" I tried.

"That's a start. But what was the intention of creation? The source of intention?"

"So, the source of the intention of the creation of the universe is the most powerful force?" I continued the idea.

"The Creator," Mardavian attempted.

"And what is the Creator?" Vorseth prompted us. We three students looked at each other, stumped.

"Love," he finally answered for us. "The most powerful force in the universe is love. The Creator is love. The creation of the universe and the intention of the universe is love."

The silence was audible. Then Mardavian laughed. His greedy silver eyes combed over his sister's body. "Love, the most powerful force in the universe," he repeated sarcastically.

Fear fleetingly flickered across her face. Heavy footsteps stopped in front of the door. The king, along with his wife, Mardavian's mother, and her stepmother, came inside.

The queen oozed disdain all over her stepdaughter. Her hatred and jealousy made her otherwise attractive appearance ugly. "How's my stupid, good-for-nothing stepdaughter faring under your tutelage, Vorseth?"

"Quite well," Vorseth answered, respectfully.

*"You are **quite** too kind," she said viciously. "I don't even know why my good husband insisted she take these lessons with the boys. He is*

quite too soft-hearted to deny such a dim-witted brat as her. Now, Mardavian, I'm sure does **very well**."

"He does…well, your majesty," Vorseth hesitated.

"You mean **very well**, do you not?" her tone rose dangerously. She took this tone right before she exploded in a rage of fiery fury and the breaking of whatever items were nearest her reach. If Vorseth didn't appease her now, there would surely be hell to pay.

"Mardavian is a brilliant student. His intellect is like the brilliance of the sun, your majesty."

She smiled now. "Brilliant like the sun. I like that. And this," she made a sweep of my body, "boy is no doubt…an alluring addition," she gave me a loquacious grin, her tongue licking her upper lip like a hungry animal. I felt my stomach curdle.

King Yaldaboath put his hand reassuring on his daughter's shoulder. Jumping at his touch, tears sprung into her eyes as his hand lowered itself to just above her heart, a little too intimate for comfort.

Something broke inside me. Should I say something? Should I defend her to her stepmother? Should I tear her father's hand away and threaten him? Looking into her carefully composed, refined features, held tightly in place; I could see the struggling beneath the surface to maintain control. Saying something may well make it worse…so I said nothing. She looked up at me, a hint of reproach shining in her eyes, as doubt gnawed at my heart.

The memories in the mirror moved me on, like the ocean takes hold of the tides, carrying the water up and away. The mirror of the past took me to that moment of love, so long ago that still haunted me…

Laughter erupted from her cherry blossom lips, like twinkling stars in the moonlight. "You love it!" said the girl, with a sly smile. Lifting her spry limbs through the air in a wide circle, her feet flew in twirling arabesques. Throwing her body upside down in the air, she landed abruptly on her feet.

"That wasn't fair! It's never fair when men use their superior strength to teach us ladies—superior in every other respect—a lesson!"

"You love it!" I smiled slyly back at her. Playfully slapping my shoulder as she moved towards me, I pulled her into me—into a sudden kiss that took both of our breaths away. She was trembling in my arms, and I was hungry for the movement of her tongue, hungry for the taste of her breath, hungry to crush the sweet cherry blossom of her lips.

Waves of desire swept over me. I reached up to grasp and finger the layers of her silky dark tresses. My heart was exploding in my chest.

Love constricted and pumped my heart, every vein beating in my body beat for every moment I spent with her. I lifted her again, this time carrying her towards the culmination of our passion under a canopy of weeping willows along a riverbank that soon became familiar to our passions...

The mirror shimmered. The scene became the moment my fear of spiders was born...

Mardavian had me bound and tied at the bottom of a dungeon in his castle, full of varied sizes and types of spiders crawling over the walls and windows and soon, my body. A giant black widow spider slowly labored her way towards me, as Mardavian glowered at me safely from another room with an open window into my room, turned into a sea of clambering spiders.

"Stay away from my sister. She's mine," the boy warned. "Stay away from her or I'll kill you."

"You're so sick. I'm not going to let you—or your father—hurt her anymore, Mardavian!"

"You want to bet?" he smirked, releasing another net full of swarming, biting spiders over my head, creating in me an unnatural fear of arachnids, as he laughed at my screams, and grinned at my terror. The torture went on through the night...and into the next day, until his sister, my love, found and released me. We both knew that the end was near...

I didn't want the memories to be over. I wanted to stay there in the past and change it—to make things right. But I knew I couldn't. So I blinked away my tears, and forced myself to walk away from the last scene I couldn't bear to see.

Varawynn came into the room, choosing the last mirror as Jonlin had. It was the mirror of the future, and the one most commonly chosen. She was probably wiser than I was, to look to the future, and not keep looking back, held back by the past. But the longer a person lives, the more they realize that the ghosts that haunt us represent unfinished business, unlearned lessons, mysteries yet to be solved, and truths yet to be uncovered.

* * *

The mirrors called to me in shadowed whispers...I would have taken hours to look into each mirror, if given the chance, for I had fantasized about these mirrors and what I would see in them, all my life. Since I was a little girl, I'd imagined the beauty of the Crystal Castle. But the reality of a Castle made entirely of crystals, gems, marble, and glass, was far more spectacular than my wildest imaginings.

Unfortunately, I was only allowed to choose one mirror to look into. So, I chose the last mirror, the seventh mirror, revealing the future. The rainbow diamond mirror stood before me, the scene beginning with an embrace between myself and Eliju. The mirror did not just evoke images, but feelings. When I witnessed embracing Eliju, a feeling of longing and desire came upon me.

Then the scenes came faster, in flashes.

There was a flash of me crying in my homeland over Lake Avalon in the Isle of Apples. The Oracle, Ileona, was giving a speech and Eliju was beside me, but it worried me because it felt like she was officiating a funeral.

There was a flash in the mirror of me running, being chased by a man on a black stallion. I tripped and fell, then he was upon me. I remember the sound of his heavy boots on the ground coming down from his steed and upon me. I struggled.

There was a flash of me crying next to a beautiful yew tree.

There was a flash of me with an athame in my hand covered in blood, with the ground beneath me a pool of blood. There was blood all over my hands and fingers. There was blood everywhere. There were the heavy black boots.

A tall, grey stone castle stood behind me and the group of Chosen Ones. A woman pointed her wand at me, to curse me. There was a flash of a pile of ashes on the ground beneath a woman with long, black hair.

Ashes, ashes, there were so many ashes. Gathered up. There was nothing. Then a spark turned the ashes into embers.

I felt my heart breaking in my chest. Eliju was pulled from my embrace.

There was a flash of my body, but the raven birthmark was different. There was a flash of a sleek, grey seal, swimming in deep waters.

A lighthouse stood alone along high cliffs.

A light shone down, where I pulled myself safely onto the bank. I followed the light.

A flash of blinding light. A feeling of bliss. Green grass beneath my feet. Water surrounding me. Slippery grey skin.

A kiss was obscured by the light, blinding light directly in my eyes. The light that shone through the mirror was so bright I could no longer see what happened next, as if my future was obscured by this light.

I stood there for a while more, as the light splashed itself around the room of mirrors, like the waves of the water.

Then the mirror went blank.

I had seen so many things I didn't understand. The tears came to me unbidden, and I suddenly longed for the comfort of Eliju's presence. I was overcome by the things I'd seen, and though I didn't understand them, I felt their inevitability.

* * *

"What is it? What did you see?" he asked Varawynn, as she came from the room of mirrors, eyes shining as if she'd been crying. A large black raven flew around them, making annoying shrieking, screeching sounds, annoying to Eliju at least.

"Shoo, get away, shoo, shoo, get out of here!"

"Caw, caw, caw," cried the raven, its glistening black feathers with a bright red streak down its back ruffling angrily.

"I said SHOO!"

"What?" Varawynn asked.

"No, not you, this confounded bird!"

"That's no confounded bird, that's my Raegar!"

"Your *what*?"

"That's my raven!"

"Yes, and you forgot me back at the castle," it said now in a deep, accusatory way.

"Well, I didn't have time to get you, Raegar—we didn't even have time to eat!"

"You still shouldn't have left me," the raven insisted, his voice ever lower in its displeasure.

Eliju's eyes bulged. "The raven is, is *talking*."

"Yes, of course he is! This *is* a magical land, and in a magical land you should expect nothing less!"

"Shouldn't I?"

"No, you shouldn't. Now close your mouth, Master Eliju."

He did as he was told, retorting, "Well, you stopped crying at least, but what in the world upset you so much?"

Her lips pursed together. "Remember what the Oracle said? We're not supposed to talk about what we see in the mirrors."

"Oh, yes I remember, but do you really believe all that?"

"Yes, I do Eliju, and you should too! How can you be surrounded by so much magic, and not believe in it?"

"I do believe–in part."

"Believing in part is not believing at all!" Before he could defend himself, Wandering Wolfe came through the door looking dazed. A small, sad smile played about his lips, and his eyes shone with moisture.

"Why did you choose the first mirror, Wandering Wolfe, when it's the least important?" Varawynn asked him, exasperated that their self-imposed leader should choose such a useless mirrored vision.

"It's not the least important to some," I chimed in.

"I agree with Varawynn," Eliju stated in her defense. He was probably the only one loyal, or perhaps foolish enough, to openly disagree with me.

"You *would* agree with her Eliju, for you're like two flames from the same fire," I laughed at them. They looked at each other with uncontained glee.

"I think I know a reason why Wandering Wolfe wanted to see his past," Alondria chimed in from behind them.

"Yes, Alondria?" I asked, turning my sunlit eyes upon her.

"Maybe it's because he misses something from his past."

"Or someone," Jonlin interjected.

"That's enough, children," said Wandering Wolfe sternly. "Now it's time for us to go." He was very careful not to look long at me, or to meet my eyes, as he had warned the children not to.

I smiled at them mischievously and nodded. "Yes, shall we?"

Chapter Eleven
Dream Weaving

Late November-December, traveling East through the regions of Northern Europe—

"What do you mean Ileona?" Wandering Wolfe stammered.

Eliju moved closer to the Shaman, a subtle show of support. His concern for his mentor was all over his face.

"I am one of the fourteen," I answered with an amused smile. Oh, this was so fun causing such a stir!

Wandering Wolfe's face went pale. "How, how do you know?"

"Do you really need me to drop my dress and untie my corset to show you the Sphinx on my spine in the middle of my back, Oh Wise One, or could you be losing your touch?"

The children stared at us in wonder, as Wandering Wolfe blushed crimson. "You haven't changed much, have you Wandering Wolfe? You look as young and able as when I first met you, but you also still hold the condescending air of the 'All-Knowing, All-Wise Shaman.' You continue to lead those around who know less than you, like lost sheep. I'm sure you're even still threatened by anyone, in particular a *woman* who might know more than you do."

Now Varawynn looked at the Shaman with narrowed eyes. Eliju was speechless. Wandering Wolfe himself, in that moment, looked as flabbergasted as a child. Jonlin and Shadow Rain looked at each other helplessly. Alondria was pretending not to notice the tension in the air.

"I have what I need, and I'm prepared to go with you now," I continued. "I'm one of the fourteen whether you like it or not, old sage one. I have the mystical Sphinx's mark. Perhaps we can lead the troupe together, or, since I've bested you once before, are you willing to hand over the 'Mentor Role' in its entirety to myself?"

"It will be a cold day in hell that I give anyone else control over the mentoring of these children!" the Shaman shouted, grappling at last to regain some semblance of control. The children gaped at him.

"We're wasting time. We'd best be off, don't you think, oh Great Master of All-Knowing?" I laughed. It was glorious poking holes at his dignified airs and deflating his colossal ego. It felt like old times. With few others did I like to get the goat as much as I did with Wandering Wolfe.

"I...I...I...."

"Spit it out, Wandering Wolfe! You're always so provincial around me! There's plenty of time to discuss this later, but for now shouldn't we start out in the direction of the Mountains of Mourne?"

"How did you know that was where we were going next?" he demanded.

I laughed. "It's not all that hard for me to guess, Wandering Wolfe. Come along now children."

"Hold on just a minute, Ileona! We ought to settle this here and now. I was entrusted and appointed to be the children's leader. Your expert knowledge at deciphering riddles will surely be invaluable to us, but I must still insist upon maintaining the leadership role of this troupe."

"Thank you for that sensible speech, Wandering Wolfe. However, considering that I've already defeated you once before, I believe that gives me some right as to the teachings of these children. Or would you like to have a rematch right here and now?"

I was well-aware that my appearance as Oracle was as feminine as blooming lavender, with my pale blonde hair and long glittering silver dress and dainty crystal shoes, many people saw me as delicate and frail.

Inside I was as powerful as a lioness and took immense pleasure in taking people off-guard with my aggression, in such contrast to what I appeared to be. No doubt my will was as fierce as the Shaman's, it was just expressed differently.

"And does your superiority to me in that one battle, render all my other knowledge useless?"

"No, but nor does it take away my own right to instill some knowledge into their impressionable young minds."

"So, what do you suggest?"

I paused, biting my lower lip in concentration. I just wanted to be in charge, not necessarily the leader. "You're right. I don't want to entirely take away your authority over rearing these children. The sole responsibility would wear on me eventually, but I *would* like the opportunity to teach them magic I know, which you do not."

"What do you propose teaching them?"

"That is my right to decide, Wandering Wolfe."

"I'll agree to this as long you give me your word you'll do everything in your power not to lead them astray."

"You should know me better than that! And now you ought to feel grateful to have me. You know that at least my skill in charm magic and fighting is expert."

Winking at him playfully, I turned to the still shocked troupe. "Now it's best we be off. As Wandering said, we're on a tight schedule."

~ *** ~

Ileona agreed to cook and prepare the venison we caught for our travels, while the rest of us were learning from Wandering Wolfe. We liked to prepare as much food as possible ahead of time, so we could hike about 10 miles every day, without needing to stop and prepare food for each meal.

The Oracle liked to do the cooking and required some time alone every day to recharge her batteries and do her spiritual practices. I envied her a little, all that time away. It grated on my nerves being around people too much.

As the slants of the early morning shone down on the Shaman's face, he looked at us condescendingly. "Today I'm going to teach all of you to center yourself through nature. ALL of you," said Wandering Wolfe firmly. "Including the Bard of Hebron, Jonlin."

Jonlin was apologetic. He didn't like being thought of as stubborn, and I really didn't think he was. As usual Wandering Wolfe was being too hard on us.

"I honestly wasn't trying to be stubborn, Wandering Wolfe. But perhaps you're right. I really don't think there's much harm in my learning something like this."

Wandering Wolfe smiled his smile that grated on my nerves because it was just so self-righteous. "So, we're in agreement?" Jonlin smiled back gently his sweet smile, "Yes, sir, we're in agreement!" The Shaman was clearly relieved.

"Now my children, there are many ways to center, but I think centering through nature would be the best place to start. The river will be a good site for this particular exercise."

I loved the rivers and lakes and streams. I loved the forests surrounding us. I loved the trees with their dignity and majesty that have told me the stories and histories of the people of the past since I was a little girl.

I loved the elements. I loved the storms and the snow and rainfalls. I loved the spring and the fall and the changing of seasons. I came to life with my bare feet on the ground. I loved to touch the earth with my bare fingers. In the summers, as I grew up, I used to love to pick wildflowers and make them into a bouquet each evening for my mother. These were good memories, and I smiled to myself as I reflected on them.

After we walked to the river and stood at the water's edge, with the energy of the water immediately calming my spirit, Wandering Wolfe instructed, "As we stand in the light of the sun, shining on us through the trees, be aware of the currents of the wind breaking up the intense heat. Feel the lightness of the earth beneath your feet. This first exercise will help you focus your energies, making it easier to hear the sounds of nature."

The earth itself was my element. In the sky, I was free as a bird. In the woods and the mountains, I was a white-tailed fawn. I was just like a mermaid in the water. I didn't care what anyone thought of me.

I slipped off my shoes and walked barefoot along the riverbank, pressing my bare feet into the earth, connecting me to it. Lost in the exercise at hand, I began to dance on the ground alone, lost in my own song, still with the others, but apart. My eyes were closed in concentration, and my arms and legs moved to the music in my mind.

My lame leg did not deter my movements. Somehow my handicaps only made the movements more unique, but still graceful. I loved to dance. Wandering Wolfe let me do my thing, and Jonlin and Shadow Rain were concentrating with Wandering Wolfe, but I felt Alondria's and Eliju's eyes on me as I danced.

I didn't dance for them. I didn't dance for anyone. I danced because I felt the urge to dance, as an expression of my feelings.

The Shaman gave me some time, before continuing with his instructions, "Relax your body, paying close attention to your jaw, the muscles in your stomach and the strength of your legs. Pay attention to your slow, even breaths. Feel your breath moving to the back of your body, connecting with the sun overhead and going down the front of your body allowing you to connect with the earth beneath the soles of your feet." I walked back to the group and began to center and ground my body.

* * *

Shadow Rain tightened her eyes in concentration. Jonlin was silently praying. But my mind was wandering. Eliju and I were clearly spellbound by the movements of the exotic Celtic Priestess. Varawynn's dancing had captured my imagination.

She was so incredibly lovely, but I think what had inspired me the most was the sense of her freedom in every movement. It was difficult for me to focus on these exercises sometimes. It made me feel constricted. And my spirit longed to be free, as free as hers was.

The centering exercise only took fifteen minutes, but it felt like much longer. Then we watched as the Shaman made a wide circle of stones in a large clearing.

"The second lesson I'm giving you today, is the Shaman's Medicine Wheel. This includes 36 stones precisely arranged. I want you to watch how I arrange them. Each stone represents a state of mind that together makes up the whole. At the center of the Medicine Wheel, is the Creator. I'm not asking any of you to incorporate this into your belief system. I AM asking you to be open to experiencing it." He looked at Jonlin pointedly.

"By Creator, you mean God?" he asked.

The Shaman smiled, taking his question to mean he was going to stay. "A rainbow by any other name would be as colorful."

"I'm not sure what that means," Jonlin said. Wandering Wolfe shrugged and chuckled, plowing forward.

The next half hour or so, Wandering Wolfe arranged the stones in the Medicine Wheel. We sat down in the grass and relaxed. After the centering exercise, silence felt more comfortable…but my spirit still longed for movement, not stillness.

"To work with the Medicine Wheel powers, we'll use a new loaf of bread, smudging materials, a bit of parchment from the Prophecy, and I'll drum as you journey. Journeying in the purpose of this ceremony is to allow the spirits of the Medicine Wheel to work with you, guiding you to where you want to go, or to something you need to learn."

"I don't know what you mean by journeying," I told him.

"Journeying is a fairly complicated concept with lots of moving parts for Shamans, so we're going to start with something simple. For you, Jonlin, and Eliju, this is just about quieting and emptying your mind and letting it take you to another place, filling your mind with something ethereal, in a similar way as food fills your stomach. Varawynn and Shadow Rain are more advanced and understand the concept, so I will expect their journey to be more intensive. Alondria, you may do as you wish. I trust your judgment. May you all learn to follow your instincts, which is really our higher consciousness guiding us."

It made me feel good that the Shaman trusted my judgment. I felt very validated and respected by him. I also liked Ileona. I thought that they were both good teachers in their own way. I hoped that we could all learn to get along.

Wandering Wolfe carefully smudged us. Smudging was a way of cleansing and clearing your negative energy—like resistance, using sage. Carefully moving the smoking sage up my arms, back, and legs in the front and the back of me; he concentrated around my face and eyes. The smoke was heavy and sweet at the same time. The smell of the smoking sage and Wandering Wolfe's focused movements calmed me.

As I slowly breathed in and out, I felt myself relaxing enough to begin the ritual. Jonlin told me he loved the smell of the sage. The heady smoke drifted through the air, moving gracefully around and among us. It immediately set us at ease. It didn't make any sense, and we couldn't have explained it with words, but its calming affect was real. I felt my spirit lift in serenity and bliss.

* * *

My mind was wandering again. I started thinking about the woman in my dreams. Did she wish me harm? When would I finally meet her? I'd been hoping she was Varawynn, and certainly there were similarities…but there were also too many differences for them to be the same person.

When Varawynn was dancing, I felt my body responding to her movements. I couldn't deny my attraction and desire for her. She was just so beautiful.

I could tell by the look on Shadow Rain's face she was right at home. This was her Destiny after all. I imagined she was homesick, and these experiences comforted her. I think it was even more meaningful to have Jonlin with us, as he had never joined us in a spiritual exercise before. Varawynn was now so deep in a meditative state, a wild coyote in our midst wouldn't have taken away her focus.

"Pick positions that feel right to you in the moment," Wandering Wolfe instructed. Standing by the final stone of "Unity," I took another steadying breath as the Shaman started drumming, speaking his instructions through the pounding of the drums. To my surprise, the rest of the group followed my lead and stood behind me and the stone of Unity.

"With your inner eye go around the Medicine Wheel, making a complete circle of the outer stones, then in counter-clockwise motions, walk around the circle of inner stones. After you've gone around the inner stones, go down each path; walk on the outside and the inside of the circle, until you reach the center. Do this until you've honored each stone in the Medicine Wheel." As I gave thanks for the stones in the circle, a supernatural pop exploded in my mind.

"Feel the power of the stone calling out for you, and with your inner eye reach out to this stone. What is this stone calling you to do? Sit? Kneel? Bow, lie down, or stand up? After you've felt the answer, and are in the position most comfortable for you, make an offering of bread to this stone. Thank the spirit of this stone for allowing you to learn of the position it wanted you to take."

The explosion in my mind turned into a pounding hammer, bang, bang, bang, bang, BANG! Every third or fourth pound the pulsating was so severe, a vein was pumping out the side of my head. It was so painful, I fell to my knees.

Wandering Wolfe was oblivious to my discomfort, intent upon his teaching. The Shaman's rhythmic drumming was strong and sure in the practiced movements intended to bring us to a higher level of awareness, but every hit of his drum seemed to be pounding into my skull.

"I see that some of you are kneeling now, and that you all have stood behind the Stone of Unity. I want each of you to kneel together and cup this sacred stone between your hands. Thank the Stone of Unity for allowing you to share in its power today. Tell the stone that you are open to whatever message it wishes to impart."

Wandering Wolfe continued drumming as we were supposed to be "journeying," even though I still wasn't sure what that was. But instead of emptying my mind, I felt my mind filling, pulling at the ends of my body and mind. Our hands were touching one another's hands along with the cold, smooth white stone.

My body was being lifted—all the sounds and sights of the earth became just vague memories and images. The intense pain from the pounding of the drums vibrating with the pounding in my skull felt like centuries ago...

A peace that passed all understanding overcame me, as I felt myself expanding to become a part of the air, the sand, Wandering Wolfe, the trees, the fields, the animals, the insects…in total unity with every living thing…in total unity with the group around me.

I saw the details of their particles and atoms. Seeing past the atoms into the energy behind them, my body was without substance, moving into everything, as a part of everything, yet I also stood outside of everything, watching the movements of life, watching all of life breathe; all of life's existence a part of One cosmic energy.

"After you've received the stone's message, use your third eye to visualize yourself following the same pathway you followed before. Make a complete circle of the outer and inner stones and then go back to where you began. Thank the entire Medicine Wheel for imparting its wisdom. Thank the stone that spoke out to you."

Wandering Wolfe's voice slowly brought me back into myself, just myself, and the details of what all living things are composed of, and the unity of all living things, closed themselves up again. The beating of the drum was slower now, and the even tone of the Shaman's voice brought my spirit gently back into my body.

"Come back into your physical body, making sure you're centered and grounded. When you're completely in your body, stretch your arms and legs in all positions. Take a deep breath and open your eyes." Rubbing my eyes, I inhaled deeply, stretching my throbbing limbs as the drumming completely stopped.

"That was an experience!" I exclaimed.

"Why? What did you see?"

"It was the power. It was like I became one with the infinity of the universe, but I could also see the finiteness of what every living thing was made of."

"That's amazing Eliju! I'm quite pleased. It looks as if you truly journeyed," Wandering Wolfe smiled.

"There was such peace in the unity of it all." I smiled back, blinking in amazement. Wandering Wolfe looked deeply into my eyes. "You've done well today, Eliju. I'm very proud of you, lad. Now we'll rest and prepare for weapon training tomorrow. You children may rest while I prepare tomorrow's lesson."

I noticed Wandering Wolfe didn't ask anyone else about their experiences. It probably bothered them how close the Shaman and I were, but I was grateful for it.

When we got back to the camp, I read from the Torah and meditated for the rest of the day, deep in thought and reflection of my experience in the stone circle, the "Medicine Wheel."

~ *** ~

Jonlin, Shadow Rain, and Eliju all internally decided to go along with whatever the Shaman and I decided for them. Until they could process all that'd transpired, they thought it wise not to comment on our power plays.

Varawynn and Eliju meanwhile became even closer, thick as thieves. Varawynn was enamored by my power and always had been. Eliju began to neglect his other friendships, in his fascination with the Priestess, Varawynn.

"I wish you could've seen more of my land, Eliju. I'm sure you would have loved it! If we could've stayed longer I would've shown you more of the forest and the lake surrounding Avalon, not to mention the mountains leading up to Camelot."

"I would have liked that."

"I would have liked that too." Varawynn and Eliju smiled sweetly at each other.

Rain glanced over at them and glared. "You say that now, but just wait a day or two."

"Wait a day or two for what?" Varawynn's temper flared.

"Wait for Eliju to get into one of his miserable moods because of his nightmares and insomnia."

"Rain! How could you tell her that?" Eliju stared hard at her, feeling betrayed. "Maybe I get a little cranky from lack of sleep, but it isn't that bad." Really, it wasn't. And he was surprised she offered up anything about his nightmares. He'd trusted her with that.

Shadow Rain's face beat red-hot as the shame came over her. She shouldn't have said that. "Oh, I'm sorry Eliju. I shouldn't have said anything. You're really not like that."

"Well, you *did* say it, and it wasn't very nice to Eliju, Shadow Rain," said Varawynn coldly, looking at Shadow Rain as if she were a careless puppy who'd just stepped on her delicate kitten's tail.

"I'm really sorry," Rain said again, as the tears welled up in her throat.

"Why did you say that, Rain? I thought we were friends."

"*Varawynn* happened, I would wager," I interjected shrewdly, watching the children's actions and reactions analytically.

"I'm *not* jealous!" Rain exploded.

"Well, how else do you explain it, my dear?" I laughed at her.

"I'm telling you I'm *not* jealous!" she shouted, as Varawynn and Eliju laughed with me. Clearly Rain was of the type who couldn't laugh at herself. But we weren't really laughing *at* her, as she suspected. Her reaction was just so cute.

"FINE! DON'T believe me!" she said, stomping off.

"Should I go after her?" Eliju asked me. "I didn't mean to hurt her feelings.

"No, don't give in to her childishness," Varawynn insisted. "You'll only encourage her."

"It would help if you tried to understand Rain better, Eliju," I answered him. "And you, Varawynn, are misunderstanding her. I'm afraid we've all hurt her feelings by laughing. You've got it all wrong my pet." I gave a glowing look to my favorite pupil from our land.

"It seems to me that she was the one being hurtful just now," Eliju said honestly.

"She's only acting this way because she has a crush on you," I explained to him.

"You've got to be kidding!" Varawynn puckered her mouth in distaste.

"No, I'm not; I think it's pretty obvious, Eliju."

"Ileona, I think *you've* got it all wrong now. Rain and I are just friends. If anything, we're like brother and sister, and we're very protective over each other. Really, she's probably just afraid of Varawynn hurting me."

A flash of memory about Rain's emotions and hurt feelings in the fourth mirror swept over him like a tidal wave. He felt a moment of doubt that left him as soon as he looked over at Varawynn. I could read his mind like an open book.

"You both really ought to be more considerate of her feelings," I said again, looking hard at my darling Varawynn.

Eliju looked irritated. "But weren't you the one who started us laughing, Ileona?"

Varawynn sighed. "And come on, Lady Oracle, I have the utmost respect for you, but Rain hasn't exactly been welcoming to me. Doesn't she have some responsibility in this too? If she knew me, she wouldn't think I'd ever hurt Eliju. Not on purpose. Seems to me, she's the one who never gave *me* a chance!"

Not one to admit where I could have been wrong myself, I ignored part of what they'd said, and insisted, "It's a misunderstanding, that's all."

"I really hope it's not what you think it is, Ileona. I think she's a sweet girl—usually at least, but I could never like her as more than a friend." Smiling warmly at Varawynn, Eliju reached over to take her hand in his. I witnessed their brief affectionate display with troubled eyes.

If Eliju *had* gone after Shadow Rain, she would've told him what was really bothering her: that Varawynn had taken her place. He would have seen the tears in her eyes that she was too proud to shed in front of *her*. Maybe she would have shed them if Eliju had gently taken *her* hand and asked her what was wrong. But Eliju had stayed with Varawynn and Ileona, thereby choosing *their* friendships over one with Rain. At least, she thought of it that way...

* * *

Truthfully, I *was* jealous of Varawynn, *very* jealous; jealous of her beauty, jealous of her charms, jealous of her compatibility with Eliju. *I wonder how he feels about her...* Eliju seemed fascinated by her exotic beauty. He couldn't take his eyes off her.

"It's just a little crush. It'll fade with time." I almost had myself convinced. I felt like an utter fool for feeling this way at all. I wasn't used to feelings like this, and they were causing me to act out.

In my tribe, I'd advised others when to plant their seeds by the position of the planets, when to get married and conceive babies and perform burial rites. I had so much knowledge about how people feel and think and why they act as they do. I remembered once seeing a love triangle and thinking how immaturely the one who was unloved in the threesome was acting.

Now that the same romantic emotions were coursing through my veins, I felt as immature and inadequate as the young man I'd counseled to get a hold of himself. It was like love itself had turned me back into a child.

Later that day, Jonlin and I talked about Varawynn and Eliju. "What do you think of her, *really?*" I was almost afraid to hear the answer.

"I think she's misunderstood," he replied.

That was a weird way to describe her. "How do you think she's misunderstood?"

"Some people may believe she's cold, but that's only because she's trying so hard to control the depth of her emotions."

"By some people you mean me, right?"

"Perhaps, but not just you. I think many people don't see her as she really is."

"So, you think I'm being hard on her?"

"Maybe a little."

"Then what about her? Is she being hard on me?"

"Oh yes, and probably more so."

"Thank you for saying that. I was beginning to think you were just like Eliju, and had been lost to the dark side!"

"Rain, I hardly think that Varawynn is the dark side."

"Well, that's how it feels to me, Jonlin! I know she's beautiful, but doesn't what's inside matter even more?"

"Yes, of course it does. And you, Rain, are beautiful from the inside out, and genuinely caring, and I love that about you. I'm only trying to explain to you that Varawynn doesn't possess your courage."

"My courage?"

"Yes, the courage you have to be free, to be honest, and to be real."

"So, you actually see me as stronger than Varawynn?"

"In this sense, absolutely! You're stronger than her on the inside, in the final analysis, when it comes to the emotions. For some people, for me even, it isn't so easy to be emotional and honest about my feelings. I admire your ability to express yourself. You're so…full of life! I really appreciate that about you, Rain." I smiled; his words were encouraging to me. I was coming to depend on his kind assurances.

"I feel so out of place here, Jonlin. I'm not used to being with a group of people traveling all around the countryside for unknown purposes."

"None of us are used to this, Shadow Rain. We just have to try to make the best of things and get along as well as we can."

"It's only Varawynn I don't like, Jonlin."

"I think your real problem with Varawynn arises from her closeness with Eliju."

I averted my eyes. "Why do you say that?"

"Because you've been angry with him all the time lately—ever since Varawynn arrived. I think that's because he's not acting as you wish he would act towards you. And now that Varawynn is here, and they had such an instant connection, it's that much harder for you."

Turning away, I knew he could read the feelings in my eyes, and I really didn't want him to. "Look at me, Rain," he said kindly. It was hard to say no to someone being so sweet, so I did.

I knew he was reading my emotions. "I *know* what you're really afraid of. You're afraid of your feelings about him, and that he'll never share them."

With his analysis, so dead-on, I couldn't control the tears welling up in my eyes. "You can talk to me Rain. You can tell me how you feel, and I'll try to understand. I won't tell anybody what you tell me in confidence."

Jonlin was my best friend. How I appreciated his kind words! "I'm afraid..."

"What are you afraid of?"

"I'm afraid you're right, that I do like him, and that he doesn't like me, and that he never will." He hugged me gently and caressed my boring, straight brown hair, so plain next to Varawynn's black curls. "Maybe he *could* like you—only you're going about it the wrong way."

"How do you mean?"

"Well, you keep picking fights with him. Maybe if you were more sympathetic–"

"I tried that."

"And what happened?"

"And Varawynn got in the way!"

"Then don't *let* her get in the way!"

"Oh, who are we kidding? He'll *never* like me as much as he likes her!"

"Yes, but does he love her?"

"I'd say there's more of a chance for them than for us. They're more alike."

"But opposites can attract."

"Or there can be so many differences, you have nothing in common."

"Oh, I wouldn't say that. I'd say you and Eliju definitely have some similarities."

"Maybe that's true, but if it is, then our similarities, like our emotions, are what makes it so hard for us to get along. And really, we're both emotional, but in different ways."

Jonlin sighed, "You can be very stubborn; you know that, Rain?"

"I'm sorry," I said, still trying not to cry. "I just know in my heart that Eliju and I aren't well-suited for each other, and yet I can't seem to help the way I feel."

"You don't choose who you love, Shadow Rain. But I'll try to help you okay?" Jonlin put a consoling arm around my shoulders. "There has to be a way we can get Eliju interested in you."

"And is he just going to forget about Varawynn?" Jonlin gave me his gentle smile that brightened his dreamy eyes. "I have a feeling that it won't work out between them."

"But, how do you know?"

"I *don't* know. It's just a feeling I have. Trust me okay?" And suddenly, when I looked into his warm brown eyes with flecks of gold, I did.

~ *** ~

Slowly, but surely, the children and I were developing a routine along with our daily traveling. I found routine reassuring. Ileona had surely put a damper on my authority with the young people. But I held myself with dignity, refusing to allow her impetuous and insistent need to thwart my authority like a petulant child, deter me.

Today was an important day because I was going to teach them methods to control the elements. The levels of the children and their knowledge of magic varied, but they all had room to grow in their elemental knowledge. Alondria and Jonlin were gathering kindling and wood for our fire, Ileona was doing her weaving, and so my afternoon was dedicated to the teaching of Varawynn, Shadow Rain, and Eliju.

I began with a centering exercise. "Take ten slow, deep breaths. Slowly exhale after each breath. Connect with the space on your forehead between your two eyes. Feel the invisible third eye in the middle of your forehead. Concentrate on feeling your third eye and slowly allow it to open. Imagine yourself holding out your hand and lightning erupting from your fingers. You will say these words to release the thunder and lightning, 'Alam nuom serium solice.' Say these words to call forth the rain, 'Furium noum torin solice.'"

Lightning struck the tree next to Eliju. "Who just did that?" I demanded.

"I don't know," Varawynn said quickly.

"It wasn't me," said Eliju.

Shadow Rain stared down at her moccasin-clad feet. "Was that you, Rain?"

"Yes, I think it was me," she admitted reluctantly.

"You have great elemental power, Rain. You must use that power well."

"Yes, Wandering Wolfe," she agreed, as Varawynn looked at Eliju and rolled her eyes to make him chuckle.

I took a deep breath, trying not to allow the Celtic Priestess to get under my skin. Clearly, she was in the Oracle's camp, and had determined to undermine me just like her mentor. This was a test just like anything else. A test for patience. A test to understand and rise above those who would upset the apple cart as much as they could.

Ignoring Varawynn's rudeness, I gave a special look to Shadow Rain, patting her on the shoulder. At this point, I could see Eliju and Varawynn were getting jealous, but neither one said anything.

"Girls, I want you to raise your arms into the sky and imagine with your third eye, lightning coming forth. Eliju, I want you to do the same, only imagine rain being released from where you're pointing into the sky. I want you to say, 'Frenion freniyew, alaba, alabu, serion. Girls, I want you say jiniour, jinua, grindiyer, grindyia! Now, on the count of three! One, two, *three!*' "

Only drops of wet, sputtering spit oozed out of Eliju's wand after his words. After Varawynn's chant, sparks of electricity shot out about three feet. Shadow Rain managed to slash Varawynn through the side, as a wide bolt of lightning erupted from her words.

"Shadow Rain, that was amazing for your first try!" I encouraged her.

"*Amazing,* she almost *killed* me!" Varawynn screeched.

"Please try to be more careful, Shadow Rain," Eliju said, rushing to Varawynn's side, "You could really hurt someone." Eliju didn't want to hurt Rain's feelings, but her emotions were getting out of hand. I could tell he was fighting back his urge to yell at her. His respect for the female gender kept him in check.

"Well, it was an excellent first attempt. She just needs to learn how to control it," I insisted, as I walked over to Varawynn and inspected her wound. "No harm done, Varawynn, it's only a shallow cut; it will heal up nicely, and it won't leave a scar."

"I think I've had enough elemental lessons for today," said the wounded Varawynn, perhaps wounded more by the lack of concern from me, than the wound itself. It's not that I didn't care about her, or that I wanted her to be harmed, but her attitude towards me was rather disrespectful, and she was slowly infecting Eliju with it.

"As have I," stated Eliju loyally, feeling a strong urge to get away from Shadow Rain before he lost his temper, in spite of his best intentions.

"Fine, then I'll work with Shadow Rain alone," I answered pleasantly, deep down glad to see Varawynn go.

"Great, then *we'll* go to learn from the Oracle," Varawynn said with a humph. I did regret losing Eliju, and I could see from the creasing of his eyebrows that he regretted it too. But still I stayed with Shadow Rain, and Eliju followed the Celtic Priestess.

* * *

I was weaving a gossamer dress in the middle of a large, empty clearing when they found me. My face was bent down toward the spinning wheel, and my long, light hair covered my face and moved softly with my movements, like waving wheat before harvest. Flipping my long blonde tresses to the other side of my face, as my hands danced on the spinning wheel, I looked up expectantly at the sound of their approach.

"Wandering Wolfe is favoring that little beast again," Varawynn complained. She looked over at Eliju who looked conflicted and confused. "We were supposed to be getting our group lessons right now," continued Varawynn. "But since Wandering Wolfe doesn't seem to care that Shadow Rain almost killed me with a stray lightning bolt, we thought we'd get some lessons from you instead."

"I'm quite honored, though I hope your wound is not too deep, Varawynn. And I do have a lesson in mind for you today."

"No, it's not too bad, but I appreciate your concern. What lesson do you have in mind for us?" she asked eagerly.

"Dream weaving."

"Dream weaving? What's that?"

"You see this spinning wheel?"

"Yes?"

"This spinning wheel is weaving more than my clothes. I'm weaving dreams into these garments."

"How are you doing that?" Eliju asked in amazement, impressed with my abilities in spite of himself, and his loyalty to the old Shaman.

"You see that one?" I pointed to a dress of deep royal purple, with long princess sleeves and a bell-bottom skirt. The waist had a cinched corset stitched with silver thread creating an intricately seamed pattern of diamonds atop diamonds forming shapes that looked like stars.

"This is a dress for a coronation. I have it in my mind for a wedding celebration. And this next one—"

Picking up a dress of gold so light it looked like glitter, without full shape or form or substance, I said, "This is meant for the birth of a baby. In my mind, I imagined it for the birth of a little girl. I'm saying a blessing over her, and as I imaged the event in my mind, I embroidered the dreams into the clothes. As I weave the dreams into the clothes, I chant ancient Sonar words from the sea to ensure they come true."

"Wow," said Eliju, clearly so impressed he was almost speechless.

"For Eliju, I had in mind a cape, and for Varawynn a cloak. These are easy things to start with. Varawynn, I think yours should be emerald green with a dark-toned sheen. Eliju, I think yours should be red, a bright, vibrant red." Eliju just nodded, wide-eyed.

Varawynn wove her cloak first because she already had the skill of weaving, if not the skill of dream weaving. Eliju couldn't help but notice the feminine beauty and grace of the spinning wheel as it whirled.

Her fingers were moving upon the wheel faster than his eyes could perceive, her eyes closed in focused concentration. Both Varawynn and I chanted words over the spinning wheel, our contrasting beauty like the green and thorny stem against the bloom of the white rose.

Several hours passed as the cloak took shape. After Varawynn took the cloak from the spinning wheel, I tied the cloak's ribbon with a deep, midnight blue. Varawynn sighed, "That was a lot of work...but it's beautiful."

"You did very well," I assured her.

"Thank you, but if you don't mind, Eliju, I'm not going to stay to watch your dream weaving. I'd like to go lay down now. I need to rest. I'm exhausted."

"I understand," said Eliju. "I think I'll do better without your eyes on me anyway. Please try to take it easy and feel better." Varawynn left them to the spinning, more than ready to get some rest from a day's work of weaving and lessons in magic.

Now it was Eliju's turn to try his hand at the spinning wheel. He looked shy as he approached it, and me, rather awkwardly.

I was patient with him as I showed him what to do. He was a quick learner in spite of his fears, and got the hang of weaving quickly. In his mind, as he weaved his red cloak, he was imaging Varawynn dressed all in white. To his surprise, his hands moved as if by a will or knowledge of their own…

She was coming toward him, Wandering Wolfe stood beside him. Dagda, Varawynn's father, was walking her toward the chuppah. She looked so beautiful. Eliju grinned with the images in his mind, which I could read as easily as a scroll as I watched him.

"OOOOWWWW!" Eliju shouted, as the palm of his hand collided with the eye of the needle. Bleeding profusely, his cut hand stained the ruby red cloak with his own red blood…at least it should have been red…but it looked more yellowish than red. How curious.

I didn't notice what happened at first, and continued chanting the words of Sonar magic over him, my eyes closed in concentration. It was as if both of us had been in a trance.

Before he'd had a chance to catch my attention, the red cape, now stained and ruined, ripped in half while he held it. The rip sounded as deep as an earthquake, and the vibration of its being torn reverberated in the earth beneath us and in his body. His shaking hands unwittingly allowed the bloodied cloth to fall to the ground, shredded and ruined.

"Is that why you chose red for my color, Ileona? Did you guess I would cut my hand and it wouldn't matter so much if my blood stained an already red garment?" Eliju laughed nervously.

I looked down at the torn cloth, the yellow blood, and back up at him. This did not bode well for the dreams he'd been imagining coming to pass. "I guess you chose the wrong dream."

~ *** ~

Chapter Twelve
All the King's Men

From King Mardavian's Fortress in Ireland—

"Where have you been all this time? It seems you're always disappearing."

"Isn't that my own business?"

"In other words, you're refusing to answer me." I glared at him. "You would think by now I'd be used to your inexplicable absences."

"Everything I do is for your benefit, mistress."

"Is that so?" My sarcasm held a warning note.

Fidgeting uncomfortably, he consented, "If you must know, I'll tell you. I've been training *your* men."

"Oh, really?"

"Yes, my mistress."

"Well, I can easily corroborate that with my Captain. And yet I wonder why you claim that training my men was your own business and not mine?"

Studying him intently, I added nothing more. His swiftly recurring disappearances had always been one of his countless idosyncroncies, but they were occurring more frequently, and something didn't set right about it in my gut.

* * *

I knew she suspected me, but I couldn't tell her the truth. From now on I would only leave the boundaries of the castle and her influence while she was sleeping. Captain Keirnan would cover for me. He had before.

"What have you learned today so far, my mistress? Have you studied the legend?"

"You know very well I know the legend by heart." Purposefully, she picked up a skittering spider scampering along on the edge of her desk.

Looking her directly in the eyes, I insisted, "But you *were* having trouble with some parts of it."

"Yes, I was, and of course you would not consent to share with me your own interpretation. And yet you always seem quite interested in my interpretations."

"It would be better for you to have your own opinion—even if it's the wrong one, my dear."

She liked to make her points with actions—the meaning in her words were often subtle. It wasn't as much what she said, as *how* she said it that got her point across.

"You remind me of this spider, Vorseth," she murmured, with her deceivingly seductive mannerisms. Between her two long pointer fingers, she squished the wildly moving spider, desperately dancing for its escape.

I cleared my throat. "And that is unfortunate, but I won't be changing my ways, not even for you."

Lightning struck the window and shattered the glass. Rays of light emanated externally from the woman's eyes, directed towards the wizard who refused to cower before her.

"I can see that you're angry with me."

"I'm concerned about you—sometimes I wonder whose side you're really on."

Studying me again, as if I were a stranger, it began to rain outside the broken window. Some droplets fell into the room. I was cold, and shivered involuntarily—more from the chill in her eyes than the actual temperature.

"When should I leave to take them?"

"I thought you'd just be taking him?"

Wiping the remnants of the squished spider off her fingers, with a finely embroidered cloth she brought forth from the elaborate folds of her dress, she answered, "I've decided on taking one of the girls too."

"Why?"

Her eyes narrowing in annoyance at being questioned, she barked, "Because I'm afraid of what Mardavian will do to her of course!"

"What are you talking about?"

"I *know* him. *You* know him."

"Meaning?"

"You were there two thousand years ago, surely you can remember what he did to me?" Her narrowed eyes seemed to peer into my soul.

Closing my eyes for an instant, I allowed the memory to cascade over me, like water rushing over a dam. In my mind, I probed through her walls to allow myself to feel for a moment the shame this trauma had caused her.

"Yes, I suppose I do, but still–"

"Are you actually blessing me with your opinion for a change, Vorseth?"

"Yes, mistress—so listen. Leave the girl there for a time."

"How long, not long enough for him to–"

"Yes, long enough for the Prophecy to come to pass."

She closed her eyes, as she meditated on my words. "But how and why would I let her go through what I have gone through?"

"Because that's the way it will be, regardless of whatever actions you take to prevent it. Besides, the hurts we suffer are as important to our lives as our blessings, and more important to our character. Only those who have truly suffered, have the ability, or even the capacity, to become extraordinary."

"Are you saying that what Mardavian did to me built my character?" She was clearly revolted by the thought.

To be fair, this was a point of contention for most people. To allow others to be in pain seemed unnatural, but pain was necessary for growth and maturity.

Taking a deep breath, I measured my words carefully for her benefit, "What he did to you changed the course of your life and in some ways defines you even now does it not? Would you be as powerful and invulnerable today without your…experiences with your brother and father? If I, or anyone else, had tried to step in, do you really think it would have changed what you were born to suffer?"

I paused a moment, before asking her my final rhetorical question. "Or that without this suffering, you would have grown into the formidable woman you were destined to become?"

She looked surprised and perplexed with the concepts I offered her. "Born to suffer…so are you saying no one could have protected me, and I won't be able to prevent Varawynn from suffering as I did, because it is our destiny…so why should I even try?"

"It was your destiny and it is the girl's destiny. It was written in the stars before your births. You can try, my mistress, if you can find some use in futility, but not even you have the power to prevent Fate." Looking up at me, her dark eyes were like sparkling stars with the echo of memories and unshed tears.

~ *** ~

December, traveling North through Europe from England—

Our traveling was wearing on the young Shadow Rain, but Varawynn had raised Eliju's spirits considerably, and he no longer suffered from nightmares. Much to Shadow Rain's chagrin, Eliju now bounded out of bed, practically jumping up and down with excitement to begin each day.

Crossing the channel in our small wobbling boats that the Shaman rented for us, we encountered some wind that did some damage to our stomachs. Being as land bound as Shadow Rain was, the inclement weather and bouncing boat we had a hard time controlling, caused her to throw up.

I held her hair back as she leaned over the boat, throwing up into the water. Once we'd crossed the little over twenty miles, onto the other side of the channel, the group still seemed to be under a dark cloud.

The days began to blur together. The lessons with Wandering Wolfe and Ileona were all that made them distinct. We each had lessons with both teachers, separately and together.

The Shaman spent every night by the campfire, keeping watch, while the rest of us slept in our tents. Sometimes, not as much as before, but sometimes, Eliju still joined him in sleeping outdoors and keeping a look out for danger. But Wandering Wolfe and I rarely exchanged a hello without someone else in the group being present.

Sometimes I felt a little on the edge with the group. I was Shadow Rain's best friend, but since Varawynn's entrance into the group, the growing brotherhood between Eliju and I, had all but become stagnant.

I admired Alondria, but from afar. I was often too shy to speak to her much. She was too beautiful. I was just a common bard, and she was a Princess, part muse. We had so little in common. But being around her often motivated me to write poetry, prose, and music that was growing better each day with practice and inspiration.

I was often alone writing. I was often isolated even while traveling in a group. To some extent my solitary nature caused this separation. I was not so lonely as most would have been in my situation. Still. Sometimes I *was* lonely.

One day when Varawynn and Eliju had gone to learn a lesson from Ileona by the water, and Shadow Rain had gone into her tent to lay down and take a nap before dinner, Wandering Wolfe had the rare opportunity to speak with me alone.

"That creature we met, the Nephilim—he taught you something important didn't he, Jonlin?"

Of course, he had, but he'd also instructed me not to share it with anyone, so I said, "I don't know what you're talking about, Wandering Wolfe."

"You were honored beyond compare. The Nephilim have notoriously hidden their ways from every creature on the earth for thousands of years. Only the unicorns could compete with them in their ability and skill with magic."

Wandering Wolfe hesitated, trying to decide if he should press me further. "Why are you hiding from us what he taught you?"

His honest question made me want to come clean. "He told me I had to. What Ramuel taught me is meant for me alone, Wandering Wolfe," I finally admitted.

"It will protect me from offensive attacks because I'm not meant to fight. I would prefer to not even defend myself, for even in this there's some action taken against someone else. I believe in nonviolence because I've seen the results of violence and even in defense, the repercussions are far-reaching, and often permanent. Violence disturbs me at a core level and creates patterns in families and cultures that are difficult to break. I'm sorry, Wandering Wolfe; I don't see how someone with my philosophy on fighting will be much use to all of you. I'm a singer and a musician—a bard, not a warrior."

"Jonlin, are you peace-loving for the sake of peace itself? Or is there another reason behind your philosophy?" I think he must have sensed there was more to my story. But I wasn't sure I was ready to share it with him just yet. Being so lonely here, and so apart from the rest of the group, I challenged myself to be more open with him in this rare opportunity for a private conversation.

"My little brother was accidently killed because he got in the middle of a sword fight, I was having with my friends a few years ago. It was only a stupid game we were playing. None of us were angry. It was meant to be harmless fun. But he wanted to join in—and it was because of me he died. I vowed after my brother's death that I would never fight again."

Wandering Wolfe's face softened, he could see those words had cost me much in the relaying. I felt like all the blood had drained from my face, though no emotion was revealed in the telling.

"I'm sorry for what happened, Jonlin. And your reaction is understandable. But different circumstances require discernment. What happened to your brother was a horrible accident, but if you allow evil people like King Mardavian to harm others, you're as much a part of the evil done for standing idly by, as if you'd participated in it. It's not right to base an entire way of thinking on one incident. Rather, to look at what happened as part of a greater whole."

"I can appreciate what you're saying, Wandering Wolfe, and perhaps my perception is skewed, but it's useless for you to try to convince me to go against my vow to never fight again. My brother's death was the most significant experience of my life. Besides that, my basic nature leans toward creating harmony and keeping the peace. Have you ever read my part in the Prophecy? What does it say my purpose in the group is?"

"You can't know that yet. None of you are meant to know your purpose in the Prophecy until your part is fulfilled. I don't even know *my* purpose in its entirety."

"Why?"

"Humans have a funny way of being contrary. Often when someone is told they're one way, or are meant to do something, they stubbornly choose to go another way. That's why it's good for *none* of us to know everything. But I will tell you this; we're all going to have to overcome our weaknesses in the end."

"I draw strength from my faith, and from God. God works through me. I don't know how to fight, and I don't want to learn."

"Would you consider learning some basic skills in weapon training, or experiencing some of the Shamanic practices, or defensive training at least?" It touched me that the Shaman kept trying. It showed me he cared.

"Even if you don't use it," Wandering Wolfe continued, "I would like to teach you just in case. Even if you don't believe in magic...couldn't you consider there is good magic and bad magic and that it might help you to learn it?"

I didn't enjoy being difficult, so I agreed to sleep on it. "I'm meant to be your master too, Jonlin. I'm going to do my utmost to protect all of you from King Mardavian."

"But apart from magic and weapon training could you still be my teacher?" I saw in his eyes how much he wanted to be.

"You make a good point. I may not be your teacher in weapons and magic, but perhaps I am meant to be your teacher in life, Jonlin.

There's something for me to teach each one of you, and there are a lot of lessons I'm sure you could teach me too. The lessons I teach *you* may not be the same as those I give to the others. But I believe the lessons I have for you are of even *greater* worth than lessons of magic and fencing."

"You were born with more wisdom than many people die with, Jonlin, so I can speak with you on a level of which I can't with very many others. Wisdom can be sharper than the blade of any sword, and more potent than the magic of any wand. The source of the greatest power is from the human mind."

"That's high praise, but I don't believe I deserve it."

"Your humility is wisdom in and of itself, Jonlin. I would be glad for us to talk like this again; I believe we both could benefit from these conversations. And I would like to be closer to you."

His words meant a great deal to me and were an answer to my prayers. "That is very gracious of you and I would be honored to get to know you better, Wandering Wolfe." The Shaman's eyes held unshed tears that glistened by the firelight. Though they didn't fall, I saw them, and was beginning to understand what they meant...

~ *** ~

As Jonlin and Wandering Wolfe were talking back at the camp, Shadow Rain, Alondria, Eliju, Varawynn and I had begun to gather food and kindling for dinner when a group of King Mardavian's men happened upon our group, catching us unawares. Eliju drew his sword, pointing it at the men.

"One, two, three, four, five, six, seven men." I quickly did the math. "I have the perfect spell," I said, more to myself than to anyone in particular. Varawynn had drawn her bow and arrows and Shadow Rain her wand.

I pulled a crystal scepter from my bag of tricks and began to dance. The children watched me as dumbfounded as King Mardavian's men. Dancing in twirling movements of color and light, the scepter emitted ray after ray of color whose substance was like steel.

Winding itself around the men whose eyes never left my sensuously moving form, they barely noticed or cared that I was binding them with my rainbow magic. Prancing around the men on their horses like a tireless child at play, I laughed and laughed at their folly. The sound of my voice was enchanting them as much as my movements.

It didn't take long for the colorful steel rays to bind the men and their horses. "Come along children," I said, with one last laugh at the men's misfortune.

The men were so spellbound by my enchantment, that their eyes followed me as we left the grove; it was as if they could've cared less about their capture, in the glory of seeing my sexuality.

"The charm will last for only 24 hours, so we'd best be moving on, and travel through the night," I warned them.

"I don't know how you did that," said Shadow Rain, wide-eyed and awed.

"You forget I'm not entirely human, my dear," I smiled at the acolyte apprentice.

"You defeated those men so effortlessly," Varawynn complimented, impressed.

"Seven is not very many men for me to enchant, my dear, and it was the perfect number for that particular enchantment. I want you to take a lesson from this, children. You can often get much further in combat much faster, through the sweetness of a rose than the bitterness of an herb. So, keep some sugar in your repertoire of weaponry," I told them with a wink.

Alondria smiled at me and winked back, with her ancestry of the muses, she already knew well the power of charm. Meanwhile Eliju and Jonlin, poor fools, couldn't say a thing, for they were under my spell now too, content to follow me around like puppies, until the spell had run its course.

~ *** ~

From a cottage in Caledonia, on the Isle of Skye—

"They will find *you*, my dear. How many times do I have to tell you that?" It was a dismal day. Dark clouds, dark skies, the sun as hidden and obscured as my words.

"Trust me," I said simply, words she'd heard so many times before she wasn't really listening anymore. Watching the wolf outside her window whose dark eyes bore into hers, neither human nor beast looked away.

"My dear, pay attention, you must be ready when they come."

"Ready for what, Vorseth?" she asked, still staring at the wolf.

"Ready to show them just how powerful you really are. You're meant to reveal that you're more powerful than any living wizard or witch on this earth."

Turning to me eagerly now, she asked, "More powerful than you even?"

"Perhaps."

Ignoring my evasiveness, she asked, "And how will I show them this?"

"By breathing life into the dead."

She rose quickly before me, shaking with excitement. I had won her full attention now. "Can this be done?"

"Yes, but only for those souls who were created as immortals. Also, it requires a sacrifice."

"A sacrifice?" she questioned, suddenly suspicious. "From whom?"

"From you, my dear, of course."

"What sort of sacrifice?"

I thought back to the throne room in the bowels of the caverns in Caledonia, with Arlillyth. "That you will learn in time."

~ *** ~

Chapter Thirteen
The Celtic Shepherd King

Late December, heading North from England into Caledonia—

"Do you think Alondria is prettier than me?"

"Of course not," Eliju assured me, though Alondria's beauty as a partially magical being, was greater than any of us had ever seen, beauty is more than just of the eyes. There is a beauty that is felt in the matching of soul mates, and nothing physical can alter those soul ties. Varawynn was my Twin Soul, and so her beauty enchanted and haunted me, more than any other beauty ever had, or could.

"Really?" I asked him again, proud and yet insecure all at once.

"Yes, of course," he insisted, giving me that special look that filled my heart with bliss, and magically uncovered my mask of calm composure and self-assurance, to reveal my vulnerability.

"Don't worry, ani ohev otkha," he said, in Hebrew. I didn't ask him what he said; I didn't need to know the words to understand them.

"The Shaman gave me some books yesterday he'd gotten in Mount Carmel before we left the area. He said he'd been waiting for the right time to give them to me for the past few months."

"Hmmm?" I asked sleepily, so relaxed laying in the grass that I felt near slumber. Languidly stretching my arms beneath my head, I lay like a lazy cat on the ground next to him.

"They're ancient books about the Kabbalah—Jewish Mysticism."

Pulling my left arm beneath my right arm, and looking up at him, I was paying more attention now.

"He told me about a tribe of Jewish mystics, the Essenes. They were persecuted and killed, but some of them managed to escape to the mountains of Mount Carmel."

"That's fascinating."

"There's more…some people believe that the Essenes taught Jesus some of his abilities, like his healing touch and ability for levitation. This man is the founder of Jonlin's religion and the reason for a lot of the recent persecution of my religion."

"Holy star of Orion's Belt!"

"This Christ was supposed to have been around Mount Carmel during his eighteen 'lost years' that weren't written about in the Christian's Holy Texts, with this hidden, royal line of Jews."

"Poseidon's trident!"

"And the books Wandering Wolfe gave me are about all this, and the Kabbalah, which is the spiritual study of numbers that's part of the particular magical knowledge of the Essenes."

"This is really interesting, Eliju."

"Then you think I should read them?"

"Of course, you should read them! This is your heritage and birthright we're talking about!"

"It's a part of it."

"What do you mean?"

"I don't think my father was Jewish...he had red hair and green eyes."

"No, that definitely doesn't sound Jewish," I laughed.

"There's something else. Something I've never told anyone before."

"What is it?"

"In the hut where I lived, I kept the spare blankets under my parent's bed..."

"And?"

"And one winter when I was getting a blanket out from underneath it, I found a loose floorboard."

"And?"

"And there was a book underneath it."

"What was the book?"

"It was a book with Celtic spells for each Celtic holiday."

I sat up fully now. I felt like the cat that had caught the canary. "I don't understand! Why would a Celtic book be hidden under the floorboards in your parent's home?"

"Written on the inside of the cover there was an inscription," Eliju closed his eyes and saw it in his mind, reciting:

My dear brother Kenneth,

May you never forget where you came from, and one fine day, we shall look forward to your return.

Blessings Be,

Your sister

"That means your father was Celtic by blood! And *that* means part of your ancestry is the same as mine!"

"I know," Eliju smiled. "That makes us even closer now, doesn't it?" I smiled back at him. Of course it did.

"Indeed, Master Eliju! But why would your father leave that book behind? Unless...unless he *wanted* you to find it and recognize the other half of your heritage!"

"Do you really think he left it there on purpose?"

"How could it not have been on purpose? It seems to me he *wanted* you to study Celtic magic! Would you like me to teach you about our rituals?"

My words tumbled out with the overexcitement of the proposition. Oh, to become Master Eliju's teacher! To be a teacher to the King of All! What an illustrious honor! And I would probably do a much better job of it than Wandering Wolfe ever could.

Hesitating, Eliju felt unclear; his culture's strict traditions were still flowing strong in every fiber of his being, in his blood, in his veins. Yet I knew his growing love for me and the points I'd made about his father led him to agree, though I sensed there were still doubts and fears in the far corners of his mind.

* * *

Reassuring myself as I'd done with Wandering Wolfe at the outset of this journey, with the promise that all I learned would be weighed against reason, intention, and outcome, I agreed to learn from her. Just like in the beginning, I had misgivings about opening myself up to this other side of myself and heritage.

Yet the truth was that I loved learning about other people and cultures. The knowledge I'd learned so far of magic had done nothing except fill my soul with expansive love. I'd never felt so close to God.

In the next weeks of our traveling, Varawynn and I walked and talked together a lot apart from the rest of the group. She taught me Celtic history, as well as the history of her own family, and the legends of where she'd grown up. She taught me a lot about the various magical creatures in England, like the fairies, banshees and phookas.

"What are phookas again?"

"Phookas are shapeshifters, men that can turn into different animals and the like, to play practical jokes on people, kind of like the fairies do. Only they don't get along with each other. Probably because they're too much alike! They love wreaking havoc on the farm animals where I come from. They like to spook them."

"I'm glad they're not further south—I've had enough troubles protecting my lambs from the snakes!"

We laughed together often. Varawynn had a way of tickling my funny bone, and she made me feel safe to be my real self.

In the night, I often dreamt of sleeping with Varawynn. It wasn't about the physical intimacy. It was more about the softness of her face against my bare chest, a stray piece of her hair tickling the growing stubble on my chin, my hands caressing her bare shoulders. I fantasized about her face nestled against my chest, stroking her shiny hair, looking into her sparkling jade eyes, and the tenderness I felt deep inside, finding physical expression.

Mainly I imagined the moment she would fall asleep in my arms. Even in my dreams, I didn't touch her sexually, just watched her sleep, treating her with the respect a Celtic High Priestess deserved. Knowing none of my dreams could come to pass yet, I tried to show her my feelings in other, more subtle ways that I hoped were just as meaningful.

Before dawn, I woke from my dreams and begin sketching Varawynn's face on a piece of tree bark that I'd stretched in some spare hours a week before, from memory. A little while after dawn, Varawynn opened her tent flap to tell me breakfast would be ready soon. She could tell by my stance and the alertness of my eyes that I'd been awake for some time.

"Eliju, how long have you been up?"

"Since about an hour before dawn," I replied, not looking up from my sketching. Her eyes widened as she looked down to see what I was drawing.

"Is that me?"

"Yes."

"You've made me flawless."

"You *are* flawless"

"To you perhaps."

I put aside my sketching and looked her intensely in the eyes. My intensity made her look away.

"Look at me, Varawynn," I said, with a note of command in my voice.

"Why?"

"Because, I need you to, and I asked you to." With my words I moved to take her hand. "What do you see in my eyes, Varawynn?"

"I don't know."

"Yes, you do."

"I can't talk about this right now, Master Eliju."

I squeezed her hand. "What are you afraid of?"

"I don't know." I stared at the soft, smooth luminosity of her porcelain skin for a moment more, before dropping her hand and stroking my first stubble of a beard.

"Things would be so much easier if I fully shared in the birthright of your religion and its culture."

"Eliju–"

"Come on Varawynn. Breakfast is sure to be ready by now. We should start our day."

She wanted to stop me. She wanted to express her feelings for me. I could see them shining on the surface of her eyes. I could feel it burning in my own, and yet neither one of us could push through the barriers.

"Master Eliju, please wait." She looked up me, still trying to push through her fears to show her feelings. She tried. She wanted to. But she just couldn't express her emotions in words.

She moved sensuously like a black panther into the warm broadness of my chest, burying her face in the crook of my neck, kissing my skin with such devoted sweetness, my heart melted and burst at the same time. For the first time in my life, I got caught up in the moment.

With a rush of sudden passion, I bent her face down, kissing her lips hungrily. Fire exploded between our pressed bodies. As we kissed, my body came alive in ways I hadn't known were possible.

I would look back at this moment as the first vision to come to pass from the mirror of desires in the Crystal Castle—when Varawynn and I embraced in the third mirror. I would remember and recall this embrace with Varawynn many times, for it was to be a desire that was satisfied but once...

I think the group sensed something had happened between us in my tent that morning. We were even closer than before. More and more we excluded ourselves from the rest of the group, though Varawynn had taken Ileona as a confidant since she was from her homeland.

~ ~ ~

Varawynn was using her raven Raegar to send messages back and forth to her parents, and the morning we kissed she wrote her parents a revised account of what had happened. Tying the letter onto Raegar's leg, she gave him a gentle nudge goodbye. "I'll see you in a few days Raegar. Be careful with that letter; it's important!"

"I will be ca-ca-careful," boomed Raegar, in its strangely deep cawing voice, taking off into the open sky. And she felt it; deep in her soul—that nothing could ever kill the love she would feel for the Celtic shepherd boy destined to become their King, for the rest of her life.

~ *** ~

As we traveled to the caverns of the dwarves in the highlands of Caledonia, one of the most important of my religious holidays was coming up—Chanukah. My spirit thoughtfully contrived gift ideas to show each person I understood them, and I loved them.

I was never so happy as on this Chanukah, for I had always prayed and hoped to have a big family to give gifts to. Every other "Festival of Lights" I had spent alone. This was the first time since I was ten-years-old, I had anyone to share my life with.

I wanted to get something intimate for Varawynn. I decided on giving her a carving of the pagan God Woodwose in front of the others and a more personal gift in private. I'd hand-carved a wooden flute for the Bard of Hebron, Jonlin, out of boxwood, and crafted an intricate jewelry box comprised from unique pieces of wood I'd vigilantly collected from the forests and towns we'd passed, including my own hometown of Haran, containing a vial of snake venom which could be used as an anti-poison solution, I gave to our beautiful healer, Alondria.

I had little money as a poor farm boy, so every penny spent counted. But a silver necklace was purchased for Rain in one of the latest towns we rested in, a silver necklace of a crescent moon with a turtle in its center. It had been just too perfect for me to pass up.

An onyx stone from the desert, which couldn't be found in the forests of Caledonia where Ileona was from, was given to the Lady of the Lake, lover and collector of gems that she was, and a new staff for Wandering Wolfe, engraved with ancient, arcane words, and symbols were carved into the bark that Varawynn had taught me and made from the powerful oak tree—which I felt was more fitting for the greatest Shaman on earth, than the sacred, but in some ways weak, birch wood.

Feeling shy about giving them these gifts at breakfast, I walked in with the rather large bag of presents and stood before them with an awkward smile. My joy could not be contained. This was a dream come true. Every year on this holiday in my culture where gifts were presented to your loved ones, I'd had no one to give anything to. This year there were so many...

Walking around the circle where everyone was eating, I dropped off their presents one-by-one, even remembering Flint, as if I could forget the wolf that had saved my little lamb. Throwing the wolf, a huge bear thigh bone I'd been saving since we'd been with the Cyclops, Flint grinned and immediately started chomping down on the marrow, rich in calcium.

At first their faces were dumbfounded. Then Alondria broke into her heavenly smile. "This is so kind of you, Eliju. Thank you so much."

Ileona looked impressed with the thoughtfulness of her gift. Shadow Rain was surprised at first, then happiness and gratitude transformed her features and brightened her essence. "I love this, Eliju; I won't ever take it off. It's perfect for me."

Alondria helped her with the clasp as she put it on. Leaning in closer to Rain's ear, softly enough for only her to hear, I whispered, "I'm sorry for how I've treated you...and I want you to know that your gift cost me the most."

Her eyes spilled over with tears, as she spontaneously flung her arms around my neck. I laughed merrily. Varawynn glared over at us disapprovingly.

Jonlin grinned, expertly placing his fingers on the holes of the flute I'd carefully carved him. The bard played for us a high and lilting jig. Alondria lifted her layered skirts to dance, laughing gleefully.

Flint ran in circles around the clearing and barked. Wandering Wolfe's eyes twinkled seeing Flint's joy. Grabbing me into a bear hug, he said gruffly, "You did well, my boy."

A wave of pain-filled joy overcame me. The words from Wandering Wolfe meant more to me than anything. I had longed for a father's pride and approval, and to belong, to have friends, to love, and to be loved. In that moment, I felt as if all the love I'd ever longed for, was mine.

This was the best moment of my life. Sitting there at their feet, taking it all in, something broke in my heart seeing their happiness, the result of my generosity. Now this was Chanukah, the Festival of Lights.

I leaned close against Varawynn to whisper, "I have something I'd like to give to you in private."

I needed to leave the circle of love I felt there, and somehow make Varawynn understand that my love for the rest of the group didn't make my love for her any less. Somehow it made my love for her even greater. The more my heart loved others, the more it expanded to love everyone more.

Even though it was what I'd always wanted, when confronted with it, my instinct was to leave that powerful love, as uncomfortable with the bittersweet feelings welling up inside me, as much as the unfamiliarity of it scared me, and the fear of losing it hurt almost as much as never having it at all.

So, we stole away to a quiet place along the riverbank. The creek was half-frozen with the cold, but still peaceful and serene near the water. The cattails were wet and squishy; their stems frozen mush filled with ice. Our shoes were getting soaked on the edge of the riverbank, but we sat down in the tall, wet grasses anyway.

She was more quiet than usual, and I understood why. She was hurt.

I handed her the stretched hide. On it, was an exact replica of her face. Not just her face—but the essence of her being. It was if her soul was in the simple sketching, as if I'd captured her life force with the charcoal and grass for the green of her eyes, flower petals for the cherry of her lips, charcoal and flint for the romantic dark tendrils of her flowing mane of hair.

"How ever did you give it all these colors?" I could see that Varawynn was touched and impressed by the obvious time and effort I'd taken to paint her.

"For your green eyes, I used wet green grass like what we're sitting on right now. For your hair, I used soot from the dead fire and charcoal. For your lips, red Rowan berries, and for your skin, crushed petals from a rose and the Rowan's berries. It's the best drawing I've ever done. Your present took me the most time to complete."

Varawynn was better at controlling her emotions than I was, but when she looked up from examining the portrait, tears were streaming from her eyes, and she made no attempt at hiding them. She knew this was my unspoken way of saying I loved her.

The sincerity of the gesture softened her jealousy, which was only a fear of losing our connection. I think she knew that the portrait I'd made of her said more about how I felt about her than my words ever could.

I'd never felt like this before—and neither had she. I knew that. Varawynn knew in that moment without a doubt that she would never love anyone as much as she loved me. I read it in her eyes. The same way I'd captured the essence of her soul on the canvas.

We sat together on the edge of the riverbank, in silence for a long time. Everything we had needed to say had already been said, without words.

~ *** ~

Chapter Fourteen
King of Broken Hearts

From the major stronghold of King Mardavian's Castle in Caledonia—

Walking through the lowly town square, I enjoyed seeing the looks of fear on my people's faces, the way they cringed backwards at the infamous "King Mardavian," the way they bowed their heads as I walked by.

My fear-inspiring presence found tangible expression in the way I prowled like a lion, moving upon my unsuspecting prey, muscles atop of sinewy muscles, moving and flexing in succinct motions creating the perfect predator. In the distance, I heard a dog barking and two children fighting.

"He's mine!"

"I saw him first!"

"No, I did!"

"I did!"

"I did!"

"I did!"

"Nah ah, I did!"

"What's all this about?" I demanded, in my deep bass voice, walking in quick strides towards the ruckus. The children respected me of course, but they were too young and brave to realize that they should fear me too.

"Do I take it that you both want this pup?"

"Yes, sir, King Mardavian, sir!" they agreed in unison, while glaring at each other.

"Then the solution is easy," I said, almost kindly, belying my true intentions.

How I loved the looks on their faces…the look of surprise, then fear, then shock, then horror and then, best of all, the pain, the exquisite pleasure of their agony, as I raised my sword in quick, sudden motions—too quick for them to stop the fast plummet of the blade, down, down into the pup's back. The priceless tears from the youth, and the last howling cry of the sublimely weak, insipid animal were music to my ears.

Acknowledging with pride that I'd taken the innocence of the two boys I left behind, as I walked away, I knew the image of the crying children and suffering animal would be the highlight of my day. This day, but then there was always the trouble of tomorrow. What tomorrow would ease my constant desire to kill and to give eternal pain to those I deigned to let live?

I thought for a moment. A smirk passed over my features, as I thought about all the suffering to others that my tomorrows would bring.

~ *** ~

In the morning, I dressed quickly. Once a month I checked on the progress of my commission. I moved quickly through the passageways and tunnels beyond the castle and the town. The tunnels in the ground went miles in every direction, like the endless sprawling of spider legs. They could take me to the woods far beyond the castle's gates, throughout the town, all the way to my sister's main castle dozens of miles away, in the span of mere hours.

My machine was kept in a remote location just past the town. The scientists I'd hired had been hard at work on it for years. It would be ready soon. It had to be. Today I needed to find out how soon they'd have it ready. I'd have to put some pressure on them again, but I knew it would pay off.

These scientists weren't like the farmers and peasants of the towns. These were learnt men. Money impressed them more than brawn. And after all, I couldn't just dispose of them like the others. I needed them. These were the best inventors of the day. They wouldn't be so easily replaced.

"Tally ho, Franco!" I called, as way of greeting when I stepped into the campsite where my scientists were working on what I'd commissioned. He glared and barely looked up. I shook my head. My familiarity clearly did not impress him. He regarded me darkly.

"Hello Franco," I tried again, more seriously. These men had no sense of humor.

"Hello Vanwert, Urcell, Newt," I nodded at each of them. "I've come to check on Zorkog and its progress."

Newt nodded, "Yes, sir, of course."

"We've come into some complications with its release of webs, sir," Urcell began.

"How long?" I asked, trying to cut to the chase.

"That, and the web's attachments," added Vanwert.

"How much longer will this take?" I asked again.

"Of course, you want us to make sure that the webs will do what we have designed them to do, sir. You don't want to rush the process," said Franco.

I sighed. "Let me put this another way—*how* much more, men—in gold?" The men looked at one another.

"It isn't that sir—really," said Vanwert.

"Really?" now I regarded them darkly.

"Really," Urcell assured me.

"I want it ready in one year's time, men."

"A year?" Vanwert screeched.

"That's going to be difficult sir," said Franco.

"But we can do it," said Newt confidently. "However, that will require a few more materials for us to make our trial runs with."

"How much more then?"

Newt, the scientists' leader smiled. "The materials are quite expensive of course."

"Oh yes, of course." I nodded, feigning understanding and consideration for their arduous work.

"And with the inclement weather we've been experiencing lately, the men who bring the materials will be wanting compensation."

"Naturally."

"And—"

"And how much will it take, Newt?"

"Say, ten additional bags of gold?"

I grimaced. I'd gotten the men seven more bags of gold only two months prior. But this was no time for haggling or negotiations. I needed the machine completed. NOW. There wasn't much time left…

"Done," I agreed. "Now get back to work!"

Walking away in quick strides from their campsite, I sighed. This meant asking for more money from the damn old wizard again. Resentment put a knot in my stomach.

"Oh, confound it all to hell!" I cursed.

Throwing a rock against the window of a dirty hovel as I passed by, I broke it in sheer frustration. The loud shattering of glass and the looks of fear from people rushing past and away from me soothed me a little. Breaking things and causing problems was nice enough, but after my next rendezvous with Vorseth, I knew I'd need more than this to make me feel better.

~ *** ~

The following day I met with Vorseth in our meeting place—the tallest tower on the grounds overlooking the sanctuary where I'd been christened and baptized as an infant. Though I had never accepted any religion as my own, he knew I found the history of my life there comforting.

"How are your plans coming for Zorkog?" Vorseth asked me, with his usual manipulative ability to get the first—and last word in.

"Very well, Vorseth, very well," I nodded. It still grated on my nerves, cow-tailing to the old wizard, but it was a necessary evil.

"Excellent. Did they say when the machine would be ready?"

"A year or so."

"Very good."

"Yes." I put my hands in my pockets and cleared my throat. Being around the wizard made me feel nervous and fumbling, like a teenager, even after all this time. I prided myself on not being a man easily intimidated. But Vorseth intimidated me.

"I don't enjoy meeting with you without my sister's presence," I admitted.

"Oh, really?" Vorseth looked at me quizzically. "But you were the one who wanted to keep Zorkog a secret from her."

"I realize that, but...just the Zorkog, and, anything that pertains to the old Shaman. You know why."

The wizard nodded. "Yes, I know why."

"So...I don't want to discuss the dwarves without her."

"I understand," agreed Vorseth. "Then is there anything else, or shall I take my leave?" he asked shortly.

"Yes," I said reluctantly. "I, well, I need your help with something." Vorseth gave me a look as if to say, *and what is it this time?* Damn the old man to hell! "With a couple things actually." It took every ounce of my will not to strike the condescending look from the wizard's face.

"Yes?"

"Well, firstly I need some more gold and gems."

"For?"

"Well, to pay the scientists for one."

"And for another?"

"For the dwarves."

"And for another?"

"Another weapon I've been trying to get my hands on. It's this really fantastic mace."

"Don't you already have Zorkog, Mardavian, which you have been working on for quite some time now?"

"Yes, but I need more!"

"And for what other reason do you need more money, Mardavian?"

"That's *my* concern! And I resent having to ask you for money at all, Vorseth!" I'd finally lost my temper—he'd pushed me too far. If my mother were alive, she would have thrown him out of Kingdom, and maybe off this ledge, the way he was talking down to me.

Vorseth sighed patiently and looked at me indulgently, as if I were a misbehaving child. "Now, now, Mardavian. We both well know why it has been set-up this way. You breezed through your inheritance in the first few years after your parents' death. And now you're eating through your sister's. She's the one who put this little arrangement between us in play, so I am going to have to ask her—"

"What about everything I've looted from the towns I overtook?" I demanded. "What happened to all of that?"

Vorseth looked at me pointedly. "Your guess is as good as mine," he answered.

"Fine! Ask my sister. You know how to handle it. Tell her I'll pay her back after I overtake my next conquest."

"I'll tell her. And what else did you want to discuss with me, Mardavian?"

My mouth twitched. I kicked a bit of dirt beneath me. "This is a little messier. It's a legal dilemma. With one of the Lords."

"And?"

"And I'm getting to it!" I burst out impatiently. "Let me talk, damn it!"

"I'm sorry, please continue." Again, Vorseth looked at me as if I were an immature boy he was indulging.

I glared at him, for making me *feel* like that child again who could never outwit my sister, and who Vorseth only pretended to respect because my mother would have had him killed if he didn't. "It's more about the Lord and his wife really."

Vorseth nodded. "Ah, I see."

"Yes, well..." Straightening and pulling at my cloak uncomfortably I added, "He's rather making a fuss."

"I'll take care of it for you," nodded Vorseth.

"I'd do it myself, only coming from me it would look rather suspicious."

"Of course. How would you like it done?"

"I think it would be best to appear their deaths were an accident."

"*Their* deaths?"

"Yes, the Lord, his wife, and their children for good measure. Just to be safe."

"I see. That's a lot of people for one accident."

"I know."

Vorseth thought for a moment. "I think a carriage accident would do the trick...a slippery wheel, a spooked horse, off a high cliff into the sea."

"That's a clever idea..."

"It's done. Anything else?"

I smiled, relieved. At least the old wizard did my bidding in the end. "Not at the moment."

Vorseth gave me one last piercing look. "Until next time then," he said, with a wide flip of his cloak, as he climbed down the stairs of the tower, and was lost in the shadows. I stood there looking out into the woods for a long time, wondering how Vorseth made me feel as if he was the real King in charge of our fates, wondering how he always managed to have the last word.

~ ~ ~

The day was nearly done. After being emasculated by the wizard, I really needed to unwind. Of course, I could always go down to the brothel and drink and while my time away with the prostitutes, but after the stressful days I'd had between the scientists and Vorseth I deserved a special treat.

I smiled my smirky smile. No, today was *the Day*. Tonight, was *the Night*. I'd been contemplating this and planning it for some time. There would be a broken heart in Caledonia tonight, in the little hovel where the lovely Bellerica dwelled...

I knew the way. I'd been there many times before. I could still recall the way she looked when I first saw her in her parent's cottage. She'd been fourteen at the time, young and happy and free, pretty like a spring daffodil. There'd been something in her expression that'd reminded me of my sister when she was very young.

This girl, Bellerica, was different in that hers was an angelic beauty. My sister had been dark, sarcastic even then. Bellerica, by contrast, had long, wavy, blond hair, warm brown eyes, and the sweetest smile I'd ever seen.

There was something in her smile that made me—or any man for that matter—keenly aware of her innocence. Only a virgin could have such a smile. It was almost completely absent of guile.

She was sixteen now, which was the perfect time to enter her parent's house and collect my due. My debts were always paid–if not in life, in death. And Bellerica's parents' debt was high—I'd carefully seen to that. The bill would be paid tonight in full, with their daughter's delectable innocence.

I'd waited two long years for this night. Persuasively tempting the girl's parents to borrow ever higher from me until the debt was impossible for them to ever repay—this had been the result of much clever planning on my part. Now at last Bellerica was the same age my sister had been, the first time I lay with her—sixteen, the perfect age to be broken. Smirking to myself, I found a perverse pleasure in thinking about the faces of her parents when they realized what I was going to do.

Their cottage looked particularly run down tonight; their thatched roof was sparse and bare in its center and around some of the edges where the rain and snows had damaged it. The exterior walls looked haggard, as if they'd collapse at any moment. Knocking on their door, I waited impatiently for the man of the house to answer it.

As Bellerica's father peered out of the door's peek-hole to see who was standing there, he hastily unbarred the door for his King, bowing deeply. The mother and Bellerica's six younger siblings kneeled at my feet as I entered.

Bellerica was at the fire stirring a small pot of foul-smelling soup full of rotted and thoroughly bruised vegetables in dirty, turbid water. Jumping to her feet when she saw me, she quickly prostrated herself before me as well.

"Send all the children into one of the bedrooms, and send Bellerica into another–by herself. We'll settle this between us."

"As ye wish, me lord." The father obediently agreed, as the children immediately dispersed. "Have ye come fer what we owe ye, me lord?"

"Yes, dear sir. Indeed, I have."

"We doesn't have the money wight now, m'lord," the man

answered me, as his wife fretted in the corner, pulling at her hair and dress.

"Good, because it isn't money I'm after," I told them with my twisted smile.

The husband and wife looked at each other in obvious confusion. "Then what, m'lord, could you possibly want from us that's worth as much as our own great debt?"

"Oh, that's just it, dear sir. What you're giving me will be worth far more than the debt of money. In fact, it is *I* who owe *you*," I said, throwing down a heaping pile of gold on their crude table. This would sully my time with Bellerica, and equate her to a prostitute. I found the thought irresistible.

The mother's eyes widened in greed, but the father's eyes narrowed. "Now wait jest a moment, here, m'lord. What is it ye is asking us fer?"

"Oh, but I'm not asking. I am *taking*—with or without your permission."

"Give him anything he wants. Anything he takes ain't to be worth as much this here gold," the mother said merrily, rushing to the table to play with the gold. She didn't even have enough manners to wait until I was gone to pour the gold from hand-to-hand, fingering the cold pieces and biting down on one of the coins to discover its value by its purity.

"Enough of these mysterious thingys, me King, sirs. What is it thee is speaking of?" Usually a man speaking to me in anger would give rise to fury in my proud heart, but now I simply laughed, taking pleasure and amusement from the game. They were simple folk to be sure, but it was fun to toy with them.

Watching the mother covetously kissing the gold for a moment more, I replied, "I'm speaking of your eldest daughter, Bellerica." The father's eyes clouded over, and the mother's gluttonous face took on a look of horror.

She was greedy all right, but not greedy enough to give willingly her eldest daughter's virginity, particularly when the loss of that said daughter's innocence deemed her ineligible for any other man's bed— and she'd been counting on Bellerica's absence. One less mouth to feed in these trying times was a priceless gift. Even if her plucking was done by the King himself, surely the plucking in and of itself would deem even someone as young and lovely as Bellerica, worthless.

"No, never!" Bellerica's father growled furiously. "NO."

"Please, *oh no...*" Bellerica's mother begged desperately, dropping the pieces of gold from her grimy fingers.

"Yes, oh yes, and it will happen tonight—now in fact."

Moving rapidly to the table where they'd been cutting the fly-eaten vegetables for the soup, Bellerica's father grabbed the knife from the table and held it up against my throat.

"Ye will never take her!" he shouted, with all the love in a father's protective heart.

I only smirked, reciting an easy spell that bound the two parents to the chairs at the table. "Please stop! Don't!" the father yelled, as I walked towards Bellerica's bedroom door. The mother screamed, and I murmured another spell under my breath to bind their mouths shut, wanting no interruptions when I took her.

I found Bellerica lying on one of the beds, quietly resting with her eyes closed and her pouty lips pursed in a romantic reverie. Her long, blonde hair was pulled up into a practical bun and her rosy cheeks gleamed even in the dim lighting.

"Bellerica," I said softly, to alert her of my presence. She looked up at me, flushing at my expectant expression.

"Where are my parents?" she asked.

"Don't worry, my dear, they won't be disturbing us."

"Whatever do you mean, your majesty?" At my look, she cast her eyes down. Oh, the glory of her modesty! "Please, sir, I think I know what it is you want. But it isn't mine to give."

"Whatever do you mean, Bellerica?"

"I'm promised in marriage to Arthur Smithson. We're to be married this fall."

"So?"

"So, he won't want me if..."

"On the contrary, Bellerica, I think any man would be honored to know the King had unfolded his flower's honeyed nectar first."

"Please, your majesty—don't do this."

"Now, now, I'll have no more protests, young lady." She quietly began to cry. "You will do as I say from here on out," I continued. "Agreed?"

"Agreed," she said tearfully.

"Take down your hair." Without hesitation, she pulled it from its band.

"Such lovely golden tresses," I purred, stroking the length of it, moving my hands to her chest to undo the top button on her dress, to reveal the top of her corset.

"Please, don't do this," she beseeched me again, as the tears poured out of her warm, brown eyes.

"Hush girl. Be silent. You don't want your parents, or brothers and sisters to overhear us, now do you?" At my remark, her eyes opened wide in fear, as she shook her head vehemently.

"I will be quiet, your majesty," she promised.

"Good, now take off your blouse, then your skirt. Good girl, just like that, and now your corset." Bellerica cried as she did as I commanded her, but they were brave and silent tears.

* * *

Even in that moment, especially in that moment, I thought about Arthur. I remained in my love for him. As King Mardavian came me into the bedroom, I sensed what he wanted. I knew there was nothing I could do to stop him.

To him, to this kingdom, to this village, perhaps even to my own family—the sacrifice of my reputation, and from that the fate of my life, didn't matter. But God was still good. Life still had meaning. Hope was eternal.

I hoped that Arthur would forgive me for being broken by the King. I prayed that he might still want me—lowly though I was, with poor parents, overcrowded in our home like rats. I thought of Joseph and Mary, how even though she was only a young girl, pregnant and unwed, Joseph had faithfully believed her story of a divine conception and married her anyway.

I hoped that my Arthur would show me this same sort of trust and devotion. But even if he didn't, and the King's actions condemned me to a spinster's life, bound to the slovenly home of my parents forever, I would find what I could to be grateful for, and do what I could to enrich the lives of those around me.

In the moments, even when King Mardavian was violent and cruel, I felt pity for his soul. For how wrought with insanity and pain must a person be, to bully and abuse another person? How unworthy must he himself feel of love that is given freely and not taken? Who had twisted him into this perversion he had become? If I allowed myself to become bitter or take my own hurt out on any other, then I was merely perpetuating this pattern of abuse and darkness.

God did not create these traumas. But in this moment of trauma, God was with me. He made me strong. I remained in love, standing above and apart from what was happening, like a spectral ghost floating above myself, with him on top of me, floating above and watching below, sending love down to myself, and to him. Sending healing down. So that somehow my soul was made purer for his sin.

* * *

As I softly began to caress her naked form, she shivered and cringed at my touch. I only smiled at her disgust. No, she was not like my sister after all. My sister had fought me all the way, every single time, until the day she grew so powerful I knew to stay away from her.

Bellerica was only a simple country girl. Perhaps she was a little smarter than most, a little sweeter, a trifle prettier, but there was no passion or great depth of pain in her countenance. She was grateful for her pitiful life, grateful even to the King who sought to destroy it.

At that moment, I almost abandoned my plan. She'd disappointed me so greatly I was revolted by her. But the beauty of her youth compensated somewhat for her lack of feeling. Her supple skin, her womanly curves, the warmth of her body would suffice for the gold that lay on her father's table.

I realized that in one respect this peasant girl was stronger than my sister. When my father and I had raped my sister repeatedly, she had lost her sweetness, her innocence. Her youthful, plump cheeks had waned and the sparkle in her eyes had dimmed, like the slow decline of the light and sparkle of a falling star.

Bellerica would never lose her purity, or any of her love. I would never be able to break her spirit, for her innocence was not the outcome of her virginity, but her faith.

This probably angered me the most, and my thrusts grew hard and violent as I tried with everything in me, to break her spirit and destroy her soul. Even though Bellerica lay beneath me, I sensed that she was not with me at this moment. Her heart and mind were with the young boy she loved, and she would always stay pure and intact for him. Her sweet spirit could never be broken, destroyed or stolen. Not even by me.

~ *** ~

In a cottage in the woods of Caledonia on the Isle of Skye—

Looking outside my window at the dense, green wood, the wolf howled in the distance, but I wasn't afraid, though wolves often attacked humans in this part of the country.

They killed out of hunger, as the truest of wild, untamed spirits. But this wolf came near to the cottage so often, I had almost begun to consider it a friend.

It was a dark, moonless night, and the planets had aligned in such a way that revealed the time was nearing. I felt patient and impatient all at once, both restless and at peace. I wanted to go find them, but Vorseth kept insisting they would come to me. I'd waited long enough.

For nearly two centuries I'd been awaiting the moment when it would be time for me to find him, and *her*, and then, *them*. My whole life had been spent waiting. It was part of my Destiny to wait, but not forever. Soon my power would reach maturity. Then when I'd fulfilled my part in the Prophecy, I hoped I would finally get to *live*.

This was my only hope. I didn't mind participating in underhanded means to get to the desired end. For after the end, I felt as if my life would finally begin. For me, the end would always justify the means.

~ *** ~

Chapter Fifteen
The Mountains of Mourne

January, traveling through Caledonia, crossing into Ireland and into the Mountains of Mourne—

The night before we reached the Mountains of Mourne, the group of us sat and talked around a large fire drinking rosemary lavender tea and eating venison. The night sky was as clear as the song of a nightingale cutting through the sounds of the darkness. Our voices echoed in the quiet clearing.

I explained to everyone that we were going into the mountains to see a dwarf friend of mine, Norgorian, who would provide us with fresh provisions and bequeath us with a special jewel we'd take to the Land of the Fairies, Astarra, as trade.

"Will Norgorian be joining our group?" Jonlin asked me.

"No, he isn't one of the fourteen, just a good friend who's willing to help us out. He owes me a favor."

"For what?" Eliju piped up.

"For saving his life."

Varawynn interjected angrily, ever-ready to engage in verbal combat with me, "So you were willing to die for this dwarf? Did you ever stop to consider what would've become of *us* if you'd died?"

"There is no greater love than this, that a man be willing to lay down his life for his friends," Jonlin quoted.

"I think that's your answer. I saved him for friendship and love, as I would have done for any one of you. In the moment, I was only thinking that if I could save his life I would, and I did. Thankfully we were both able to survive the attack, but when you truly love someone, and they're being threatened—you defend them without taking stock of what it may cost you. The true measure of love, unconditional love, is being willing to sacrifice yourself for someone, or something, greater than yourself. It's not that one life is worth more, or less, than anyone else's, Varawynn."

"Except Master Eliju's life—his life is worth more than our lives," Varawynn whispered softly. Eliju didn't like it when Varawynn said things like this, and I knew that it bothered him to think that one of them might die to protect him.

"But how can you say that? Isn't Eliju's life worth more than any of ours because he's the prophesied King?" Alondria asked, saying openly what Varawynn had hinted at to Eliju.

"All of *us* are equally important because we're meant to protect him," Jonlin concluded.

"That doesn't make any sense! How could the Knights of the Round Table mean more than King Arthur himself, who was meant to unite all kingdoms? No, surely, the *source* of power is the most important," Varawynn insisted.

"The scriptures do say that the student isn't greater than the teacher, but that eventually the student will become the teacher…" said Jonlin.

"We all have something special to contribute here," Ileona interjected, throwing her opinion into the mix. "Good leaders are only as strong as the people they surround themselves with."

"Does the sacrifice of one soul for another, make the soul who sacrificed themselves more important than the soul who remains?" Shadow Rain interjected.

"Yes, Rain," Alondria said, with a nod and a smile. "I agree with your line of thought. Isn't the person who made the sacrifice, in a sense, the true source of the saved person's power?"

"If the source of the act of sacrifice is love, that's the greatest power. There's no greater act or choice, or state of being than love. Loving is always the best way to be, and love is always the best action to take. Eliju is not the *source* of our purpose or power. He is merely the answer to the problem," I finished.

Ileona smiled at me approvingly. "On this, I can but agree."

"I think I'm starting to get it," Shadow Rain said.

"Well, I don't understand it all," said Varawynn darkly.

"Is one life, in exchange for another, worth less than the one who remains?" Ileona asked her, as she tried to help her understand their points.

"Maybe not worth *less*, but how much value is the worth of someone who's dead?" Her intense green eyes glistened with the inner workings of her mind.

Ileona's light gold eyes flashed. "His worth is in the accomplishments of the person who he saved. None of those accomplishments would've been possible if not for the sacrifice."

"Yes, but if our lives are truly of the same value, and we really are all equal, then what about the good that would've come from the life of the one who was sacrificed? That still proves Eliju is the most important!" Varawynn persisted.

It was Jonlin who spoke up now. "But if the greatest act of love is sacrifice, there's nothing the one remaining could ever do that would be greater than the act of the person who chose to die to protect him. It's a new way of thinking than you're used to, Varawynn, but my religion is based on this concept. There's nothing greater than the grace to live because of that sacrifice, for without the sacrifice we cannot be blessed with redemption and grace."

Varawynn looked at him oddly. He was right. It was a totally new way of thinking than she was used to. Ileona and I looked at him oddly too. We'd shared our beliefs with the children, but it took us aback when we learned from our students.

Ultimately Jonlin had the final word in the argument, although his Christian values and beliefs were foreign to the rest of us, or perhaps because they were so unique. Eliju was curious about this word grace and what it meant. He told me he intended to speak with Jonlin more about it privately.

~ *** ~

We traveled into swamp lands and around murky waters, where odd mounds of caverns rose up among the dirty water, hidden by the brush, moss, and seaweed, and the dark purple swamp flowers beset along the way. I'd never seen mountains like this, nor swamp lands. I found the various landscapes along our travels fascinating.

"We're almost there," Wandering Wolfe said, more to himself, forgetting for a moment that the rest of us were looking to him for guidance.

"How much longer do you think we have to go, Wandering Wolfe?" I asked.

"Rest assured, dear boy. As long we put our best foot forward, we'll reach our destination by noon!"

"Noon, oh thank the Goddess!" Ileona said with a dramatic sigh.

As we came to the stone opening at the bottom of the Mountains of Mourne, a metal door with wooden handles seemed totally out-of-place. That's what made it clear that this was the doorway which would lead us into the mines of the dwarves' kingdom.

As Wandering Wolfe knocked on the door, a slot opened at the top of the metal doorway, concealed among the brush.

"Who's there?" asked the dwarf guardian of the mines.

"We've come to see Norgorian. He is expecting us. We are among the group of Chosen Ones."

"Prove it," countered the dwarf. "Speak the appointed message and I will let you pass."

Wandering Wolfe thought for a moment, then recited: *"Alev eleete gonolda, sur gonolda urlit alev."*

"And what does it mean?"

"All as One, for One is All."

"Yes, One is All...gonolda urlit alev," the dwarf agreed. Opening the door for us to enter the mines, at 4'6, the guard was tall for a dwarf—stocky too.

"Norgorian is feasting in the ninth passage under the Mountains of Mourne. I can't leave my post; can you find your way?"

"Of course, I can. I've been here before," Wandering Wolfe replied.

The dwarf nodded, and we followed Wandering Wolfe around long, winding tunnels, entering spacious cavernous rooms of rock. Deeper and deeper within the cavern's depths we went, and deeper and deeper under the dense swampy waters of the Mountains of Mourne. It was darker and colder under the earth than the snow storm was in Andorra.

We came to a crossing that divided in four ways. "Which way to the ninth level?" the Shaman asked himself aloud.

"The third path t'will bring us there," a voice echoed from behind us.

We turned around to see a 4'4" dwarf with a ruddy complexion and a long red beard. "Heyo, my name is Beiarnon, but everyone just calls me Red Beard. I don't think we've met before," he said with a merry grin, as he stuck his hand out politely to Wandering Wolfe.

"No, I don't believe we have," Wandering Wolfe smiled at him in surprise and gratitude, as Red Beard shook his hand heartily.

"You must be the Chosen One," the dwarf said to me with a special nod.

"Yes! Finally, someone has gotten it right!" I liked the dwarf immediately for recognizing me.

"I can tell by your eyes and the way you carry yourself," he replied, with a sly wink, making me like him even more. His good-humor had a way of cutting through the dark caverns surrounding us and lightening our sober moods.

* * *

"Come on, I'll take your brood to Norgorian."

"Thank you so much, Red Beard," Wandering Wolfe said.

"Of course, it t'would be my honor." I looked up at the Shaman, tall and dignified. His bearing was both proud and humble. But it was Eliju that captured my attention. There was something wild in his spirit. Something honest and strong that was truly noble in its essence. When our eyes met, I felt the soul stirring of the recognition of a fellow kindred spirit.

Walking ever further down the tunnels, we entered a grand room where a hundred of my comrades sat at a magnificent table edged with gold and countless gems. The room was open to the tunnels in the high ceiling around us.

It never ceased to amaze me, how in the depths of the mountain's core, the ceiling could be so high as to appear as wide open as the sky. The workmanship and craftmanship of my kind were unparalleled by any other race.

This being the center of the mines, my fellow dwarves could be seen scurrying in and out of the tunnels hundreds of feet above us. I was lost for a moment, watching their movements. Some carried heavy loads—pulling or pushing barrels of jewels or building materials. Some of the dwarves I recognized, but many I did not.

Of course, I knew Norgorian and King Drakkin well. At the head of the table in the middle of the imposing room, sat our King, wearing his jewels and royal garb, and at the other end of the table stood Norgorian, wearing his shining silver armor, as if he was ready for battle to ensue at any moment.

King Drakkin slammed his fist down on the table, shouting curses in our ancient tongue. Rain winced and Alondria and Jonlin looked disturbed. I threw a reassuring grin Eliju's way.

"I am King, and as such *I* will make the decisions around here!"

"*They* are here, your Excellency," said a short, round dwarf, dipping and bowing to the King. Immediately King Drakkin turned furiously towards us, and with a forced smile more like a grimace, he beckoned us to where he was sitting.

"We've been expecting you. My name is Drakkin, and I am the King of this dwarf clan, if you hadn't surmised that already."

Before Wandering Wolfe could greet the King as leader of the troupe, Ileona rudely cut in, in a haughty, take-charge manner, "It is a pleasure to make your acquaintance, my Lord."

Her gossamer silver gown and billowing soft blonde hair lay in stark contrast to our surroundings. It was clear the elegant, "Lady of the Lake," disapproved of our kind, but her delicate beauty was in no comparison to the hearty dwarf woman who were as aggressive and fearsome as the men themselves.

Let her disapprove of us. There were more lasting treasures than beauty. Like kindness. And there were few things more distasteful and uglier, than conceit.

* * *

I had always heard of the dwarves' legendary rude manners and gruff natures, but before this, I'd never had the misfortune of making one's acquaintance. Red Beard seemed polite enough. Perhaps Red Beard was an unusual case, but clearly the "King of the Dwarves" was not.

The room's opulence was overdone and ostentatious, not at all like the effortless elegance of my Crystal Castle, next to the lovely Lake of Avalon in the Isle of Apples, and was clearly focused on an obvious display of wealth and a hedonistic love of eating, as the heart of the room was a grand table encrusted with crudely chiseled gems of all sizes, shapes and colors, and the room itself was inlaid with unrefined gold.

I—along with everyone else—assumed the armored dwarf sitting to the right of the King was Norgorian. We were right.

"We are so honored to make your acquaintance," I murmured graciously.

"We've prepared a banquet every night of this past month in anticipation of your arrival. You must be hungry, please sit down," King Drakkin replied to my graciousness, with thinly veiled hints at just how much they had been put out. Wandering Wolfe must have apologized to King Drakkin for twenty minutes before he finally allowed us to eat. Sometimes I really found the old Shaman's humility embarrassing. Where was his manly pride?

I was mistrustful of the dwarf King's obviously fake, courteous attitude, but this was not the time to voice my suspicions. Besides, we'd run out of supplies, and everyone was weak with hunger. Forgetting their manners in the hunger of near starvation in the company of the dwarves, the children were messy in their intake of the poorly prepared feast, mainly comprised of meats—not that the dwarves noticed this, or seemed to care much, in the light of their own uncivilized ways.

It was difficult to hide my distaste of the greasy, meaty food, and the rude and slovenly ways of the dwarves, for the dankness of our surroundings was so very different from the rainbow crystal radiance of my castle's feminine beauty.

The Dwarf King showed a complete lack of social etiquette when he criticized us so severely for our late arrival, as if we could have so easily planned the length of time it would take us to arrive to his dark dwelling in winter, whilst traveling with a large mix of humans and magical beings.

It was classless to show my disfavor and dislike of the dwarves, but sometimes I couldn't help but wrinkle my nose at a sordid smell or a bit of food left in the corner of the mouth of some messy dwarf who'd missed his mouth in the rapt enjoyment of shoveling the grub down his throat, as quickly as his dirty, short arms and small hands would allow.

* * *

I came from the wealthiest kingdom of everyone in the group. Our city of Andorra in the Pyrenees Mountain Range was beautiful, but I didn't mind the dwarves' ways or the cold caverns. Dwarves' body heat tended towards the warm side, so they loved the cavern's dank cold. I laughed with them, enjoying their blunt and honest humor, easily becoming friends with them.

Even though we were quite different, I had a knack for fitting in—finding ways to relate to everyone, even other races. Sometimes a loud, raucous roar from one of the little men made me jump in my seat and widen my eyes, but I was otherwise unperturbed by their ways.

Eliju too, got along well with the dwarves, partly because he lacked many social skills and airs himself, partly because their personalities suited him. He liked that they didn't live under false pretenses. In a way, the ostentatious display of their gold and jewels, expressed their social naivete better than anything else did. He found their blunt ways humorous, and their unpretentious airs comforting. Their untamed wildness was like his own.

Jonlin was always friendly and kind to everyone he met, but he also tended to be shy with strangers. He was polite, but quiet, as he usually was when we were with a large crowd of people he didn't know.

Shadow Rain and Jonlin talked mainly to each other and kept to themselves, and Wandering Wolfe, who knew many of the dwarves already, laughed heartier and talked more excitedly than we had ever seen, reminiscing with many of them about adventures and escapes in faraway lands.

Eliju clearly liked Red Beard the most. Sitting together and laughing all through dinner, Eliju wished Red Beard could join the group. Even if he wasn't one of the fourteen, he would always be good for a laugh.

* * *

I was quietly observing everyone throughout dinner. Something about the evening felt off to me. At one point, I saw Norgorian discreetly shift something wrapped in fine linens to Wandering Wolfe, whose head was drooping in exhaustion, but whose eyes were alert as he took the hidden treasure into his possession. But by the time Norgorian guided us to our chambers, I was too tired to tell Ileona I felt something was wrong with the Dwarf King.

It can wait until the morning, I thought to myself, as I settled down to sleep, losing my resolve to warn the Oracle, in the softness of the plump sheets. Really, it was only a bad feeling anyway, which didn't leave much to go on…

* * *

King Drakkin and I stood face-to-face, anger and disdain dripping from my stoic warrior's face, greed and self-righteousness oozing from the King. We stared each other down for several minutes before speaking.

"What is it you're planning?" I demanded.

The King's tone dripped with sugary sarcasm. "Planning? Whatever do you mean?"

"Or should I say plotting?"

"You are being rather dramatic, Norgorian."

"Am I? I have a source that has told me you have sold this group who came here for safekeeping to King Mardavian's men!"

"Perhaps you should consider your source."

"I owe my life to Wandering Wolfe, Drakkin! How dare you put this group in jeopardy!"

King Drakkin dropped the pretense, "The loyalty owed to Wandering Wolfe is yours, not mine."

"So, it's true?" I countered.

"You'll know that soon enough, now won't you? If it is true, it's far too late to stop it now."

"I can't believe you've sold them out like this! Worse still— you've sold yourself out and cast a shadow over the whole dwarven race."

"Again, you are being rather melodramatic, Norgorian. You know very well we were out of gold and gems for our progressive improvement project. I simply exchanged them for what we needed."

"Meaning?"

"The trust Wandering Wolfe placed in your friendship, for the necessary materials to complete my project."

"You rotten piece of swamp slime! How could you—" I couldn't get out my next words, before a group of King Mardavian's men had placed their hands over my mouth and a hood over my head.

"You are free to do what you like with him," King Drakkin told them. "He is no longer welcome in the Mountains of Mourne in the Dwarven Realms. *I* rule. Keep him or dispose of him, but I wash my hands of him and this ridiculous group of 'Chosen Ones,' who have excluded the noble race of dwarves from their folds."

I struggled against the men as best I could, but there were too many of them to escape their capture. Damn King Drakkin for his betrayal! And to add insult to injury, now I was no longer welcome among my own kind, even if I did manage to escape! My only hope was that Wandering Wolfe wouldn't believe that it was I who had betrayed them...

* * *

Damn Norgorian and his novice principles! Damn him for trying to guilt trip and manipulate me! Damn the "Chosen Troupe" that had excluded our race! Who did Norgorian think he was? Who did Norgorian think *I* was? I was the King of the Dwarves after all! This was my Realm! How dare he tell me what I could and couldn't do, and how I could or couldn't use my power and authority?

We would see which race would rise to ultimate domination in the end! I was being strategic to ally myself with King Mardavian, who was currently the strongest leader in the world. Eventually, I planned to rise above him.

I would find the perfect time and way to kill him and overtake his thrown. Then Norgorian would understand what I did and why I did it! He, being a warrior dwarf, must understand the principles of war. Then he would come back and thank me for the decision I'd made to hand the group over to King Mardavian's men.

At that time, perhaps I would forgive him for his insubordination. Only after he bowed at my feet, kissed my boots, and admitted my actions had been right—would I consider it. Until that time, let King Mardavian's men do what they might with the insipid dwarf. He deserved to learn a hard lesson or two about the pecking order of our royal lines.

* * *

I'd gotten a bad feeling from King Drakkin's treatment of the group during dinner. I had followed Norgorian and King Drakkin when they stole away. I overheard their conversation and watched as King Mardavian's men took the warrior dwarf away.

I vowed to follow my comrade, and when the time was right, aid him in an escape. I would notify Flint of the group's captivity as I left the caverns, and I would manage to discover what they did with Norgorian and help him to overrule this power-hungry greedy King of ours—to redeem his reputation, as well as the reputation of the dwarves themselves. I, Red Beard, would not be overcome by these betrayals and disloyalties, without a fight.

* * *

It wasn't long after I'd fallen asleep, that I woke to sounds of shouting and a struggle in the corridor. Grabbing my sword, I left the bed quickly, not taking the time to get dressed. I didn't have long to wait before the chaos was brought into my room.

Alondria and Wandering Wolfe tumbled in, fully dressed, and soon after came the rest. Tall, hooded men held them in their grasp, with knives at their throats and hands gripped at the nape of their necks.

"Get your clothes on!" one of the hooded men shouted at me.

"What's the meaning of this? Who are you to come barging into the Dwarf King's caverns and—"

"We are the *true* King's men. *King Mardavian's* men," spit out another man. "And we have an arrangement with the King Dwarf in these caverns. All of you for ten bags of gold and jewels."

"Drakkin *sold* us for ten bags of gold and jewels?"

"It's time you got dressed, boy—or else we'll have to slit this pretty one's throat," a man said, as he brought the knife to Varawynn's long swan's neck. Making a small incision on her lily-white throat, a line of blood trickled down her shoulder onto the floor.

After that, I dressed quickly. A black rat scurried beneath my bedroom door and I barely caught a speck of orange on its back before I was blindfolded.

Flint was still waiting for us outside the caverns. Raegar sent messages to Varawynn's parents all the time. I clung to the hope that they could save us—as we were taken prisoner.

Hoods were placed on our heads, so we wouldn't know in what direction we were being taken. We soared through the dark, unseen night in a carriage flying across the terrain, run by steeds of unusual speed and smoothness.

Led into a castle by the dim light of an awakening dawn, we were thrown into a dreary, windowless room. The air was stale and heavy. Sadness settled over us like dust.

* * *

"Do you think Norgorian had anything to do with this?" Jonlin asked.

"No, I don't think so. Not Norgorian, but perhaps King Drakkin."

"What do you think?" Jonlin asked Wandering Wolfe.

"I agree with Eliju," he answered.

Ileona wrinkled her nose, "I really don't put much stock in any of them myself."

"Who do you think captured us?" Shadow Rain asked.

"Didn't you hear?" said Varawynn. "We were taken by King Mardavian's men!"

Shadow Rain burst into terrified tears, and Varawynn took a deep breath to steady herself and not punch the girl in the nose amid their other troubles. It was then they heard the heavy booted footsteps down the hall. Waiting breathlessly to see who would open the broad oak door, they barely blinked in anticipation of who would enter in.

When the door finally opened, the tallest man they'd ever seen came striding through the door. Looking to be about 6'6", maybe even 6'7," he towered over even Wandering Wolfe. With jet black hair, eyes so black you couldn't see the pupils, and unlined olive skin, he was highly exotic in his features.

His meticulously tailored clothes, height and air of command, gave him a powerful presence. When he spoke, his voice was low and deep, like the gong of a mammoth church bell, with an arrogant, sarcastic lilt that grated on Eliju's nerves as much as Raegar's low-pitched cawing.

"Hello dear friends. You came late to the dwarves mine. I was afraid you'd decided not to come at all. But of course, I should've known your leader wouldn't have the instincts to sense the danger there."

"On the contrary," growled Wandering Wolfe in a severely hateful tone, I wouldn't have thought him capable of.

King Mardavian laughed in disdain at Wandering Wolfe, and all he stood for. Wandering Wolfe glared at King Mardavian, for all he was. After a moment of uncomfortable silence, the King turned to face Eliju.

"And you...*you* must be *the chosen king,*" he said sardonically. Eliju only glared his response. "Answer me boy," Mardavian insisted with an edge of bitterness ringing so savage, Eliju shuddered.

"Yes," he answered him brazenly, standing as tall as he could and still several inches shorter, "I am the *man* who will conquer you and overtake your lands and rule over them as the *true* King."

"You little beast!" King Mardavian's eyes flashed dangerously. Wandering Wolfe's eyes warmed and twinkled with Eliju's display of confidence and courage.

"I'm not afraid of you, *King Mardavian*. Neither your power, nor your steel, nor your magic," lied Eliju.

"You will fear *this*!" he shouted, striking Eliju down onto the cold stone floor, and with his bare hands he beat the boy senseless. Eliju heard one of his left ribs cracking with the brutal force of Mardavian's fists. Just as he'd begun to lose consciousness, he felt himself being dragged from the room, while I watched them, hidden and unseen...

~ *** ~

I took the Chosen One to my castle in a carriage run by sleek black horses, while he was unconscious. I brought him to the very room from my childhood where the traumas had occurred. Evil actions taken in the night, that still haunted me.

I left him to go to my new quarters and try to get some sleep myself. But I was restless. Restless that Eliju was here. Restless about what tomorrow would bring. Restless that a moment in the Prophecy was coming to pass.

I stood at the window, staring out into the night. The cold winds beat against the window panes, making melancholy sounds like the white noise of a silent scream.

The sound stirred my soul in a strange, familiar way. It reminded me of my own silent screams, in the silence of this room, after my father left me in the darkness—the first time. The screams inside my head had never left some part of my consciousness.

It was terrible how the sound of his footsteps down the hall still haunted me sometimes, late at night, right before I fell into the dreams of illusions that briefly stilled the haunted memories of his steely boots coming towards my room, down the hall. Sometimes in my sleep, I was jarred awake—the sound of footsteps making me sit up in bed and pull up the sheets, sweating in a state of panic, as if I was that defenseless girl again.

Shaking my head, I tried to clear away those disturbing memories. Even now, they were always so near—those footsteps echoing upon the caverns of my psyche. For just a moment, when I remembered the sound, I was that ten-year-old girl again who so was so cruelly turned into a woman by my own father.

Then later, that girl of sixteen lying broken beneath another; betrayed and violated by my half-brother, Mardavian. Another familial betrayal nothing I ever did could make me entirely forgive…or forget.

Sometimes during some menial task, I would recall the horror of the smell of their sweat. Now every time, every single time I lay beneath another man, I remembered their smells.

With the taste of fear, I felt fragments of my soul fleeing in shame every single time I let a man inside of me. Something pure and true within me was lost forever into the darkness that never fully left me, after what they'd done.

Yet there'd been one who'd loved me long ago. I'd tried to love him back. I'd tried to open-up my heart to him and fall in love. But even then, a part of me was repulsed by his love, for they'd claimed to love me too.

Maybe then what I wanted even more than love, since I didn't place much value on it, since I didn't really believe in it—was protection and defense. Of course, that was how I'd felt when I was still a girl. Now that I was a woman, I believed I'd learned how to protect *myself.*

He hadn't protected me; the man who'd claimed to love me— Wandering Wolfe—was as bad as my father and brother in the final analysis. Maybe worse—since he'd pretended to be something different, something better. I realized then that love was an illusion that was never meant to last.

I used sex for its power, to unite political parties, to gain strength by gaining a little bit of the other person's soul in each conquest. But I was aware how every time I lay with a man, I also lost a little bit of my own soul.

My heart was never in my actions, my emotions and body were disconnected. No attempt at love penetrated the fortress I'd built around my heart, to protect myself. Sex was the enemy of love. So, I used sex, to ensure I would never have love, or be loved again, because love hadn't done for me what it had promised.

I took a deep breath. I tried to shake away these introspective musings and just be.

As I lay with my head against the window pane, and felt the wind undulating the glass with my face and slender fingertips, an unnatural longing overcame me. A longing I hadn't felt since I was a child—the child before the footsteps down the hall.

There was a flashing in my mind of certain, familiar eyes burning with a fire and intensity, a fire so unlike my own. This fire was red-hot; whereas, my essence was akin to the blue of the flame. His intensity burned with passion, and my intensity was spiritual and mystical. He was the one who'd made my heart ache with a strange and urgent need, so long ago, but only in my dreams.

What this feeling was I didn't know. What this feeling meant I didn't want to know. This was a rare feeling I only felt when my mind was not active with plots and plans, with spells and dream-weaving, with the small, manipulated conversations of my life. This feeling had been inside of me before I became the girl of ten, when my innocence had been so brutally stolen.

I wanted to believe that I was above fear, above love, above even death. I wanted to believe that as I'd once been destroyed, so would I destroy others. I wanted to believe I'd grown too powerful to ever be destroyed again.

This feeling, it was a weakness, that much was certain. I hated weakness in others, and I wouldn't tolerate it in myself. Nothing was as vile or repugnant to me as my own vulnerability. Nothing gave me fear, except the loss of the control I carefully wielded over others, to feel in control myself.

I had learned that what one fears; one must either destroy or be destroyed by. I had endeavored to find the source of this weakness and destroy the man who made me feel my own blue heat.

But even with my determination and the strategic plan in play, the ache returned when I thought about the Chosen One lying in my old childhood bed. The green-blue of his eyes burned themselves into my mind, making my heart pulsate.

The truth was that those eyes haunted me almost as much as the resonating echoes of those heavy, uncompromising footsteps down the hallway to my chambers long ago, where Eliju now lay unconscious. Those eyes and heavy-booted footsteps continued to haunt me, whether awake or asleep.

~ *** ~

Chapter Sixteen
Secrets Come to Light

January-February, from the Castle of a major stronghold of King Mardavian in Ireland—

After Eliju was taken by my sister, I decided to weaken their power by placing them in separate sections of my estate, understanding well the principle of division as one of the greatest weapons for destruction. Thus, Alondria and Jonlin were put in the uppermost room of a tower in the east end of the stone castle. Varawynn, Shadow Rain, and Ileona were locked in the cold, small confines of a dungeon, with one window high and barred, but still open enough to let in the cold elements of the frigid winter winds.

Wandering Wolfe, my old friend, was placed in an obscured cell in a passage none but the royal family had ever been permitted to enter. I let a few days pass before coming to pay my respects to my old boyhood chum.

It had been a long time. I was curious to see how time had altered him. There was magic in all of us, that much was certain—some ancient magic that had kept all four of us alive for so long. I knew the magic that was inside of my sister and I, but I still did not know how the Shaman was still alive after over two thousand years. The origins and ancestry of the wizard, Vorseth, after all these years, was also still a mystery to me.

The jailer unlocked the door, and I found the Shaman meditating, his face turned towards the barred window, as the sparse sun shone on his upturned face. He had aged worse than I had. But his face still bore that condescending expression, I so disdained.

He thought so highly of himself, didn't he? He'd always thought so very well of himself. Damn him for that, and for so many other things.

"Hello, *old friend*."

"We were never really friends, Mardavian. You know that." Wandering Wolfe opened his eyes, his back to me and the door.

"Maybe not, but we've certainly had the same taste in women. Think that's why we've never been friends?"

Wandering Wolfe clenched his fists and tightened his jaw, turning towards me. "I'm *not* going to lose my temper with you, Mardavian, no matter how hard you push me to."

"Oh, of course not, Wandering Wolfe. You're above that sort of thing, now aren't you? But you forget that I've known you before you were the greatest, as well as the *oldest* Shaman on earth. Even if you're still strong and look fairly young—I know your *real* age."

"That's just because I'm *almost* as old you are, Mardavian. And I knew *you* before you were a King. I knew you when you were an unintelligent, inexperienced underling who was always too big for his britches. But you've done pretty well for yourself, filling your monster of a father's boots, aye?"

"Oh yes, things are very different now."

"You're right. You've grown from that foolhardy, cruel young man into a tyrant worthy of the title of dictator."

I laughed at his insults good-naturedly. Indeed, they brought me pleasure. "Oh, it's so unfortunately rare to meet a worthy adversary; especially one you knew as a boy."

"One who's hated you since you were a boy."

"We were all friends before–"

"Before what you did to your sister—you and your sick father."

"And what exactly did we do that was so horrible, Wandering Wolfe?"

"You know perfectly well what you did, don't make me say it! But whatever happened to your parents, Mardavian? Soon after...what you did, I heard they'd been killed."

I smirked. "You really can't bring yourself to say it, can you old wandering one?"

"Answer the question, Mardavian!"

"My parents died soon after I came of age," I answered elusively.

* * *

"And what killed them?"

A shadow fell across King Mardavian's face, as what happened to his parents played out in his mind. "They were murdered."

I raised an eyebrow. "Who could have been powerful enough to kill *them*?"

"There was only one with the magic to end their reign," King Mardavian answered mysteriously.

Something in the way he said that, made me change tactics. "Why are you even here? Why are you making me remember all this? Have you only come to torment me? Why are you dredging up all these horrible memories?"

Mardavian looked as strong and striking as ever. His dark hair had only a few strands of gray at the temples. A few lines creased his forehead. But it was disconcerting how young he still looked. It was disconcerting we were all still alive after so much time...But that smirk. That infamous smirk of his—I was suddenly overcome with the desire to punch it off his face.

"Why? Because I've missed you, old chap."

"My God, is there any part of your soul left that holds a spark of humanity? Or have you become pure evil? Do you have any heart left at all, *King Mardavian?*"

He smirked again. "Your flower was lovely, Wandering Wolfe." Mardavian deftly changed topics, but I was confused. I wasn't sure what he was talking about.

"Don't you remember? After what happened with my sister, you went back to your tribe. I watched you there for quite some time. I watched firsthand, as you fell in love for a second time with that young girl who smelled of the sweet musk of heather. She surely was a lovely young thing, Wandering Wolfe. Snow Lily...mmmmmm..."

"What the hell are you referring to, Mardavian?"

"Surely you didn't think the massacre of your tribe was some random act?"

"I assumed your parents orchestrated it."

"Your assumptions were wrong. It was after my parents' death I acted against you. My father was a brilliant king, but it is I who have advanced our kingdom across continents."

"It was you then, it was all you...you were the one who killed my tribe and..."

"Yes, in fact, that massacre was the very first action I took as King. Well, after partaking of your young, sweet thing, Snow Lily. Strange, how I tasted and lay bare both your loves before you did."

My horror was swiftly turning into a fury and pain I'd not felt since the loss of the women I'd loved, and the tribe that had raised me. "She was going to be my wife. How could you do that to such an innocent girl?"

"For one so extolled for his wisdom, you understand little."

"What does that mean, you bastard? Tell me what that means!"

"Your future bride meant nothing to me. She barely struggled as I took her. It was all so easy, too easy. But my sister, she was special—a hellcat. I loved her more than anyone or anything. Or rather, I *love* her more than anything, except power. My sister is the most beautiful creature I've ever seen. She has a rare beauty that truly becomes more beautiful with time. That Indian girl would've eventually lost her bloom. But with age, my sister blooms more divine from year-to-year, season-to-season. She is living proof that beauty is timeless."

"What're you saying Mardavian? Why are you talking as if your sister were still alive?"

"Because she is."

"That's not possible! If she were still alive, I would have known it! She would have told me she'd survived your father's attacks—contacted me somehow. I saw her beaten myself, Mardavian!"

"That's why she didn't tell you, old fool! Because you failed to protect her, Wandering Wolfe. You failed her! And I didn't. I made sure my father didn't take her life. But *you*, you proved yourself and your lack of love by so quickly moving on to the princess of your tribe. My attack on them was something I did for her sake—which is more than you ever did for her. It was a vengeance I took on her behalf."

"No, Mardavian. You killed them for yourself. You're perverted and twisted, and revel in every kind of degradation—especially rape. You don't even know the meaning of the word love."

"I know that when you love someone, you will do anything to protect them."

Jonlin's words from only a few days before, crossed my mind, *"There is no greater love than this, that a man be willing to lay down his life for his friends…"*

"What are you saying? That you saved your sister? I find that hard to believe, Mardavian. You wouldn't want anyone usurping your power or authority. You wouldn't want anyone to undermine your supposedly divine power—not your sister, not even a son—two unnecessary heirs to *your* thrown."

"You bore me, Wandering Wolfe. I didn't think I'd have to spell it out for you. Looks like I got more from Vorseth's teachings then you did, old chap. It's easy to kill what you don't love, but my sister, she is my better half. I've always known that."

"But I saw your father beat her till her body was covered in her own blood! I saw the baby taken away—lifeless! And I did try to stop it, damn you Mardavian!"

"The baby, yes, but didn't you know it would take more than mere physical brutality to murder a magical being like my sister?"

Shock flashed through me. Could this really be true? Could Mardavian be telling the truth? Then the realization swept over me— he never could have done so much damage, and conquered so many kingdoms, not without *her*!

"She *is* alive! How foolish for me not to have known it! It's *her* magic that gives you your power. You could never have been so successful without it. She *is* your better half, and you protected her because you knew you would need her. So, then she truly is, *the power behind the throne...*"

"My sister never really loved you, Wandering Wolfe. All she does is to fuel her own agenda."

"She wasn't like that when I knew her. If she's that way now, it's due entirely to the mistreatment of you, your father, and her stepmother."

"And you shoulder no blame for what she's become? I may have protected her out of necessity...but shouldn't you have protected her out of your *love*?" The corners of King Mardavian's mouth twitched disdainfully.

"That's not fair, I tried—"

"It is one thing to try, Wandering Wolfe, quite another to succeed."

For years I'd hidden my past, the bitter memories of my young adulthood, and the loss of my family, friends, and the two women I'd loved so briefly. I'd buried the pain of their losses, and built a wall around my heart and mind, which held the memories of my cruelest failing—the inability to protect the ones I'd loved the most.

Now in the face of the man who'd made these barriers necessary, my defenses and self-control crumbled. Only in the mirror in the Crystal Castle had I allowed the faces of the people I'd loved to enter my remembrance, as they did just now.

All the doubts I'd had about myself returned like a phantom menace, intent on its revenge. All the long-held guilt and fears rose from the shadows of the dungeon and my heart, as if intent on the damage it would do, as such deep-seated resentments were borne only to destroy.

"I tried to help her," I said again.

"Oh, you are so *weak*, Wandering Wolfe! It's so disappointing to find after all these years the same young man who was such a *failure!"* Lightning flashed from my eyes, just as lightning flashed outside the small window.

"Controlling the elements is child's play. It's something my sister could do in her crib. Now she does it just to get her point across."

I lifted my arm and held up my staff toward his face. The buried fury from the decades and centuries of my life was directed from the oak staff imbued with Celtic magic Eliju had given me, toward King Mardavian's forehead.

I chanted the words I needed as the lightning struck his head. King Mardavian's crown, covered every inch in jewels, fell to the hard, stone floor, some of the jewels coming unhinged from the gold and breaking into a thousand pieces, as he doubled over in pain. He fell to his knees, holding his bleeding head in his hands.

* * *

"What've you done to me?" Touching the wet mess of blood on my forehead, I stared apprehensively up at Wandering Wolfe.

"What is it? I've given you a permanent scar, old *friend.* I tattooed you with the symbol of evil, the symbol of Satan, for you truly are his brother and son."

"Then perhaps my sister is the Devil's Queen."

Wandering Wolfe reached out his crooked staff and pointed it toward me once more. This time fire spewed from the wood, lighting my clothes on fire.

The fire calmed me, as I closed my eyes and raised my hands toward the ceiling. Rain poured down on us, stopping the fire from scorching my dusky skin.

My eyes bore into the Shaman's as I chanted, "Enum alan salum, enum alan salum, enum alan salum."

"What's the meaning of this?" he demanded. He was always demanding something.

"It's the same curse I spoke so many years ago…made more powerful by the second utterance. That you shall never know love; never know the bliss of a lover's arms, but once. I offered you just one moment of love, so that you would always have the haunting memory of the way of her body, the grace of her walk, the smell of her skin, and the taste of her lips. I cursed you with but one moment of love, so brief—yet everlasting. I cursed you with a memory that will last you forever. For there is no worse pain, than the loss of love."

My forehead was still bleeding when I left Wandering Wolfe with the sting of our bitter words, and the revelations of our first conversation in centuries.

~ *** ~

As soon as King Mardavian's men had left, Shadow Rain and I turned woebegone beseeching eyes toward Ileona. "What are we going to do?" lamented Shadow Rain.

"What are we going to do? We're going to make the best of things," said the Oracle decidedly.

"How on Poseidon's beard are we going to do that?" I demanded.

"This is a wonderful opportunity—to give you girls some private lessons," Ileona smiled a wry smile, and we laughed despite the bleakness of the situation.

"I'm not like the Shaman. I don't always have to have a big production for my rituals. I don't need drums and rattles. Something as simple as," she was shuffling for something in the pouch on her side hip, "as small and beautiful as this crystal can suffice for a lesson."

* * *

She held me up in her palm for them to see—a small, but powerful, diamond-shaped crystal, shining very softly in the dim light. Ileona explained, "Sometimes crystals need to be reminded of their power…they need to be among other crystals to re-energize themselves."

So, they watched the Oracle, as she laid us out in the middle of the floor. Deftly she took out more of my crystal sisters from her pouch, laying each of us down—each stone into a carefully precise circle, putting me in the center. We were sacred to the beautiful Ileona and treated with the utmost respect.

"It helps the crystals to be together; they gain strength and power from each other."

Our mistress understood how what made us strong—our healing powers that came from love—also made us weak. We retained the memory of every creature of the world. We recorded the history of time. Science, as well as spiritual, and earth magic were each within us.

We had seen the best and worst of humanity, yet still we were the substance of love, healing and truth. All gems are crystals—and diamond crystals like me were the hardest, purest substance on earth.

To witness evil and still believe in love and the goodness of humanity, is what made us so strong. Our delicate beauty was indestructible.

As she took out each stone, she explained to the girls the properties of each colored stone in the circle: amber, aquamarine, azurite, bloodstone, emerald, garnet, gold, jacinth, jade, jasper, obsidian, ruby, topaz, turquoise, and the onyx stone Eliju had given her.

I was the clear diamond crystal in the heart of the circle. Gaining power from my crystal sisters around me, I was glowing. The other crystals shone brightly too. We crystals were above competition. We gained energy from each other. And when one of my crystal sister's lights dimmed, all our lights dimmed.

As we began to sparkle, I felt a stirring in my core, as a light emanated from my small, yet powerful form. So often it was the smallest things on earth that held the most power. Filling the room with the colored lights, I sent up a ray of white light toward the center of the ceiling.

The ray of light was white, a white energy reaching up to the ceiling and beyond, up through each story of the castle and up into the sky like a beacon. It was a message I had to be shared, from the depths of the library from the Akashic Records, about the history of the world, and man, and magickind.

The Oracle began to sing, her voice strong and clear, and as she carried the melody, Shadow Rain and Varawynn joined in harmony. Our colors were getting brighter with every note of the song. The whole room was awash with our rainbow lights. I spiraled, faster, faster, and faster still. The ray of light was moving onto the wall around us, twirling in tight spirals until its light rested a few feet above the ground on the west wall.

All of my beautiful sisters, a myriad of gems of different sizes and properties, were glowing rainbow colors, and together we formed an additional ray in the same area of the wall that my ray from the center pointed. The small spot in the west wall was flooded with colors.

Ileona went to the wall, and as she touched it, a false brick fell crumbling down. Reaching into the wall for what lay hidden there, she pulled out a small package. I was flabbergasted—it was like the colors had led Ileona to something hidden in the walls. Her abilities would never cease to amaze me.

Ileona held out in her palm a small pouch of red cloth tied

together with a simple white ribbon. I recognized it as a charm. As the Oracle moved to open the pouch, Varawynn stopped her. I sensed the fear all over her.

"You should not open that unless you were the one who made it."

"What is it?" Shadow Rain asked.

"It's a charm," Ileona replied, "which could be any number of things, depending on what lies inside it."

"But it could be a curse. Look at the blood red color. The worst thing we can do is open it, Ileona. It could be a trick." She squeezed the small, red pouch in her hand, then placed it unopened in the pouch she kept us in.

With the overriding feeling of fear pervading the room, the lights and rainbow colors from myself and my fellow crystal family, dimmed. The message we'd hoped to impart was lost, to one of the most destructive emotions of humanity: fear.

Ileona put us back into the pouch. But there was always hope, for the truth cannot be hidden forever. It was only a matter of time. And we crystals, the most magical and oldest substance upon the earth, had all the time in the world.

~ *** ~

After King Mardavian left Alondria and I alone, the young princess shivered uncontrollably. I draped the only blanket left for us in the corner of the room, over her dainty shoulders. "Are you all right, princess?"

"Yes, but I'm worried about the others. Something bad is going to happen to Varawynn, Jonlin—something terrible. I can feel it in my bones."

I nodded. In my mind, I gently stroked her almond hair to comfort her. The truth was, I lacked the courage to reach out to her as I so wanted to.

"I wish my brother was here."

She had no way of knowing that her innocent words would make me feel inadequate, and, as I always felt with her, a little unworthy.

"Do you think Aldoran will save us, Jonlin?" Gently laying her head on my shoulder, she nestled herself onto me. The jewels in her circlet cut into my shoulder blade, but I wouldn't have moved away to save my life.

"Say something. Why does it seem like I always do most of the talking when I'm with you?"

"I like to listen," I replied lightly, though really her nearness and touch took my thoughts and breath away. "I enjoy the sound of your voice. It sounds like music to me. And you know how much I love music…"

"That's the muse in me," Alondria laughed. Even her laughter sounded like music. "You're very familiar to me, Jonlin."

"What do you mean?"

"Nothing."

"Please tell me. I sense there's something behind those words…"

"There were, there *are*. But I've never told anyone about it—not even my brother."

"I thought you told Aldoran everything?"

"I did, I mean, I do, just not this."

"Will you tell me?"

"I will, someday soon." It wasn't in my nature to push for an answer, so I didn't prod her. I'd much rather patiently wait until the words were shared freely.

"But I will tell you something else I haven't shared with anyone except Aldoran because he was there. It's hard for me to talk about."

"Are you comfortable sharing it?"

"I want to tell you."

"Okay."

"It's about my friend, Oric. He was our best friend growing up—Aldoran and I. He was a stable boy and we used to go to the stables every day to ride. I just loved to ride. One day when we went to the stable the new horse, the new horse spooked and—"

She curled herself into my arms and cried. It ripped me up inside to see her so sad. "And you lost your friend." She nodded through her tears, burying her head into my chest like Shadow Rain had done months ago. I decided not to make a joke this time. This time I would share my own sad story.

"I'm glad you shared this with me, Alondria, because I can relate."

"You can?"

"Yes."

"A few years ago, I was rough playing with my friends, as boys often do—but we were playing with real swords. My little brother wanted to play, but I didn't think it was appropriate for him yet, so I told him no. He tried to join in, and he ran into my sword as I was making an offensive attack on my friend."

"Oh no...."

"Yes, I killed my own brother, Alondria. By accident. By a horrible accident. He lost his life due to my reckless violence. In telling him he couldn't play, I'd meant to protect him, but—that's when I decided I would never fight again."

We were both silent for many moments more. I was sober in my memories of my brother, Jacob. She was remembering her friend, Oric. I felt we had bonded in the sharing of our burdens and secrets.

"What do you think is going to happen to us?" she asked quietly.

"I think King Mardavian has a plan for all us—though I can't imagine what it is," I answered. We talked the rest of the day away, but as the sun set, we were hungrier than we were tired.

"I feel so weak. I hope we'll be given a *little* something to eat," she whispered. Speak of the angels; two small bowls were pushed through the slot at the bottom of the door.

"What's this?"

"It's porridge, a staple where I come from."

"Is it good?"

"It can be."

"There are no spoons, but I suppose that's as expected." Picking up the bowl and holding it between her two hands, she took a sip. "I like it!"

"And that's what I like most about you—you always make the best of things. You see the best in everything and in everyone."

"It's not hard to find the good in you, Jonlin! Don't you have any hope of getting out of this?"

"I can't help feeling how bleak the situation is, Alondria. How can fourteen people fight and win against armies from several continents, a dozen countries, and dozens more cities? We haven't even gathered the entire group of fourteen together, and now we're captives. It's unlikely we're going to escape any time soon."

"Those are the facts, but we can't give up the faith. We still have Raegar, Shadow Rain's raven, and Flint, Wandering Wolfe's wolf out there on our behalf. I'm positive they'll let Aldoran know we're in trouble."

"So, you think Aldoran alone could free us all?"

"I know my brother. He could single-handedly rescue us, as well as gather the rest of the fourteen together, and command a large army besides. Trust me; my brother was born to lead."

Alondria's glimmer of hope lit a fire in my own heart and my steady flame of faith gained heat from the warmth of her certainty. "I'm sorry if I'm moody, Alondria. My doubts are more about the insecurities I have about myself. Sometimes I still can't help but question why a mere bard like me is fortunate enough to share in the company of royalty and, and beauty the likes of which I could never have imagined."

"Yes, Varawynn is very beautiful, Jonlin."

"Yes, she is. But not as beautiful as you." I was tottering on a weak bridge and must be careful not to break it and fall into the ravine beneath.

Alondria fidgeted uncomfortably, as I added hastily, "Both of you are lovely. I'm just not used to being around girls like you. Sometimes I'm not sure how to act."

"Just be yourself, Jonlin." She smiled then; the kind of smile that could ease the weary heart of a dying soldier on a battlefield. "And it's probably in everyone's nature to doubt from time to time, especially in a situation like this one. So please don't be too hard on yourself, for me?"

"Yes, for you. Look, I don't really like this stuff, do you want mine?"

Alondria gave me a knowing look. "I'm not falling for that old line, Jonlin. Come on, you need your strength as much I do!"

"But I'm not as hungry as you are!" Alondria still didn't look convinced. "Look, I'm setting my bowl on the floor beside you and it's going to get cold if *someone* doesn't eat it."

Alondria laughed. "At least eat half of it and then you can have some of my breakfast tomorrow."

"Agreed." Taking a small sip from the bowl just to appease her, I had no intention of sharing her breakfast in the morning.

"You're sure?" she insisted. I nodded, going to bed with a hungry stomach. I'd gone many nights hungry, but greatly doubted the princess had.

Of course, Alondria would still be hungry after those small portions and the idea of her gradually weakening made me feel desperate. Alondria was a healer, but even the best of healers cannot heal themselves. So, I would give her all I had—to protect her from the hunger I felt myself.

~ *** ~

"I'm going to show you girls how to balance your chakra energies in this exercise. I'll start with Varawynn. Please watch carefully, Shadow Rain, as your turn is next, and I would prefer not to have to repeat myself. Stand up with your arms out, Varawynn. Good girl."

Ileona traced her hands along the outline of my body. When her warm hands came to my heart chakra they shook. I felt heat exploding in my chest. My heart beat wildly as she placed her hands above my chest. Without even touching me, the heat emanating from her hands were making me sweat. The pain in my heart was both emotional and physical.

Then Ileona made the same sweeping motions down Shadow Rain's body. Nodding, she said, "It seems Varawynn's heart chakra is out-of-sync, her biorhythms are off-beat and Shadow Rain's fifth chakra, the Throat Chakra is blocked."

"I'm going to go over a general overview of the chakras to give you girls an elementary understanding of them before we work with them. The first chakra, the Root Chakra governs the base chakra which is situated at the base of the spine. It represents vitality, courage and self-confidence, corresponding to your kidneys, bladder, spinal column, hips and legs. The color it resonates to is red."

"The second chakra is the Sacral Chakra which is situated in the lower abdomen and denotes happiness, confidence and resourcefulness. The physical organs it correlates to are the lower organs, such as the uterus, large bowel, prostate, ovaries and testes. The color it resonates to is orange."

"The third chakra resonates with yellow and governs the Solar Plexus Chakra, situated below the ribs. The feelings associated with it are wisdom, clarity, and self-esteem, and it corresponds to the pancreas."

"The Heart Chakra is the fourth chakra, corresponding to green, and relates to balance, love, and self-control. It governs the heart, breasts, and thymus gland." It made sense to me that this was the Chakra I had that was off-kilter. Ileona was so incredible in her knowledge.

"The fifth chakra, the Throat Chakra, resonates to blue and governs knowledge, general health and decisiveness. It's related to the throat, lungs and communication. The upper digestive tract can be affected by any imbalance in this area. It's helpful for both the Throat and Heart Chakras to wear the turquoise stone. I will give both of you girls some turquoise jewelry to wear for the next few days—unless we get out of here before then!"

Ileona's optimism in the face of our captivity really astounded and inspired me. I had been feeling depressed and heart-sick worrying about everyone. If Ileona hadn't been with us, I probably would have spiraled into one of my dark moods of depression and despair, believing we would never get out of our imprisonment. My emotions were something I struggled with every day. The Oracle and I were very different in our personalities, but I admired her differences. I especially admired her optimism.

"The sixth chakra governs intuition, mysticism and understanding. It is the Brow Chakra or the Chakra of the Third Eye, located in the center of the forehand, corresponding to the color indigo. The related organs are the eyes, lower head and sinuses, and the pituitary gland, the spiritual center of our bodies."

"The color violet resonates to the seventh chakra. The seventh chakra is called the Crown Chakra and is located at the top of the head. It relates to the mind and the pineal gland, denoting beauty, creativity and inspiration. These seven chakras relate to the body as the foundation. There are higher chakras as well, related to the spirit realm."

"Now, Shadow Rain's throat chakra is out of balance. Could you be afraid to express your thoughts and feelings, Shadow Rain? Are you afraid to communicate?" Rain cast a fearful, furtive glance my way. Ileona looked over at me disapprovingly.

"What did I do?" I demanded, glaring at Rain.

"Well, you're always snapping at the poor girl for starters, aren't you, Varawynn?"

"I really can't believe how you're turning on me! Aren't I the one who's always on your side?"

"That's just it, Varawynn. There shouldn't be sides. We're all on the same side."

I shook my head, on the verge of tears. "What about the way she snaps at Eliju? Why don't you get on her case about how poorly she treats him, Lady Ileona?"

"Because, my dear, it's as I told you before. Shadow Rain snaps at him so much because she likes him." Shadow Rain turned several shades of purple. "Go on my dear," the Lady of the Lake said to the apprentice Medicine Woman. "Best to get these things out in the open."

The idea of being totally honest horrified Shadow Rain's sensibilities. Sputtering she said to me, "You first." I glared scathingly back at her, gritting my teeth, ready for a good fight. I didn't like the idea of being total open myself.

"Ah, now we're getting down to it. You *both* love him don't you, girls? And that's why your heart chakra is out-of-balance, Varawynn and why Shadow Rain's throat chakra is closed. Shadow Rain cannot communicate her love, just as you, Varawynn, cannot express it."

My face flushed crimson; Shadow Rain's was a painful shade of violet. How could Ileona expose us in this way?

"It's perfectly understandable that you would both have a crush on Eliju, girls. But you must come to some sort of understanding and compassion for each other, so we can begin to work together as a team." When neither of us answered her, Ileona commanded, in her forceful, regal way, "Please take my hands girls."

As I grasped her left hand, Shadow Rain took her right. Light emanated from our hands. Shadow Rain's thoughts and self-doubts, worries, and shadows of fears were transferred into our minds. My excruciating pain of unexpressed love and desire shot waves of anguish through our hearts. I clutched Ileona's hand harder, as Shadow Rain's hand trembled and faltered.

"Now that you understand what each has been enduring, do you think you might find it in your hearts and minds to become friends?" The words were barely out of her mouth before Shadow Rain and I had come together. Shadow Rain cried, and I held her.

"I'm sorry," I whispered in her ear softly.

"I'm sorry too...do you think, do you think we can be friends now?" I smiled back at her shyly, and Ileona grinned like the cat that'd caught the mouse.

~ *** ~

Jonlin and I had already been captives for a week when we first saw the servant who brought us our food. He seemed a poor and fearful young man, living in fear of King Mardavian's shadow. No matter how hard I tried to talk to him, he practically ran from the room as soon as I looked at him.

"Do you think we could convince him to help us?" I asked

Jonlin one day.

"I'm afraid he's too much under King Mardavian's control."

"But if we could get him past that—"

"And do you really think we could?"

"I'm not sure, but it's worth a try."

"It sounds like a long shot."

"Well, if nothing else, I'm giving it a shot in the dark. It may be our only hope."

"Okay, then let me help you." Locking eyes, we made a silent pact to stick together as a team. The servant helping us was unlikely, but miracles did happen.

~ *** ~

Chapter Seventeen
Crowns of the Conquered King

February-March, from the castle of a major stronghold of King Mardavian in Ireland—into Andorra, the Kingdom of the Franks and heading South into the deserts and plains—

A sense of urgency carried me up and away, into the wind and above the mountain peaks of the Andorres Mountain range. I bent and curved myself with the flow of the wind.

I dove with the current of the air, like a mermaid dives into the currents of the water. I flew as fast as I could. I was worried about my beautiful person, Varawynn. I could see her with her long dark curls and emerald feline eyes, beseeching me to find a way to rescue them from their captivity in the castle in Ireland.

Sweeping down over the mountains and plains, I found Aldoran in the mountains over his home, training in the art of war with his newest weapon master, Kenju. Aldoran caught a glimpse of my orange streak down the length of my back and told his teacher he'd have to take a break.

"I think that's Raegar, the pet of a person in my sister's troupe. I'd better see if something's wrong."

Kenju nodded, bowed and went into the sweat house to give Aldoran his privacy.

"What is it, Raegar? Is something wrong?"

"Alondria is in trouble. Caw caw. They all are. King Mardavian caw caw has taken them prisoner caw caw."

"What can I do to help them?"

"Caw caw gather up the rest of the group. We'll come up a plan to get them out. Caw."

"Where are they being held?"

"In a castle in Caw Caw Ireland."

"Do you know where to find the remaining group?"

"Some, but Wandering Wolfe entrusted, caw, one of the prophetic scrolls to me, caw, caw, and I'll give it to you to help. Caw caw."

"I'll leave immediately," he agreed, as he stroked my orange feather. "I just need to go into the sweat house and tell Kenju I'm leaving straight away."

"Hurry caw, Aldoran. Caw caw. My mistress is in grave caw caw caw, danger." I felt certain Aldoran would find the girl in the Prophecy and help rescue my mistress, Varawynn. I flew past him and the Andorres Mountains, on to the land of the elves...

* * *

I'd never met Varawynn's raven before, but Eliju had told me all about him, as Raegar was the first talking animal he had encountered. After the raven flew away, I read through the scroll it left me, hoping to find a clue to the rest of the group's whereabouts and save my sister and the rest of the group:

"The Philosopher's Daughter"

She speaks in naught a whisper
Of the terrors she has seen—
The massacre of her family,
And the end of their regime.

The blood of all her sisters
Upon the foreign castle's steel grey walls;
The people who fought in brave defiance
Who died within its halls.

Her father caused their destruction,
All that's left is rot and decay.
The scholar had one choice:
To fight and die or run away.

So she hid in the same walls that were
Covered with her family's blood,

Because she'd hidden to protect herself
She lived to give purpose to their love.

The blameless kingdom lay in ashes,
But her mother lived to say:
"'You must survive to tell our story
You must bring this kingdom glory.'"

"Remember how we worshiped—
Remember how we prayed—
Remember how we loved—
Remember the lives we gave."

"Carry our knowledge upon your shoulders,
Honor our blood coursing through your veins.
Remember you're the daughter
Of the souls who died for you, to save."

Then she closed her eyes in death,
As the young girl shook and cried.
She prayed that some might live—
That she'd restore their kingdom at a future time.

She promised herself that evening,
Without steed, wandering aimlessly in the night—
That she'd overthrow the King
Who had needlessly taken these people's lives.

Her father, the Greek philosopher,
Ruminous, an adviser to the King

WHERE THE SHADOWS MEET THE LIGHT

Worshiper of many goddesses and gods
Brilliant scholar of the Prophecy,

And knowing the language of countless cultures—
Had used his skill and expertise
To help King Mardavian conquer and claim—
As the lands once free because of him were said to waste.

But when Ruminous saw what the King
Had done with his wisdom and his skills,
A spirit of omnipotence overtook him,
And he worshipped one God, after submitting his will.

For years he tricked King Mardavian,
Subtly thwarting his every move—
Until one move was made too soon,
And the King realized he'd been used.

Turned defiant and betrayer,
Ruminous was caught in the castle with a lie.
The people of this kingdom were in the wrong place
At the wrong time.

His daughter vowed to carry out her father's mission
In everything she did.
She'd become a servant to the memory
Of the spirits that had lived.

One last tear fell down her face,
And she swore she'd cry no more.

Her future lay with the Chosen One
From the Prophecy she'd studied ancient lore.

Maybe the Chosen One could explain
Why these innocent people had to die;
Maybe he would be able to help her
Bring purpose to their lives.

This section of the Prophecy concerned me more than I could say, for what if King Mardavian tried to destroy my beloved homeland as he had done to this one? But it was more than that. I felt empathy for the girl in this story, but I had no idea where to find her.

"Go south," was all Raegar had told me, before he began his journey to the coast. "Head to the cities of the desert nearby the villages of Jonlin and Eliju, toward the Grecian shores where the girl in this Prophecy comes from." So, I went, trusting the universe to guide me to her.

~ ~ ~

After a few weeks of travel over the mountains of my homeland, I'd arrived at the forests where my people and I went on our hunting expeditions. Eventually, after several more days, the earth became flat and dry. Fewer and fewer patches of grass were growing, and there were far less trees to provide shade. Water became sparse too.

I'd traveled on this terrain for no less than a week, when I stumbled upon the ruins of a castle. Much of it had been destroyed, but some 100 yards away a grander castle was being built.

As mine was a curious nature, I went into the ruined castle to explore. What I'd taken to be rocks from a distance were actually decaying bodies! Putting a hand over my mouth to keep from gagging, the realization swept over me like the shock of a cold wave.

"This is it. This is the city where the girl's family died."

Going back outside, beyond a small hill, men were gathered around a massive bonfire, throwing things into it to feed the growing flames. On closer inspection, the objects being thrown into the fire were parts of bodies and limbs from the battle that had taken place beyond and within the castle's walls.

I realized the Prophecy Raegar had given me had only recently come to pass. I'd inadvertently stumbled upon the scene of the crime.

The smell of their burning flesh threatened to gag me. Staggering backwards, I leaned against a boulder, and gripped my stomach to keep from losing my last meal. Another group of King Mardavian's men were working on the construction of the new and much grander estate.

Guess King Mardavian is the bigger and better type. I shook my rich mane of hair at the idea.

Someone was approaching me from the direction of the great fire. Quickly, I ran back into the old castle, clambering up the stairs, burying myself behind a fallen dresser in one of the bedrooms.

"I swear I saw someone standing just beyond that ye hill," a man growled.

"Well, I certainly didn't see anything, Grendin. Come on, it's getting late...let's shove off for the night. King Mardavian won't know the difference."

"Will too. Them here bodies have been here too long already. They shud'of been burned a fortni'ght ago."

"Nightfall is only half an hour away. Come on, Grendin, let's shove off."

The two men continued to bicker, but to my immense relief, they took the argument outside. I was glad I'd had the forethought to tie up my horse, Miko, a safe distance away.

Now that the two men were gone, I took the liberty of looking around. A woman was lying beneath a small, wooden table. Clearly, she'd been hiding before she'd been killed...

A long pool of dried blood trailed the floor beneath her. Nearing the decaying body, I realized with a sudden shock that she was the Queen of the Kingdom. Her crown was made of flawed jewels in a crudely constructed setting, making it clear that hers were a poor people.

Something about the girl in the poem, the love she'd had for her family and these people she didn't even know, but had almost died with, made me do something I never thought I'd do. Gingerly, with great care and purpose, I pulled the woman's wedding ring off her finger, and took the crown from her hair.

I put the crown into my knapsack, and the ring carefully in a pouch from my pack, after wiping it with a rag I found lying haphazardly on a table, as if left there on some half-completed task.

I don't know why I did it. Perhaps some part of me didn't want King Mardavian to have these pieces of history. I felt that the crown belonged to the girl of the Prophecy, though I couldn't have explained how.

I took one last look around the room and turned to go. Putting my ear to the outer door to see if anyone was just beyond it—to my surprise and dismay, I heard the whinny of my horse, Miko.

"Damn it!" I cursed under my breath.

"Told ye I saw somebody Captain—where there tis a horse there tis a rider. Probably a spy to boot!"

"You were right, Grendin, okay? But that doesn't mean he's a spy!"

"I were right before, aye?"

"Aye," the more educated man agreed begrudgingly.

"You and thee others check the grounds. I t'will check this here castle meself, Captain Nathaniel."

"Agreed," Captain Nathaniel said, and with lightning speed, I ran from room to room until I found a long, spiral staircase, which I climbed several stories high. Hiding in the closet in one of the topmost bedrooms, I silenced even my breathing, standing as still as a statue.

Several minutes later I heard Grendin in the next room. I'd have to do some quick thinking. Remembering the girl's story in the Prophecy, I explored the closet more thoroughly. My fumbling fingers found a trunk, hats, and shoes. Feeling for a wall behind me, in a castle such as this, as stipulated in the Prophecy about the scholar's escape, surely–yes, I had found it!

Towards the back of the large walk-in-closet something hard and round was sticking out. Pulling on the knob, a thin door opened. Quietly, I went into the tiny, hidden room, shutting the door silently behind me, just as Grendin opened the door to the room I was in. Soon enough Grendin peered into the very closet that had housed me.

Satisfied no one was in this room, Grendin went to inspect the next room. I let out a sigh of relief. I realized this closet had saved both the girl of the Prophecy and me.

Some time passed while I searched the tunnels to see where the passageways led. Why had only the daughter of the philosopher Ruminous hidden within these concealed rooms? Had there been so little time when King Mardavian and his men came that no one else could've found time to hide within them? I doubted many of the people in this kingdom had even been aware of these passageways. So how had *she* known where to hide?

Hours passed until I believed it was safe to leave the hiding place. Vigilantly, I left the castle to find my horse and get as far away from here as possible.

It was totally dark as I left the safety of the castle walls. In the darkness, I made out the campsite over the hill in the distance. Making my way to where I'd left my horse, in what I'd believed to be a safe distance from the men's campsite, I heard a whinny coming from where the men were talking.

Grimacing, I snuck towards them only to discover—my horse Miko was chained in the midst of Grendin, Captain Nathaniel and the other soldiers. I lay on the dirt ground, listening to their conversations, and formed a plan in my mind as they spoke.

"They never did find that their betrayer Ruminous' daughter now did jay?"

"Farin, or something errr other? No, they haven't. King Mardavian was furious when he found out she'd escaped."

"Why's that?" Grendin asked.

"She's one of the fourteen," answered Captain Nathaniel significantly.

Grendin whistled. "And how'dja know a purty thing like that?"

"I have my ways," Captain Nathaniel said, with a sly chuckle.

"None of the royals here lived then, aye?

"Nope, there's just a handful of peasants left. Maybe some ladies of the court and a few of the fighting men, not many at all really."

"You reckon King Mardavian will turn jem into servants like he did wif all jay others, Captain?"

"I reckon, yes, sir, Grendin," said Captain Nathaniel, with a wicked laugh. In a flash, Grendin was on his feet and had his fingers around Nathaniel's throat, lifting him off the ground.

"Don't ye ever make fun er me again, ye here?" The Captain gurgled out a yes.

"I can snap yer neck a dozen different ways and never leave a mark," Grendin growled threateningly, as he dropped the man to his knees.

"I wasn't making fun of you, Grendin!" the injured man insisted, rubbing his throat.

"Aye, will, just en case, mate, just en case."

"Look, it's getting late, we should get some sleep."

"Forgetton about the trespasser have ye?" snarled Grendin.

"Fine, you stay up all night and watch. *I'm* catching some shut-eye," growled Nathaniel irritably, as he lay in his makeshift bed and flipped on his side, turning his back to Grendin.

Grendin only sat up straighter, looking about him sharply. Captain Nathaniel was clearly better educated than Grendin, but Grendin had the gut instincts. Hours passed until his head finally drooped. An hour after that, his head was on his shoulder and he was slumped down and snoring louder than anyone.

I stalked stealthily towards my horse. Seeing the chains were magically tied, I put my hands on them until they vibrated and shook, turning colder and colder, then "Bull's-eye!' I exclaimed softly.

The snores stopped for a moment, continuing again in a few minutes as if nothing had happened. The chains were frozen. With one touch they would crumble.

They were brittle when I gently put my hands on them one more time, disintegrating into my palms like fluffy flakes of snow. Just as I was about to mount my steed, I noticed a pile of the people of this kingdom's belongings. On the very top of the immense stack, was a crown: *the King's crown.*

On some insane, impulsive whim, I made an internal decision to gather the set of the King and Queen's crowns from this foreign land for the philosopher's daughter. Even as I walked towards the pile, I knew the attempt was absurd, yet I was inexplicably compelled to move forward.

Circumspectly, I stood to my top height, of a rather respectable 6'4", and reached charily for the golden, bejeweled crown. My chest pressed against something sharp, as my hand gripped the crown. Losing my grasp, the crown fell to the ground with multiple loud clanks, rolling several feet away. There was a moment of screaming stillness, then it was as if the entire world had sprung to life. The camp of King Mardavian's men came charging towards me all at once.

Rushing to the ground and grabbing the crown, I hurriedly ran back to my horse, jumped on him, kicked him in the side, and shouted, *"Ride!"*

"Hurry, he's got the crown! Let's get him!" those behind me were shouting.

"North or south, which way did she *go*? "*South,*" was the answer that came into my mind. "*Go south.*"

"Then for the time being, I'll go north," I murmured to myself.

Turning my horse in that direction, we rode with the wind through the night. Close behind me, Captain Nathaniel, Grendin, and many of King Mardavian's men followed in relentless pursuit.

"La turn, ta la fur tu," I whispered into Miko's velvety ear, as we galloped faster than any of the other horses and soldiers following behind us were capable of riding. When we came to a T in the road we turned left, hoping the men behind us wouldn't be able to guess which way we'd gone.

After galloping another mile, I commanded Miko, "Go into the prairie grasses. *Now!*"

Leaping off my horse's back, we both laid down in the tall grass. The horse whinnied in protest, but did as he was told. I'd taught the horse how to lay on the ground, just in case of this type of pursuit.

Miko and I lay in the tall grass, keeping as still and quiet as possible. To save the King's crown, without even thinking about it, I'd set it on my own head. Now it was glowing with a golden halo.

Realizing if the other men went this way, they'd see the light, I yanked it off my head, setting it down beside me. It glowed for a moment more before the light went out.

I could hear King Mardavian's men arguing at the T in the road. "Which way do you reckon he went?"

"There's nothing to the left but prairie grass and hills," Grendin growled. "I reckon he went right. There's a small village that way and berns to hide in and such."

"You were right about everything else, Grendin. So, let's go right," agreed Captain Nathaniel. I breathed a silent sigh of relief.

The men sped in the opposite direction. For three more days I went north, out of my way, staying a safe distance from the path. Then I went east a little and found the dirt path once more, resuming my southern bent. Following on the path was my safest bet on finding a town and I would need fresh supplies soon.

A few days later, I found such a town. As soon as I'd tied my horse up in the barn, I went to the tavern to get something to eat and drink. I bought a simple meal of sourdough bread with a rich, creamy potato soup. After the heavy meal, it didn't take long for the fatigue of constant travel to catch up with me

Checking myself into the inn, I was too tired to notice I'd been watched the whole time. It was so nice to lie in a nice, warm bed even if the sheets and blankets had a few holes in them and smelled vaguely of rotten potatoes.

In the morning, I bought more supplies and decided to keep heading south. But before I left, I bought one last decent meal at the inn. This time I ordered a hearty breakfast of biscuits and gravy, eggs, bacon, and sausage.

"What's a man like ye doing in a place like this?" someone asked from the corner. I hesitated. If I didn't answer the man it would seem rude, and maybe a little suspicious, so I quickly answered, "Seeking my fortune."

"*Here?*" the man asked with a laugh.

"I'm just passing through this town." I began to eat a little faster.

"Well, pass through it a little quicker then. We don't care for men like *you* in these parts."

"Men like me?" I asked, feigning innocence. I took a big gulp of milk, some of it dribbling down my chin in my haste.

"Rich blokes who think they're better than everyone else."

"But I'm not—"

"Rich? I can smell the stench of gold on ye a mile away!"

With his last angry words, I took one last bite of biscuits and gravy, and one last gulp of milk to wash it down with, and left the inn, hurriedly wiping the milk off my face with the back of my hand, as I rushed away. The angry man with a chip on his shoulder, yelled obscenities after me. "You ain't better than the likes of me, you yellow-bellied coward!"

Knowing I'd overstayed my welcome, I went to the barn, paid the stable hand, mounted my steed, and rode south once more. As I was leaving, I heard the man calling back at me in the wind, "And we better never see the likes of ye back in these parts again!"

In a few more days, the dirt roads and prairie grasses gave way to the sandy ground of the deserts. My horse moved slower and slower through the dry earth it was not accustomed to. I started giving it not just the horse's share of water, but part of my own rations as well.

After two days in the plains, I consulted my magical compass (which conveniently always pointed in the direction I wanted to go), and realized we were going west a little too much. Readjusting the direction of our traveling, Miko and I continued.

A few more weeks passed. I was already running low on the horse's grains, due to the added helpings, so I decided not to ride him anymore, to conserve his energy. I was even carrying two of the smaller packs on my own broad shoulders. My horse just wasn't meant for this kind of traveling.

I often felt like I was being watched. After a couple more days of traveling, the intense quiet had begun to unnerve me. As the day waned, the strange silence erupted into the loud, long whines of the wind.

The wind picked up speed, swirling around me, faster each minute until the hot sand pelted my body and face, burning my skin. Something flew through the sky, hitting my horse square in the rear. The horse whinnied in fright and before I could stop him, Miko ran blindly towards the setting sun.

"Miko! Miko! Come back, boy! I don't want to lose you! Miko!"

Desperately trying to move against the sand-filled wind to get to my horse, the power of the wind, and the impact of the earth picked up. I was thrown all about, the sand pummeling against my skin made me barely able to stand, let alone move.

I'd have to find shelter soon or—no, I wouldn't let myself finish that thought. The soil had gotten into my mouth when I'd called my horse's name. Now it was getting into my eyes and I could barely see.

The wind knocked me off my feet and into the sand. Pulling my arms over my head, I dragged myself on the ground until I found a small mound of earth and buried myself next to it. As I moved my arms up to put the pack over my head to protect my face from the hard pelts of flying earth, I felt something strike me on the back of my head.

The pack fell into place above me, as I lost consciousness. But the last thing I heard before losing consciousness, was strangely not the whine of the wind, but the slow, threatening hiss of a snake...

~ *** ~

Chapter Eighteen
The Captives

March, from the castle of a major stronghold of King Mardavian in Ireland—

"Now girls," Ileona began, in her bossiest of voices, "For our lesson today we're going to practice the Celtic Weave. This is a fine way to connect the energy we strengthened through the chakra exercise."

Clearing her throat loudly, to make sure we were paying attention, she continued in a voice meant to entrance and enchant us. although sometimes I found her dramatic displays rather over-done. "The body's energies spin, spiral, twist, crisscross, and curve, weaving themselves into beautiful patterns of extraordinary beauty."

"By our movements, we can lace through these energy patterns to create a harmonic resonance within our own force field. The Celtic Weave will pulse your aura's energies outward and fortify them, in a unique way from the chakra work we did, in continuation of that energy medicine work. This is a very simple exercise, but I warn you not to underestimate simple exercises, which aren't any less meaningful as Wandering Wolfe's long-winded and complicated practices are."

"The Celtic Weave draws all energies together, as a web of communication, so that information within the body can freely travel to where it needs to go, to lend itself more energy. When the energy from your back, to your feet, to your hair, to your teeth, are all working together in cooperation and synchronicity, you will feel charged and powerful. If you do this correctly, you will notice a quiet humming within your own body that sounds like the resonance of music, like the echo of the harp's chords after a symphony." I must admit that the Lady of the Lake had a lovely way with words.

"Think about the varied Celtic patterns and designs, and this is what we're attempting to do with our bodies. But before we begin, I'm going to perform an energy test on both of you."

Moving her hands from either shoulder, to the opposite hip, in swift, sweeping motions, while barely touching my body, and then going in the opposite direction from the hip to the opposite shoulder, this was the energy test she performed next on Varawynn.

With her hands, she traced a figure-eight pattern starting over the torso of my body. Moving her hands freely, with a different speed and rhythm for each of us, she made dancing figure-eight motions all over our bodies.

"I've just demonstrated for you girls, the movements I want you to make, as well as performed the energy test for the Celtic Weave. Varawynn, your stress level and alignment of chakras is poor enough that I'm going to recommend you do the figure 8s in both directions. Shadow Rain, you're not quite so tightly wound, so I'm going to recommend you perform the figure 8s in right-hand, circular motions. The Rhythmic 8's will allow us to relax enough, even in our captivity, to let go, bringing balance between the creative and logical sides of our minds."

Varawynn and I moved our hands in the rhythmic eights. Making several more Celtic designs with our arms and hands, we could feel our bodies relaxing and strengthening at the same time. The tightness in Varawynn's upper shoulder loosened, and I felt like I could finally think, and focus again. No wonder Varawynn was enamored with the Oracle!

After several minutes had passed, Ileona nodded at us approvingly. "You both have listened and done well today."

We smiled at each other. All this energy work wasn't only uniting the energy within our own bodies, it was also uniting us. Somehow, because of Ileona, Varawynn and I were finally becoming friends.

~ *** ~

As the weeks wore on, Alondria and I grew closer and closer, and our food grew more delicious and plentiful. In the mornings, we were given two hearty bowls full of Alondria's newfound love—porridge, and sometimes in the afternoons we were given stew and, in the evening, hearty helpings of meat and potatoes. Indeed, at times there was too much food for us to eat.

It was always the same lowly servant who brought us our meals. We'd never seen his face through the mound of his matted hair. His hair was so dirty, we had no idea even what the real color was. His clothes were dirtier than his hair and reeked of dead pigs and rotten vegetables.

He seemed a shy lad, for when Alondria tried to thank him for bringing us such hearty helpings; he only looked at the floor and ran from the room.

One day Alondria took courage and put a restraining hand on his wrist. "Who prepares the food you bring us, sir?"

"Yous, yous call me sirs?"

"Yes of course," Alondria told him kindly. "Now, who prepares the food you bring?"

"I's does, missus," the boy said with a bow.

"And what, pray tell, is your name, good sir?"

"I does not know."

"How do you not know your own name?" I asked him gently.

"I does not remember, nows I needs to go," the peasant said, violently snatching his arm away from Alondria's grasp. But before he'd run from the room entirely, he turned back long enough to say, "I likes yous. Yous is very nice to me."

"Jonlin," Alondria said, turning toward me after the servant had rushed away. "I think we need to help him."

"I don't know. Perhaps..."

"We just *have* to help him. I can't say why, but I felt a kinship with him when he spoke, even though I know that couldn't have been his natural voice, or way of speaking."

"But Alondria, how could someone like you have kinship with someone like him?" Alondria recoiled at my words. "I didn't mean it like *that*, Alondria! Really, he seems very sweet. But I don't understand why you feel such a strong need to help him."

"Because I know he *needs* our help. I don't understand why *you* don't want to help him! After all, I thought you enjoyed helping everyone?"

I didn't understand it either, but I was hesitant to help King Mardavian's servant. Not wishing to openly disagree with her, since I had no real basis for my reluctance, and remembering our silent pact to work as a team, I answered, "Okay, I'll try to help him, Alondria. King Mardavian's castle is no place for anyone, even a servant."

~ ~ ~

The next day, when the servant brought us our hearty breakfast, Alondria put her hand on the young man's scrawny shoulder and asked him to stay and talk. He didn't shrink away from her touch this time, but still seemed very frightened.

"King Mardavian won't find out, sir."

"King Mardavian finds outs ev-er-ything, missus."

"Please, stay." Alondria handed him her bowl. "Eat with us."

"Yous, yous givin this to me?"

"I will give you much more if you stay." The servant's eyes widened. "What...what shoulds ya gives me?"

"Friendship," Alondria said, with the kind of smile that could light up a twilight sky after the sun had set.

At that moment, the young man visibly melted, only gurgling out a feeble, "Okay."

I thought Alondria reserved that type of smile only for me. Was this what they called jealousy? I'd thought myself incapable of such a base emotion. I'd always detested men who were controlling and possessive of the women they loved.

I would have to pray about this and hope the feeling would pass. I'd never forgive myself if such a sordid emotion like jealousy prevented me from helping a person who could really use it.

"Have you always been a servant, sir?" Alondria asked pleasantly.

"I's, I's don't remembers." Alondria and I exchanged glances. There was something very odd about the servant's complete lack of memory.

"Is there any way we can help you to remember?"

"I's, I's does not know, missus."

"Ileona is an Oracle of the Celtic race and the daughter of a magical creature of the waters. She would have ways to help you, if anyone did."

"I's is not ersking no favors of them women," the servant said stubbornly.

"But Ileona could help you. Don't you want to remember who you are?" The servant seemed to think about this for a moment, confused and undecided, deeply suspicious.

"Give the women a chance," Alondria prodded him softly. "I really think they would know how to help you. They know a lot of magic."

"Magic! Is theys magical like mys master then?!"

"They *are* magical, but they'd never use their gifts to hurt people like he does!"

The young man looked her over doubtfully. "And how's does ye know that?"

"Because I know *them*. They're not like that. Let Ileona help you. Let *me* help you…as your friend."

"I's goes now. Thank yous for the porridge."

"You're very welcome, my friend."

The boy blinked. "We is weally friends now?"

"Yes, we're friends now," I said quietly from the corner. "All three of us."

The young man looked at Alondria, visibly melting again at her smile. He frowned at me suspiciously. The wretched feeling welled up in me again. I sensed the same negative feelings I was experiencing in the servant, feelings he was unable or unwilling to fight.

~ *** ~

The two girls ate in silence; exchanging confused glances as the servant sat watching them eat. After I was through, I asked the servant politely if there was something he needed from us. "Missus said yous could helps me," the sullied servant answered.

I was taken aback. "May I ask what you want me to help you with?"

"I's don't remember my past or whos I am. Is there a spell yous could per–per–torm over me to makes me remembers?"

"Yes, there, is. But I would need a body of water to perform it."

"And whys does yous need that for?"

"It's part of the cleansing process. I recite the spell, lay ashes on your head, which represents your lost past, and then dunk you into the water. When you emerge, you'll be back to your true self and will have regained your memory."

"I's can't let chuse goes."

"Then I am afraid I don't know how to help you… Unless–"

"What?"

"Do you know *how* you lost your memory?" The boy was clearly frightened and looked as if he would bolt out the door any minute.

There were ways around things. I was very good at maneuvering myself out of tricky situations. It was only a matter of matching wit with opportunity. I gave Alondria a lot of credit for her charm. We were working together, even as we were being held captive apart.

"I can't help you unless you answer the question."

"The King won't like it if I's–"

"Shhh, that's all you had to say. Now," I said, immediately changing into my take-charge mode. "If you bring me a hair from King Mardavian's head, I'll be able to make up a spell so that he will no longer have control over you. It won't reverse the damage, but it will at least restore your ability to think for yourself and make decisions for yourself."

"A hairs?"

"Yes, a hair."

"But how's does ya supperse I can does that?"

"Why, you'll have to trick him of course." Just as I would trick the servant even as I helped him.

"Trick him?" The wide-eyed peasant boy looked terrified.

"Or you can simply ask to sweep his bedroom and find a hair in his bed or on the floor. It's up to you as to the *how*."

Looking relieved he said, "I can does that. Thank yous."

After he'd gone, I turned to Varawynn and Shadow Rain. "*You* girls were quiet while he was here."

"I didn't think we should interrupt. Are you really going to help him?" Varawynn asked me.

"Yes, I think I should."

"Why?"

"He brings us our food, doesn't he? And besides, there may well be a way out of this dungeon for us by manipulating this servant." Shadow Rain and Varawynn both stared back at me in astonishment, then all three of us burst out laughing.

"Who do you think told him to come to you for help?" Shadow Rain asked nervously.

"Why, Alondria of course! Who else would have the desire to help him, the charm to make him come to me for help, combined with the strategic brain power to recognize a chance for escape?" We looked at each other and burst out laughing again.

I stopped laughing and looked at the girls very seriously. "And this may be our only chance, so keep your eyes open for ways to help me."

~ *** ~

I seen how well Jonlin and Alondria got along. I didn't like it. I played tricks on the bard. But he was so damn easy-going, he ignored me trying to bother him.

I spied on them, when I gots my works done early. On Jonlin's birthday, I watched Alondria and Jonlin talking, listening outside the door. I couldn't get the girl out of my head. Sometimes Is even neglected my other chores to listen to their fancy talk. The closeness betwixt them set me alight with anger.

* * *

On Jonlin's birthday on March 16th, I decided it was time to come clean. We'd really bonded since becoming captives, and I felt comfortable opening up to him now.

"I'm ready to tell you something you asked me when we were first taken prisoner."

"Oh?" Jonlin asked, his ears perking up. "Are you finally going to tell me why I'm so familiar to you?"

"Yes."

"Go on." His dreamy eyes now held an edge of excitement.

"It was when I was trying to heal my friend when he was dying, a long time ago. Remember, I told you about the accident with Oric?"

"I remember," he nodded. "And I'm so sorry you went through that." Jonlin's sweetness always had a way of setting me at ease.

I reached out and placed my hand into his, knowing he would never have the courage to reach out himself. My skin was softer than a baby's skin, and I think my touch quieted his nerves. His touch certainly helped to quiet mine.

"I was so young when all this happened. And as I was kneeling over my friend trying to heal him, a strange vision appeared to me. It was a vision of *you*, Jonlin."

"*Me?*"

"Yes, your face was clear, but your body was a shadow, and you were calling out to me, calling to me from a place of death and destruction. I never knew what this vision meant or even if it was real, but then when I saw you, I knew there would come a day when you would save my life."

Jonlin inhaled a deep breath and whistled. "What else did you get from your vision?"

The fact that he believed in me, meant the world to me. "I believed you would be an important person in my life."

"How important?"

"*Very* important. In fact, vital…to my, to my every happiness." I felt how everything in him wanted to embrace me, but he was still too shy and afraid. Yet there was a sense of urgency to touch him that was only growing stronger with time.

"Alondria."

"Jonlin."

I lifted my head. Our lips were an inch apart, and yet neither of us had the courage to move forward, or back.

Tears sprang into my eyes. I had no idea why, and why his eyes looked so sad. Just as we were both about to kiss, the servant burst into the room, exclaiming triumphantly, "I haves the hair! I haves his hair!"

"Who's hair?"

"Thes King's hair o'course!"

"Is Ileona going to perform a spell for you with that hair?"

"Yessus Yours Majesty!"

"That's wonderful, dear friend," I congratulated him, smiling my most sunny smile, and throwing a regretful glance back at Jonlin, with my heart full of longing.

~ *** ~

Chapter Nineteen
Battles in the Lost Kingdoms

March-April, in the plains of Southern Europe, and into the desert—

When I opened my eyes, two slits so black they were the complete absence of color and light were glaring back at me. Promptly backing away, I pulled out my sword simultaneously from my side.

The...*thing* hissed with coldness, "Put that away, it will do no good on me, I am much too fasssst for youuuu."

"Who—what are you?"

"Can't you sssseeee? I am a ssssnakke, a cobra, the Queen of all sssseeerrrrpantsssss. And my name is Onessssa."

"Why are you here? What do you want with me?"

"Don't worrrrry. I do not wisssshhh to tassste your undoubtedly sssssweeet blood. I am here to hellllp youuuu."

"Was it you that struck me on the back of my head just before I collapsed?"

"Yessss, with my taaaaail."

"But why?"

"I have commmme to helllp you, Aldoooran." As I stared hard at the serpent, I felt nothing good in it.

"What issss that compasss arooounnnd your neccccck?"

"It's nothing!" Clutching the compass in my hand tightly, my palm ached with the force of my grip.

"Let me sssseeeee it."

"*No.*"

"Fiiinnne," the snake hissed resentfully.

"You never answered. What do you want with me?"

"I have cooommme to helllppp you finnnd whooo you sssseeeek."

"I'm doing well enough on my own, thanks. Who sent you? Who will you answer to if you fail?"

"I annnssssweeer to onlllyyy one. But my onlllly masssssteeer is mysssselllf."

"Who do you answer to?"

Onessa slithered in and out, up and down, and around my body, my arms and legs, my neck. Wanting to scream for her to get off me, I sensed this was some twisted test, so I didn't move a muscle or even breath.

"Pleassse, let me ssseee your commmpasss."

"No!" I'd finally had enough. Using my right hand before she knew what I was about, I flung her slithering body off me violently. Hissing threateningly, she slithered back to me, very near my face.

"It would be foolissshhh to anger the Quueeen of the ssserpentsss, Aldooraaaan."

"And it would be foolish to anger *me*!" I barked back at her, standing and drawing my sword and pointing it toward the snake in warning.

"But you arrrrre going the wronnng wayyyy."

"I most certainly am not! You're just trying to lead me in the wrong direction, and it's *not* going to work! Now go, before I cut off your head!"

"Youuu areee not fasssst enougghhh."

"Do you know that for sure? You'd better *go*, skit skat, cadaddle. I'm sick of your slithering!"

"You sssshalll ppaaay for thiisss ruddeeessss!"

"And you shall pay for your lies and trickery! Now I said *go*! And I meant it!"

Taking a swing at the snake, I had no real intention of hurting her. Onessa slithered off reproachfully, as the flaps around her face fanned out, and she hissed at me spitefully, slithering away into the underbrush. I wondered if hers was the presence I'd sensed watching me these past few weeks.

I spent the day looking for Miko. I wouldn't leave without my horse. By the late afternoon, I spotted him under a lone, small tree. He looked as relieved as I was that I'd found him.

A few days went by, but I was positive I was on the right track, and didn't falter from where my compass led. Gratefully, I saw the lights of a city in the distance. It was dusk by the time I arrived. Wondering if in this remote town any taverns would still be open, I said a silent prayer for a good night's rest in a soft bed.

When I got to the giant gate, the guard wouldn't let me through. To change his mind, I gave him a single gold coin. The man's eyes glowed with a glint of greed. "Surely if yous can spure one coin, yous can spures threes."

Pretending this was a lot for me to give (so the guard wouldn't ask for more), I reluctantly consented to give him the three gold coins. When I entered the gate, I asked the guard if the tavern was still open at this hour. "Everythang closes early here, mate. You'll have to wait 'til morning."

"Surely the inn isn't closed at this time as well?"

"Sorry, that's is toos, goods sir." I felt near tears at the guard's words. I'd been so looking forward to a good night's rest in a feather bed. *Oh well, maybe I'll just make myself familiar with this town in case I'm ever here again in the future.* Secretly I hoped I'd never see this desert or dirty little town ever again.

I set off to make the most of things. Exploring land and traveling was in my blood, as the ancient Essenes had been forced to wander, mystic nomads who'd found refuge in the mountains. It was likely that some of my ancestors had walked these same roads and eaten in these same cities. So, it was natural for me to pioneer these lands and towns, even towns like this one where I doubted that I'd find much to claim my interest.

Wandering aimlessly around houses and trees and shrubs, I hadn't the faintest idea where I was going, and didn't really care to know. I was just killing time until I could get a hot meal and a warm bed. Surely, I could've lain down on some soft patch of sand and rested a bit, even if I couldn't fall sleep. But the later it got, the more anxious I became. I began to search the town more purposefully, listening, and not just looking, though I knew not what for—as if something in my gut compelled me to press on...

Near three o'clock in the morning, in the alleyway between two abandoned buildings, I heard a soft whimper, not a scream, but a whimper—eliciting a pronounced protective urge, even more than a scream would've done.

Following the sound, I heard a young feminine voice say, "Please, please don't..."

Then a perverse laugh echoed in the dark sky, sending goosebumps of warning down my spine. Running toward the source of the sound, I thought, *please, please let me get there in time, before they...*

I made it. They were in a back alley, and her dress was torn half off, and her corset was ripped, but I'd made it. The girl was on her knees, her head was down, and six men were surrounding her, half-dressed themselves.

"Please," the young girl said again, with no tears in her voice. It was a numb sort of pleading, almost totally bereft of hope. Almost.

"Leave her alone," I growled, in the menacing voice I usually reserved for those who threatened my sister. The men turned to see who was interfering in their fun.

Their leader looked at me with an inviting smile. "Hello mate," he said pleasantly. "Care to join us?"

"No, I care to stop you," I growled again. The man just laughed, almost gleefully. "And how do you plan to stop us, stranger? We're six and you're one. Oh, I know! You think this little weakling will help you?" and with that he gave the girl a hard kick on her side.

I seethed with anger. "I'm warning you now; I will seriously maim you if you dare to touch this girl one more time."

"I'd like to see you to try," the man said, suddenly calmly serious, verging on anger himself. I immediately pulled my sword from its sheath, pointing it at their leader.

But two others charged at me before I could make a move against their leader. The first two men were always the easiest to disarm because they didn't expect me to have much skill, but although I was still young, I'd been well-trained, and as young as sixteen had been considered a master of swordplay and combat.

* * *

My first two men charged ferociously towards the stranger, but he quickly disarmed one then sliced the top of the right shoulder of the other, as Hackney dropped his sword, grasping his bleeding shoulder and howling like a banshee.

"I warned you I wouldn't spare you physical pain, did I not?" the outsider said to me calmly. Hackney's shoulder bled profusely, and he stepped back, but my man Nick, quickly retrieved his sword and this time three men in my gang came at him from the front and both sides.

Turning the sword toward Nick, while he was still recovering his sword, the stranger put his sword through two inches of William's left leg. Aaron came from the left, narrowing in on him quickly, so the stranger threw his sword in the sky and caught it in his left hand, then cut Aaron's face with a finesse that exhibited the ability to have cut him straight through if he'd so chosen.

The strange man's blade was as sharp and fine as the utensils the dwarves used to carve and fashion jewels. His skill was off-putting. His training was clearly the combination of several cultures, when the white culture's swordplay was the best, so why bother learning everyone else's techniques?

With all his strength, the foreigner shoved aside Aaron's sword so hard, the young man dropped it, and, shaking, his shoulder blade already sore from the strength of his pushing the sword from his grasp, he withdrew himself from the fight.

Once again, the outsider threw his sword in the air, with prideful glee, catching it with his right hand, now fencing with William, just as Kyle and Abel came up from behind him. All the while I hung back and watched, growing more and more incensed at his egotistical displays of fencing

* * *

I was showing off how easy it was to best them, just to make a point. I hadn't even broken a sweat. I wanted to make them feel weak and inferior, as they'd made this poor girl feel. I wanted them to feel like the cowards they really were—to rape a young girl because they were too pathetic to attract a real woman into having a real relationship. I'd been raised with much more respect for the fairer sex.

Faster than you can say, "magic," I had wounded the two from behind, and Kyle was with the other two wounded men on the ground, with a gashing cut across his forearm.

But it was their leader I wanted most. I'd heard one of the men refer to him as Darsio. I wanted to make Darsio pay for trying to rape this young girl.

* * *

We'd never encountered a man with his level of expertise, though I prided myself on being the best fencer in many lands. Would my skills hold up against this foreigner?

When my five men had all retreated from the fight, wounded and frightened, only then did I step forward. My silver sword flashed by the light of the moon's soft illumination, and the outsider's sword flashed gold. My movements began slowly, as I warmed up my body, and to test my opponent's skill, giving him a false estimate of my proficiency.

* * *

Certainly, Darsio's ability was better than I'd expected in this remote, backwards town. But this man didn't have just motives, like I had. Surely, he'd not been trained by the masters from ten cultures. Surely, he didn't have the magic of Andorra up his sleeve.

As Andorra bordered the Visigothic Kingdom and was so close to Spain, some of my first masters had been from those regions. But masters from all countries of the world had come to teach me. As such, my skill in fencing was formidable.

* * *

We continued to test each other, gauging the level each had of speed, of paring, learning each other's styles, marking each other's strengths and weaknesses. Just as the Outsider was gaining confidence, I picked up speed in less than a second flat, coming after him with the full force of my hatred.

I hated him for his rich man's clothes. I would never wear such fine things. I hated him for his prissy horse. I'd never been able to afford such a fine steed. I hated him for his training. I'd had to train myself, and I was gifted. Surely even this wretched Outsider could see that!

As I lunged at him, he closed his eyes, and just as quickly off-put my attack on him, even with his eyes closed. I continued to pursue him as the aggressor. My rage was deep and blind.

* * *

With my eyes closed I could anticipate Darsio's moves. I continued to elude every attempt Darsio made on my person. Murmuring under my breath a special chant, my sword shone with a brilliant golden light once more.

The light emanated from the sword, until every time my sword touched Darsio's steel, he faltered, his arm weakened. As all that I was, and all that I am, and all that I will be, outlined my form in a halo of radiant light.

Darsio staggered backwards, in awe of the power from within me, multiplying onto my sword, and the focused energy of my movements. The power of the light was weakening Darsio's resolve as no other tactic could've done. His mind was clouding over with the weight of his feelings, confusing his resolve.

"Stop this!" Darsio cried.

* * *

The light was so bright, too bright. It was invading the crevices of the darkness. The girl was mine! She was a toy, a doll, a play thing—to be used, to be shared, or not shared—possessed, then thrown away once we'd outgrown her familiarity. She was an object. Girls were made to be used, to be broken. As I had been.

This wretched man was entering my psyche; my life was being exposed by the brightness. I saw my father go into my sister's room when she was 9-years-old. She was a tiny little thing. Frail and gentle, compliant and obedient, and even though she hadn't wanted to have sex with our father, she was too soft-hearted to put up much of a fight. I was horrified when I'd watched it, but then...

The dark things I'd done were playing out in my mind, and for the first time, I lived my actions through my victims, from their perspectives...

My father had urged me to join in with him when she was about 11. He felt ready at that time to share her. I hadn't wanted to. He'd beat me for weeks before I finally gave in.

We shared her body for one year, and by the time she was 12, she'd gotten pregnant. Both she and the baby had died in childbirth. Her body was just too young and delicate to handle it. I remember holding the blue baby in my arms, too small, much too small.

It had taken one gasping breath of air. Just one. Then it had died. The little girl baby had lived and died taking its first and last breath with my sister's last breath...

I hadn't wanted to!

Feeling the pain of my own regret, and feeling my sister's pain, both physical and of the heart, feeling her death, and the death of the baby that had had no real chance to live, I cried out, "Make this stop!"

"It's this, or physical pain," said the cruel stranger.

"Anything but this! Give me pain!" I shouted out again, at the rotten scoundrel with my last breath of will.

He was cheating. Magic was cheating! I hated magic-users. Cowards, one and all! Yet another reason to kill the man.

* * *

The glowing dimmed, as all that I would be departed, but all that I was and am remained. Now I went on the offensive, using all the skills of my latest Chinese mentor, Kenju.

Surprisingly, Darsio was excellent at defending these maneuvers, but perhaps because I was not yet as good as the best of the Samurai. I switched to tactics I'd gleaned from the cold, frozen lands of the Russian warrior, Azkeck.

But still Darsio persisted.

Something in me knew that it was not me—a stranger—he hated so much. Something in me knew that in fighting me, he was fighting himself.

I tried something of the ancient legends of Camelot, and yet Darsio continued to fight me off. At last, I, the master swordsman, tried something of my own, and quicker than you can say "magic" Darsio was on the ground, bleeding in three places.

"I warned you."

"This isn't over yet!"

"I say it is."

Picking up Darsio's silver sword before he could stop me, I said, "Now leave here before I kill you with your own sword."

* * *

Darsio limped off bitterly toward his home, and this noble man, for the first time in an hour, turned to look back at the girl he'd so valiantly saved.

I hadn't even lifted my head to watch them fight. I was still on my knees—my arms held tightly around me, my light hair spreading over my face like a fan.

It had been hard to go on without my family. Something in me had died with them. I'd never had a lot of fight in me. Now the strength in me was gone. I only had strength enough to pray. My prayers had been answered.

"My name is Aldoran, and we've won my lady. You may rise."

I rose to clutch his hand in my own two small ones. I looked up into his warm brown eyes. I touched his pressed, fine clothes, and I pressed my hand into his, to bring from his skin a little bit of his warmth and life, into my wane spirit and numbed heart.

* * *

As her delicate hands gripped tightly onto mine and she lifted her face up towards me, her hair parted, and her face was revealed. Staring down at her, at the tears in her eyes she was trying so hard not to cry...I knew in that instant, without a shadow of a doubt, that she was the one I'd been looking for. I'd found her.

In the brief moment our eyes met, and our hands touched, I saw the massacre of her family in the foreign land they'd been visiting. I saw the deaths of all the innocent people there. I saw the closet where she'd found a secret hiding place. I saw her beloved horse who'd run away from King Mardavian's battle and was now lost, but more than this, I saw *her*, more than, perhaps, anyone else ever had.

* * *

"Thank you, sir," I whispered breathlessly. He was looking at me as if he'd known me all my life, as if he was reading my soul in the orbs of sea green.

* * *

Something about her, something in her innocence, her dainty, doll-like form, made me softly caress that soft, light hair, but she moved away. "Please miss, I have only come to help you–"

* * *

After what Darsio and his men had tried to do to me, I recoiled at his touch. It frightened me. I didn't know who this man was. He had protected me, but that didn't necessarily mean he didn't wish to harm me himself.

"And pray tell, what is your name, sir?" I asked him cautiously.

"Aldoran. And what is yours?"

"My name is Pharean, sir."

* * *

Pharean! Then it *was* her! She was the girl I'd been searching to find. Surely God worked in mysterious ways.

"And why have you come to these parts?" she continued. I barely heard her. "Aldoran?"

"I'm sorry. My sister is in danger, and I'm…looking for some other people to help me rescue her."

"I think you would do well rescuing her yourself," Pharean said with a graveness that made me laugh.

"My sister's name is Alondria."

"I think that's the most beautiful name I've ever heard."

"I was just thinking that about your name, Pharean. Do you have any markings on your skin from birth?" It was hard for me to mask my excitement.

"Yes, an owl on my right foot, why?"

"Do you know what that means?"

"Yes, I do, and do you?"

"I know about the legend of fourteen and that you've been chosen from birth because you have the marking of the owl. And do you know the legend?"

"Yes. I've always known I was Chosen. Are you one of the fourteen Chosen Ones as well?"

I just couldn't believe my dumb luck in finding the girl. I found it ironic that I never would have found her if I hadn't helped her. "No,

I'm not, though I wish I were."

"I find that strange."

"But my sister is, she's one of the fourteen Chosen Ones, and I've come to find you—to help bring the predestined group together and break my sister and the rest of the group out of captivity."

Pharean nodded. "My father was an advisor to King Mardavian. I know him personally. My father was the Greek philosopher, Ruminous, and through him I became a scholar of language, geography, astronomy, and I'm also an expert on the Prophecy. His education did not exclude the teaching of females, you see."

"Impressive. Then you probably know more about the Prophecy than I do."

"I would imagine so, Prince Aldoran."

I laughed. She blinked in surprise.

As she turned away, I caught a glimpse of her profile: thin, wane, no shape or curve. She'd lost a lot of weight wandering alone in the desert sands. But she was so young, surely, she'd recover. Feeling an intense desire to feed her warm, hot foods, and healing liquids, I suggested we find shelter now and rest.

"I'll give you the last of my rations, and in the morning, we'll replenish them and eat in the tavern across the way."

"Don't you think we're no longer welcome here?"

"Because of what happened with Darsio and his men?"

She looked so weary and downtrodden. Suddenly I saw just how tired and hungry she really was. Beseeching her to sit and rest a while, she said she wanted to go to the General Store and get the food now.

No sooner had she said this then she collapsed into a deep sleep, waking in just a few hours with the first soft rays of the sun. I gave her the last of my rations when she woke up, sparse though they were, and we made our way to the General Store.

Filling our sacks with food and taking from a dusty shelf an even dustier bottle of a healing liquid for Pharean, I hoped the owner wouldn't try to overcharge me. The man that owned the store said he was unwilling to sell to us at all, however.

"I can offer you *five* gold coins, sir," I haggled, confident the owner would serve us now. "You is the one the guard spoke of," the man said glaring. "And you hurt Darsio. I wouldn't serve ye for all the gold in the world."

By the sounds of it, the whole town had arrived outside the General Store with his words. I placed six gold coins on the counter for the goods I'd already loaded into our packs and grabbed hold of Pharean. She was looking at a book in the back of the store, when I dragged her outside with me.

* * *

In Aldoran's haste to get us out of the town safely, he didn't notice that he hadn't given me a chance to put the book I was looking at back when he grabbed me to go, so I'd had to stuff the book into my corset.

"Hurry, Pharean, we don't have much time. Run as fast as you can. I know you're tired and starved, but you were right when you thought we weren't welcome here."

Fortunately, the General Store was close to the desert opening, but unfortunately some of the men were on horses, and it was hard to sneak past them. We made it to the gate, but the guard wouldn't let us through.

"How does four gold coins sound, good sir?" Aldoran asked the guard hurriedly. "Makes it twenty and you've gots yourselfs a deal," the sly man bargained.

Realizing this was a foolish time to barter, Aldoran laid the twenty gold coins into the palm of his hand, and we narrowly escaped into the desert, but not before I saw the guard stab himself with his own sword to make it look as if Aldoran had hurt him to escape.

* * *

I took one more look back. The men on horses were gaining on us. Then I saw something very beautiful out of the corner of my eye. It was my horse, Miko!

"Thank you, God!" I cried, pulling a bewildered Pharean toward the horse.

The men were closing in. They almost had us cornered. Lifting Pharean onto my steed, and mounting it myself, I yelled, "Run, run like the wind, Miko!"

The broad, black stallion butted his way past the other horses, running faster than their eyes could perceive. In the preoccupation of getting away, the book Pharean had inadvertently stolen was the last thing to enter my mind. We wouldn't know for some time how important that act of accidental pilfering was, or how much the importance of the book itself would come to mean in time.

~ ~ ~

The next few weeks brought us back to the town where I'd been unwelcomed before. "Why do we have to come here, if they ran you out the last time?" Pharean questioned.

"This is the only town for a long distance, and we're in need of fresh supplies again. I couldn't manage getting much from the last town. I promise we won't stay for long. You shouldn't be worried anyway; you know I'm perfectly capable of protecting you."

"You certainly did last time."

"I did the last time and I always will. You've got nothing to fear when you're with me."

I tried to put a reassuring hand on her shoulder, but she winced at my touch. The massacre of her family and hundreds of innocent people was still a fresh wound in her heart. And Darsio and his men had scared the poor girl half to death. I understood that.

I tried not to let it hurt me that she hated to be touched because I understood why. She reminded me of a doe evading the chase of the huntsman, or a rabbit bounding away, to not be caught in a trap.

* * *

I knew my aloofness must have hurt him. But I'd been through so much with my family being killed, wandering aimlessly through the wilderness with so little food, water, or sleep. Darsio and his gang had nearly scared me to death. I was so grateful Aldoran had rescued me, but I couldn't be too close to anyone right now. I hoped he understood.

I'd never been a touchy-feely person anyways. I didn't take comfort in hugs and caresses. I'd rather be shown concern in actions, over time.

At first, when we entered the town, nothing seemed amiss. We headed to the supply store and bought lots of feed for the horses and enough food to last us for a few more weeks.

"That's an awful lot of food," said the storekeeper warily. "Where are you off to?"

"We're going to seek our fortunes up north. I met my sister in the south where we're from, to accompany her as her escort, as we seek our fortune elsewhere in a more prosperous land."

"By the look of your clothes and fine horse, I'd say you were prosperous enough as it is!"

"We spent all our money on fine clothes, so we'd be well-received in another kingdom," Aldoran answered quickly. He was not dull, that was certain.

"If you spent all your money on fine clothes then how do you expect to pay me for your supplies?"

Aldoran grimaced at his careless remark, but I decided to help him out. "We spent all our own money on clothes, but our father left us some money in his will that shall help provide provisions for our journey. We are collecting the money from his will, where his solicitor lives."

"Your father's dead, aye?"

"Yes, and our mother passed long ago." Tears glistened on the surface of my eyes. To Aldoran's surprise, the shopkeeper patted my hands comfortingly.

"Tis sad, alright miss. My own daughter t'would be lost if I myself passed on to the netherworld."

"Oh yes, I'm sure she t'would be lost without you. I know that I am lost without my good father. All I have left is my dear brother and this horse. We were forced to sell our farm too, you see. This horse used to plough the fields. It may look fine now, but believe it or not, just a brief time ago it was nothing more than a common work horse."

The shopkeeper patted Pharean's hand again, as she continued, "And I have but one small drawing of my mother and father. That drawing is more precious to me than all the money in the world." She was struggling not to let her tears fall. She turned away, and pulled from the folds of her bodice, the drawing of her two parents.

"Here," said the shopkeeper, as he turned to pull a small package from his drawer and handed it to me. "It's a picture frame and it's on the house. Treasure your parents' memory my dear child."

"I certainly shall, dear sir. You are too kind."

"Here's the money we owe you," Aldoran interjected, handing the shopkeeper a handful of gold.

"I was overcharging you before. Please, dear sir, give me but half that."

"Half? All right, there you go." Aldoran gathered the supplies, and we loaded his horse, Miko, outside the store.

* * *

"That was a fine act you pulled on that man." Looking at her with a half-raised eyebrow, I started to wonder if her father's years of lying to King Mardavian had worn off on her. Her family had lived a lie for so long, what if she'd gotten used to living in deception?

"Act, what act?" Pharean's eyes shone innocently.

This wasn't the time to pursue a discussion like this, as we were getting angry looks from the townspeople. "Come on, we'd better get out of here, Pharean."

I had to pull the lever myself to open the gate, for there were no guards standing watch as we approached it, though as we rode away there were men gathering 'round the gate. Thank God we had left before they could start something.

"Why do they seem so angry with you, Aldoran?"

"I don't know. It must just be the way I'm dressed."

Pharean looked worried about something.

"You're remembering that we have to pass through the Kingdom where your family was killed aren't you?"

She didn't answer. I could already tell she would be in no mood to discuss much of anything, until we'd passed the ruins of the castle where King Mardavian had killed the people of that city and her family.

~ *** ~

Aldoran and I had traveled for a week or so through the desert, and were getting closer to the prairie lands, when I asked to see the compass he wore protectively around his neck. Seeing no problem in letting me look at it, he took it off and handed it to me. I fingered the gold and sapphire, feeling sad.

"What's wrong?"

"I'm just remembering some of my father's magical items."

"I'm sorry you lost them, but I have some other things that may take the edge off."

"What do you mean?"

With swift, deft movements, he pulled both crowns from the Kingdom where my family had been killed, from his pack. My light eyes widened.

"Aren't those the crowns of the King and Queen from the Kingdom that were killed because of my father's betrayal to King Mardavian?" Aldoran nodded. "However, did you get them?"

"They were no trouble to get."

Aldoran was smart, that was clear, but he was a horrible liar. Gently, I took the Queen's crown from his hands, and on a strange whim, placed it on my own head. The crown glowed gold.

"The King's crown glowed on my head, just as the Queen's crown is doing on yours right now." I started at his words. I'd heard the legend of that City while I was staying there, before King Mardavian and his men had closed in on us.

"What's wrong? What did I say?"

"It's nothing, nothing." Hurriedly I took off the foreign Queen's crown.

"I'm tired now though, Aldoran, and I need to go to sleep." I'm sure he wanted to make sure I ate a little something before bed, but he knew better than to argue with me. And I really was tired.

When I laid my head down on my pack, I fell asleep almost immediately. In my unconscious state, my sisters were alive and well and we were dancing, having a party. I was prancing among them, wearing a gown of the snowiest of whites, with long bell sleeves, and pearls and lace intricately designed upon the dress' silk foundation, making it almost appear to be a wedding dress.

Dancing with my sisters; throwing our heads back and leaping through the air, it felt like we were gravity-less in our state of exaltation. My father had tears glistening in his eyes, and my mother's happy tears fell freely as they watched us, making no move to hide their feelings, or to conceal their pleasure.

When I woke up, my eyes were moist, but I had no time to consider this before feeling a hard nudge on my shoulder blade and a loud whinny.

"Be quiet, Buttercup," I said, shoving the horse's snout out of my face. "Buttercup? Buttercup! Oh, Buttercup is that you?"

The horse looked thinner and her lovely butterscotch mane was quite dirty and matted, but her eyes shone adoringly as she looked upon her mistress.

"Oh, Buttercup, wherever have you been?" Throwing my arms around my horse's mane, I kissed her again and again, inhaling deeply that heady horse scent I loved.

I woke Aldoran up with my loud exclamations. His eyes widened at the pretty animal. "This is your horse I take it?"

"Yes, I think she was trying to get back to the castle and the prairie lands!"

"Well, she's a welcome addition; my horse could really use help carrying the load right now." Buttercup whinnied accusingly, but I hushed her with another kiss.

"I'm glad to see your friend is with us now, Pharean, but I think we should probably try to get back to sleep."

"You're right Aldoran," I agreed. "Goodnight, Buttercup." Giving her one more kiss, I lay back upon the prairie grasses smiling. The horse whinnied one more time, and then she too fell silent.

~ ~ ~

Despite the weariness of our travels, and the weeks of aimless wandering I'd endured before Aldoran found me, the hooting of an owl in the dead of night woke me straight awake yet again.

"Mordorn..." I murmured. The dark owl with burning eyes swooped down upon me with his familiar hooting call.

"It is I," he spoke out deeply in the darkness.

We hastened to a discreet clearing a safe distance out of Aldoran's earshot. "It's been months since I last saw you."

"I was protecting those elsewhere," Mordorn replied in his elegant, low voice.

"What message do you have for me this time?"

"Do not lose heart when the 13th falls to dust. Can you recall lines 16-20 of poem 133 of the Prophecy?"

I recited, almost mechanically,

She who bears the raven mark
Shall be the first to fall and rise again.
From fire and coal, out of embers and shadows,
She is made more than whole in the resurrection."

Mordorn nodded his furry bush of a face. His large amber eyes penetrated my soul and mind. "You will need to remind them. Death is not always the end of life."

"Remind who?"

"Those who bear the birthmarks foretold in the Prophecy."

"But Mordorn—can't you be more specific?" The owl cocked his head, his great horns an extra sensory perception. His eyes, with their x-ray vision, stilled the questions stirring in my mind.

"You must be their hope—with your expert knowledge of the Prophecy, remind them of these words and I will lead them to the one who will perform the resurrection. Take particular care of her ashes, and believe that beneath the ashes, the embers of life and true love burn in the spirit forever."

In the face of his unfathomable wisdom, in the mysterious magic of his small, dark form, I could only nod. "Yes, Mordorn. I'll remember. But when will I see you again?"

Looking at me with limitless power in its piercing expression, he answered, "That, I have just told you." Allowing me one brief caress on the nape of his furry neck, he flew with broad, shadowy wings, up and away, into the immeasurable recesses of the mysteries of the night.

~ *** ~

Chapter Twenty
Omens in the Sky

February-April, from the forests, valleys, mountains, and seas of the Olde World—

While Aldoran fought through the desert to find the scholar, Pharean, and while Alondria and Jonlin learned more about the servant, Luquinn, while the Shaman met with the evil King Mardavian, and while Varawynn and Shadow Rain became friends through the teaching of energy taught by Ileona, my dark wings flew over many lands, to find the Ones of Olde, on the borders of the sea...

I flew past the countries of men, past forests of great depth and mountains of great height. I flew above desert sands shifting like the fields of wheat in autumn, then back amongst the thick, dense woods like endless canopies of emerald green. Flying like a seagull above an ocean vast in its pure blue waters, whose home lies in the undulating tides, until at last I came to the banks of the sea elves' crystalline shores.

I descended upon the land of the ancient ones, of seekers of truth, of warriors of peace, of merchants of jewels, of the leaders who governed the seas. There amongst the elves of the water, I found an elder—one of the eldest sea elves that now lived.

She was as deep as the ocean's depth. She was as wise as the moon, from which she bore her name. She was as true as the clear light of day, and she was...the personification of grace and truth.

With her gift of insight for which she'd been so blessed, she knew, she *knew*, as most who live their lives flittering and purposeless would never know, the precise moment I would arrive. She had only to look upon a night full of stars and planets in specific positions of the sky, to see.

Raven and elf communed, as humans cannot...through the mind, without the handicap of words—where meanings were too often lost in misinterpretations and misunderstandings. For the heart knows that for many truths, words get in the way of thoughts and feelings best said unspoken.

In this way, I told the elf of my mistress, the Celtic priestess,

Varawynn, of the shepherd boy destined to become our King, Eliju, of the great Shamanic teacher, Wandering Wolfe, of the kind Bard of Hebron, Jonlin, of the beautiful healer and Muse, Alondria, of the brave warrior, Aldoran, of the powerful Oracle, the Lady of the Lake, Ileona, and of the Legend of Shadow Rain. I beseeched this great elf to find the most noble and magical creature of all races, the unicorn.

Moving like the wind, she lifted her long graceful arm, for my legs to perch on her elegant white hand. Her silvery blue hair swayed like the branches on a willow tree, and as this haunting beauty fixed her watery blue eyes upon me, her words were accented with the ancient, universal language that I still remembered.

Illumina spoke in tones as fluid as her movements, as strong as the intuitive perceptions of her mind. "I will find the cursed black unicorn, Silvandrin. Then we will travel across this beloved sea, and I will return to the land of men. And I will save your mistress, Varawynn, and I will meet again the wise Wandering Wolfe, and I will join the Chosen One, Eliju, who will become the King of Men and Elves alike."

* * *

And so, after Raegar, the deep, dark creature that Shamans say are the messengers of the dead, had received the assurance he needed from me, we said goodbye. I watched him fly away until his tell-tell orange feather was no longer a speck marring the cloudless sky.

I would have to say goodbye to my people, but not before I called a meeting of the elders, so I could name who would take my place in my absence. Calling the group of Twelve Elders to the holy marble table, "The White Sinore," the elves were respectfully silent as I began my speech.

"Hello, my dear friends and leaders of Olde. I am leaving my home on behalf of the greatest charge. My destiny is at last coming to pass, as I find my place amongst the humans who are our future. The Chosen One, Eliju, has been found."

The other elders looked at each other, some in surprise and excitement, others in fear and trepidation.

"This is a critical time for the sea elves. Our fate hangs in the balance between eternal life and extinction. Everything rests on the shoulders of a young and inexperienced boy, and on the group that was Chosen before time began, to accompany him on his journey. As you all know, I am one of those predestined to be a part of this glorified troupe."

The elves gave each other looks, some of awe and reverence, others of barely concealed jealousy and resentment. "This is a great honor, as you all must know," I continued. "I honor you, by being one of the chosen fourteen. I honor our kingdom by leaving it."

Many of the elves looked angry I was going. "But I will not leave you with a broken Sinore. No, I will name someone to take my place in my stead. She is a worthy and beautiful sea elf who has been waiting for this moment for many years. I am sure she will honor me in my absence and will also honor all of you and the others in our kingdom: my beloved daughter, Sadrena."

At the mention of my daughter's name, those elves who were angry were instantly relieved and at peace. Sadrena had long been a favorite amongst the elves, and there'd been talk for centuries about adding her to the Table of Elders. Her soft and pleasant personality would lend harmony to the White Sinore. She did not like to make waves.

"So, without further ado, I invite Sadrena to talk where I now talk, to sit where I now sit, and to stand where I now stand."

Sadrena appeared in the doorway, a little shy, but clearly humbled and honored. Walking toward the table like the cool breath of a mother's kiss on her child's forehead, she stood at the head of the White Sinore, as the other eleven elves clapped their hands in a physical display of approval.

Smiling her sweet, guileless smile, her eyes looked faraway and dreamy; tears came forth from their cool, blue-green depths, but she would not shed them here. She would not stain the sacred table, the White Sinore, with her fears and the sadness of her mother's absence. The table must remain unmarred, even from the lonely tears of the kind of love that makes the broken whole.

"We must feast!" A sea elf named Helynra exclaimed loudly, joyfully. "We must feast as a celebration for Sadrena being named an elder, and for pride that our very own was selected to bring us to our glory!"

"Or our doom," an old elf named Kinlindore retorted gloomily, but no one heard him over the cheers of happy exaltation.

The elves set about making a grand feast that would hearten me on my journey to find the unicorn. There were breads, round and square, white and brown, and wheat and leaven. There were cakes tall and wide, and round and sweet. There were dishes prepared with special herbs that tasted of the salty sea and the earthen grass and forest. There were no meats, for all sea elves are vegetarians, just like our wood and mountain elven sisters. Sadrena, and my daughter's husband, Whitmore, feasted by my side, laughing and talking, hugging and loving.

Was I sad or eager to leave my race of sea elves behind? Among a few of the elves, was a sentient foreboding that something was amiss. The result of this journey did indeed hold the outcome of our fates. We all sensed it—and I sensed their thoughts.

~ *** ~

Even if the group was successful, how indeed did we know that this human, Eliju, would be a benevolent ruler? How indeed did we know if he would not hate the elves, as other humans had done in the past? Would my mother, in all her sanguine glory, manage to express to Eliju the worth of such magical creatures?

Before she left the next morning, the elders of our Kingdom said a protection spell around the carriage that would safeguard my mother's mode of travel. The carriage was in the shape of a great ship, white with silver trim. Designs of the elfin folk and symbols of the Olde Magic were carved upon it, and carried forth by a hundred white doves, the messenger birds, and the anthem bird of sea elves: the dove itself a symbol of peace and water's healing purity.

Hence the greatest of the sea elves, my mother, set forth into the day, into the light, with hope in her heart, and wise humility in her soul, willing and ready to find the most infamous of the unicorns. She was the last hope for our kind. But she was also my mother, and I prayed for her victory.

~ *** ~

I'd been on many quests before and had visited the Kingdom of the unicorns on more than one occasion, but tonight an ominous sign hung in the sky: a red full moon. A red moon could only mean one thing: bloodshed. By the look of the star's alignments it wouldn't be long in coming. Danger was ahead, but when it would come to pass was uncertain. I just knew it would be soon.

Days and nights of travel wore on me, even from the comforts of my plush carriage flown by the doves. After all, I hadn't traveled in many moons. It would take some time to get re-accustomed to the wear and tear of constant motion again.

As a younger elf, I'd loved to travel. I'd even gone on a quest once with the Shaman, Wandering Wolfe. We'd both acquired a treasure at the end of the hunt. I had fond memories of the old Shaman. I could remember him when his beard was short, and his eyes twinkled with mischievous youth. It had been many years since we'd seen each other. The last time was when he came to tell me about the Prophecy, the group of fourteen, and my part in it.

I'd taken it all in stride, looking forward to this day. My birthmark was of the Selkie, a half-woman, half-seal on my left ankle. It was evidence I was one of the Chosen Ones in the elect group of fourteen, though the meaning, or purpose, of the birthmark itself was still a mystery to me.

After a few weeks of travel, I'd come to the edge of the forest where the unicorns roamed. This was the Forest of Eleethion, named after a legendary unicorn that'd been alive since the beginning of time, but his horn had been cut off by an evil sorceress. He had died a few hours later, unable to live without the magic that gave life to his soul.

In the middle of the forest, two rivers intersected and swept across the depths of the forest. These were special bodies of water that only flowed within the borders of Eleethion.

At the edge of forest, I drew from the folds of my robes my white horn, and blew it seven times. Everyone known by the unicorns were given a white horn to sound upon arrival at the Forest of Eleethion that only the unicorns could hear.

This was called "Blowing the Ithor." You were instructed to blow the Ithor seven times because seven is the number of spirituality and creation, and of course, there's no creature more magical or pure than the unicorn.

After the seventh blow, a unicorn named Dumorias came out to the clearing to see who'd blown the horn. As he recognized me, he stomped his hooves and threw back his mane in excitement.

"You must have come for Silvandrin!" he said with a whinny. "It's so wonderful to see you again, Illumina! Please let me have the honor of taking you to Silvandrin! Is it the foretold time then, my friend?"

I nodded and thanked him for guiding me to Silvandrin. I'd met the infamous Black Unicorn, Silvandrin, on previous occasions, but every time I saw him, he took my breath away. This occasion held no exception.

Standing a good ten feet from the ground, as the most legendary of unicorns, his mane and body were of the deepest black, his horn so silver, it sparkled in the light. His blackened body and silver mane glowed with a sheen quite unlike the hair of any other unicorn. Born of pure white as all unicorns are, his white body had been turned black in cursed shame. Most unicorns have gold horns; Silvandrin was the only unicorn whose horn, mane, and hooves were silver. They'd turned that color when he'd used his horn to save the life of the very sorceress who'd taken the life of Eleethion.

For many years Silvandrin had been an outcast, but time had given him a reputation for nobility and good standing in the community of gracious creatures. Now he was the leader of the unicorns, if indeed such peaceful creatures ever claimed positions of power.

"Illumina," he said, in a voice rich as butter, soft as velvet, deep as the drums of Ithica.

"Silvandrin," I replied, in a voice blue like the sea, light like the moon's pale beams, gentle like a spring breeze. Both elf and unicorn smiled and as one, we embraced.

"Is it time already? It feels as if only a few moons have passed since the beginning of this earth."

"It is time, Silvandrin. It is *our* time."

* * *

Looking down into the eyes of the dainty and elegant elf, I nodded to myself. "Surely you, too, have seen the signs in the sky, Illumina?"

"Yes, I have. But have you discerned when, how, and what precisely shall be?"

"A battle, and someone we love will die—someone very significant to us."

"You mean to say, one of the fourteen?" I gave the elf a meaningful look that made her shudder.

"Haven't you read that part of the Prophecy?"

"No, Silvandrin. Please, recite it for me." In a voice heavy-laden with the burden of knowledge, I recited:

"The Chosen Ones"

Fourteen come together,
Each wise and brave and true.

Humans from all walks of life—
Elf and Oracle too.

The brilliant Bird of Eden,
Only one left, of the single pair God made—
A creature holding the memories
Of every story and life in the human race.

The Trickster of all shapes and forms,
Who's known and yet unseen.
Who's learned what can't be taught,
What's so priceless it cannot be bought?

And the infamous black unicorn,
Who in his shame became one-of-a-kind;
The truths and mysteries of the earth
Are reflections from behind his eyes.

One will be sacrificed—
One will betray—
One will say goodbye—
One will run away.

One will break a curse—
One will change their form—
One will teach them all—
A lesson they must learn.

One will hold a secret
That will help them win the war

One will teach them how to fight,
Using powers to make what was wrong, right.

One will heal the wounds
By guiding them from the darkness into the light.
One will see into the future,
With eyes that ever dream.

One will see into the past,
Revealing that which must be seen.
One will lead them into danger,
But shall save them in the end.

Showing them the righteous way;
One shall be their leader,
Whose choice of mercy
Shall bring them glory in the end."

"How did you come upon this legend?" Illumina asked, but I avoided her eyes. "It sounds like one of the last verses of the Prophecy."

"It is. However—" There were spies everywhere. I felt their eyes upon us. "Come with me. It's not safe to talk here."

"Not safe, in the Forest of Eleethion?"

"We're being watched."

"By who?"

"There's only one place where her ever-watchful eyes cannot see us."

"Where?"

"In the Nine Towers of the Planets we built after Eleethion's death."

"I've never heard of these towers."

"Let's hurry," I said, urging her away.

Illumina looked up into the sky, lost in a reverie. "What is that?

Do I see an owl flying in the middle of the day?"

"Come along Illumina, we must make haste."

"I wonder if it has been watching us all the while."

"Illumina, please, we need to go."

"It is so cold today." Illumina shivered.

I sighed and said, "Well, it is winter, dear elf."

"Silvandrin, why are we just standing here? Didn't you have somewhere you were taking me?" Laughing and nodding to myself, I'd almost forgotten how absentminded Aquarian folk could be.

* * *

Despite Silvandrin's enormous size, he moved as swiftly and silently as any elf. When we came upon these magnificent towers, I felt dazed. I had to take a moment just to gaze upon their beauty.

They were different shapes and sizes, signifying the various planets amongst the stars. One was the Tower of Mars. It was flaming red and tall. It was the boldest tower in design.

Another was the Tower of Venus; it was a dark, lovely shade of blue, with flowers hanging in all its windows. It was the prettiest tower. The Tower of the Moon was a translucent white composed of pearls and clam shells, gleaming translucent different shades of colors in the various phases of the moon. It was the most peaceful tower.

The Tower of the Sun held the most windows and was full of light. The Tower of Jupiter was the tallest and the most imposing. Mercury's Tower was yellow and light green and Saturn's Tower was an earthen brown. Neptune's was a lovely sea-foam green, and the tower of my own ruling planet, Uranus, was a glittering silver that sparkled brightly even in the night. Pluto's Tower was dark grey and ominous.

"When the following three planets are discovered, we will build the rest of the towers. Now, hurry Illumina."

"Which tower are we going into?"

"The one which offers us a sanctuary—my own ruling planet: The Tower of Venus, ruler of love and peace, nobility and harmony."

Entering the beautiful tower where flowers bloomed everywhere—falling in cascades from the window sills, in the folds of the midnight blue velvet curtains hanging on the windows, down to the stone tables and chairs that provided visitors a place to sit and rest, the sweet fragrance of flowers permeated the large, open room.

Illumina asked, "Can you tell now me who gave you this part of the Prophecy? Are we safe to speak here?"

"Yes, we are safe here, my dear friend. This poem in the Prophecy was given to me by the very sorceress who killed Eleethion—the very sorceress I saved."

"Oh, Silvandrin, how could you? This Prophecy's been tainted!"

Silvandrin shook his silver mane. "The Prophecy cannot be tainted simply because it was held by evil hands."

"On whose hands the blood of an innocent unicorn was spilled? How could you have saved her Silvandrin? I've always been too afraid of offending you to ask...but, how could you?"

Sighing deeply, he replied, "I've been asked that question many times, Illumina. More times than I care to remember, I've wondered it myself. I was there when she used her magic to cut off Eleethion's horn. Only someone who possesses great magic can do such a thing."

"Black magic you mean; no magic any *decent* wizard or sorceress is willing to use."

"Yes, of course, it was very powerful black magic that allowed her to kill him. But as she lay there on the ground beneath me, she looked up at me with these eyes, these eyes that haunted me. Her eyes were so dark and deep, I couldn't even make out the pupils, and her movements were like shadows."

"But there was something else in her eyes, something in the expression...and I just knew she couldn't die. I knew I had to save her. To this day, I don't know exactly why I did it. I knew even then that it would cost me everything, but I also knew that if I didn't save her, it would cost me more than my status and reputation. Saving her meant more to me than saving my own life. Somehow I knew it would cost us everything if she died."

"You're speaking in riddles, Silvandrin. But I don't doubt you were right in what you did."

"Can you sense I was right, or do you just trust me?"

"Sometimes, I have strange visions, Silvandrin, and sometimes they come true. I've dreamt of who you are speaking about, and I believe we will meet her one day, sooner than I expect I'd like to."

"Of course, my dear, for you are a seer. I've always known that about you."

"I was born with a gift, but it's something that comes as natural to me as breathing."

"But you shouldn't take any gift for granted, Illumina. I hope you will remember this."

"Of course," I answered him defensively. Silvandrin looked at me intently for a moment, then added, "I'm certain of one thing, Illumina. I'm quite certain of who you are in the Prophecy: 'she sees into the future, with eyes that ever-dream.' I just meant to say that I have faith in your gift, Illumina."

"And I have faith in you," I acknowledged.

Silvandrin thought it was safe now after our conversation for us to leave the Nine Towers of the Planets and rejoin the other unicorns. Unicorns are vegetarians like the elves, so we feasted on all the plants of the forest that night. In the morning, we set out towards Ireland, where the captives were being held.

~ *** ~

Chapter Twenty-One
How the Mighty Fall

January-late April, from a castle in Caledonia—

"Let us go, Mardavian!" I growled. "Or I promise you'll live to regret it!"

King Mardavian's laugh sounded like the cat-call of hyenas. "Think it's sensible to threaten your captor, you foolish boy?"

"I'm not a boy, I'm a man!" King Mardavian only laughed harder. I wanted to punch that disgusting smirk off his face.

"Even if you were of age, you'd be too immature to *ever* be called a man." Before I could make a retort, the arrogant king kicked me in the chest, to teach me a lesson.

He kicked me in the sides and abdomen until I spit out blood. I didn't cry out in pain. I kept the screams inside my own mind until I was nearly unconscious.

I barely noticed the sensation of being dragged out and away from my friends. I heard a woman say from the doorway, in even tones, as if unmoved by the blood and bruises upon my body. "That's enough, Mardavian."

"It's enough when I say it's enough," King Mardavian barked.

"I say you've had your fun. Let me take him now and I'll leave you with the others."

"But...I want the boy."

"Don't go back on the arrangement, Mardavian. You'd be asking for trouble to back out on me now. So just go away. Torture the others as you will but leave Eliju with me." He shot her a dirty look before he left us alone together.

I stared up in the doorway at her long, dark silhouette. Unable to make out her face in this darkness, her cold finger brushed the corner of my lips. There was something fine and grainy on her skin that felt like the texture of sand, but tasted sweet.

Losing consciousness, this time for good, when I came to, I was in motion. My hands were tied so I could not feel for where I was, or what I was moving in. There was a mask over my head, so I couldn't see, but the sound of horses' hooves helped me to recognize that I was in a carriage.

Days passed. It could have been a few days of travel, or maybe a week. I was in a great deal of pain from the wounds King Mardavian had inflicted on me. The motion helped me to sleep.

Then at last when I awoke, I was no longer in movement, my face was not covered, and my hands were not tied. All evidence of King Mardavian's rage was gone. Looking my body over, I couldn't find even one scrape or cut or bruise, and I felt no aches or pain anymore.

"Good, you've woken up. Right on schedule."

Looking around, I tried to gather my bearings. "Where am I?"

"You're in a bedroom; you're lying in a bed."

"Well I can *see that*, but *whose* bed?"

"Your bed."

Her voice was familiar. She reminded me of Wandering Wolfe, the way she avoided giving direct answers. "Won't you come closer, into the light..."

Slowly she stood, coming before me in the smooth, languid movements of a cat. I recoiled in shock and familiarity. No, it couldn't be...

"It's you."

"Yes."

"The woman that's been haunting my dreams..."

"Yes."

I was overcome, overwhelmed. "The woman that's been coming to me in visions?"

"Yes."

"You're really here. I'm really with you?"

"Yes."

Part of me just wanted to sit there and look her over. She was the One. The One I'd both been longing and terrified to find.

"What do you want with me?" I'd asked her the question countless times in my dreams and visions; it was surreal to be asking her this in person.

Hesitating, to carefully measure her words, as if trying to decide how truthful she'd be, and how much she would reveal, she answered honestly, "I want you to join me."

"*Join* you? You mean you want me to turn my back on my friends? Who *are* you anyway? I don't even know your name."

Hesitating again, at last she voiced the name I'd coveted to know for so long, "Darlillyth...Queen Darlillyth."

"What a beautiful name." I said it before thinking, and then was embarrassed. I hadn't intended to pay her a compliment.

"Eliju, I could teach you so much more than the Shaman ever could," she pressed on, ignoring and avoiding my embarrassment.

"No one knows more than the Wandering Wolfe."

"Then why didn't he see through my trap?"

Ignoring that train of thought, I countered back, "You were behind all of this?"

"Of course."

"Then how could I ever trust you?"

"No one on this earth has ever seen through one of *my* plans, Eliju. I want you to *join* me. I want to be your teacher, your master...your partner, that's why I had all of you captured," she pressed on.

"I already *have* a teacher."

"But he's not worthy for one as great as you are destined to become! You are the Chosen KING and you should have the best, the most *powerful* teacher of all!"

I was quiet for a moment, letting her words sink in before I spoke. The old Eliju would have answered her back rashly. But the Shaman had taught me the power of a pause. "The power I am looking for can only be taught and given by the Shaman."

"Eliju, you don't have to give me an answer now. Just think about what I've said, and perhaps in time, I will prove my powers to you so that once and for all, you'll know who the true mistress of magic is."

She left me then, and I was glad to see her go, for her words were unsettling. Yet as the days passed without her, my curiosity got the better of me, which it often did.

I wondered what exactly she had in mind for me. She frequented my thoughts constantly. *The Mistress of Magic...Darlillyth, the woman who had haunted my dreams while I was sleeping and coming to me in visions while awake.*

After a week had passed, late one night after I'd fallen fast asleep, I was jarred awake by smoky breath on my lips. Her chiseled face, etched like a flawless marble statue, were mere inches away from mine. She stared at me with a purposeful, resolutely cold expression on her face. Shivers moved like beetles up and down my spine.

"You startled me!"

"Have you been thinking about our conversation?"

"Isn't there a better time to talk about this than the middle of the night?"

"Have you considered my proposition?"

"Even if you *were* the most powerful, that doesn't necessarily make you the *best* teacher."

"Of course, it does!"

"No, it doesn't because evil can never be the best, in the end, evil is always defeated by good."

Laughing her cool, confident laugh, for the first time she looked me directly in the eyes. "You sound more like a Christian than a Jew." Anger exploded in my chest as I sat up in bed and glared at her.

"You say that again and I'll have to teach you a lesson." My words were impetuous. I never intended to strike her, maybe just give her a good talking to, but Darlillyth just laughed again and fired back, "With what? You fight with knives and swords, bows and arrows and you have none of those here. I've already taken all your weapons, even that dagger you keep tied to your ankle."

"I guess all I have left is the strength of my spirit and will— and you won't ever be able to take those!"

"Well, I can try to show you, to teach you, to mold you. Perhaps I will show you a lesson, the first of many if I have my way..."

"I'd like to see you try!"

Closing her eyes, Darlillyth moved her hands up and down, in quick motions, making the area in front of her a wall of water. I let out a brief cry as her motions ceased. The bruises and cuts had returned. I was painfully aware of the wounds inflicted on me from King Mardavian.

I had a broken rib in my chest where King Mardavian had kicked me, and bruises down the length of my body where he'd beat me. My whole body felt like it was being prodded with red-hot pokers. I wanted to scream and beg her for some relief, but I determinedly contained myself, knowing the worst thing I could do in her presence was to show weakness and lose my self-control.

"I would like to see you try and hurt me *now*, Eliju."

Grinding my teeth to hold the pain at bay, I knew I had to be quiet and humble, or her punishment of me would only get worse. "Very well."

With a different sort of pride, I attempted to move toward her before realizing there was a wall between us. Wherever I turned, even backwards and away from her, a wall boxed me in. She'd easily gotten the better of me, but it didn't really matter: freedom was a gift of the spirit—she could never trap that.

"Can your Shaman do that, Eliju? Anything of what I just did?"

"I don't know. But he can do other things."

I could barely control my features. The physical pain inside my body was so severe, but when she put down Wandering Wolfe, I couldn't bear what that did to my heart. Wandering Wolfe had changed my life. I could never be disloyal to him. "Could you take away my wounds again?"

"I can–but I won't. I told you I would teach you a lesson. I will tend to them, however," she continued, snapping her fingers as solvents appeared.

Lighting a candle, so that she could see what she was doing in the dim light, she pulled away my shirt. My muscles shimmered in the candlelight, as I flexed them unconsciously from habit.

* * *

For a young man, his arms were well-built, and he'd only continue to get stronger as he matured. His skin was olive, a sensuous olive. His hands were rough, but the rest of his body was supple and bulging with muscles.

"How old are you, Eliju?" I asked him, unwittingly aroused as I bandaged his wounds. My hands were cold like ice, burning him more than the ointment.

"I just turned twenty."

"When was your birthday?"

"December 17th."

"The number seventeen suits you. Seventeen is the number of Immortality."

* * *

I was intrigued. I considered asking her for more information, but then I realized that would only encourage her. I didn't want her to know how alluring I found her...both her knowledge and the excitement of her nearness. I felt like I was fighting both my curious mind and my treacherous body.

"Lay down, so I can bandage up your face," she commanded.

Laying my head down on the silky black pillows, I pulled the black sheets up to my neck, to hide my body from her roving eyes. I didn't like her eyes on my bare chest. It made me feel vulnerable and exposed.

"You were talking about numbers...the meaning of numbers is called numerology, right? But the power of numbers is also in the Kabbalah, isn't it?" Okay, so I couldn't resist asking, but better to expand my mind, which would hopefully silence my body.

"Yes. I know the Kabbalah very well, Eliju. It's just one more thing I could teach you if you decided to stay here with me. Wandering Wolfe doesn't know it. It's a knowledge that requires more than skill to study. It requires a mentor who has studied it with a mentor. In this way, the knowledge is passed down. The students are carefully chosen by their masters."

Wandering Wolfe did know the Kabbalah and had offered to teach me it before we'd been taken prisoner, but I decided not to share this knowledge with her. Knowledge was power. I didn't want to give her any more of mine.

"Who did you study with?" I asked her, still trying to distract my body from her surprisingly gentle touch.

Her hands shook slightly as she replied shortly, "My father." Something in her voice made me decide not to press her further about the Kabbalah. Her cold hands had been warmed with the heat of my body and were now a soothing balm against my face.

This was the brightest light I'd ever seen her in, and I found myself staring up into her face, taken aback by her uniquely stark beauty.

She had waves of black hair, falling in long layers down the entire length of her back, and long black eyelashes to match the onyx stones of her powerfully exotic eyes. Despite her coldness and forceful way of speaking, her face was feminine, though more angular than rounded. Her olive complexion lay in brilliantly lush contrast against the distinctive red fullness of her lips.

In my dreams, her face was always a blur; now I could make out every nuance of her form. Probably sensing my appraisal of her every inch, she wouldn't meet my eyes.

She seemed to be all-knowing and all-powerful, but as she stood before me, the haunting phantom of my dreams in mere flesh and bone, my fears dissolved in the sudden shock of her beauty...and my attraction to it.

"You're stunning." I said it without thinking, as if I couldn't control my words in the shock of seeing my vision come to life.

Recoiling backwards as if I'd slapped her, she stood upright and stepped away from me, but I gripped her wrist, holding her down.

* * *

This was so unlike me. Usually it was everyone else who was too intimidated to meet *my* eyes. But something distinctly masculine in me felt like dominating her.

"Look at me—please. I want to see your eyes." Defiantly I met his gaze, but masked my thoughts.

* * *

I almost thought I saw some fear and some…but no, that had to be my overactive imagination…

My eyes burned into hers until I was reminded of the Oracle. They had very different eyes. Totally different in shape, size and color, yet there was something similar in the expression, if only that they were both so hard to read.

A strange emotion came over me as I looked at her, unlike any I'd ever had before. I was in awe of her. Her beauty, her power, the way she moved—like liquid on land, confident and flowing, graceful and fast.

"I'm done bandaging you now, Eliju."

"Already?" I asked, sorry to see her go, despite myself.

"I'll be back tomorrow to bring you fresh bandages."

"Come back during the day next time so I can really see you."

"I take orders from no one, Eliju."

"It wasn't an order, it was a request."

"We'll see."

The next afternoon, Darlillyth brought a bowl of hot stew with tender beef and celery, carrots, tomatoes, and onions, along with a crust of thick white bread on the side. Donning a beautiful, black lace gown, v-shaped with silk overlaying the bodice, her body was the most dramatic hourglass I'd ever seen.

Trying to act nonchalant, I said with a wry smile, "I was afraid you'd come in the middle of the night again."

"You need your sleep to heal," she said. I felt my smile widen. I knew she had to say that—so I wouldn't believe she'd done what I wanted her to do. Reddening for an instant at my smile, the moment passed as quickly as it had come, and I wasn't even sure it had happened at all.

I tried to be strong, but I winced as she took off my shirt.

Darlillyth said nothing as she poured the warm liquid over my cuts and bruises and broken rib.

Sitting on the edge of the bed when she bandaged my face and leaning toward me...I found myself staring at her ample chest, until a stray strand of her lanky hair fell across my nose. Closing my eyes, I inhaled the heady fragrance...her hair smelled like sandalwood and smoky musk with a hint of jasmine.

I was overcome with the desire to taste her skin, and as her hand neared my nose, I inhaled that too. The air around her skin smelled like hyacinths.

"Are you quite alright?"

* * *

"Yes," he answered quickly, too quickly, as his eyes fluttered open. I smirked to myself. Did the boy think I'd been born yesterday?

But when I looked into his eyes, I felt again that strange sensation I'd had the night before.

I stood and backed away.

"What is it about my eyes that has you so frightened?"

"I'm not afraid, Eliju." But his eyes were so honest. They shone with something pure, that made me remember...

"Are you sure? My eyes seem to make you anxious and I've always been told I have very unique eyes. They can change colors to blue or green. What color are they with you?"

"Both green and blue."

"Really? They're usually one color or the other. What don't you like about them?"

"They burn, with a strange fire..."

"As do yours."

"Not in the same way. Yours are so warm...red-hot, though the color is...it reminds me of the sea in Caledonia where I spent my childhood. When I was a child it was my favorite color."

"What's your favorite color now?"

I hesitated. "Indigo." Indigo for the skies in the Isle of Skye. Because the deep green forests and green grass of Caledonia, and the haunting blue-green highlands, and the tempestuous blue-green sea had failed me. I did not want to look down and remember. So, I looked up, into the purple skies, which held the future.

"Really? I wonder why..." I didn't answer him, so he continued, "When my eye color was your favorite color we probably were more alike."

What a childish comment to make. "It's frivolous nonsense talking about your eyes and colors, Eliju."

"Fine, then I will talk about yours."

"Mine?"

"They are the darkest black I've ever seen, so black I can't find the pupils. I'll admit they're cool, but I believe beneath your mask is a fire even warmer and deeper than my own."

"Yes, a fire intent on vengeance."

"But something else too."

"There's nothing else.

"I can see there's something you desire more than power and the control it gives you."

Could he possibly see into me as he was saying he did? I didn't want anyone to see into me. I did not want anyone to know me.

"No, there's nothing else, nothing I want more. You're wrong. Be quiet now. I'm trying to change your bandages, Eliju."

"Love."

I was overtaken with fury. Making an angry, guttural sound, I snarled at him, "There's no such thing as love, Eliju. You reveal your immaturity when you say things like that."

"But I love Wandering Wolfe and—" his eyes clouded over as he looked away.

"Varawynn?" There was a shrillness in my voice that unnerved me. Why was I so overcome with anger when I thought about him…loving her?

"How do you know about her?" he asked me, his feelings written plainly all over his open, expressive face.

"I know all about your *love* for her." Now it was his turn to avoid my eyes. Incensed, I haughtily turned to go.

"Wait!" he called after me. But I was already gone, the job of redressing his wounds only half-done.

~ *** ~

I wasn't sure I would see her the next day, but she came. Wearing a beautiful sapphire-blue dress made of the finest silk, she was no less then dazzling. We were both silent as she took off my shirt. Roughly, she removed my bandages. I knew she was still angry with me.

"I love her very much. She says we're Twin Souls."

"Who?" Darlillyth asked.

"Varawynn."

"Do you love her enough to marry her?"

Fidgeting uncomfortably, I remembered the obscured dark hair of the woman who stood beside me in the seventh mirror, in the Crystal Castle foretelling my future, as she pressed the ointment into a particularly tender cut, particularly hard.

"Ouch!" I exclaimed, a note of reproach in my voice. *Varawynn would never have done that.*

Darlillyth smiled viciously, as if she'd overheard the thought. "Answer me," she demanded menacingly.

"I'm not sure," I answered honestly.

Darlillyth's hands became gentler as they reached for my face, such a carved angel's hand, with long, slim fingers, warm olive though she rarely ventured out of the cold stone walls of the castle, where heavy drapes obscured the sun.

Varawynn's hands were the same shape, but were paler. But their hair was the exact same shade of black, with the exact same fine, rich texture, the exact same thickness. Though Varawynn's hair was curly, and Darlillyth's hair framed her face in long waves. Something in Darlillyth reminded me of Varawynn, though I couldn't fathom why, or how...

Why does the tenderness in her fingers remind me of my mother's last kiss goodbye? Why does looking at her make me feel so different about everything and everyone? What do these feelings mean? Maybe she wasn't truly evil...maybe she could be my teacher, maybe...

NO! I can't let her break my will, I can't give in to her manipulations, or all we could ever accomplish would be lost, all the Shaman's work would be for nothing.

But her hair is so fine, so dark, so soft, and so beautiful...

"What're you doing, Eliju?" Darlillyth asked, in muted tones, as I dropped the strands of her hair.

"I'm sorry. I don't know what came over me." I was red-faced and shocked at myself.

Sitting down in the chair beside me, she asked abruptly, "Have you thought more about my becoming your teacher?"

"Yes."

"And?"

"And the answer is still, and always will be...no."

* * *

I wouldn't give up so easily. "Eliju, can't you see what a wonderful team we'd make? You have it in you to be as physically powerful as my bro–as Mardavian, and as spiritually powerful as *me*. Few are capable of such power..."

"Wandering Wolfe taught me to be all that I am, and there's much more he has to teach me."

"You're very loyal. But sometimes being loyal isn't wise."

"But why? It could never be unwise to be faithful to Wandering Wolfe!"

"He'll let you down, wind up disappointing you—mark my words."

Eliju was furious. "You're free to speak about disappointment regarding Shadow Rain, but never, NEVER say anything against Wandering Wolfe!"

"And Varawynn?"

"Nor her."

"They will disappoint you, Eliju." My heart felt as cold as ice. He should know the truth. *The ones we love disappoint us the most.*

"You've finished. Could you leave now?" Turning his back, many moments passed until he felt sorry for his callous dismissal. Eliju had never been able to hold a grudge for long, unfortunately I held the edge on grudges, and by the time he'd turned back to me, I'd gone, leaving as silently as I'd come. Though there was not a moment that he was not being watched.

~ ~ ~

March, from the castle of a major stronghold of King Mardavian in Ireland—

Wandering Wolfe had been completely alone for three months. In that time, he'd received food and water only every few days. Due to the lack of company and sustenance, and the inability to sleep in the cold and harsh conditions, he'd started losing his mind. He'd been talking to his staff, the walls, and even the floor, for days.

By this time, even King Mardavian would've been welcome company. He wondered how Eliju had survived such isolation as a small child and young man. He'd discovered a newfound respect for Eliju and his unique brand of strength.

This was the state he was in when I came to his dungeon. The guard unlocked the heavy door, and out of courtesy, I knocked. Emerging from his reverie, he called out eagerly, "Who's there?" I didn't answer right away. "I said who's there?" he called out again.

"Someone with whom you haven't seen in many years."

"Come in, if you will," said Wandering Wolfe, getting back to his distinguished, dignified self in a hurry.

"I thank you, I shall," I answered him cordially.

As the door opened, I was surprised how nervous I felt. I was surprised to feel anything at all.

* * *

When I saw her, I couldn't believe my own eyes. It looked as if she hadn't aged a day since I'd last seen her! How was it she looked the same? How was it any of us were still alive after all this time?

That feeling came over me again, that fear. I knew of course, ancient black magic and blood coursed through the veins of Mardavian and Darlillyth, but what about me, why did I still live? What magic lied unknown and dormant within my own ancestry? She was still dark and beautiful in the strangest of ways, more so even. "Darlillyth..."

"Here," she said, handing me a plate of heaping hot food. "I've brought you some dinner."

"Then there's good in you yet, but I can't believe you're really here, that we're together, when I thought you were dead all this time."

"Yes, it must have been quite a shock for you when my brother told you I was still alive. But eat up now, while I talk."

Taking the food, she handed me, I marveled, "Just a few months ago I thought you were dead. Now here you are standing before me, as if not a day had passed since the last time, we were together."

"You've weathered the years well yourself I see."

"Yes, we're both ageless, though I couldn't begin to explain why. For my part, I'm relieved the Prophecy is at last coming to pass."

"That's why I'm here. I've come to speak with you about your student, Eliju."

"Oh?" I asked, taking a large bite of roast beef. I was trying to eat politely, but was ravenous after months of starvation.

"What is the chosen boy like, Wandering Wolfe? I'm curious."

"That's difficult to put into words. Why do you want to know?"

"I don't remember you ever being at a loss for words,"

Darlillyth chuckled. "What is it that means the most to him, Wandering Wolfe?"

"Not a thing—people mean the most to him."

"People? Who?"

"Certain people..."

"But where is the darkness in him?"

"I don't know what you mean, mistress," I said, calling her by the title of my boyhood.

"I haven't heard that title from your lips in many years. Don't flatter yourself you'll be able to bend my will to yours, Wandering Wolfe. I have my own agenda."

"So, I see."

"I am behind this...all of this."

"I already guessed that."

"Mardavian is nothing without me; surely you of all people must realize that, old friend."

"I do realize that now. But we were never friends, Darlillyth."

"No, we weren't, were we? We were more..."

"You could have been my wife. We should have been married."

"Married," Darlillyth snorted. "I would never marry unless it were to further my power and ultimate agenda. Now, back to the Chosen One...allow me to make my question clearer, what are his weaknesses?"

"As if I would tell you! Why should I confess to you the boy's weakness? Why don't you let me in on what *you're* planning?"

"As if I would tell you!" Darlillyth's voice cruelly imitated my words. "We're no longer lovers, Wandering Wolfe. I have no obligation to you—not then and not now."

"You're only speaking this way because of the horrors your family inflicted on you. The girl I knew would never have used others for her own gain. Why should you side with Mardavian—one of the men who so hurt you?"

"It's not as if you'd been around or tried to protect me when they—"

"I didn't even know you were still alive! And I did try to protect you—"

"But you failed."

"Mardavian said it was a very powerful sorcerer who killed your parents. I was afraid to ask if he meant you."

"Oh, Wandering Wolfe, you have no idea what I'm capable of.

I've done far worse things in my life than my family has."

"How can you say that? They brutally raped you! They killed…" I stopped myself before I went too far. She flinched. "So… you still think of her?"

"She's dead, long dead. And I was better off without her. *We* were better off without her."

"You don't mean that!"

"Oh, don't I?" Her bitterness was like a cobra inside her own heart, striking at me, and slowly poisoning herself to death.

"I believe there's still some good in you," I insisted.

"What you believe is merely what you want to believe. It is an illusion founded by your own desires. All the good in me that once was has been destroyed long ago, and I'm better off without it. I was never the girl you imagined, or wanted me to be."

"Then why have you brought me food? Why have you come to see me at all?"

"I told you! I want information!" she shouted angrily, yanking the empty bowl from my hands and throwing it across the room, its loud, clattering noises clanking down the length of the stone floor in the dungeon.

Looking at her intently I asked, "Is it information, or is there a part of you that missed the love we once shared?"

This time, her vixen's laugh was cruel and lasted for several moments. "Wandering Wolfe, I never *truly* loved you to begin with. To be honest, I've never truly loved anyone at all."

I was stunned. "You don't mean that. You agreed to marry me, Darlillyth."

"I was never going to marry you, you foolish old man. I was only using you to glean the bits and pieces of the Prophecy you knew."

"That's a lie."

"Is it? We're talking in circles. You haven't changed much I see. I didn't come here to discuss our past. I don't think about our relationship. I don't care that it came to an end. If I cared, wouldn't I have let you know I was alive at some point in these past centuries? I came here only to discuss the Chosen One."

"You've grown bitter and rough with age, Darlillyth. Even if you look as perfectly ageless and beautiful as you ever did."

"And you've grown senile and befuddling, despite your external muscles and clear eyes! You still speak in riddles, and I haven't the time, or patience for riddles! Isn't it enough the Prophecy is a riddle? I was always best at deciphering the riddles, so stop wasting my time, and speak to me directly."

"Why do you think I'd help you break Eliju?"

"Because I can make your stay in this dungeon very difficult for you, Wandering Wolfe. I can make the past few months of starvation seem like life in the Garden of Eden."

"What happened to you, Darlillyth?"

"That's not your concern. Now answer my questions. Have you been teaching Eliju magic?"

I did some quick thinking. My head was still spacey from months of starvation and lack of proper sleep and air, but I wouldn't let her get the best of me. Still, she wasn't going to leave until I gave her something. She wanted information. Then information she would get. "Yes, of course I have."

"Does he have a strong suit?"

"He's wonderful at controlling the elements, but absolutely horrible wielding weapons. Shadow Rain is just terrible at elemental work, on the other hand."

"What about the boy Jonlin? What is he good at?"

"Generally speaking, Jonlin can do most everything well. He's our jack-of-all-trades. Shadow Rain is particularly good at shape-shifting and deriving the future in astrology and astronomy."

"Ah, a girl after my own heart!" said Darlillyth with a sugary sweet smile, oozing in insincerity and discontent.

I smiled slyly under my beard. "Yes, you love astrology too, don't you? And you've always been good at all types of magic, haven't you?"

Ignoring the question, she asked, "And what about the Oracle?"

"Ileona, of course, is our weapon master. Alondria is a natural crystal ball worker. I only wish one of us were a healer."

"And Varawynn?" Something greedy and hateful in her eyes gave me pause to measure my words carefully. "Varawynn…works with runes."

"Is that all?"

"No, she knows the Elven and Dwarven languages, and is a natural tracker."

"Thank you, Wandering Wolfe. It's been…interesting seeing you again."

"I've thought of you so often. Have you really never thought about me, in all this time?"

"It didn't take you long to become engaged to someone else, now did it, Wandering Wolfe?"

"Your brother took care of her though, didn't he? He killed my fiancée, and most of the tribe that raised me, in one fell swoop!"

"I'm sorry, Wandering Wolfe," said Darlillyth seriously. "My brother has killed many innocent people. But it is hard to remember with fondness a man who exhibits such a great display of disloyalty."

"I thought you were dead, and until now, I have continued to love you. Snow Lily was a marriage arranged by her father and the chief who raised me. It was the chief's way of fully integrating me into the tribe. But it was always you I loved. And it was you I've missed all this time." I could see my words had affected her.

She was very close now, and I stole a moment to inhale her fragrance. After all these years, it still made me falter. Her heady combination of smoky musk and sandalwood, with a hint of something sweet, made my heart beat faster and my palms sweat. No one smelled like that. No one looked like her...

There was something about her that drew men. Something powerful and magnetic, irresistible. I felt a mad desire to kiss her.

"I have to go now, Wandering Wolfe, but I'll be sure you're given meals regularly now."

"Thank you for coming, Darlillyth," I said gruffly. "I'm glad to know you're alive."

* * *

I said nothing more as I turned the knob and left him, but not the memories, behind. He looked different, aged, but still the same. I'd tried to let go of the memories. I'd tried to forget all the time we'd spent together, learning from Vorseth.

But I remembered the times he'd shown me compassion for what my father and brother were doing to hurt me. He hadn't stopped it, but he had shown me compassion. I remembered now that when my father beat me that day, when he'd discovered us...that Wandering Wolfe *had* tried to stop him...but I put that out of my mind. Feelings would never mean as much to me as power, and the fulfillment of the Prophecy.

After I'd left my brother's castle, I smiled to myself, knowing I'd gotten the better of him. Of course, I knew everything he'd told me were lies—but I would work hard to decipher the real truths.

* * *

I smiled to myself as she left me. I hadn't trusted her in one moment of our conversation. Her beauty still moved me, but I'd finally learned to see past her flawless façade.

I'd managed to feed her lies about the people in the troop, and was pleased that despite the weeks of starvation—no doubt in preparation of this encounter, that even in my weakened state, the shock of her being alive and seeing her in the flesh, and the feelings I still harbored for her—that I hadn't betrayed the people I loved. The false information I'd given her, would only serve to thwart her unsavory agenda, and the Kingdom she shared with Mardavian.

~ *** ~

Darlillyth didn't come to visit me again for over a week. By the ninth day, I was nearly in a panic. When nightfall came, she brought dinner. It was the first meal I'd had since she'd left.

I was relieved to see her. I didn't care about the punishment she'd given me in my happiness over seeing her again. Smiling warmly at her, as she handed me the steaming soup, she wouldn't meet my eyes. So, I spoke my feelings in words.

"I'm sorry."

"You don't owe me an apology."

"Evidently I do. I didn't mean to turn you away. I didn't really want you to go, I was just hurt by what you said."

"You weren't hurt, you were angry. And why wouldn't you want me to go? I'm only the warden in your prison cell after all."

"I *was* hurt, and you're more to me than that."

"What could you possibly mean? You're nothing but a means to an end to *me*."

"Then why are you so gentle when you touch me?" She resembled a frightened doe in the woods, but just for a blink of an eye most would've missed. I knew I had seen it this time.

"If I'm gentle with you it's only because you're special. You are the Chosen One."

"I don't believe you're truly evil."

"Who are you to tell me who and what I am?"

"You're just like me."

"We're nothing alike, Eliju."

"When you're hurt, and when someone sees something inside yourself that you don't want to see, good or bad, you get angry."

"Stop it!"

"Stop what?"

"Stop making assessments about me when you don't even know me."

"But I do know you…Darlillyth."

"How in the world can you claim to know me?"

"Because you've come to me in my dreams for so long now."

"For the past year, yes, but—"

"No, it started before then."

"Occasionally, yes—"

"No, many times. I saw you, sometimes when you weren't looking, when you weren't trying to make me afraid or plant lies in my mind. It's so strange, with everyone but me, you're this strong woman—a force to be reckoned with. But with me, I see your vulnerability. With everyone but you, I feel so stupid and inexperienced. But with you, I'm the one who can do the saving."

"Save me?" she laughed. "Save me from what?"

"Save you from the hurt that's destroyed the best parts of you. I want to save you from yourself."

"*I* don't need to be saved."

"Yes, you do."

* * *

"STOP IT!" I shouted. Damn him for his sentimental words! I would show him who I was. Reaching out my hand so a bolt of lightning went from my finger to his heart, I gave him a shock as powerful as a small heart attack.

It took him several minutes to catch his breath before he could speak again. "That was unnecessarily cruel."

"I AM cruel."

"You're more than your actions."

"You sound like Wandering Wolfe. When did you start pretending to be so wise?"

"I'm only like this with you."

"You don't understand me, Eliju, and you never will. But I understand you. And you, like me, will choose the darkness in the end, and we will rule together."

"No, I *will never* choose evil."

I hated his stubbornness. I hated his loyalty to Wandering Wolfe.

"But you have rage inside you, just like I do. Hatred and bitterness for the parents who abandoned you. Bitterness will eventually eat away all the good in you. I would know."

"No, it won't. I'm learning to control my emotions, and eventually I'll learn to forgive them, so the bitterness won't steal my joy...*you* will teach me that."

"How can I teach you something I don't believe in myself?" He reached out his hand to take my hand into his. This time I was the one who felt the electric shock.

"You may be the Chosen King of all, but I was chosen too, Eliju."

"Yes. Your destiny is as important as mine. We're eternally linked. Two opposing pieces in a puzzle that together make the puzzle whole."

"No." I stood up. I had to get away from him. I walked in slow, seamless movements to the window. Staring out into the mountains, into the forest, I felt an odd presence that disturbed my peace of mind. Overcome by that familiar ache—the old loss which occasionally still caused my heart to ache. I hadn't felt it in so long...in eons.

Why did this foolish, rash young boy make me feel that wretched pain and longing once more? Why did this stubborn, intrepid boy make me remember all the things I'd worked so hard to forget? He had a way of making me feel, making me remember, even more than my time with Wandering Wolfe back in Ireland had.

"I do understand you," he said again. *Better than you understand yourself,* he thought in his mind. But I, *I* who could read minds was furious with his thoughts, so as I yanked off his shirt, pounding my hand ruthlessly into his cuts.

His silent scream made me recoil backwards.

"You read minds then, don't you? You can hear me when I'm not saying anything."

"Yes..."

"Then hear this..." Opening his mind, he let me hear all that was in his heart.

* * *

Smiling knowingly, cruelly, she pressed her cold, olive finger on my chest, pressing down until the pressure reached my heart. My heart constricted. I couldn't breathe. "What are you doing?"

"I'm making you *feel* your words more deeply." My heart was being so constricted that I was afraid I was going to have a heart attack.

"My thoughts aren't supposed to give me pain."

"But your thoughts of Varawynn give you pain. And your thoughts of me give you pain too. Now still your thoughts and feelings and let me dress your wounds."

"Darlillyth, I... how?"

"Shhh," she whispered. "You're just like all the others."

"I thought you said I was special?"

"You are special because of who you are; your place in the Prophecy."

"I don't think anyone else ever felt about you the way I do."

"All you feel is an illusion, but illusions will suffice for reality; if you really trust what you feel, you'll let me lead you into the darkness. Perhaps you were right. Perhaps we aren't so different after all, in the final analysis. What about the vengeance you seek? What about the justice against your parents?"

I knew her clever mind would eventually best everyone she argued with. But the best arguments didn't necessarily guarantee a victory. A gentle word can bend an iron-clad will. Only the weak man strong in love, overcomes the strong and brilliant woman full of hate.

"I'll never follow the darkness. Don't you understand?"

* * *

Looking deep into his steady, loyal blue-green eyes, I finally recognized that his convictions were stronger than my will.

"You want me to join you Darlillyth, but I have this feeling you're meant to join me..." he whispered.

Something in him had a way of piercing my masks, but I was just as stubborn and strong-willed as he was. "If you refuse to follow me, perhaps another will," I whispered, too quietly for him to hear.

He looked at me with a tenderness that permeated the air around us. I knew I had the power to make his heart ache in a unique way. I was the master of manipulation and I wouldn't let him, I would let *no one* deter me from the path I'd chosen so long ago.

Not even Wandering Wolfe's compassion. Not even Eliju's...love.

* * *

Her eyes were the last puzzle piece of my visions. In that moment, when she'd relented to my will, when I'd gained the small victory over her no one else had been able to manage for centuries, a flash of insight burned into my third eye.

Popping open like the breaking of a dam, a thousand *future* memories flooded my perceptions, as I recognized now, without the shadow of a doubt that *she* was the one who was standing by my side in the seventh mirror in the Crystal Castle.

It was *her* eyes, *her* hair, *her* face, *her* body, in the mirror that had shown me my future. Queen Darlillyth was destined to become my wife.

She was the woman I'd dreamt of my whole life. I thought at first it could've been Varawynn, but I knew now that it had been Darlillyth all along.

I wanted to touch her like a man touches a woman; I wanted to feel her naked skin against my own. I wanted to make love to her, make her feel the pain I felt every time she walked out of the room. Make her long for me, the way I'd longed for her before I ever even knew her name.

Was this even possible? Could a person really fall in love so fast? And was it too soon if I'd been seeing her in visions and dreams my whole life?

She looked the same as the woman in my dreams, but somehow, seeing her in the flesh made the aching and longing in me *so much stronger.* Some people, *she,* claimed she did not believe in love, did not believe any man on earth could ever truly love her. But I wanted to believe that she could love me back.

* * *

The truth was I'd seen him before too, seen the blue-green eyes, the careless handsomeness of his brown hair, the honest, expressive face...since *I* was a girl, and long before the gods had breathed his flesh to life.

But it wasn't possible for someone like me to feel love. I would fight it, deny it, hide it, bury it and ultimately kill it—the same way I used my will to bend other's will——the same way I destroyed what other people loved——I would turn that vengeance upon myself before I ever surrendered to it, and the inevitable vulnerability which was its consequence...

It was a trap, it was all a trap, and he was too blind to see it. He was ruled by his heart, and everything he did was clouded by his feelings. I was ruled by my mind, and all I felt was clouded by cool, detached logic. I would never let passion rule me, overtake me, and all he was—his very essence—was passion. I was like a black panther and he, a wild stallion. Like the green, earthy forest and the ocean.

He believed he could change me—that he could turn me, that he would find whatever good was left in me, and nurture it to make it grow. I could feel it. I could feel his desires. He believed in me the same way he believed in himself, but my will was stronger than any of his feelings.

We were equally strong-willed, but willed in different directions. I, towards evil due to righteous vengeance turned to sin. He, of righteous suffering, driven by nobility and high-minded purpose, towards redemption. Even though I didn't want to, against my will, I respected him for that. And it had been so long since I'd found a man who elicited anything in me other than contempt.

* * *

She'd never learned to overcome fear by surrendering, and thereby transforming a weakness into strength. After what she'd been through, she had no strength to surrender to anything or anyone. Security for her was to be in control. But somehow, understanding this, I loved her even more for her weakness.

I wouldn't, couldn't believe she was evil at her core. I wouldn't give up on her because giving up on her would be like giving up on myself, or worse, like giving up my faith.

For by the faith of a mustard seed, you can move mountains. Faith is hope in things unseen. I'd never seen any real goodness in her. But that didn't make my faith in her goodness any less. My faith in her over the months that passed grew every day, until it became as majestic as a mountain, so that in my love for her, I believed I had the power to move the world...

As the time passed, slowly my wounds healed. She didn't want it to, but my gentleness towards her made her more tender to me. Every move she made seduced me—making me fall even more in love with her.

I had loved Varawynn, but I'd never loved like this. It was the kind of love that would change me into the man I was born to become. In time, her words and actions made me believe she loved me too. But alas, it was only the trick of a sorceress, to play into the plot destined to define my future.

One night as I lay in bed, tossing and turning, thinking only of my want—my incessant need to have Darlillyth body and soul, I fell into a dream more real than reality. Every night was like this one, every night the need grew worse, but this night was different, this night she was there in a long lace gown, right there beside me, on the black satin sheets.

"Darlillyth, is it really you? Have you finally come to me?"

"Yes, Eliju, yes," she murmured, kissing me with voluptuous movements, starting softly and continuing with erotic expertise that left me gasping for more. It was a kiss unlike anything I could have imagined. Better than my greatest fantasy, it was a kiss between a man and a woman, not a boy and a girl. But there was something grainy and fine on her tongue, with that faint sweetness that reminded me of the night we were taken captive by King Mardavian.

The kiss empowered me with masculine force and passion, and yet weakened me at the same time. I found her intoxicating, irresistible; her heady smell, her soft skin. Cupping her beautiful face in my left hand, twisting her dark tresses round and round my fingers, it was hard not to hurt her with the fierceness of my desires. The feel of her hair was more dreamlike, for how could hair be as light, as fine as silk, soft as the ethereal airy caress of velvety rose petals?

"Stand up," she commanded me. Two figures stood obscured in the doorway. In a haze, I stood with Darlillyth. Words and chants were spoken, which in my foggy dream-state, I couldn't fully grasp.

Someone addressed a question to me, but I couldn't comprehend it. Someone else nudged me. As if by instinct alone, I murmured, "Yes, yes…" though I was unaware of what I'd just agreed to. The two tall figures left the room, and Darlillyth pulled me back towards the bed.

I explored her body with my hands, in-between the black satin sheets, and despite the will of her mind, I felt her responding in a way I wanted to believe she hadn't with anyone else... My touch...electrified her... Her touch...it was magical, and as our bodies, hearts, and souls fused into One body, heart and soul, I knew I'd never been more alive, more in chains, or freer than in this moment.

* * *

It was the moment of twilight, when the day and the night become One. It was, perhaps, a defining moment in both our lives, not *the* defining moment perhaps, for this was not the end, it was not yet the time for Eliju to choose between good and evil, but an evil came out of our passion that night.

Darkness comes after twilight. It was darkness that came out of our twilight, for me at least. But for him, for Eliju, it was the dawn—the beginning of becoming a man worthy to be called the Chosen, a man worthy to be crowned our King…

~ *** ~

I brought thee three females a hearty stew wif lots er meat in it, waiting until they'd finished eating to show 'em thee prize I'd gotten: a strand of black hairs from me master's head! They'd never know the trouble it'd been on me to get it.

"This is excellent. I'll perform the ceremony right away!" the woman in charge said. As I turned to go and finish thee rest of my duties for thee night, she stopped me.

"I need you with me to perform the ritual. I will need four blue candles and a blue chalice filled with water."

It took me another hour to get thee additional items, and for the head lady to set-up. I was worried they'd know I'd been gone a long time from me chores. I had so many of 'em I often didn't get to sleep. With all the time this was takin', I worried I wouldn't get 'em done at all today.

Suddenly I was afearful. What if this magic lady did bring back me memories? What would I do then? Go back to thee chores?

* * *

May, from King Mardavian's Castle in Ireland—

Laying the four candles around the chalice in the center with careful attention to the symmetry of the spacing between the objects, Ileona held King Mardavian's hair over the water and chanted:

"You have stolen this servant's memory
Of all that he once was,
You have taken him away from the truth
Of the ones he's dearly loved.

Now with this piece of you we hold,
We remove your power from this man.
We drop this piece of hair into a cleansing consecration,
Of which you cannot find a way of penetration.

His power is no longer bound

To the evil King of these many lands,
He will no longer be your slave,
And he will remember his true name.

We bind your power with all our might,
To the place of the dying night,
Where the shadows meet the light,
And the wrong you've done is made right."

Ileona dropped the strand of King Mardavian's hair into the chalice of water. Blue flames burst forth from the water's shallow surface. Shadow Rain watched the ritual, awestruck. But I felt a deep foreboding pass over my spirit, as the flames were fanned into a fire.

The flames took on a liquid form, spreading over the wet stones and the castle's walls, until the whole dungeon burst into flames. Heat and smoke filled the room fast. The fire flirted with the bars on the window, until it lunged back at us, as a predator lunges, to overcome its prey.

How were we going to get out of here? Was this a part of Ileona's plan all along? Or had the plan gone wrong?

* * *

As the walls caught fire, I felt the transformation back into my true self begin to wash over me. The three ladies coughed and hacked, as I rushed to open the door to let them out.

"Are you taking us to another dungeon?" Shadow Rain asked me, still gagging.

"Just go," I urged her, "You've helped me, so now I'm helping you."

"But what about Jonlin and Wandering Wolfe and Alondria and Eliju?"

"I'll get them out of here, just *go!*"

"But–"

Cutting off her next words, I grabbed Varawynn and Shadow Rain by their wrists and pulled them away from the burning cell, dragging them out into the light of freedom. Ileona came rushing after us, having paused for a moment in the echo of my altered voice.

~ *** ~

May, from Queen Darlillyth's Castle in Caledonia—

After my exceedingly vivid dream of our night of passion together, I fell into a deep and blissful sleep, and when I awoke, to my surprise, and I am ashamed to say, disappointment, I was outside. The castle was at a distance, and my lost comrades were asleep at my side! How had she moved me without waking me up?

I heard Rain stir, just as I realized there was something in my pocket. Putting my hand into my pocket, I felt the familiar dryness of parchment paper. Could it be a letter from Darlillyth?

"How did *you* get here?" Rain asked, in surprise. "All this time we never even knew where you were, Eliju."

"I'm not sure how I got here. How did *you* get here?"

"There was a fire in the dungeons, and one of the servants let all of us go."

I saw Alondria, Jonlin, Ileona, Rain, Wandering Wolfe, but... "Where's Varawynn? We can't leave without her." I was worried. Why was everyone there except Varawynn?

"Of course, we can't go yet," answered Wandering Wolfe, sighing. "So, part of the legend has come to pass."

"What part? What're you saying?" I shouted at him, not intending to yell, but I was panicking as I remembered Shadow Rain's nightmare about Darlillyth, who told her in a dream that one of us was going to die.

"I know where she is," said Wandering Wolfe.

"So, she's not dead?"

"No, but she may well be in a state worse than death."

"What? Why?"

"I didn't understand that part of the legend fully until just this instant."

"*Well*, explain it to *us* then!" demanded Shadow Rain, who had come to view Varawynn as a friend, and was genuinely concerned.

"I'm afraid something terrible has happened to our Varawynn."

"But *what, what happened?*" Concern creased Ileona's forehead too. "Mardavian has, has...hurt her," Wandering Wolfe answered gravelly.

"How?" Shadow Rain demanded.

I felt realization dawning on me. "No..."

~ *** ~

Chapter Twenty-Two
Healed by Song and Sea

May, in the wild forests of Ireland, beyond King Mardavian's Castle—

Varawynn was just finding her way out of the dungeon and the castle, when she stumbled over a large rock. It only took a moment, before she was separated from Ileona, Shadow Rain, and the servant. She had barely looked up before they were several paces away. Varawynn tried to call after them, but between the burning castle, and the shouting townsfolk and soldiers trying to put out the flames, her voice was lost.

Then she heard a voice say her name in the darkness. "Varawynn, I know where you are. Your Oracle's feeble spell has bound you to me."

"Who are you?"

"I'm your first, but I won't be your last."

"My first what?"

Fear was suffocating Varawynn, as she ran blindly away from the sound of the voice, as best as her lame leg would allow. The sound of horse hooves pounded toward her. Her heart raced like a frightened rabbit. Panicked and unthinking, she ran blindly, not seeing or caring where she was headed. Her only concern was to get away.

Stumbling on the stone-strewn path, she managed to continue running through sheer will. In her haste, she dropped her cane, fumbling clumsily in the night and the unfamiliar landscape. The sound of the horse was getting closer now, and she was limping away faster and faster, when her useless leg got caught on a dead tree branch, and she fell again.

It was only a second later that the man and his horse were upon her. She was overcome with a fear so great, she nearly couldn't see. She sensed the loss of her future self she was trying to protect.

"What do you want with me?"

"You'll know that in the next moment, my dear."

The Celtic Priestess, who bore the mark of the black raven, fell beneath the Highland King, as had happened in the same place in another time. And he broke her from the inside out, so that she would never be the same. Her story was in the Prophecy, and what he did to her, had already been written…

"Prophecy of the Yew Trees"

Underneath a tree with arms far-spread,
Lies a fallen girl with a crown upon her head.
Her crooked leg with a raven mark
Saw the violation of a virgin's heart,
As once again he took the innocence away
Of a young girl who was born the same.

He took her limp body, defiled and aged,
To the holy yew trees of the Celtic race.
Ironic he took her to a place that would heal—
Where the wounds he inflicted, the earth could feel.
Bless that sacred cathedral, above those sacred trees—
Where two halves of a whole were together made free.

The scene was played out in the sorceress's head-
Blood on the heather, sharp thorns for a bed.
It was too late to stop it, too late to go back,
Too late to undo the future of the past.
Yet what is yet to be, is sometimes meant to be,
For out of suffering, the most extraordinary of souls

Are refined by the fires of the tests and trials of Destiny.
This violation was the inevitable Fate of the futures tied
To the one man who saw past their deception and lies:
The Chosen One with the consecrated dream—
To unite all countries, creatures, and creeds—
By becoming their leader, their servant, their king.

~ *** ~

Almost six months had passed since we'd been taken prisoner. It took six months for us to escape and find each other again. Through the "Prophecy of the Yew Trees," I knew where to find her. Varawynn's body was sprawled at the foot of the Celtic yews, whose entwined branches had been immortalized in Celtic folklore. Her face was buried in tears, in the roots of those ancient entwined yew trees of Deirdre and Naoise.

For although those two star-crossed lovers could not be together in life; in death they were forever united. The two yew trees that represented their two hearts, had grown together, until even their roots were entwined. The High King had separated their graves, but their souls had become the yews whose branches and roots had joined the lovers together in eternity.

~ *** ~

I loved her. The way her small, heart-shaped face curved so delicately onto her long, swan's neck. The way her wild tangle of dark curls framed her face. Almond-emerald eyes, full of life. The way she could make me laugh, even in the worst of circumstances.

We had to get away. We had to run. It was the only option. When I looked at her, my chest swelled with possessive pride. I longed to protect her, her beauty, her untamed spirit, her magical soul, her generous heart, which I had loved before, throughout the lifetimes.

I took her to another realm, to the mountains in Caledonia, where we lay together in long nights, overflowing into ever longer days of love-making and ecstasy. We lived on an island of love, where the only thing that existed was us, and the only thing that mattered, was our passion.

I knew it was unlikely we could live forever this way. But I hoped that we would always be two steps before the High King's hound dogs, or that I could kill the High King and take his place.

* * *

I loved him. From the first moment of our meeting on that fateful Winter Day, when a raven landed to feast upon a fallen rabbit in the snow. These were the three most sacred colors to my people— black for the raven, red for blood, and white for the pure, clean snow.

I said to my foster father, "Fair would be the man upon whom these three colors should fall: his hair like the raven, his cheek like blood, and his body like the snow."

My father told me that a man such as this did exist, and that his name was Naoise. We met, and it was an instant, soul mate recognition. There was no doubt that I had loved him before. I felt as if I had been waiting my whole life to find him, and that when I did, my life had at last begun.

I cared not about the cruel High King's feelings. I only wanted to run away with Naoise, run far away, where he couldn't get to us…into the remote Highlands of Caledonia, into the deep green, getting lost in the sweet, wet rain storms, lost in the pools of his loving jade eyes, and raven hair.

* * *

I could not live without her. I could not live an eternity in death without her either. I could not live, and die, without love. She was my love, my only love. She was my everything. The very air I breathed.

She was my bone and my marrow. She was my missing rib. She was my other half, my better half. I was useless without her. It was not good for man to be alone. Without her, I would always be alone. There would be no replacing her.

The High King could take my body, but he could never take my heart and soul, that beat in time with hers. He could not take away the nights and days we'd spent in bed, entwined within one another, in perfect love and bliss.

I'd rather fight with her, with that fierce Celtic temper of hers which often resorted into thrown cups and shattered glass, than make love to any other girl. She was my North Star, guiding me always in the right direction. I was dependent upon her touch…always reaching out for her. I could not imagine a day in Time without her body and spirit next to mine.

And so, I prayed, as I was slain down to nothing, down to death by the jealous High King, who could not live with the one he so coveted, loving me. I prayed to the gods that my dearest love, Deirdre, would find a way back to me, so that we could remain in each other's arms, linked, and entwined by our love for all eternity. I prayed for the gods to make a way for us, to forge a way by magic, for us to be together forever.

~ *** ~

How I suffered when Naoise was killed. He and his brothers were beheaded in front of me. I never smiled again. I was taken back to the High King's castle in Ireland with my hands tied—not much more than a slave to his violent whims. I was pining away, living in a prison behind a veil of silence and grief.

I wept myself to sleep every night. My dreams were always full of Naoise, and so I woke up crying. The days were spent in more silence. A year passed like this. Until at last, I could take it no more.

I threw myself into a chariot, and in the instant before death, before my head struck the rock and there was no more pain, I prayed to the gods, to bring me back to my true love's embrace…where we could share forever…

As I died, I had a vision of a raven shot by an arrow, lying fallen on the white snow, drops of red blood next to the broken body. I saw Naoise, black raven hair, red cheek, and body like the snow. I closed my eyes and felt my spirit lift.

~ *** ~

Naoise and Deirdre were granted their request. Their bodies were buried next to each other. Their bodies were overcome by magic on a Strawberry Moon night long ago. Their bodies hardened into bark that was never chipped by the rain and the snow and the storms, never struck by lightning, or able to be cut down by the envious High King. They became two yew trees, entwined around each other, in an eternal embrace.

Not far from what is now the Church of Armagh in Ireland, near the borders of Caledonia, lay the resting place of the two star-crossed lovers, Dierdre and Naoise…for as long as the earth meets beneath the endless sky. And in the roots of the Yew Trees of Naoise and Dierdre, hundreds of years later, lay Varawynn, who bore the black raven mark, broken in white body and soul, marred by her own blood, by another High King, in another Time…

~ *** ~

In the struggle, King Mardavian used me to strike the Priestess Varawynn. Though she was slender, and weaker in body than most, with her limp leg, she had fought the King valiantly.

But in the end, he used me, a small grey rock, to hit her until she was unconscious. Her blood spilled on the ground around us. A little of bit of her blood dried on my hard form.

I had been made witness to many battles, and much pain. I knew mankind to be an angry, violent race. I had found comfort in the love of the Yew Trees of Dierdre and Naoise, and their love that had stood the test of time, and life, and death.

I could only hope that the beautiful girl, Varawynn, would also find some comfort in their love, and that upon the earth that had been made witness to her violation, we would do what all nature was created for—to give healing, inspiration, and hope to all mankind.

* * *

We saw the High King attack the beautiful young girl, Varawynn, whose heart and soul belonged to the Chosen One, Eliju. But we knew that Eliju's heart and soul belonged to another. We'd seen the devastation that occurred when love was not returned. For was it not jealousy from the High King that had turned us into the Yew Trees?

Together, we bore the pain of battles, from whose blood filled the earth, and went down into the soil, and into our very roots. We witnessed rape and murder; we witnessed life and death. And we began to understand how humanity's evolution rested not so much in science and new technologies, but in compassion, forgiveness, and love. The kind of love that gave of itself, asking for nothing in return, like an apple tree bearing fruit.

* * *

I lay motionless, awake, but catatonic. I felt dead. Empty. Numb. Wandering Wolfe was the first to reach my side. Gently, he shook me, until I opened my eyes. I stared past them, looked through them.

I was spent. Worn. Gray. All the blood and color had left my cheeks. My face was as white as snow. Many moments passed. No one knew what to say, how to alleviate or approach me in my suffering.

"We should be moving on," Wandering Wolfe murmured softly, to break the heavy silence.

"Can you move your leg?" Eliju asked me, as he tenderly reached out to touch my twisted leg, ever so carefully. I winced. Every touch hurt right now.

Shadow Rain rubbed my back, needing to caress me, wanting to comfort me. She was so caring. She had become a real friend.

"I can gather some herbs that might help," Alondria offered kindly. None of us would have gotten out of the castle, if not for her. Before Wandering Wolfe had a chance to respond, the cry of a bird sounded through the skies—melancholy, holy, and reverent.

It sounded like the bird was singing the melody of the Psalms without words. But I did not bother to look up. I did not care about the beautiful song above me, or the beautiful scenery around me. There was only sorrow now, throughout me.

* * *

All but Varawynn raised our heads to the sky, where a bird of vibrant colors: red, orange, green, purple, and blue flew like lightning through the heavens. The bird was so bright, it seemed to burn, like a streak of fire in the sky, diving towards us.

Flying a little behind her, Varawynn's raven, Raegar, cawed. Alondria's breath caught in wonder, and Eliju gasped. Jonlin had tears in his eyes at the lovely wordless song, and the awesome beauty of the majestic, one-of-a-kind creature. I hoped that it could heal my friend, Varawynn. What had been done to her was unthinkable, and I couldn't bear to see her in so much pain.

"What is that?" Eliju asked Wandering Wolfe. "*Who* is it?"

"It is Celestria, the Bird of Eden, the only one of her kind."

"The Bird of Eden...is it from the Garden of Eden then?" Eliju asked, as Wandering Wolfe nodded.

The sacred bird continued singing its haunting melody, until tears had filled all our eyes. Still Varawynn would not look up. Wordlessly, Jonlin took out his psaltery, a ten-stringed instrument, and perfectly accompanied the bird as she cried. I couldn't play an instrument, and my singing couldn't compare to Jonlin's or Alondria's, so I quietly chanted for Varawynn, a chant for healing and peace, I lifted up like a song, or a prayer.

The bird stopped singing the healing melody of the Psalms, and cried a song of the Oracle Ileona, of the enchantress of the waters. When Varawynn's head still hung low in her state of shame and grief, Celestria's song altered its course, taking on the high lilt of the winsome melodies of the Celts, Varawynn's own people.

Somehow our musical bard knew the melody of even this, of places he'd barely been, and people he'd never known. Many more moments passed, until the bird sang a song Varawynn had composed herself, for a special ritual of healing. Varawynn had never shared this melody with anyone before.

Without pause, Jonlin's fingers knew the notes to play, and the Bird of Eden's wordless song at last moved Varawynn's heart to lift her eyes. The bird was so bright as she flew, it was like a thunderous firelight in the sky. It was as if the sky was caught on fire with her colorful beauty.

Celestria's eyes bore intensely into Varawynn's, as our group witnessed through the Bird of Eden's laser eyes, all that'd happened to the Celtic Priestess. The images exploded between us, as real and tangible, as if King Mardavian stood in front of us...

* * *

Varawynn ran wildly through the forest, using her cane to help her run. Her cane got stuck on a wayward tree branch, and she fell, hurting her leg in the process. Then suddenly he was upon her, grinning, laughing, joyfully relishing the thrill of the chase, and the ecstasy when the chase was over, and he could catch and torture his prey.

Springing off his horse, he went to her and roughly gripped the mane of her curly black hair. "Varawynn, lovely Varawynn. You remind me of my sister."

He moved closer to her face. "Emerald eyes, a feline twist, such beautiful, cat-like eyes. They're so much brighter than hers. Life has been kind to you—until now." Varawynn glared at him savagely, pushing his hands away.

"And what beauty lies beneath these dirty clothes, Varawynn? I see you've lost some weight. But you are still curvaceous for an eighteen-year-old, aren't you my dear?"

"My body, my eyes, they do not belong to you!"

"Then who do they belong to, dearest?"

"I belong to myself alone!"

"To yourself!" he laughed. "Is there no one who you love, no one who loves you?" Varawynn's eyes clouded over, but she refused to answer him.

"Ah, so there is someone!"

"I never said that! Leave me alone. Just leave me ALONE!"

"I'm afraid I cannot do that, Varawynn. I would not waste your beauty and innocence on anyone other than myself. No, my dear, that delectable beauty of yours should be put to good use. I will be your first, just as I was many others first."

Peering at her closely, he added, "And if you cannot give up your obsession with Eliju, I am surprised to find that I may also be your last." Varawynn's eyes were hard and dry.

"So strong," Mardavian said with his customary smirk. "Just like my sister. So very proud. And I'm sure you will fight me when I take you, even if your leg is useless."

"I will fight you every step of the way!"

"But you see I enjoy that, my dear. I enjoy the struggle," he

said, beginning to remove her clothing.

"You're sick," Varawynn spit out him. "And you'll be punished for this! I promise you that!"

"You're so spunky right now, I wonder if you'll be so fierce with your clothes off."

* * *

What happened next, only I saw, for the rest of the group turned their heads away, closing their eyes to the moving images being transmitted from my eyes. They didn't want to witness her pain.

But I understood how the truth commands witness. I knew that love didn't look away from the burden of another person's pain. Pain, when shared and accepted—dissolves into forgiveness and absolution.

As I witnessed her story, I cried the "Song of Varawynn." It felt like shades of blue and emerald green. It felt like violet and indigo were sewn in the threads of the melody. It felt like ravens in flight and water creatures in the depths of the ocean. It felt like tears making up a river of pain. It felt like loss. It felt like rain storms. It tasted salty with regret. It was beautiful. It was perfect. Just as she was.

I saw her Whole—her lame leg moving freely, her heart as it had been as a child—carefree, freed of the burdens of the pain others had inflicted on her. I saw her for what she was. I knew her from the beginning. I also saw her for what she was destined to become.

Laying my beak on Varawynn's leg, kissing it, I took her pain into myself. The blood on her leg dried with my beak's kiss, and her intricate dark raven mark stood out like a sore thumb against the fairness of her snowy skin.

I felt it all. I saw all she been through. I had been a witness to humanity from the dawning of Eden. I had seen how humans hurt and loved each other, unable to recognize that as they hurt each other, they were really hurting themselves. And that in the end, only the love mattered, and remained.

* * *

"Could you please restore my memory to me now?" the servant asked quietly. We had forgotten all about the young man and how he'd helped us to escape. I suddenly remembered the spell I had cast over him, and the fire that had led to him helping us escape the castle. I had promised to heal him completely by water.

"By water, Ileona?" Wandering Wolfe asked me. I shook myself from my reverie, lost as I had been in the Bird of Eden's wordless songs.

I nodded to him, but my thoughts still dwelled on the images that had unsettled me, "The sea isn't far and will act as a powerful catharsis. Follow me, and I will revive your memory."

"Thank you, ma'am," the servant said. "But King Mardavian must not find me here, with all of you."

"You want us to hurry?"

"Yes."

"Don't worry, son," Wandering Wolfe said to the servant. "I think King Mardavian will leave us alone, for the time being at least. Ileona, I'd like to purify this land when you get back."

"By smudging?"

"Yes, but the Shamanic version, not the Celtic version." The Celtic smudging process would be more fitting here. But it was important to pick your battles, so I didn't argue. I would just do the smudging I wanted to do when I walked the servant down to the river.

* * *

The Oracle took hold of the freed servant's arm, and we walked down to the sea with them. Shadow Rain, Alondria, Jonlin and I came with her. Wandering Wolfe stayed behind to get the ceremony ready. The meadow of heather filled my senses, until I was drunk with the bitter sweetness of the scent. The familiarity came upon me as suddenly as a rainstorm. The smell was in my dream of nearly a year ago now. I'd been here before—in visions.

* * *

Ileona gathered some herbs on the way, grinding them together. I watched her precision. When we got to the river, she said a spell, and dunked me in the water. Releasing the herbs over my head, she rubbed them into my body and face, and then dunked me in the water six times more. The last time I came up, gasping for breath, my memory was fully restored.

* * *

As he came up from the water the final time, into the sun and air, he radiated like the sun itself. His blonde hair shone like gold in the bright light of day. His grey eyes were soft and gentle, like lamb's wool. He wore the clothes of a doctor.

His skin was golden pale, as the soft haze of dim light before the sunrise. The girls gave a start at his handsome appearance. It was so hard for me not to be jealous when Alondria's eyes widened like she'd never seen a man before.

Then I saw it—*he had the birthmark of a beaver on the back of his left hand!*

"Shadow Rain, Alondria look! Eliju...look at his hand. He belongs with us!" They gasped, as they saw what only I had seen.

* * *

I remembered who I was. A doctor. And why I had become all that I am. "Thank you Ileona, for restoring my memory. I want to thank you, as well as the princess, for making me trust you, and leading you all out of King Mardavian's castle during the fire. I can find no words to express my gratitude...and how sorry I am for what King Mardavian did to Varawynn."

"Who *are* you?" Ileona asked, clearly astonished.

"My name is Luquinn."

"Luquinn—this might shock you, so please prepare yourself." She paused for dramatic affect. "You belong with our group. That birthmark on your hand is written in an ancient Prophecy. All of our birthmarks were foretold."

I found my eyes searching for Alondria's eyes. Her eyes met mine, and the idea of belonging with them—with her—gave me peace. I knew nothing about this Prophecy the Oracle spoke of, and yet I felt grateful to be a part of it, so that I could become a part of the group that went where she went.

Ileona stepped dramatically into the light. "That special birthmark on your right hand is evidence you've been chosen as an elite member of our group of fourteen." I was shocked—as was everyone else in the group.

"But I never would've guessed you would be one of us!" Alondria gasped.

"Nor would I!" added Shadow Rain. We slowly made our way back to the clearing, in a daze. We found Wandering Wolfe brewing some tea over the fire.

"I think Wandering Wolfe knew all along," said Eliju with a glint in his eyes. He shared a closeness with the Shaman I didn't understand.

"What do you mean?" asked Shadow Rain, wide-eyed. She was such a sweet and innocent girl. Anything she did wrong was out of ignorance, not malice.

"Don't you remember when King Mardavian first captured us, and Wandering Wolfe said he knew this was going to happen all along? We never could have gotten Luquinn OUT of the castle if we hadn't been captives IN it!"

When Wandering Wolfe looked up at us, his warm brown eyes twinkled, and the deep rust in them sparkled like the glowing of embers in a hearth. Even Ileona looked impressed. His smug expression was answer enough to Eliju's surmise.

We walked back to Varawynn, and I surprised the group by saying, "May I bandage up your leg, Miss Varawynn? I am a doctor."

"Oh, all right," she relented, testily. Exhibiting great skill with my gentle techniques, I impressed the group with my abilities. I hoped I could serve them well.

"This is wonderful, now we have several types of healers!" exclaimed Alondria. "I'm really looking forward to learning from you." It felt significant to me that it was Alondria and I who were the healers—I was a doctor through technical training, and she was a healer through magic and inspiration. Her birthmark of the cross was on her right palm. Mine was of the beaver on the back of my left hand.

"And I, you," I smiled back at her.

But in the distance, a massive black figure stood on the edge of the horizon. "Oh, no…" Shadow Rain whispered, anticipating a fight.

"What is that?" Jonlin asked, to no one in particular.

"Or who?" added Ileona, drawing her dagger and standing in a position ready for battle.

An unusually shaped figure was moving towards us. The body of a horse…no…it had a horn…

"It's a unicorn!" Alondria exclaimed. "A…black unicorn?"

* * *

At last the figure was upon us—blackened body, silver hair and hooves and horn, he was ten feet high, and as wide as a full-grown Cyclops. At his side, an elf with delicately formed and pointed ears stood by his side. Her long, willowy silver blue hair was as light and gossamer as fairy wings. I had always wanted to meet an elf. Elves were so beautiful.

"My name is Illumina, and this is Silvandrin. We've come to join you," Illumina said to us, in a lyrical voice. "We're two of the fourteen."

"Welcome!" Alondria rushed toward them, sweeping the elegant elf up in one of her spontaneously warm and affectionate embraces.

Illumina was knocked off her feet by her exuberance, and the unicorn whinnied his surprise. Humans were not permitted to touch a unicorn, staining them with their impurities, yet when Alondria hugged his mane, her touch did nothing to harm him. Silvandrin was as surprised as any of them by this.

"You're truly one-of-a-kind," he said to her, in his deep, booming voice of warm velvety butter. She answered him with a radiant smile that took our breath away. She was descended of the muses. We could not help but be affected by her charms.

Climbing past a hill in the opposite direction of Silvandrin and Illumina, came her brother Aldoran on his steed. Someone else was riding on a horse by his side.

"Aldoran!" Alondria shouted, moving into a dead run towards him. Aldoran kicked his horse's side to hurry to her.

Jumping off his horse, with the skill of practiced movement, he pulled his sister into his arms and twirled her higher in the air than Silvandrin at his full height. I couldn't understand the love between two siblings, having never experienced it. But I envied it.

"She must be another member of the group?" I asked Aldoran, motioning toward the light-haired girl that rode with him.

"Yes, my name is Pharean, and my father was an advisor to King Mardavian, before he realized how evil he was. So, I think I have some inside information about him that may be useful to all of you," Pharean finished rather shyly, as if longing to find her place among us, wanting to belong. I smiled at her encouragingly, knowing how that felt.

"Wait, but aren't we still missing someone from the group?" Shadow Rain asked Wandering Wolfe.

Speak of the devil; a shadowy man appeared, his shaggy black hair covering his face. My eyes almost bulged out of my head. "It's you! I saw you talking with Wandering Wolfe all the way back in Haran!"

Wandering Wolfe nodded approvingly. "What an astute memory, lad."

For a moment, I felt myself brought back to the beginning, when it was just me and Wandering Wolfe in my small, humble hut—

before all the others had joined us, before our travels and subsequent capture, before everything in my life had changed. An intense longing overcame me to return to that time and place, before Wandering Wolfe had come, when I was unaware of the Prophecy and my part in it. I yearned to return to the simple life I'd had, before I knew what great evil there was in the world—that there were people like King Mardavian who destroyed innocence for their own pleasure.

But I knew that I could never return to what, and who, I once was. I had changed. These experiences, these people I now loved, had altered me, and the course of my life. And yet, at heart, I was still the shepherd boy of Haran—whose visions led me to the light, amid the impatience, anger, and uncontrolled passions that made up my shadow side.

~ *** ~

Chapter Twenty-Three
Fourteen Come Together

May-June, in the forests of Western Europe—

After the various emotionally charged events of the day, the group was weary and subdued. It was twilight by the time they decided to set-up camp a little way from the sacred yew tree. There were now so many people in the group, they would have to share tents.

Eliju and Wandering Wolfe were in one tent. Luquinn and Jonlin were in another, and Shadow Rain, Alondria, and Varawynn were in the third. Ileona had her own tent. They were just roasting some meat Luquinn had had the wherewithal to snag before they left, when they heard noises deeper in the forest.

I chose to remain apart from the group. I had my own agenda to take care of, for there was still someone missing. That, only I knew. They, only I could find.

* * *

I watched as the shaggy-haired man, Orzenith, stole away from our group, and sighed to myself. I still knew so little about that man. There was so much I did not understand about the Prophecy. How could I lead the group when I remained in the darkness?

"We should set watchers up tonight, to make sure we don't get captured again. I'll take the first watch. Luquinn, would you like to stay up and watch with me for a while?" Luquinn was nervous and slightly put out, but agreed. I'm sure he was very tired.

* * *

I was glad I'd get to sleep in private, and would have rather slept in the same tent as Eliju, instead of Luquinn, if they'd given me a choice. It wasn't that Luquinn was all that good-looking, I decided. It was just that he looked so different cleaned-up. By tomorrow, or the next day, the girls would have calmed down, and it would be back to lessons as usual.

But deep inside, I knew it would never be the same. As the fourteen had come together, our dynamics were forever altered. For so many reasons, it could never be as it had been before.

I had a tough time sleeping that night. I guess I was wrestling with the shadow of jealousy. I guess I was wrestling with love for a girl that wasn't mine. I prayed for God to forgive me, finally falling asleep while an owl hooted, and outside my tent Wandering Wolfe and Luquinn talked quietly by the flickering light of the fire's flames.

* * *

"So, your memory has finally come back, has it Luquinn?"

"Yes, sir."

"What happened to you? How were you taken prisoner?"

"I was just in the wrong place at the wrong time, to be honest. I was dining at a local pub, unwinding from a late-night sick call, being entertained by a bard. We left at the same time. Unfortunately, the bard was so handsome and talented, many men in the place were jealous of his skill and the affect it had on the women in the town. So, they attacked us both."

"During the brawl, King Mardavian's men overtook the town, erasing my memory and taking me as prisoner—which you evidently knew all along. How did you know where to find me, sir, out of curiosity?"

"You may call me Wandering Wolfe, Luquinn. Everyone else does. Do you have any idea what happened to the other people at the tavern—the bard for instance?"

I noticed he had ignored my question. "I think the bard's name was Larsius. I assume many were turned into servants like me—or were made into warriors at best—killed at worst. But really, I've no idea, sir."

I bit my lower lip, I'd meant to call the Shaman by his name, as he'd requested, but I didn't feel comfortable doing that just yet. In my line of work, professionalism was an essential asset. It was hard to dismiss my stiff nature and training in social decorum.

Noticing my discomfort, Wandering Wolfe assured me, "I'd like you to relax with me, Luquinn. I know you don't know about the legend, but you're important to it."

"So, you know all about me through this Prophecy?" It felt strange to be known by a man I didn't know. "How did you know who I was before we'd escaped? How did you know how to find me and that I was a part of the group? I never even met you…I wasn't even the servant that served you in your dungeon."

I was suspicious of Wandering Wolfe's evasiveness. While I appreciated politeness, I also hated undo pretenses that were foreign to the details and exactitude of my station.

"You'll soon learn I know of many things no one ever told me."

"What does that mean, sir—errr, Wandering Wolfe?" The Shaman's elusive ways continued to grate on my practical nerves.

"It means I've learned to trust my intuition. It is seldom, if ever, wrong."

"I find that difficult to believe," I replied stiffly, never putting much stock in anything I couldn't see, touch, smell, taste, or analyze through logic.

"Haven't you ever had a feeling about something, or someone?" I felt like Wandering Wolfe was searching inside my mind, for some secret part of me that I had never shared with anyone before. I don't know why something in me wanted to give it to him.

"I knew I was meant to become a doctor…and I knew I could trust Princess Alondria even when King Mardavian had me in the fog of his curse," I reluctantly admitted. "But those are unusual occurrences for me."

"Then I would encourage you to entertain the notion of developing these intuitions, so that they may become more frequent."

"I suppose I can admit to understanding the basic premise of your theory, though I think reason should trump gut instinct personally."

Wandering Wolfe laughed. "Okay then, what made you trust Alondria?"

"Her open sincerity and caring. Not many people are like that."

"True. Alondria is very special in that way."

"She's the most beautiful girl I've ever seen too."

"And what did you think of Jonlin when you were the warden to his cell?"

"Jonlin? Oh, he's nice enough," I answered guardedly.

"He's a very pleasant person, wouldn't you agree?"

I laughed gruffly. "He wasn't so pleasant when I was getting to know him. I don't think he likes me much."

"What makes you say that?"

"Just a feeling I have. I guess I do sometimes have intuition."

"I've never known Jonlin to dislike anyone, Luquinn."

"Maybe it isn't me he dislikes, but how much Alondria likes me."

"You mean he doesn't like sharing her attention? But he's had to share it with Eliju all along, and Eliju is the Chosen One."

"But it's different with me than with Eliju, isn't it?"

"I don't know. How do you think it's different, Luquinn?"

I sighed. "I'm tired now, Wandering Wolfe. Do you think I can get some sleep, and we can discuss this in more depth at a more opportune time, say, tomorrow—earlier in the day? I'm really a morning person, and I don't like being up this late at night. Though I've made an exception to help you out by keeping watch, I'd like to go to sleep now, and let someone else take over the next shift."

"Yes, I get your point, doctor. And despite this inopportune time, would you mind please waking up Jonlin, and sending him out here, before you get some much-needed shut-eye?"

I nodded, yawned, and went into the tent I'd be sharing with the Bard of Hebron. Bard and doctor…an odd pair of opposites.

Opening our flap tent, I poked at Jonlin, who'd only just fallen asleep. He was thrashing around in a nightmare, and violently hit me across the face as he was waking up.

"Ouch!" I shrieked.

"Are you okay?" he asked me, concerned, but groggy. "Why are you waking me up?"

"Because Wandering Wolfe wants you to keep watch with him now."

"Oh yes, of course, and I'm sorry for hitting you…" Jonlin said sheepishly, gathering up his blanket to bring it with him outside into the chill air. My eyes narrowed, glaring at his back as he left the tent, rubbing my swelling face. I wondered if his attack had really been entirely unintentional.

* * *

Wandering Wolfe was poking at the fire, and Celestria was asleep on a nearby tree branch. I yawned, and sat down beside the Shaman. It felt so wonderful to be in his presence again. I had grown rather fond of the old man.

"Have you or Luquinn heard any noises since it got dark, Wandering Wolfe?"

"No, thank the gods. Just the sounds of animals moving around in the forest brush—no signs of danger."

"That's good," I said with another yawn.

"Have you given any thought to our earlier conversation?"

"About the fourteen becoming thirteen?"

"Yes."

"I think the fourteenth is Luquinn."

"And are you speaking with your heart, or your mind now, Jonlin?" Why was Wandering Wolfe trying to get at me—inside of me? What was it he wanted from me?

* * *

I wanted the truth. The sandy-haired boy looked up at me sharply. "But this part of the Prophecy is perhaps uncertain."

"In Christianity there are twelve disciples, with one leader."

"Yet there are many leaders in our group, are there not, Jonlin?"

"Yes, but you are our master."

* * *

"*I* am the master?" Wandering Wolfe said with a raised eyebrow. "Shouldn't the Chosen King be the master?"

I sighed. "It's too late at night for this kind of talk, Wandering Wolfe."

"Then allow me to get to the point. What do you think of the newcomer?"

I didn't understand why Wandering Wolfe was trying to decipher information from me. Why would he want to know my thoughts and feelings about Luquinn? And yet for some reason I felt compelled to confide in him.

"He doesn't fit in. I hate to say it, but I don't like him—I really don't like him."

"He hasn't been given a chance yet to fit in…Are your feelings perhaps clouded by someone else in the group?"

"Who?"

"Alondria."

* * *

Jonlin avoided my eyes. That was answer enough. There were problems here. The jealousy between the two boys was obvious. They both liked Alondria. That was the source of their animosity. It wasn't like Jonlin to feel this way. I had a hunch it wasn't quite normal for Luquinn either. And yet here we were.

"I think we're done here, Jonlin. I'm sorry I had Luquinn wake you. Could you please wake up Eliju, and tell him it's his turn to keep watch with me?" Jonlin blinked in surprise. "You're done talking with me?"

"Yes, we can talk more when your training begins in the morning. Please come to my tent when the sun is rising, Jonlin."

"Yes, Wandering Wolfe," the boy said respectfully, already dreading the little sleep he would have that night, but then thinking about how I hadn't gotten any sleep at all, and feeling bad for me.

A few moments later Eliju came out of his tent, bounding toward his beloved mentor. I smiled to myself. I'd missed him most.

* * *

"Eliju, I've missed you very much, my son," Wandering Wolfe said with tears in his eyes. We embraced for a handful of heartbeats I treasured, for he had undoubtedly become the father I'd never had.

"Let's sleep out here, next to the fire, Eliju, as we once did in Haran. I have a feeling we won't be disturbed anymore tonight, and it's very warm here by the fire. I feel as if I've been cold for centuries in Mardavian's dungeon."

"Of course, Wandering Wolfe, I'd be happy to sleep out here with you." I fell back asleep quickly, but Wandering Wolfe was up for a while longer, pondering what King Mardavian and Queen Darlillyth had in store for all of us.

~ *** ~

The next morning, although Jonlin was very tired, he woke me up just as the sun was beginning to rise. While everyone else in the group was fast asleep, we began the practice of defensive training. Although I'd only gotten a few hours of sleep, the sun revived my energies.

Alondria was the next to rise, and kindly made everyone a delicious breakfast we were all infinitely grateful for. Then we packed up our things and set off towards the east. This time Aldoran was staying with us, as a fellow warrior and protector, regardless of not being one the fourteen. We all loved Aldoran. We were happy to have him with us.

"What's our next course of action?" Silvandrin asked me when the rest of the group had wandered ahead of us.

"We're going to Astarra."

"The land of the fairies? Why?"

"There's a scroll there of the Prophecy which will tell us what our next course of action should be. We have a jewel to trade with them, the dwarf warrior, Norgorian, gave me before we were captured." Silvandrin nodded and said nothing more.

~ ✳✳✳ ~

The journey to Astarra was not far. I only hoped we wouldn't come upon anyone wishing to do us harm as we traveled, but the old Shaman knew what he was doing. As the days passed, the members of our group were slowly finding their places. Only Varawynn stood alone, silent and moody. I mentioned to Wandering Wolfe that she could probably use someone to talk to.

"She's closest to Eliju, but Eliju has been deep in his own thoughts lately. Ileona is from her homeland and would be good for her to confide in."

"That poor girl. She'll never be the same after what King Mardavian did to her."

"I've noticed that of the humans you seem partial to Alondria, dear friend. Of course, she's not fully human either."

I nodded. What was the use in pretending that the pure, sweet girl was not my favorite? "She's just as I once was, pure and innocent before Eleethion..."

Wandering Wolfe put a reassuring hand on my broad, black shoulders. I neighed loudly to clear my throat before going on.

"I don't mean to be hard on Varawynn. Nor do I intend to compare her with Alondria. That wouldn't be fair. I do feel a great deal of compassion for the girl. Though I do wonder...after all, the true mark of goodness is in the kindness shown to one's enemies. My cursed black mane is here to prove that."

"Not everyone shares that philosophy, Silvandrin."

"No, I realize that. I often wonder if I did the right thing when I showed compassion to that sorceress. If what I did was right, why did my beautiful snowy white mane turn silver and my body turn black?" I felt my heart cave in within itself, when I remembered how beautiful I had once been, with hair and coat of luminescent white like pearls.

"Black is not necessarily a color of evil, just as white is not necessarily a color of good. Rather, I believe it is in the fusion of the unity of all colors where the real source of power and enlightenment can be found," said Wandering Wolfe.

"But isn't white the inclusion of all colors?"

"That's true. And yet there is a spirituality in the process of emptying that black represents."

"The process of emptying?"

"There is a process after the emotions are spent, after the 'dark night of the soul,' when we are emptied of all the pain and angst…and that's when we are filled with love, with acceptance and with forgiveness."

"The human emotions have much to teach us all," I bowed my head to Wandering Wolfe. There truly were wisdoms and lessons to be taught by all races.

I meditated on Wandering Wolfe's words in peaceful reflection. Occasionally, certain members of the group would hear footsteps in the forest, but most of the younger humans didn't notice.

"Illumina and Ileona told me they saw giants not far from our campsite. I think they are the Watchers who have been following us," I mentioned to Wandering Wolfe quietly.

"Describe these creatures to me just as they were described to you."

As I described them, he nodded thoughtfully, "It's just as I suspected, they've followed us from the beginning."

"What do you think they want with us, Wandering Wolfe?"

"They want only to survive, Silvandrin," he sighed. "As all of us do."

~ *** ~

Night was upon us, and the moon was full in the sign of the Crab. I knew how to read the positions of the planets and the stars in the sky, to understand the progression of time. I understood that when each constellation moved into another sign, it affected everyone on earth. When the moon was full, emotions were high. With the moon in the planet it ruled, emotions were even more dramatic.

My sign, Aquarius, was the most impassioned and detached. We observed, aloofly and apart, more than the other signs. We found emotionalism distasteful. It wasn't because we didn't care. We just showed our caring in other ways. I was cerebral. I identified myself more with my thoughts and ideas, rather than with my feelings.

Shadow Rain, being of the sign of Cancer and the Crab, had snapped at Eliju all day, and during her private session with Wandering Wolfe. She had finally managed to fully control the rain, thunder and lightning. Due to Rain's dark, yet powerful mood, it was storming unceasingly around us.

Setting up camp for the night, we couldn't manage to get a fire going with all the rain, not even with magic. Forced to dine on stale bread, most everyone went to bed grouchy and hungry. I took the storm and the bad moods of those around me, in stride.

"They're coming tonight," Wandering Wolfe whispered to Silvandrin and I covertly. "We'll need to sit outside the tents and wait for them."

"They want only to survive?" said Silvandrin.

"Yes, and that's why they want Shadow Rain to die."

Silvandrin looked at the Shaman in surprise. "Why would they want such a sweet young girl to die?"

"I already told you. Survival."

Silvandrin whinnied impatiently. "Explain yourself, Man!"

"Yes, Wandering Wolfe, none of us know what you are referring to." Ileona swept her long, blonde hair over her shoulder. I stood a few feet away from them, listening.

Wandering Wolfe sighed heavily. "She was foretold to bring about their destruction."

Silvandrin whistled out his nose. "It's all in her name then isn't it? The 'Legend of Shadow Rain'—foretold to bring about their downfall."

"Precisely."

"Then shouldn't we let the girl face them herself?"

"No, it's not time for that yet. She's not ready. We've got to face them for her tonight."

"He's right," Ileona agreed. "We all heard something following us in the woods. It's them. They're not going to go away until they meet with us." Her lovely face looked pensive.

I'd already sensed and seen some of the tension between the Oracle and the Shaman, so I knew Ileona would not agree with him unless she really believed it. I trusted their judgement.

So, after the young humans had fallen asleep, the rest of us who were waiting together outside of the campsite, heard twigs breaking in the distance. "We need to follow the noises. Before they sneak up on us, we should surprise them."

Stealthily, Silvandrin, Wandering Wolfe, Ileona, the wolf Flint, and I crept deep into the forest. The moon cast eerie lights, as moving shadows swept around us. Suddenly the shadows materialized into the tall, dark forms of the Nephilim.

"We know why you've been tracking us," Wandering Wolfe began.

"Give us the girl," the half-fallen angel, half-giant hissed.

"We'll never give her up," Ileona said, in a purposely bating tone. I admired her courage.

"Give us the girl, or *you* will die!" another angry Nephilim shouted.

"We wish you no harm, but I warn you we won't let you hurt her," I said quietly.

The Nephilim hissed their displeasure, and I felt pricks of needles throughout my body that I knew the others were experiencing as well. Silently screaming my pain psychically, I was unable to move. Silvandrin kicked at the shadowy figure near Wandering Wolfe, but his kicks did them no harm. The Nephilim were like phantoms in the night, untouchable. Wandering Wolfe was bleeding from his arms, legs, chest, and even his face.

"Stop this!" Silvandrin commanded.

"Can't we come to an agreement?" I urged persuasively. The bleeding of Wandering Wolfe finally stopped. Flint quietly licked and lapped up his wounds.

The Nephilim who had attacked us asked, "What agreement can there be made? The girl is in our Prophecy. She is foretold to bring about our destruction."

"Then let us change the Prophecy," said Ileona slyly.

"How?"

Suddenly Silvandrin's horn glowed silver as the moon shone down on us, brightening and illuminating the ground upon which we stood.

"After we've gotten what we came for in the land of Astarra, I'll write on a parchment an emendation to the Prophecy," said Ileona.

"And what will it say?" the Nephilim asked suspiciously.

"There will be some of you who will live after the Shadow Rain."

"Which of us shall live?"

I answered intuitively, "Thirteen of the oldest and wisest and the youngest and fittest, and you will form a new council apart from Mount Hermon."

"How shall you create this new Prophecy?"

"I will consecrate the words they write with the touch of my horn, and that will make the scroll permanent and indestructible," promised Silvandrin.

"Can you do this?"

"Yes, I know we can," said Ileona. Wandering Wolfe gave her a warning look.

"Then so be it," the Nephilim hissed. "I'm glad we didn't have to kill you. It would bring a great curse upon us to kill a unicorn, even one of cursed black and silver hooves and horn."

After the Nephilim were far from ear shot, Wandering Wolfe exclaimed, "What have your foolish lot done? You know as well as I do that no one, nothing, can alter the Prophecy! Why have you all agreed to do something impossible?"

"We don't think it is impossible," I answered him calmly.

"With all of our magical powers combined—" explained Ileona.

"With my horn to consecrate the words Ileona writes—," insisted Silvandrin.

"And with the words written with my magic blood upon the parchment—" I gave the unicorn a mysterious smile, for few knew the secrets of Elven blood.

"We will alter the riddle by just enough so that a few Nephilim will live on," finished Ileona.

"Good try," Wandering Wolfe hmphed. "But if the Nephilim are foretold by the Prophecy to die, then they *will* die."

"But not if we give the few that survive a new name."

Wandering Wolfe's eyes rose. "Very clever, very, very clever indeed, Ileona."

"I've bested you before, and I've bested you once again," the Oracle smiled haughtily.

"And much more importantly, we've protected the girl," said Silvandrin, his voice full of compassion. I rested my arm on Silvandrin's black shoulder. Flint bounded up ahead, full of glee, his tongue dangling out of the right side of his mouth in an insane grin, making Wandering Wolfe chuckle, and momentarily setting our worries at ease with his carefree love of life.

This could work. Even if it had never been done before. I looked over at Ileona, considering her skill. She *had* bested Wandering Wolfe once before. And we can't put so much faith in the Prophecy as to doubt that there are powers greater than prophesying—when misunderstandings and misinterpretations of our visions are always possible. After all, nothing really is impossible, even altering the history of the future, or past...

~ *** ~

Chapter Twenty-Four
Ashes to Ashes

June, in a cottage on the Isle of Skye—

Sometimes there are things we have to do to get by in life, which we may find to be distasteful, but which are a necessary evil. There are times that the end justifies the means. When it came to the fulfillment of the Prophecy, the end definitely justified the means.

A moment had come that would define the sorceress, my pupil, and dictate her future. She was at a crossroads. If she would do what needed to be done, then the path that had been set before her from birth, was that much closer—that much more certain.

* * *

I could see the wheels in Vorseth's mind turning as he looked at me. Studying me. I had no idea what he was thinking about, but he was thinking hard.

When he spoke, it was with measured words. "You've never left the Isle of Skye, have you?" I shook my head. "Do you remember the part of the Prophecy that spoke about the resurrection?" he asked. I shook my head again. He recited:

"The Resurrection"

"She who bears the raven mark
Shall be the first to fall and rise again.
From fire and coal, out of embers and shadows,
From the pit of death, her brother's thigh bone
Makes her more than whole in the resurrection."

Again, Vorseth stared at me with measured eyes, seeming to look into me, searching for something inside me. "You are the orchestrator of this Prophecy."

"How? I do not bear a raven birthmark."

"No, but you are meant to bring about her resurrection."

"How?"

"From the pit of death...her brother's thigh bone," he whispered.

Now it was I, who studied the wizard with narrowed eyes. "What exactly are you suggesting, Vorseth?"

"You wish to murder King Mardavian for killing the couple who raised you."

"Yes," I answered, with unflinching conviction. "To avenge their deaths."

"Let this be a test then, to see if you are worthy and capable of such a feat."

We stared at each other for a few moments more. "I want to take you off this island for an outing. I want to take you to the Isle of Apples—not too far away, to take the thigh bone of the brother of the girl with the raven mark. A girl in the Prophecy."

"Where is the brother buried?"

"He is not yet dead."

A heaviness filled the room. I inhaled one deep breath, before I answered. "When shall we depart?"

~ ~ ~

Vorseth guided me off the island in a boat. I relished every moment leaving my home. I had never been more than a few miles from my small cottage on the Isle of Skye.

He took me to the Sword in the Stone where once Exacalibur had been held. "You will meet me back here once the deed is done." I nodded.

"How will I know where to find him?"

"Take the boat and cross to the other shore. You will find a small, stone castle. Cross behind it and you will see a garden of flowers where a young man, Aengus, will be tending them. He has a connection with the plants of the earth."

I followed Vorseth's instructions like a machine. I did not pause in my pursuit. I found the castle, the gardens and the young man exactly where he told me I would.

I knew that it would be best not to engage the man in conversation, but to catch him unawares. I watched him for a few minutes. Then I came up from behind him, with movements of stealth and silence, wielding the knife blade into his back, piercing his heart.

Gus faltered to the ground, onto his hands and knees. He looked up at me with a look of utter shock and betrayal. "I don't even know who you are. Why are you doing this to me?" Gus asked, with such sorrow in his voice, it gave me a moment's pause.

"I'm doing this to save your sister. For the Prophecy." His expression changed. There was a light in his eyes. Peace passed over his mien. He fell into the hands of death, with complete surrender. I felt his spirit lift, as he took his last breath.

* * *

I died among the plants I loved. The plants that had been my friends, more than people had ever been. I died for the Prophecy I believed in. I died for the person I loved the most, my sister. I died so that her part in the Prophecy might be fulfilled.

* * *

I took a few deep breaths, then took the hatchet from my pack and cut off his left leg. I cut his leg at the knee. I placed his long thigh bone into my black bag.

I went down to the river, took off my dress, removed my corset and undergarments and bathed the blood of Aengus off my body. Then I met Vorseth back at the Sword in the Stone. "Do you have it?"

I nodded my head, handing him the bag. He gave me a small smile, with a glint in his eyes. "I have taught you well." We moved through the woods, back to the boat, back to my home, isolated and alone on the Isle of Skye.

After the day away from my home, I realized I had never been cut out for travel. I preferred to live a solitary life, on an island that was my heaven on earth.

How did I feel after what I did to little Gus? I tell you, I felt nothing. Nothing at all. I was glad to have pleased Vorseth. I was glad to be one step closer to my part in the fulfillment of the Prophecy.

~ * * * ~

June, from the woodland forests of the Celts in the Isle of Apples in Avalon—

It had been over six months since I'd sent the letter to my parents through Raegar. The letter had been sent just before we were taken prisoner and I wondered if they'd been concerned with my silence and if they'd tried to answer my last letter. I wondered how they were, and if they were worried about me.

A week later, my raven Raegar flew to me from the west, returning with a letter attached to its tail, streaked with the vivid firebird orange. But instead of coming to me, the raven delivered the letter to Ileona.

I was confused and slightly irritated on my walk to the Oracle's tent. As I went into the tent, Ileona pinned down the flap of the opening. An odd range of expressions passed across her face as she read through the letter.

When her eyes lifted, something in them overwhelmed me with anxiety. Reluctantly, she handed me the letter. "I'm sorry," she said softly. "But you're not alone in this. I think that's why Raegar delivered the letter to me."

Eliju was waiting for me as I emerged. He probably sensed something was wrong. I was not alone. Wasn't that what Ileona had said?

* * *

She was as pale as the first snowfall. She didn't look at anything after she came out. She didn't look to see if anyone was waiting for her. She just moved forward, moved on—looking straight ahead, in a barren trance—with a lost look in her eyes as unsettling as an unmarked grave.

I called out her name, but she kept right on walking, unhearing or uncaring; she ignored my presence. Walking slowly, somehow, I still couldn't catch up to her. It was just like the time when I'd first met her, and she'd led me to the other shore. But this time it felt very, very different. It felt sinister.

Hours passed this way. I tried desperately to catch up to her, but she continued to ignore me in a totally desolate state of being. The sun was setting, and the blue-grey mist swept across the horizon. There was something melancholy in another day done. Something caught her eyes and she stopped dead in her tracks. Cautiously, I moved a few feet from where she stood, as my eyes followed her line of sight.

An owl sat perched on a crudely constructed wooden cross, beneath which lay an altar where something small and greatly detailed lied. Varawynn moved toward, it as if possessed. She knelt upon the altar and lifted and clutched the object tightly in the hands she held up in prayer.

Holding the object so tightly that her pale hands turned a light pink and then purple, her down-turned face lifted upwards, as tears fell freely from her face onto the altar. When she opened her hands, I saw that she was clutching a delicate rosary, which fell back onto the ground as she released it.

Wiping her cheeks, the sky was black, and the fog from earlier obscured the stars. In that in-between state of unknowing and waiting, I could feel how deeply alone she felt inside. I could feel her faithless faithfulness, her hopeless hope, her loveless love, as if they were my own feelings, as if she were my own self.

So much was said in the colors of the sky around us and between us without words. People who have experienced real loss don't need words of explanation. Pain needs no explanation. It needs only to be felt and released.

I didn't know who'd made the altar and the cross. It must have been made recently, because the snow was still unsettled where the objects had been placed, and the beads were not yet dirty from the woods and the elements of spring. I didn't know how Varawynn had known the way, the placement of her hands, the way she had kneeled.

It was as if the way of the foreign religion came to her simply because she had had a need for that expression of faith. A raven feather and blood-red scarf lay upon the altar, and Varawynn lifted the light feather, and softly brushed it across her face and tears, wrapping herself up in the cloth like a veil.

I was afraid to break the silence. As I stood, and as the minutes ticked by, she finally looked at me so intensely that I wasn't sure I didn't prefer her obliviousness of me.

"My brother Gus has been killed," she whispered.

Looking upon each other in one of those rare moments that transcend time, the dear and already well-worn memory of our spontaneous kiss in my tent, flooded my mind. I'd turned it over in my heart again and again, like a stone made smooth by the consistent caress of the waters, for only water and wind can change the form and shape of steady stone.

"You mean, that he's been murdered?" my voice got stuck in my throat, and my words came out muddled.

"Yes, and because of me," with those words her tears fell again, and she buried her face in her hands. I couldn't stand to see her in so much pain, but I wasn't used to being around crying girls, and I didn't know what to do. I loved her too much not to at least try to comfort her, so I went to her and awkwardly rubbed her back.

I choked a little. *Could it be? Darlillyth? Surely there were other sorceresses in the whole of the land...*

"Eliju, would you please come back with me to...to...bury him?"

"Of course," I agreed immediately. I gathered all the courage I could muster, to wrap my arms about her. She fell into my embrace, as naturally as the flow of the water rushes to the shore.

"Ileona is coming as well. She wants to pay her respects and show her support of me. But...it wouldn't be, I wouldn't feel right, without you...I wanted you to come back home with me, but...not like this."

"Shhh, Varawynn, it's going to be okay. I'll be right by your side." She gave me a weak, grateful half-smile, and slipping her hand into mine, we walked back to camp.

I went to Wandering Wolfe right away to request accompanying Varawynn to her homeland since we were so close, and it was only proper for Varawynn to bury her brother. Ileona also insisted to accompany her. She was very concerned about Varawynn, and wanted to say something for Aengus at the service.

Wandering Wolfe agreed that this was a good idea. He was worried about Varawynn as well, and hoped that being home for a little while, and being among her family and friends, would revive her spirits after all she'd been through. Shadow Rain wanted to come too, as they had become close during their imprisonment, but Rain understood how much it meant to Varawynn to take Eliju home with her, so she stayed behind and wished her condolences.

It seemed life was handing Varawynn one fatal blow after another. I wasn't sure how well she would handle it. She seemed to fold within herself, into a deep depression. We set off together, into the forests which had always been a sanctuary for her. She was silent through most of the traveling, buried deep inside herself, buried in shame and guilt, blaming herself for her brother's death.

~ *** ~

On the other side of the forest, the rest of our group was making our way to the land of Astarra. I was looking forward to meeting the fairies. I felt like we were about to embark on a great adventure—where magic and beauty ruled.

Although, my excitement was rather dampened by the murder of Varawynn's brother. It was unfathomable what had happened to Gus. Poor Varawynn had been through so much lately. I don't think I could have handled someone in my family dying very well. It was so strange and unfair to me how some people, like Eliju and Varawynn, seemed to suffer so much more that others did.

~ *** ~

"Evidently this sorceress believed she would get to me through my poor brother. She...tortured him..."

I put a comforting hand on her shoulder. "You don't need to talk about it now if you're not ready."

Climbing high above the mountains where the air was cold and crisp—even climbing the mountains in that elevated level of altitude, Varawynn breathed easier alone with Eliju and I. It was clear to me that I was her favorite teacher, and of course Eliju was her best friend. Even though we were returning home for such a tragic reason, I believed our company lifted her spirits.

For the first few days we didn't talk much. I'd known Varawynn all her life, and knew she needed silence when she processed through her feelings. The night before we were back in Avalon, Varawynn caught some fish in the stream, and Eliju built a fire to roast them. I was getting our beds ready, as Varawynn cooked the fish over the fire.

* * *

Something was pressing in on me. This feeling, this knowing, a sixth sense. Something had happened with Eliju while he was in captivity. Something that made it impossible for him to ever feel the same about me again. Something significant.

Something was twisting itself around my heart, constricting it. The pain of love lost, his loyalty pledged elsewhere. The pain of bonds being broken, and hopes being dashed. I'd lost so much more than my brother and my innocence in the past few months. I knew intuitively that I had lost the only man I would ever love.

I knew it. But I needed to know how. I needed to know why. I needed to understand. I needed to dissect and analyze how this had happened. Some perverse aspect of my nature needed to press to uncover the details of the annihilation of my hopes and dreams.

So, I asked him, while Ileona was elsewhere, and we had a moment alone, "Where were you all the time while I was with Shadow Rain and Ileona?"

He avoided my eyes. "Does it really matter?"

"Yes, of course it does, or I wouldn't ask."

* * *

Her jade-colored, cat-like eyes narrowed. The intensity of her stare made me fidget uncomfortably on the ground. How could I ever tell her the truth, when I wasn't sure of it myself?

Throwing another stick on the fire, even though it didn't need it, I thought it best to change the subject. "We're finally going back to your Avalon, but I'm so sorry it's under these circumstances, Varawynn."

Her eyes flooded with tears, and she looked away, to gain strength enough not to shed them. "It's the anniversary of Morgan le Fay's death. We'll be scattering his ashes over the water on the anniversary of my beloved ancestor."

"You really do love your homeland, don't you Varawynn?"

She couldn't help but break into a small smile—the deep green grass, purple moors, and violet waters called to her in a way that nowhere else they'd traveled to ever could. Her home was like a lover.

Her homeland was her first love, and in her reverence for it— like her feelings for me—they were imprinted on her heart like the raven birthmark was tattooed on her body. She smiled because she knew I felt the same way about her home. The change of subject worked like a charm, for as she told me more about her homeland, she forgot to question what had happened when I'd been in captivity.

~ *** ~

We slept in the open, a little ways away from the fire. I woke up in the middle of the night, to the cold. The fire was almost out; all that was left were dying embers. Stoking the fire and adding kindling, as the fire roared back to life, I looked down at Eliju in the light of the flames.

His skin was toughening due to the elements; muscles were bulging where once there'd been only strong, but tawny skin. But it was his face that turned my heart over. Like looking at the man you've spent your whole life with, before you begin that life—like I was looking into the future.

I forgot about what King Mardavian had done to me when I looked at him and thought about him meeting my parents again—this time from a different angle, for a different purpose perhaps. I guess some part of me still hoped I was wrong—that he still loved me, and one day we could be joined together.

I had let him divert the topic earlier tonight to share in the glow of the love of my homeland. He knew it comforted me to talk of Camelot and the Isle of Apples. He felt the magical beauty of my homeland too.

I was not so quickly diverted from that urging inside myself, that darkness in the air surrounding us, following us like a shadow, that warning in my soul, that the love for me he'd felt had diminished. Its absence crippled me more than the lameness I was born with. My heart was crippled now, incapable of ever loving again.

He made a soft mewing noise in response to the roaring of the fire, but he was fast asleep. Ileona was near, but I bent down anyway, unable to resist the longing of the moment. My long hair concealed my face as I stroked the short, sharp stubble of the beard growing on his face. For a moment he half-opened his mouth, as if preparing for my kiss.

As I was leaning down to press my lips to his, he murmured, "Darlillyth..." and something deep inside of me went cold. The truth had come out in his sleep. The truth often comes in the moment we want to know it least.

Going back to lie on my spot on the hard ground, I slept little and restlessly. Knowing the dreams of my future were impossible, life itself felt impossible. I didn't know now, how I could ever go forward.

* * *

The familiar stone where the sword of Excalibur had been taken, marked the boundary of their land. Varawynn's beautiful long curls fell with casual elegance across her face. Without thinking, I brushed the hair from her face, and her eyes bore into mine with such passion and silent intensity, a weaker man would've retreated. Ileona hummed a slow tune, as if to remind us of her presence, and Varawynn took my hand, to lead me to the boats along the shore...

It seemed like a lifetime ago when we first met and fell asleep on the shores of this very lake. It felt like those things had happened to different people. Over half a year's time had altered us both so much. Yet our bond was made deeper with the hardships, deeper and wider—with a chasm of distance too far to be breached.

Could it be felt by others, or just by us? Could the whole world feel the pain of two heart's separation?

"We've arrived early," Ileona said softly, rousing me from my thoughts, and the burning pain of hopes and visions that had turned to ashes.

* * *

Upon arriving at the castle, the door was instantly unbarred to us. Varawynn's parents wore grief-stricken faces of such severity that no words would reach them. They barely responded to Varawynn's touch or tears. You could feel the joy they felt at seeing their precious daughter again, just as much as you could feel their depression over the loss of their precious son.

The service was held at the water's edge. They asked me to officiate the funeral. High Priest Dagda told me they were deeply honored by this.

Wearing a light, billowing gown of white, flittering all about me like rose petals blowing in the wind, I felt again my incomparable majesty as the Lady of the Lake, the most magical enchantress of the waters, and in our culture, we wore white at funerals.

"As a descendent of Vivien, the Lady of the Lake, I speak to you now in honor of a boy who was taken much too soon. He was a young man destined for great things. Borne from the prestigious line of Morgan Le Fay, and with his parents of High Priest and Priestess rank, with a sister bearing the hallowed birthmark of a raven as one of the Chosen Group of fourteen, foretold to revolutionize our world, there is no doubt that Aengus would have made his mark in the Land of Avalon."

"With his shy, sweet spirit, he would have brought much light to the darkness, stoking the living dead to life with the embers glimmering underneath the ashes of our complacency. With his sudden, untimely death, let his passing be a reminder for us to live our lives to the fullest. Let his life be a testimony of the love and the light that never dies—that cannot be silenced or stilled, not even by death."

After my eloquent, heartfelt speech, I danced the "Dance of the Otherworld," my body bending and flowing in fluid movements, as Varawynn's mother, Priestess Boann, sang a mournful song of lament without words, like the illustrious Bird of Eden, who could only cry to make a melody, and whose words had been stolen by the legacy of her curse.

After the speeches of many others in the lands that had known and loved Gus well—mother, father and sister, held Aengus' ashes in their hands, and scattered his body's essence into the waters. I watched

Varawynn's face as the sunset turned to dusk, and the shadows deepened around her face, especially around her eyes.

The circles beneath her eyes darkened. The surface of her face became a mask. Her pain was closing in on her, trapping her in its cage of despair. I was helpless; we all were helpless, to help her to escape it.

I understood how these things, these tragedies and these traumas, changed the humans. Varawynn was still the person she was born, as the baby I had anointed and blessed. I believed she was still innocent, but scars gave humans the knowledge of the evil and the darkness. It came down and back to, our choices, and how we would let the scars of evil effect us.

There was always a choice. Even when the way was unclear. Even when we'd lost all hope, and were in desperate need of a lighthouse, of a beacon to shine out a sliver of light, on a path going nowhere on a moonless night.

We could still choose. Hope for hope's sake. Love for love's sake. Even if it wasn't the love we had hoped to have. I knew how much Varawynn had hoped to share Eliju's love, but I felt, too, that Eliju was not the same person I had first met in my Crystal Castle.

* * *

We were honored to have the Lady of the Lake, Ileona, officiate, our dear son's funeral. The Oracle's words and dancing moved all who watched her to tears.

A million memories rained down on me, as we scattered Aengus' ashes in the Isle of Apples. I remembered how he came into this world, so quietly. He barely cried as a baby, and hadn't changed much growing up.

He was so thoughtful, gentle and kind. How he had loved and admired his beautiful big sister. I knew he had chosen to die for her— using his life to protect hers.

The sorceress who had killed him had removed his left thigh bone. The rest of him, we burned down to ash. We knew that her taking his thigh bone had something to do with Varawynn's birthmark, and the Prophecy, but we still didn't know what.

* * *

It wasn't until we found our son, covered in blood on the garden grounds of the castle, he had so loved, that I realized how much I loved him, and how wrong I had been about his character. I was full of guilt and remorse. Varawynn had been my little girl, my first born, and my favorite.

Now I regretted not recognizing the greatness of my son's soul. I'd always measured bravery by courage, by action. But in protecting his sister, my son had shown more bravery than any soldier I'd ever fought with, than any leader I'd ever known, than any act his foolish father had ever committed.

I admired my son now, more than any man I knew. I would give anything for just one more moment with him, just one more conversation, to let him know, how much I truly loved him.

* * *

Standing there in perfect silence, until the sun set, and the darkness lay heavy upon us, I watched her, as a sad and simple lullaby was sung by one of the ladies in the land. An odd, misplaced song— for it was not a Celtic, but a Hebrew lullaby, like the one my mother used to sing…

I listened to it for a while. Then my body moved as if by a will of its own. I walked through the crowds, searching for the source of the song. As the singing continued, it became clear that this was the song I'd been trying to remember for so long now, on the edges of my consciousness…my mother's song.

As the lullaby continued, I recognized it was *her* voice too. Soft, and deep, and sad; there was a unique quality to it, a strand of something that was…that was her own, and also my own self, in the ethereal essence of the melody. My voice was in her voice.

Could it be? It was *her.* It was *them. They* had been here all along. I knew. I knew it was them.

At last I was upon the melody, upon her face, I was starting to make it out through the crowd. She barely looked like she'd aged a year, yet over ten had passed. There was the same graceful line of her swan's neck, the same thick hair swept up into a regal bun, the same serious expression, the same wide, guarded eyes, the same hand. A thousand memories rained down on me. So many things I'd forgotten rushed over me full bore, like a tidal wave threatening to take me under.

Memories flooded my mind. My father's bright red hair, the crisp, green eyes whose color we shared, but his held a happy magic all their own. Tears filled my eyes over my father's lively expression, his over-enthusiasm, his careless way of breaking things. It was my mother who fixed the things he broke. I remembered the way my father used to make my mother laugh. How she sang over our holy dinners.

Sitting at the little table reading the Torah, my father had placed something too heavy upon the table—that was the first time it had broken, and after they'd left, I'd never been able to get it to stay fixed. Wandering Wolfe had said there was a broken part of myself I'd been unable to fix since my father had first broken the table. As if it was something only my parents could fix.

In the stillness, the crowd had noticed my single-minded purpose. They'd parted for me like the parting of the Red Sea. All eyes were on me.

Though it was dark, there were blue and purple lights that'd been hung, so their faces could still be seen. But I was riveted on her. My mother's eyes were closed in the feeling of her singing, so it was my father who recognized me first. His eyes looked like two green saucers—wide with shock to see me here, now.

"Son?"

My stomach felt like it had jumped off a cliff and fallen down a ravine at the same time. My mother's eyes popped open. With the sudden halt of her singing, I had a wild urge to run into her arms shouting, "Chavah!" like a lunatic little child. In that moment, I could have bowled over even Varawynn to get to her.

Waiting long enough until I was sure my mother had seen me, I saw just enough regret behind her eyes to turn on my heels and march away from the crowd. Varawynn, oblivious, was still standing at the edge of the water, staring down into her brother's floating ashes.

I wasn't ready to face them. I wasn't ready to kill them...or forgive them.

I felt the urge to run. I had to go right now. I would leave Varawynn behind with Ileona if I had to. I had to get away, or I would die. I couldn't breathe.

"Are you ready to go?" I asked Varawynn. Blinking in confusion, she nodded absentmindedly, too lost in her own grief to question me, or to notice what had just happened.

Had Wandering Wolfe known? He had said he knew my parents. But did he know they were here? Had he known all along?

Gently taking Varawynn's arm, I guided her back to the safety of the boats. Quickly, I pushed the boat from the shore, and paddled with quick, urgent strides to the other side of the waters.

Away. Away...

"Eliju…" was like an echo on the wind. "Wait." Practically flying out of the boat and running back to the security of the distance of the Sword in the Stone, I got far enough away, so I wouldn't have to see or remember. We were only human. How much did God expect us to endure?

* * *

I stayed behind to speak to Eliju and Varawynn's parents. We all agreed it was time for the Chosen One to come to terms with the truth of his own life.

Deep into the night, I returned to where Eliju and Varawynn slept by the stone. "They want to speak with you, Eliju," I whispered softly, knowing he'd still be awake, but pretending to be asleep, he didn't answer me.

"I'll say this again in the morning," I sighed, lying down on the hard ground, and spreading leaves to make my bed.

~ *** ~

The morning light showed the dewdrops on the ground, and in Eliju's eyes. He got up to make some tea, and I stirred. "Eliju…What happened last night?"

As Eliju got up to stoke the fire, Ileona was already up, and the kettle was whistling. "The tea's ready and I've fired up some biscuits if you'd care for a few?"

The biscuits and honey smelled good, but my stomach felt as empty and hollow as my heart. I didn't think I could stomach any food. Serving Eliju one biscuit and a cup of tea, I sat down beside Ileona, and took one biscuit and a cup of tea for myself as well.

My head was cloudy, and I was caught up in my grief. But as I managed to eat the biscuit, I felt certain something very strange had happened to Eliju last night. He looked as if he'd seen a ghost.

* * *

In the morning's vivid light, you could make out all the tear streaks across Varawynn's face. Bits of twigs were in her hair and some of her brother's ashes had made their way onto her face and sleeves. Her usually sleek, curly hair was matted down and tangled. She really looked a fright. In spite of myself, I burst out laughing, as I took a good, long look at her. And yet somehow, she looked even more beautiful unkempt, as she did cool and clean.

Varawynn threw me a hurt look, and then to her chagrin, Ileona burst out laughing too. She hmphed and stood up to leave. "No, stay, you ought to know what happened last night too, Varawynn." Her eyebrows rose, and she sat back down grumpily, pulling at the twigs caught up in her hair.

"Last night Eliju discovered his parents have been here all this time, Varawynn. As none other than Lady Isadore and Sir Kenneth."

Varawynn's eyes bulged. "That's impossible, Master Eliju!"

"I believe you were awake last night, but I will say it again. Your parents want to speak with you before we go, Eliju."

"I can't, Ileona."

"But haven't you been waiting to confront them?"

"No, I can't. I'm not ready."

"Eliju, listen—"

"I said NO all right?" I can't face them now. I'm not ready. It isn't going to happen. If you both need to go back, I'll wait here—but I'm not going back there."

"This isn't fair to him, Ileona. If he doesn't want to go, he shouldn't have to," Varawynn defended me fiercely.

"I never thought I'd see the day when I'd call you a coward," Ileona said, with disappointment oozing from her voice like congealed honey.

"The day will come when I'll confront my parents. The day will come when I decide what path I'll take. I'm not ready to make that choice. I'm not ready to decide. This isn't cowardice, this is discernment."

"This day is the only day we have accounted to us! How do you know something won't happen to you, or them, before you've confronted them, and allowed them to say their peace? Won't you even give them a chance to explain their side to you? If you aren't ready to decide if you'll continue to hate or forgive them, won't you at least give them a chance to explain?"

A mirage of emotions passed through me. Varawynn was clearly furious Ileona was speaking to me this way, and hadn't I come to support *her?*

I looked from one to the other. It killed me inside, but I merely nodded, looking down. Ileona nodded. Varawynn held her tongue out of respect for the Oracle, but I knew she was worried about what this was going to do to me.

We made our way back to the boats, rowing purposefully to the insecurity of the other shore. It felt like the longest and shortest ride of my life. First, we went to the castle, where we spent many hours speaking in soft whispers with the people of the town and Varawynn's parents. Then after lunch, Ileona gently led me by the arm into the village. We didn't have far to go, to my chagrin.

Around the door of the small hut where, evidently, my parents had lived since they abandoned me in Haran, had the same Lily of Sharon flowers blooming. My mother had planted them at our home in Haran too. The smell of them made me disentangle myself from Ileona, to puke up my feeling in the nearest bush. Shaking violently with the intensity of my feelings, Ileona was shocked.

"Are you sure you're up for this—" but before she'd managed to finish her question, my mother had flung open the door. She was so beautiful, I felt like I might get sick in the bushes again.

She was standing there before me in the flesh, tall and slender with thick, flowing dark hair like waves and tresses falling upon each other in soft layers, like layers of shooting stars in the night. Her olive skin was radiant; her brown eyes bore into mine, penetrating every emotion flashing across my face.

As I looked at her, more memories I'd buried came to the surface. Then my father bounded into view. It took all my strength not to laugh and grin at the barely contained glee on his pale, good-natured face. His green eyes were wide and sparkling, his vivid eyes depicting good humor and kindness, which set my rumbling stomach at ease.

Ileona wasn't sure whether to enter the hut with me, so I pulled her in, physically assuring her that I wanted and needed her at my side. We entered the room, bigger than our home in Haran. The foyer opened to a large living room; the equivalent of the entire space of my old hut, and the fire in the hearth rumbled pleasantly, as if in anticipation of our arrival.

I was at a loss for words. Sitting down in the nearest chair, I tried hard to remember what it was to breathe. Ileona sat down beside me, looking as if she was beginning to wonder if she ought to have pushed me so hard to come. My father and mother stood in front of the hearth before us, their outlines haloed by flickering flames.

* * *

"We didn't want to leave you," I started. "It all seemed so cruel, but it was a part of the Prophecy. It was your destiny for us to leave you, for you to learn a skill for survival that would far surpass most human understanding. To be capable of caring for one's self fully at such an early age, takes a certain strength, an unparalleled strength that was needed for you to become the kind of man, the kind of King, who could understand, who could make the decisions that would, the kind that would..." as my voice faltered, I felt my husband wrap his arm around my waist, to take over for me. His goodness was so evident. I prayed Eliju recognized it.

"When you were born, we weren't aware what the mark on your body meant. A Shaman visited us while you were still a baby. He told us about the Prophecy. He explained to us what we had to do. We argued with him for a long time. We asked him if there wasn't an easier, perhaps a better way. We told him we refused to do it. We told him it was unnecessary, that there were kinder ways for a child to be taught."

* * *

"But God spoke to me in a dream," my mother resumed. "I often have visions in my dreams." The pit in my stomach squeezed uncomfortably.

"He showed me our future—He showed me your future. I knew through the dream you would need to learn this skill for a time, for something in the future where this highly developed survival skill could be used to save you. That was the real reason we decided to leave you. To save you. It was God's will. It took none other than God Himself to give us the strength we needed to say goodbye and abandon our only son."

"We loved you so much, Eliju," Kenneth, my father, resumed. "We treasured every moment before the time we'd been appointed to abandon you." There was something admirable in my father's courage at not shirking the gravity of what the situation had been for me—abandonment.

* * *

"I prepared all that food for you," Isadore's face was twisted in anguish. My wife's grief was visible on the surface what I knew she'd suffered every day, nearly every moment since we'd left him. Her goodness was so evident. I hoped that our son would appreciate it.

"We tried to make every moment count," I let the golden light of my love for him in my heart, shine from my emerald eyes. I let him feel the warmth of it.

"I sang to you, and played with you, and read our sacred texts to you. I tried to spend every spare minute with you, share myself with you, give you enough love to last you, in all the years to come you'd be so alone," Isa murmured tenderly.

"I'm the one that taught you at such an early age how to build things with your hands," I explained to Eliju.

"And I'm the one who taught you how to fix them," Isa laughed. We looked at each other for just a moment, but a lifetime of love was exchanged between us in that one look.

"I share a love of animals with you…" I told my son, proudly.

"I've prayed for you almost every moment since—" my sweet wife faltered again.

"Since we came here, back to my homeland," I finished for her. We were directly opposite in looks and personality, and yet moved and spoke as if one person. I guess a lifetime spent together can do that to two people who have learned to grow together and not apart.

* * *

The love they shared between them was evident, as was their love for me. After a handful of heartbeats passed, and it was clear they weren't going to speak again until I did, I stood up shakily, looked pointedly at Ileona, and walked in long strides toward the door.

Opening the door into the fresh air, I didn't look back until I'd reached Varawynn's castle. Ileona had been rushing after me the whole time, her gold eyes full of remorse.

~ *** ~

We decided to stay in Avalon a week or two more in support of Varawynn and her family. After we came to that consensus, I insisted we stay in the comforts of my Crystal Castle.

Of course, we could've stayed with Varawynn's parents in her castle, but the memories of her brother and childhood were too fresh. Besides, Varawynn had always so admired the Crystal Castle that it was quite a treat for her to stay in my home.

~ *** ~

Back at the Crystal Castle where we'd be staying for or a week or two, memories of the mirrors were brought fresh in my mind. "Eliju I'm not going to allow you to continue to evade my questions about where you were kept in your captivity…and who you were with."

"I've told you a thousand times, I don't want to discuss it Varawynn!" I snapped. "I don't nag you to tell me more about your encounter with Mardavian do I? I'm here to listen whenever you care to discuss it, but pressuring you to talk about it might well do more damage than good! And I really don't want to hurt you even more than you have been…God knows you've gone through too much lately."

"Oh? Were you hurt further when you were a captive?" she doggedly persisted. "I know King Mardavian beat you, but I hadn't known you'd been abused further. What happened to you?"

"Varawynn…"

"You're different with me, Eliju! You're so different! And I want to know why!"

I sighed, and took a deep breath. "Alright, I'll tell you. It actually first started here, in the Crystal Castle, in the seventh mirror that reveals the future…I thought I saw you there…I thought it was you at first…"

"And?"

"And it wasn't," I said simply, honestly, directly, knowing the words would cut her deeper than any knife, but not knowing how to express myself in any other way.

"I don't understand that. I don't *believe* that." Damn, she was persisting.

"You said it yourself."

"That we're not supposed to be together? No way, no way in Hade's Dorm."

"When we first met, you said that we were Twin Souls. That we were so alike, remember? That I was your *second* highest soul mate."

"Yes?"

"Yes, well, I found my ultimate soul mate. My Twin Flame. You of all people ought to know what that means."

"No, no, no this can't be right!"

How could I get her to understand without breaking her heart? "Varawynn, I do love you…but if you're not my Twin Flame, then surely you have one too…"

"For me, it's you."

"No, Varawynn, from the very beginning you said we were Twin Souls, mirror images, reflections…"

"I can't be with anyone but you, Eliju! How can you be with anyone but me?" Something dark and oppressive descended upon us— around us, and in-between us.

"Varawynn…"

But she'd already turned and walked away. There was so much she wanted to say that couldn't be said. I heard it and felt it, in the silence and the darkness that settled over the air when she left me. In silence, we packed our things and left Avalon, sorrier for having come.

~ *** ~

Chapter Twenty-Five
Creatures of the Starlight

June, in Caledonia and Astarra, the land of the fairies—

A few days passed until we came upon a forest where the waters shimmered with pure, clear lavender hues. Delicate, twisting birch trees and gently swaying willows lined the river bank where thousands of grand, twisting oaks thickened the forest beyond the river.

"When will we meet the fairies?" I asked Wandering Wolfe eagerly. I felt like a child again in anticipation of meeting such lovely creatures.

"We'll meet them very soon, my dear." Following the riverbank for miles, by nightfall we'd come upon a small, yet lovely cottage surrounded by flowers with gingerbread above windowsills full of blooming flowers.

"We're going to be staying here tonight," Wandering Wolfe informed us. We were surprised to see a fire glowing in the hearth and two rows of four beds on each row were made up, as if in preparation for our stay.

"Are they expecting us here, Wandering Wolfe?" asked Jonlin.

"Let's just be thankful for the comfort of a soft bed and the warmth of a hot fire. It is unseasonably cold and wet for this time of year."

After his words, he peered into the fire and coughed to himself. Wandering Wolfe was acting strangely, but I was too tired to figure out why. The comfort of a soft bed was irresistibly inviting after sleeping on the hard ground outside and the cold stone floors of King Mardavian's castle for so long.

Most of us fell asleep quickly, but I woke up for a few minutes in the dead of night to hear Illumina and Silvandrin whispering softly to each other. It was late morning when I was rudely awakened by something crawling around on my face and getting caught up in my hair.

"Help, help! What are you?! Get away!"

"What is it, Alondria?" Shadow Rain rushed to my side.

"There's a bug on me!"

"Excuse me?" A high, tiny voice tweeted indignantly. "I'm not a bug, I'm a *fairy!*" the creature said in a lovely sing-song voice.

I found the courage to peak out from underneath the covers and stare with widened eyes at the creature that had frightened me and woke me up. As I looked at her now, I wondered how I could have been so frightened.

She was such a dainty little creature, with long dark hair, big blue eyes, wearing gossamer threads of blue and white and purple, with little bells on her shoes that rang like wind chimes as she flew about us. Why she wasn't even half a foot long!

"I'm sorry I frightened you," the fairy chirped at me sweetly. "I only wanted to touch your hair. I've never met a human before!"

"Neither have we," a group of fairies spoke from the hearth. As we turned our faces towards the fire, we realized what we'd *thought* was a fire were the lights from the fairy's wands.

"We wanted to meet all of you, too!" the four little fairies in the hearth cried as one.

"We couldn't wait for tomorrow!" one of the fairies said merrily, with twinkles in her eyes that matched the sparkles in her dress. All the fairies laughed—as did I, as all the rest joined in the merriment. They were just so dainty and pretty and charming. I couldn't help but adore them!

"Fairies are so mischievous," Illumina sighed. I was surprised. She sounded as if she didn't find them quite as lovable as I did.

"But it really wasn't me who tugged your hair," the closest fairy to me confessed.

"Then who did?" I asked her.

"It was me!" a green-clad fairy with brazen orange hair gleefully admitted, puffing out her chest with dramatic dignity. "I wanted you all to wake up because the banquet we prepared is almost ready and I didn't want you to be late!" I had to laugh again. They were just too cute for me to resist.

"What are your names?" I asked.

"I am Mora, a Star Fairy," the blue and purple-clad fairy said.

"And I am Gwinnie!" the red-haired fairy laughed playfully.

"And we are Jasmina, Deedee, Cecil, and Noryn," the four fairies said from the hearth.

"Why don't you all get dressed, and one of us will stay behind to take you to the banquet?" suggested Mora, who was one of the leaders in the elect group of Star Fairies. "Come along girls, we'd better go now and help get the banquet ready for them."

"I'll stay and bring them over when they're finally dressed!" Gwinnie said, as she gave a discreet tug on Wandering Wolfe's beard.

"Ouch!" Wandering Wolfe barked loudly.

"Gwinnie!" Mora screeched. "Go with the other girls, and I'll bring the troupe over myself."

"Awww, fine," Gwinnie said dejectedly, though no one actually saw her leave.

Mora explained to us that there were various kinds of fairies. Some fairies granted wishes to those who were deserving, some fairies were mischievous and pulled pranks all the time—like hiding children's school work and such. While other fairies, like Mora herself, were "Keepers of the Starlight"—a magical order which studied the secrets and mysteries of the moon and stars. I asked if any fairies had been to the peaks and valleys of Andorra.

We heard a stifled laugh, and as we looked under the bed where the sound was coming from, sure enough playful Gwinnie was hiding beneath it, giggling up a storm. "I remember one of my kin telling me about pulling pranks on you!" Gwinnie said, still laughing heartily, not minding she was in trouble for disobeying the orders of Mora, who clearly outranked her. She was obviously used to being in trouble by now.

"You should've been an imp, Gwinnie," Mora said, feigning anger. "You give our kind a bad name."

"But fairies *were* in Andorra!" I exclaimed wide-eyed.

Gwinnie just kept giggling as we made our way through the deep woods, to a festival that left us awestruck. There were red lights strung from all the trees. The food was sugary and sweet, and all the drinks had something in them that made us run around like crazy people, with the pent-up energy of goblins.

We laughed, danced, and feasted all day long. At nightfall, one of the spritely fairies like Gwinnie, took center stage to sing us a song, and teach us about their kind. The blond fairy wore a bold, rebellious-red dress, with a dramatic gold crown with red roses entwined together, to make a circlet on her head. She shout-sang her song, wanting to make sure we all heard her. I told Shadow Rain that I didn't think they could miss her loud, brass singing all the way back in the West Pyrenees Mountains!

"Wee Fairies"

"This is a song of the wild and free,
Who live for the fun of mischievous glee!
Playing tricks on the humans
Who don't believe in us little folk wee!

This is the song of impish delights,
Feasting and dancing ev-er-y night!
Singing 'til four and then sleeping all day,
Living for the joy of life which shan't e'er go away!

We are the fairies, who don't have a care!
We do what we want, then, now, and there!
We romp, and we play whenever we choose,
Bringing cheer to the fellows who shout doom and gloom!

Dancing, and singing, and romping along;
These are the things for which our spirits do long!
To shine like the twinkling stars so pretty and bright,
And bring happiness and laughter in the bliss of the light!"

The fairies giggled, and shouted, pranced, and skipped, and played, as they brought our group a feast of forest delights. Simple berries, freshly cracked nuts, fresh cheeses and breads filled our stomachs from morning till night, as the fairies chattered away, their laughter and singing filling our eyes and ears. When we finally got back to the attractively kept cottage, we slept peacefully and soundly on the feather beds, finding contentment and happiness together like we never had been before.

It was as if for the first time in our journey, we'd found a safe haven—a little home-away-from-home, a place to belong. Even though Eliju, Varawynn, and Ileona hadn't rejoined us yet, and I worried about and missed them, I felt very much at peace here.

The next morning, Gwinnie brought us to the clearing where we feasted another day long. During the next nightfall, another kind of fairy got onto the stage, wearing a sparkling rainbow dress to feature their abilities, she sang the song of the—

"The Fairy Godmothers"

"We watch the people of the mountains,
Cities, deserts, wood and sea,
Until we find a soul deserving
Of the wishes of three.

It doesn't matter what their age is,
Or how powerful they may be,
Princess, king, bard or jester,
Butcher, lady, baby, or cabinet-maker.

There are few we give these blessings to,
And there are few who use their wishes well,
But we are born to grant their desires,
To see what destiny shall foretell.

What they choose reveals their character,
And how they use these magical gifts,
Will govern the world 'til the world can learn
That the magic of earth is free for all,
And does not require a blessing or wish."

The feasting, singing, and dancing again lasted far into the night and early morning, until at last we traipsed back into our beds at the cozy cottage. Most of us slept dreamlessly, but Wandering Wolfe had nightmares all night; worrying subconsciously about what was to come, and concerned we'd not yet received what we came for. He was worried about Varawynn, worried about the changes in Eliju…worried about the battles awaiting us ahead.

~ *** ~

The group was too busy feasting again the next day, to notice me steal away for an hour or so, as the sun dimmed, to meet with my friend, the great-winged bird Roc, Grifficon, in a remote area of the forest. By the moonlight, his wings spanned twenty-five feet, though he carefully tucked them around his body. He looked a lot like an eagle—although several times the size. Its feathers were grey, black, and orange with a few strands of gold.

His sulphurous-orange eyes bore into my crescent moon orbs. "How have you been, my infamous friend?"

"I've fared just as well as you have, Grifficon, I'm sure."

"How are you finding these silly little fairies?"

"I find them adorable."

The Roc made a strange noise in his throat. "Frolicsome, bothersome little creatures if you ask me." It felt like the wind had just picked up, but really the bird had only shaken its massive head.

"You've been foretold to claim a very sacred object, Silvandrin. I'm here to warn you not to use it until you're told."

"It would help if I knew what you were talking about."

"You'll discover that soon enough. Just don't use it, you understand? And guard it from the others."

* * *

Knowing Silvandrin would follow my instructions, I didn't wait for an answer. Gathering my great wings about myself, spreading out my full wing-span of twenty-five feet, I took a running leap, and soared into the sky. My wings lifted me high above the tallest of the trees.

So powerful were my wings that the rush of air it left behind me knocked Silvandrin off his hooves. The black unicorn righted himself just fast enough to watch the last of my form fly away, until my presence was nothing but a speck upon the moonlit sky, no bigger than a star appeared in the universe.

~ *** ~

They had another couple of weeks of feasting with the fairies before Eliju, Varawynn, and I had rejoined them. After we'd all been back together for a few days, Wandering Wolfe was determined for this to be our last feast day in Astarra, as he was quite ready to begin the next part of our journey, as we were now finally, fully, united.

Making our way through the deep woods to a clearing that was so gloriously prepared it took my breath away, a long, intricately designed table of oak, covered by a white canopy, spread before us, sparkling in the night.

Flowers of blue and red, violet, white, and indigo were entwined in the silver canopy sprawled out above us. To the left of the sparkling canopy and white tables clad with symbols of the stars, the purple river glistened like the glittering lights on the fairies themselves, as all about us tiny chimes rang from the bells on the fairy's necklaces and tiaras, dresses and slippers.

The sound was soft and light, and it was comforting in the way of the magic of money under your pillow from a tooth fairy. It was the kind of sound that lifted one's spirits. Astarra was so very different from the dark, dank caverns of the dwarves. I preferred these refined creatures, like myself, who found function in beauty, and power in charm.

An ornately dressed fairy in flowing robes of sapphire and indigo, with silver accessories of necklaces, bracelets, anklets, and a tiara of delicate diamonds, took the stage, covered by a canopy of sparkling lights like stars.

Singing mournfully on the stage lit with twinkling lights, her song and the sound of her voice haunted us with its poignant beauty. "We are the 'Keepers of the Starlight,' " she explained to us in her high, flute-like voice, "and this is our song:"

"Keepers of the Starlight"

"When fairies dance on the pearly wings
Of the glorious moon-beams;
Upon rivers flowing on glittering streams,
There in the currents you shall find your dreams.

As beside the river, the trees they mourn,
The flowers scent, as the bees, they swarm;
As a bell twinkles softly, a fairy is borne,
With all our hearts, we're singing so forlorn.

We sing the song, of the willow tree,
Of the white birch standing tall and free,
Of the proud, stout oak which can always see—
The price of our magnificent dreams.

We dance and weave spells far into the night,
With wisdom from the moon's illustrious light—
The seekers of truth who always do right;
We seek only the war of the freedom fight.

All that wee fairies wish to be
Is in the wisdom of the star's mysteries,

With a breath of light from our glorious dream—
To remain wild and free, like the white birch tree."

* * *

After the lovely Star Fairy sang their anthem song, the group sat down, partaking in a meal unlike any we'd experienced before. But by the end of the night, Wandering Wolfe was growing more impatient.

Everyone was enjoying themselves so much. Only Silvandrin and I were observant enough to notice the Shaman's discomfort. "You and the kids have been back for three days now," he said to Ileona. "We need to keep moving forward. We cannot afford to become complacent now."

After the Star Fairy had finished singing her sweet song, and the group was through eating, Wandering Wolfe stood and quietly, looked pointedly at the head of the Truth Seekers, staring her down.

"I want what we have come for now. Time is of the essence."

With a great deal of show, Wandering Wolfe pulled from his vest an elaborate box, comprised of Mother-of-Pearl and crushed crystals. Slowly, and in wide movements, so careful and precise everyone could see his every movement, he opened the delicate box— lifting it onto his fingers, and then high into the sky—the Jewel of the Andorres Mountains.

Holding up the perfect diamond, he let it catch the lights of the festivities. Even in the darkness it shone—a multi-prismed rainbow of radiant reflections of light.

Everyone, the fairies and the members of our elect group of birthmarked Chosen Ones, stared. Ileona looked upon the diamond longingly. She loved the crystals. I loved them too. There was a moment's pause.

The beautiful member of the Star Fairies, Mora, left the table. There were a few murmurs from the fairies around Wandering Wolfe, but we resumed our silence when the fairy returned a moment later.

"I know you've been worried about the next part of your journey, Wandering Wolfe. We have a scroll which will shed some light on the next leg of your journey. I give it to you now with all the blessings of the fairies: mischief-makers, wish-granters, tooth fairies, fairy godmothers, and Keepers of the Starlight. One and All, we wish you well." Wandering Wolfe gave her a grateful smile, as he took the ancient scroll into his hands.

"I hope you will come to understand the riddle in full," Mora added cryptically.

"The Prophecy?"

"The Riddle's Quest."

As Wandering Wolfe handed Mora the multi-faceted jewel and white Mother-of-Pearl box, with shaking hands, he took and opened the scroll. Throwing the unicorn a weak look for help, Silvandrin's voice boomed out in the darkness, reading aloud our quest in his warm buttery voice, strong and deep:

"The Riddle's Quest"

"The chosen fourteen come together,
After being captured in a web,
Escaping because of a little moth,
They travel north and west.

They learn about each other
On the journey to the land,
Where willows line the purple sea,
And the fairies sing and dance.

These glittering folks will help them understand
The lessons that have been wrought—
The West Pyrenees Jewel is exchanged for the Prophecy,
Which cannot be stolen, altered or bought.

There is a greater purpose,
That from the creation of earth has been foretold:
When the earth was borne of words,
When man's first breath of life arose.

But due to actions taken, words forsaken

Hasty choices, liars and lies mistaken
Immortal souls were bound—housed in frail skin and bones,
So that man forgot why he first arose.

Long before time began, these fourteen were Chosen,
And the beginning letters of their names
Will lead them to the answers,
None and nothing other could explain.

To understand the riddle's meaning,
Fourteen come together as if One soul
Integrated as One mind and in One heart—
All the fragmented pieces are made whole."

"So…we've got to piece together the words of a riddle, starting with the letters of each of our names," Silvandrin said.

"It's a good thing we have the Oracle to help us with the riddle," added Varawynn, smiling at Ileona with admiration.

The Star Fairy was studying Wandering Wolfe, but he said nothing. There was another long, uncomfortable moment of silence. "We'll leave at dawn's first light," the Shaman told the fairies.

Mora nodded, whispering something to the unicorn. Nodding his head, everyone resumed eating, this time more soberly, knowing it was to be our last night in Astarra.

~ *** ~

From a cottage deep in the woods of Caledonia, on the Isle of Skye—

I drew the bone of Aengus from my black velvet pouch. It was now dried out, its color fading from white to grey. Handling his thigh bone with great care, I chanted:

"Out of ashes and bones,
out of spirit and shadows,
the body of ashes is made whole.

From the blood of a brother's soul,
her breaking heart beats back to life,
beyond the veil of death into the light..."

Chanting the words as if I were sipping on a fine wine, I let the rhyme linger on my tongue, swooshing pleasantly in my mouth, as I thought about the future. Everything I'd ever coveted had never been so close...or possible. A sly smiled played around the corners of my mouth, as the wolf that haunted me, howled low in the distance.

~ *** ~

Epilogue
In the Shadows

From here, there, in, out, up, down, and all around—

I was watching them as I had always done—from a distance. Known and unknown. Seen and unseen. Within and without. I'd known them all their lives. I knew their strengths and weaknesses. Knew them as they could recognize me. I was the only one who had always been with them.

But I had always stood alone. And there was a certain loneliness in harboring the secret I alone bore.

With the birthmark of the Symbol of Unity on my neck. With the shaggy black hair and mangy ways of movement, like an animal on the prowl. Dark and strange. I lived among them and yet never spoke. Always listening. Always seeking. Always on the outskirts. An outcast. The Watcher.

Who was my friend really? Where were my kin? Where had I come from? It was as if I had emerged from the shadows themselves. What sort of man, of creature, was I?

In the hollowed tree I called my home, I heard strange sounds coming from a nearby clearing. I followed the sounds and happenstanced upon a strange ritual…

An alchemist stood above a man—or what appeared to be a man. What was he doing? Altering the course of his veins, transmuting his blood to gold. Symbols were everywhere: cauldrons, lanterns, stones, and crystals, candles, goblets—the whole clearing was lit up with arcane, occult magic.

There, a giant, the Son of God, a Nephilim, was standing over a baby, an innocent baby and murmuring words, chanting them over and over like a prayer:

From this child's line a man shall come,
After generations of suffering
He shall be the One—
To lead magickind away from man,

To save the magical creatures from human hands,
To harness the powers of heaven to earth,
To break man's curse—
To break man's curse, and bring peace to earth."

After the spell was cast, I went back to the hollow of the tree and sat down at its roots for a long time. Time was relative anyway—there was all the time in the world.

I dwelled in the roots of the ground. I was an earth dweller. I traversed the mountains, forests and swamps. I lived in the dwellings of the earth where I roamed. Really, I had no home.

My home lied with the people of the Prophecy. My home lied with the future generations of the lines of this baby. My origins were in the history of magic and Time itself. The hope for mankind and magickind lied in our futures...

..................To Be Continued In..............

The Creation Series
Volume Two

In the Origin of Time

By Crystal Wolfe

Dedication

The first scene of this book came like a flash of lightning in a waking dream. It began with the main character, Eliju, and his vision. Then over the years, my character's vision became my own.

The Creation Series came in bits and pieces over the course of many years. The story developed as I grew in knowledge and experience. Before I was even in Elementary School, I was studying history, the religions and cultures of the earth, and seeking the meaning of life.

For many years I did not know why I was so compelled to research and search for universal truths. Immersing myself in mythology and science, studying and experiencing spirituality, and the challenges of my life journey, shaped me into a unique person, capable of writing this unique series, with what I believe has real roots in the history and creation of our world.

As this book and the series unfolds, I hope that you will find the truth in these lines, the truth in the knowledge I have studied and shared. I impart all I know and feel in these books, for the universal love of humankind and magickind.

I still believe in unicorns and dragons. I still believe that unwavering faith can move mountains. This series is above all: a story about the transformative power of unconditonal love, to move hearts and change lives.

I dedicate this work to all the people in my life who have made me the person that I am today. This accomplishment is credited to my many loved ones who have never given up on me and my dreams, even in the times when it looked as if all hope was lost, and *Where the Shadows Meet the Light,* would never meet the light of day.

I dedicate this series to my mother, Lore Wolfe, who has kept me going through her faith in me and what I will accomplish with the life she gave me.

To my sister, Amber Elizabeth Wolfe, who never stopped believing I was born to be a star, and that what's meant to be will always find a way.

To my friend, Donald Hart, whose unwavering belief in me has kept me living in a lot of profoundly painful circumstances in life. I don't think I'd be alive today, and I don't believe this book would be in your hands, without these people's love and support.

This book is also dedicated to all the ones I've loved who are no longer in my life, but still haunt my dreams, and are engraved on the story of my soul. It is never too late to be who you were always meant to be.

It is faith and love that has kept me going throughout my life, no matter the circumstances. I could never have written this book without God. I believe this work was anointed by the Holy Spirit, and I hope that whatever inspiration and healing comes to those who read this series, will be to his grace and glory. Whatever good comes from this book, I give all the credit to God.

The Creation Series is written for love, as I believe all of life was created by love, for love, to love. I've written eight books so far in life, and no book took me longer to write, or will ever mean more to see in print. I believe that *Where the Shadows Meet the Light* and *The Creation Series* is my masterpiece, and I can only hope that it will bring enlightenment to all who read it.

About the Author

Crystal Wolfe attended college at Purdue University in Indiana. Wolfe has been published in newspapers across the country and has won local literary awards in the community she's from in Indiana.

Wolfe currently lives in Queens in New York City, where she's done freelance reporting for newspapers and magazines such as the New York Press, the Queens Ledger, and the Juniper Berry Magazine. She's had approximately 300 of her articles published in newspapers and magazines nation-wide. She's also written political biographies for encyclopedias published specifically for libraries in High Schools, Colleges, and Universities.

Wolfe has raised hundreds of thousands of dollars for nonprofits like the ASPCA and the NRDC, as well as political organizations such as the ACLU and Amnesty International. As one of the organization's top fundraisers, she became a trainer for the company in Los Angeles, CA and Denver, CO. Wolfe has participated in service projects throughout the nation; some of which include: beautification park projects, planting trees, literacy programs, Adopt-A-Highway, volunteering in nursing homes, sending care packages to soldiers in Afghanistan, and working in food ministries feeding the homeless across the country.

Wolfe has put her time and money into serving the homeless by founding her own nonprofit, **Catering for the Homeless, Inc.** to feed the homeless and hungry with the food going to waste from catering companies, schools, and restaurants—feeding thousands of homeless every month in Queens, Brooklyn, Manhattan, and the Bronx.

She is also partnering with other nonprofits and churches in food ministry programs, to provide thousands of toiletry items and clothes for the homeless in shelters, subways, and on the streets. Wolfe is working to make Catering for the Homeless a national program because there is enough food going to waste in America that no one in the country needs to be hungry.

Crystal Wolfe began writing *Where the Shadows Meet the Light* as a child, researching thousands of books from science, to religion, to history, to geography, to mythology over the course of a lifetime, to pen *The Creation Series.* Wolfe is also the author of *The Resurrected Dream: A Collection of Poetry and Prose from an Awakened Soul,* and a comprehensive book on homelessness, *Our Invisible Neighbors: Accounts, Causes, and Solutions to the Epidemic of Homelessness in the 21st Century...*

You can keep up-to-date with Crystal Wolfe's novels and other creative endeavors at her personal website:

www.crystalwolfe.org
crystalwolfe1@gmail.com

You can keep up-to-date with Crystal Wolfe's work with the homeless at:

WHERE THE SHADOWS MEET THE LIGHT

www.cateringforthehomeless.com
cateringforthehomeless@gmail.com

THE CREATION SERIES: VOLUME ONE